Spirits in the Wires

By Charles de Lint from Tom Doherty Associates

ANGEL OF DARKNESS

DREAMS UNDERFOOT

THE FAIR AT EMAIN MACHA

FORESTS OF THE HEART

FROM A WHISPER TO A SCREAM

GREENMANTLE

I'LL BE WATCHING YOU

INTO THE GREEN

THE IVORY AND THE HORN

JACK OF KINROWAN

THE LITTLE COUNTRY

MEMORY AND DREAM

MOONHEART

MOONLIGHT AND VINES

MULENGRO

THE ONION GIRL

SOMEPLACE TO BE FLYING

SPIRITS IN THE WIRES

SPIRITWALK

SVAHA

TAPPING THE DREAM TREE

TRADER

THE WILD WOOD

YARROW

Spirits in the Wires

Charles de Lint

TOR®

A Tom Doherty Associates Book
New York

SPIRITS IN THE WIRES

A Tor Book
Published by Tom Doherty Associates, LLC
175 Fifth Avenue
New York, NY 10010

www.tor.com

Tor® is a registered trademark of Tom Doherty Associates, LLC.

Library of Congress Cataloging-in-Publication Data

De Lint, Charles, 1951–
    Spirits in the wires / Charles de Lint.
        p. cm.
    "A Tom Doherty Associates book."
    ISBN 0-312-86971-1 (PBK)
    EAN 978-0312-86971-7 (PBK)
    1. Fantasy fiction, Canadian. 2. Technology—Fiction. I. Title.

PR9199.3D357S65 2003
813'.54—dc21   2003041410

First Edition: August 2003
First Paperback Edition: September 2004

Printed in the United States of America

0 9 8 7 6 5 4 3 2 1

This one's for my long-time pal

Rodger Turner

Break the bowl—
instead of regret,
fall back into
the potter's hands
and be reborn.

—SASKIA MADDING
"Falling" (*Spirits and Ghosts*, 2000)

Contents

Author's Note   11

First Meeting   15

How We Were Born   23

And Here We Are   67

The World Wide Web Blues   73

Shadows in the Wordwood   227

This, Too, Shall Pass   407

Author's Note

The impetus to write this book, and the title as well, was sparked by some offhand remarks made by my friend Richard Kunz concerning how, with the ever-growing prevalence of technology in the world, some of the spirits of fairy tale and folklore have probably already left the woodlands and other pastoral settings to take up residence in the wires that seem to connect us to everything: telephone, cable, electricity. No doubt they're in the satellite feeds as well.

I'd touched on this in some previous short stories (such as "Saskia," which you can find in my collection *Moonlight and Vines,* and "Pixel Pixies," in the more recent *Tapping the Dream Tree* collection), but the more I thought about it, the more I wanted to explore it at a longer length. So finally I put aside the plans I had for the next novel I was going to write and jumped happily into this one instead, even though it will be the second novel in a row to feature my regular repertory company of Newford characters taking their turn on the main stage, rather than going about their lives in the background of the books as they usually do.

Considering the origins of *Spirits in the Wires,* I should first thank Richard for those conversations, not forgetting his wife, Mardelle, who is not only a friend, but who has also done such a fine job of copyediting on a number of my books—those would be the ones without typos and the like.

I'd also like to thank:

Rodger Turner for great heaps of technical advice (with the usual caveat that any screw-ups are my fault, not his);

my coterie of friends, family and well-wishers (too numerous to name—you know who you are), without whom writing these books would be a far lonelier proposition;

my editors Gordon Van Gelder, Jo Fletcher, Patrick Nielsen Hayden, Sharyn November, and Terri Windling, all of whom are friends more than business associates;

Cat Eldridge, David Tamulevich, and the handful of readers who continue to send such wonderful music my way, as well as all the amazing musicians who, through the years, have kept my brain fertile and my spirits lifted with their music;

and last, but never least, MaryAnn for her love, comfort, and support; for the music in her heart and the poetry in her soul; for her astute reader's eye and red pen, and her sharp negotiating skills. And you know what? She's wilder than me.

If any of you are on the Internet, come visit my home page at www. charlesdelint.com

—Charles de Lint
Ottawa, Autumn 2002

Extract from the journals of Christy Riddell

According to Jung, at around the age of six or seven we separate and then hide away the parts of ourselves that don't seem acceptable, that don't fit in the world around us. Those unacceptable parts that we secret away become our shadows.

I remember reading somewhere that it can be a useful exercise to visualize the person our shadow would be if it could step out into the light. So I tried it. It didn't work immediately. For a long time, I was simply talking to myself. Then, when I did get a response, it was only a spirit voice I heard in my head. It could just as easily have been my own. But over time, my shadow took on more physical attributes, in the way that a story grows clearer and more pertinent as you add and take away words, molding its final shape.

Not surprisingly, my shadow proved to be the opposite of who I am in so many ways. Bolder, wiser, with a better memory and a penchant for dressing up with costumes, masks, or simply formal wear. A cocktail dress in a raspberry patch. A green man mask in a winter field. She's short, where I'm tall. Dark-skinned, where I'm light. Red-haired, where mine's dark. A girl to my boy, and now a woman as I'm a man.

If she has a name, she's never told me it. If she has an existence outside the times we're together, she has yet to divulge it either. Naturally, I'm curious about where she goes, but she doesn't like being asked questions and I've learned not to press her, because when I do, she simply goes away.

Sometimes I worry about her existence. I get anxieties about schizophrenia and carefully study myself for other symptoms. But if she's a delusion, it's singular, and otherwise I seem to be as normal as anyone else, which is to say, confused by the barrage of input and stimuli with which the modern world besets us, and trying to make do. Who was it that said she's always trying to understand the big picture, but the trouble is, the picture just keeps getting bigger? Ani DiFranco. I think.

Mostly I don't get too analytical about it—something I picked up from her, I suppose, since left to my own devices, I can worry the smallest detail to death.

We have long conversations, usually late at night, when the badgering clouds swallow the stars and the darkness is most profound. Most of the time I can't see her, but I can hear her voice. I like to think we're friends; even if we don't agree about details, we can usually find common ground on how we'd like things to be.

First Meeting

Don't make of us
more than what we are,
she said.
We hold no great secret . . .
—SASKIA MADDING,
"Arabesque" (*Moths and Wasps,* 1997)

Christiana Tree

"I feel as if I should know you," Saskia Madding says as she approaches my chair.

She's been darting glances in my direction from across the café for about fifteen minutes now and I was wondering when she'd finally come over.

I saw her when I first came in, sitting to the right of the door at a window table, nursing a tall cup of chai tea. She'd been writing in a small, leather-bound book, fountain pen in one hand, the other holding back the spill of blonde hair that would otherwise fall into her eyes. She looked up when I came in and showed no sign of recognition, but since then she's been studying me whenever she thinks I'm not paying attention to her.

"You do know me," I tell her. "I'm pieces of your boyfriend—the ones he didn't want when he was a kid."

She gives me a puzzled look, though I can see a kind of understanding start up in the back of those pretty, sea-blue eyes of hers.

"You—are you the woman in his journals?" she asks. "The one he calls Mystery?"

I smile. "That's me. The shadow of himself."

"I didn't . . ."

"Know I was real?" I finish for her when her voice trails off.

She shakes her head. "No. I just didn't expect to ever see you in a place like this."

"I like coffee."

"I meant someplace so mundane."

"Ah. So you've made note of all those romantic flights of fancy he puts in those journals of his." I close my eyes, shuffling through pages of memory until I find one of them. " 'I can see her standing among the brambles and thorns of some half-forgotten hedgerow in a green bridal dress, her red hair set aflame by the setting sun, her eyes dark with mysteries and stories, a wooden hare's mask dangling from one languid hand. This is how I always see her. In the hidden and secret places, her business there incomprehensible yet obviously perfectly suited to her curious, evasive nature.' "

I get a smile from Saskia, but I don't know if it's from the passage I've quoted, or because I'm mimicking Christy's voice as I repeat the words.

"That's a new one," she says. "He hasn't read it to me yet."

"You wait for him to read them to you?"

"Of course. I would never go prying . . ." She pauses and gives me a considering look. "When do you read them?"

I shrug. "Oh, you know. Whenever. I don't really sleep, so sometimes when I get bored late at night I come by and sit in his study for awhile to read what he's been thinking about lately."

"You're as bad as the crow girls."

"I'll take that as a compliment."

"Mmm." She studies me for a moment before adding, "You don't read my journals do you?"

I muster a properly offended look, though it's not that I wouldn't. I just haven't. Yet.

"I'm sorry," she says. "Of course you wouldn't. We don't have the same connection as you and Christy do."

"Does that connection bother you?"

She shakes her head. "That would be like being bothered by his having Geordie for a brother. You're more like family—albeit the twin sister who only comes creeping by to visit in the middle of the night when we're both asleep."

I shrug, but I don't apologize.

"I'm only his shadow," I say.

She studies me again, those sea-blue eyes of hers looking deep into mine.

"I don't think so," she says. "You're real now."

That makes me smile.

"As real as I am, anyway," she adds.

My smile fades as I see the troubled look that comes over her. I forget that her own exotic origins are no more than a dream to her most of the time—a dream that makes her uncomfortable, uneasy in her skin. I wish I hadn't reminded her of it, but she puts it away and brings the conversation back to me.

"Why won't you tell Christy your name?" she asks.

"Because that would let him put me in a box labeled 'This is Christiana' and I don't want to be locked into who he thinks I am. The way he writes about me is bad enough. If he had a name to go with it he might be able to fix it so that I could never change and grow."

"He does like his routines," she says.

I nod. "His picture's in the dictionary, right beside the word."

We share a moment's silence, then she cocks her a head, just a little.

"So your name's Christiana?" she asks.

"I call myself Christiana Tree."

That brings back a genuine smile.

"So that would make you Miss Tree," she says.

I'm impressed at how quickly she got it as I offer her my hand.

"In the flesh," I tell her. "Pleased to meet you."

"But that's only what you call yourself," she says as she shakes my hand.

"We all have our secrets."

"Or we wouldn't be mysteries."

"That, too."

She's been sitting on her haunches beside the easy chair I commandeered as soon as I'd picked up my coffee and sticky-bun from the counter, leaning her arms on one of the chair's fat arms. There's another chair nearby, occupied by a boy in his late teens with blue hair and razor-thin features. He's been listening to his Walkman loud enough for me to identify the music as rap, though I can't make out any words, and flipping through one of the café's freebie newspapers while he drinks his coffee. He gets up now and I give a vague wave to the vacant chair with my hand.

"Why don't you get more comfortable," I say to Saskia.

She nods. "Just let me get my stuff."

Some office drone in a tailored business suit, tie loose, top shirt button undone, approaches the chair while Saskia collects her things. I put my scuffed brown leather work boots up on its cushions and give him a sugar and icicle smile—you know, it looks sweet, but there's a chill in it. He's like a cat as he casually steers himself off through the tables and takes a hardback chair at one of the small counters that enclose the café's various rustic wooden support beams, making it look like that's what he was aiming for all along.

Saskia returns. She drops her jacket on the back of the chair, puts her knapsack on the floor, and settles down, tea in hand.

"So, what were you writing?" I ask.

She shrugs. "This and that. I just like playing with words. Sometimes they become something—a journal entry, a poem. Sometimes I'm just following words to see where they go."

"And where do they go?"

"Anyplace and everyplace."

She pauses for a moment and has a sip of her tea, sets the cup down on the low table between us. Later I realize she was just deciding whether to go on and tell me what she now does.

"You know, we're like words," she says. "You and me. We're like ghost words."

I have to smile. I'm beginning to understand why Christy cares about her the way he does. She's a sweet, pretty blonde, but she doesn't fit into any sort of a tidy descriptive package. Her thinking's all over the place, from serious to whimsical, or even some combination of the two. I think I just might have a poke through her journals the next time I'm in their apartment and they're both asleep. I'd like to know more about her—not just what she has to say, but what she thinks when there's nobody supposed to be listening.

"Okay," I say. "I'll bite. What are ghost words?"

"They're words that don't really exist. They come about through the mistakes of editors and printers and bad proofreaders, and while they seem like they should mean something, they don't. Like 'cablin' for 'cabin,' say."

I see what she means.

"I like that word," I tell her. "Cablin. Maybe I should appropriate it and give it a meaning."

Saskia gives a slow nod. "You see? That's how we're like ghost words. People can appropriate us and give us meanings, too."

I know she's talking about our anomalous origins—how because of them, we could be victim to that sort of thing—but I don't agree.

"That happens to everybody," I tell her. "It happens whenever someone decides what someone is like instead of finding out for real."

"I suppose."

"You're thinking about all of this too much."

"I can't seem to stop thinking about it."

I study her for a long moment. It's worrying her, this whole idea of what's real and what isn't, like how you came into this world is more important than what you do once you're here.

"What's the first thing you remember?" I ask.

How We Were Born

Words are like a corridor;
put enough of them in a line
and who knows where
they will take you.
—SASKIA MADDING,
"Corridor" (*Mirrors,* 1995)

Saskia Madding

I remember opening my eyes and—

You know how if you blow up an electronic image too much, you don't have a picture anymore? When you push the image that far, all you really have left is a pixelated fog, a screen full of tiny coloured squares that don't form a recognizable pattern, never mind an image.

That was the first thing I saw.

I opened my eyes and I couldn't focus on anything. A hundred thousand million dots of colour and light filled my vision. I stared hard, trying to make sense of them, and slowly they started to come together, forming recognizable objects. A dresser. A cedar chest. An armchair with clothes draped over the arms and back. A closed wooden door. A poster from the Newford Museum of Art advertising a retrospective of Vincent Rushkin's work. Close by my head on the night table was an unlit candle in a brass holder, and a leather-bound book with a pattern of pussywillows stamped into the leather, a fountain pen lying on top of it.

It was all familiar, but I knew I'd never seen it before. Just as I myself was familiar, but I didn't know who I really was. I knew my name. I knew there was a computer and paper trail tracing my background—where I was born, grew up, went to school—but I couldn't actually recall any of it. The details of the experiences, I mean. The sounds, the smells, the tactile impressions associated with them. All I knew were the bare bones of cold facts.

I studied the explosion of pigeons in the painting they'd used in the poster for the Rushkin show and tried to make sense of how I could be in my own bedroom, but have no sense of where it was or how I got here or anything that had happened to me before I opened my eyes at that moment.

And I was strangely calm.

I knew I shouldn't be. Somewhere a part of me was registering the fact that none of this was right—neither the where and how of where I'd found myself upon waking, nor my reaction to it.

I had the strongest sense of being temporary. A shadow cast by a light that was about to move or be turned off. An image in a film that the camera had lingered up on before moving on.

I held one of my hands up in front of my eyes, then the other. I sat up and looked at the reflection of the woman in the mirror on the back of the dresser.

Me.

A stranger.

But I knew every inch of that face—the blue eyes, the shape of the nose and lips, the way the blonde hair fell in a sleepy tangle on either side of it.

I swung my feet to the floor and stood up. I pulled the flannel nightie I was wearing over my head and faced the mirror again.

I knew this body as well.

Me.

Still a stranger.

I sat down on the edge of the bed. Plucking the nightie from the floor, I hugged it to my chest.

An odd notion came into my head. I had a sudden impression of some other place, a pixelated realm that lay somewhere in cyberspace—that mysterious borderland of electrons and data pulses that exists in between all the computers that make up the World Wide Web. I could almost see this deep forest of sentences and words secreted in a nexus of the Web, and as I did, I sensed some enormous entity swelling up out of it, a leviathan of impossible proportions that had no physical presence, but it did have a vast and incomprehensible soul.

The thought came to me that I was a piece of that entity. That I had been broken off from it, born there in that forest of words and sent away. That I was separate, but also still a part of that other. That it had made me up through some curious technopagan ritual, given me flesh and then set me free to make a life for myself in the world beyond the endless reaches of cyberspace.

I know. It sounds like science fiction. And maybe it was. But it was magic, too. How else can you explain a computer program that was self-aware? Some voodoo spirit, itself made of nothing but ones and zeros, that was able to create a living being out of neurons and electricity and air and send it off into the world to be its own being.

The island of calm I'd sensed before whispered to me through this whirlpool of disquiet and speculation.

In a normal person, it said, *what you are experiencing would be considered madness.*

But I already knew I wasn't normal. I wasn't even sure I was a person.

Finally, I lay back down on the bed and closed my eyes.

Maybe it was all a dream. Maybe when I woke up in the morning I'd remember my life. I'd be myself and just shake my head as I went about my morning, dimly recalling the very strange dream I'd had the night before.

But in the morning, nothing had really changed. Only the force of what I was feeling had.

I could see normally as soon as I opened my eyes. The sensations of dis-association and confusion I'd experienced in the middle of the night were still there, but they weren't as intense.

This time I was able to get up and get as far as the door of the bedroom. I looked down the hallway into familiar/unfamiliar territory. I/my body had to pee—but it was something I only knew from the pressure in my bladder. I knew the mechanics of how I would do it. I knew where to go, to lift the lid, and sit down. But I couldn't seem to call up one memory of the actual experience. The only real, tactile memories I had were of waking last night.

Panic came rolling up through my body, quickening my pulse, making me sweat, creating a worse confusion in me than I was already feeling.

Let it go, that small calm place inside me said. *Stop thinking about it for the moment. Give your body control—it knows what to do.*

What did I have to lose?

I took a deep, steadying breath. Another. I don't even know how I did it, but somehow I managed to step back from the panic and confusion and follow the voice's advice.

I was like a passenger as I made my way to the bathroom, peed and showered. Back in my bedroom, I looked in the closet and was momentarily overwhelmed by the choices. It's not that there were a lot of clothes—because there weren't. But there was still too much choice. I was still confounded by knowing exactly what all the various materials were, but not what it would be like to touch or wear them—their texture, their weight, the feel of how the fabric would hang.

I took another steadying breath and let the decision go. I watched as I chose a cotton T-shirt and a pair of jeans, enjoyed the sensation of the cloth as it covered me. Slipped on a pair of moccasins and wiggled my toes in them.

It wasn't until after I'd made toast and coffee and was still drinking the coffee at the kitchen table that the immensity of my disassociation began to ease. It came and went throughout the rest of the day, like the ebb and flow of some inexplicable tide, but the troughs and crests began to even out and calm.

The oddest thing was how whenever I had a question about something, that calm voice would speak up from the back of my mind in response. Like when I took the coffee from the fridge and I wondered about the beans as I spooned some into the grinder.

Coffee, the voice in my head said. *It's a beverage consisting of a decoction or infusion of the roasted ground or crushed seeds (coffee beans) of the two-seeded fruit (coffee berry) of certain coffee trees. It can also be the seeds or fruit themselves, or any of various tropical trees of the madder family that yield coffee beans, such as* Coffea arabica *and* C. canefora.

It was like I had an encyclopedia sitting in the back of my head. One that knew everything.

I didn't leave the apartment all day. I didn't dare. I explored its four rooms—bedroom, kitchen, bathroom, and the final all-purpose room that looked to be a combination of study, library, office, and living room. I opened the patio door that led out of that last room, but I didn't go onto the balcony. I simply stood in the doorway and studied the street below, the buildings on the other side.

Mostly I poked through the books and magazines I found, studied the contents of my purse and the wallet inside it, turned on the computer and explored its various document files.

It turned out I wrote poetry. A fair amount of it. I'd had three collections published, with enough in these files for at least a couple more, though some of the poems were obviously works-in-progress.

I also did freelance writing for various on-line magazines and wrote some op-ed pieces for *Street Times*, a little paper produced mostly by street people for street people—to give them something to sell in lieu of asking for spare change.

I found a financial program and saw that while I wasn't rich by any means, I had enough money banked to keep me solvent for a few months. When I thought about where that money had come from, my own work history popped up in my head. Dates, places of employment, job descriptions, salary and benefits. But I had no personal, hands-on memories of even one of these places where I was supposed to have worked.

I closed all the files and turned off the computer.

After a supper of asparagus, tomato, feta cheese and shredded basil on a small bed of pasta, I was finally able to go outside and sit on the wicker chair I found out on the balcony. The flavour of my meal still lay on my palate, the food itself a comforting pressure in my stomach. It was dark now, the city lit up with lights, but I was safe and unseen in a pool of shadow since I'd turned out the lights in the room behind me.

I watched the people passing below, each of them a story, each story part of somebody else's, all of it connected to the big story of the world. People weren't islands, so far as I was concerned. How could they be, when their stories kept getting tangled up in everybody else's?

But all the same, I understood loneliness right then. Not the idea of it, but the empty ache of it inside me. How one could live in a city of millions and realize that there was not one person who knew or cared if I lived or died. I searched my mind, but nowhere in amongst the neat and orderly lines of facts and work histories was there the memory of someone I could call a lover, a friend, or even an acquaintance.

That will change, the calm voice in the back of my head assured me.

But I didn't know—not how my life could have come to this, or if it even should change. Either I was so unlikable that I'd been unable to make a single friend in the—I counted out the years from the facts in my head—four years since I had apparently moved here from New Mexico—or I was some kind of freak. Neither, it seemed to me, deserved friends.

I dreamed that night that I was flying, soaring, not over city streets, but over circuit boards, and rivers of electricity. . . .

The next morning—my second that I could truly recall—I felt a little better. I still had a lack of hands-on memories and a calm, quiet voice in the back of my head that was happy to play encyclopedia for me, but the weight of a full day's experience seemed to have steadied me. Even if all I'd done for the whole day was wander around in my apartment and then get terribly depressed as I sat out on the balcony in the evening, that one day still felt as though it had anchored me to the real world.

In the morning light, things didn't seem quite so bleak, so desperately black and white, it had to be this way or that. I was able to consider that I might be different and it didn't cripple me. Last night's loneliness and despair had no real hold on me this morning. I didn't know quite how or where, but I was sure I had to fit in someplace.

Today I meant to go outside.

I finished my coffee and washed my breakfast dishes, then put on a pair of running shoes. I found my purse. After checking it for apartment keys, I stepped out into the hall.

My neighbour across the way opened his door at the same time and smiled at me.

"So there is someone living in that apartment," he said. "I'm Brad." He jerked a thumb over his shoulder. "In 3F, as you can see."

"I'm Saskia," I said and we shook hands.

He was nice looking guy, dark-haired and trim, dressed in casual clothes. I could tell he liked what he saw when he looked at me and that made me feel good. But as we stood there talking for awhile, I saw something change in his eyes. It wasn't like I had a bit of egg stuck between my teeth or something. I was just making him uncomfortable. By the time we'd walked down the two flights of stairs to the streets, I got the sense he couldn't get away from me quickly enough.

He gave me a brusque goodbye when we reached the street and headed off in the direction I'd been planning to go. I stood there by the door of the building, letting some space build between us before I set off myself. While I waited, I went back over our conversation, trying to see what it was I'd said or done to make his initial attraction toward me cool off so quickly. I couldn't think of a thing. Whatever it was seemed to have happened on some purely instinctual level—almost a chemical imbalance between us. The longer he was in my presence, the stronger it had become.

I won't say I wasn't disturbed by it, because I was. But there was nothing I could do about it now. He'd finally reached the end of the block, so I started off myself, aiming for the Chinese grocery store on the other side of the street, across from where he was. By the time I reached the corner, he was long gone.

There was a scruffy little dog tied up outside the grocery store, one of those mixes of a half-dozen breeds, but the terrier seemed strongest. He watched me approach, tongue lolling, a happy dog look in his eyes.

"Hey, pooch," I said, bending down to give him a pat.

He snapped at me and I only just pulled my hand back in time to avoid getting bitten. He was still growling at me as his owner came bustling out from the store.

"Rufy," she said. "Don't do that." She turned to me. "I don't know what's gotten into him," she added. "Rufus is usually so sweet tempered."

But I could see the same instinctive discomfort start up in her eyes as I'd already seen in her dog's, and in my neighbour's eyes earlier. Before it grew too strong, I slipped past her into the store where I picked up some milk, a bag of rice, and some vegetables for a stir fry. I completed the transaction as quickly as I could, not looking at the elderly Chinese man behind the counter. When I was outside the store again, the woman and her dog were already gone.

I stood there for a long moment, just watching the traffic at the intersection and not knowing what to do.

I was ready to retreat to my apartment, to stay there and stubbornly wait for them to show up—the people who had played around in my head and erased most of my memory, or the people who had created me and left me there to fend for myself. I didn't know which, but it had to be one or the other.

For a moment I had a shivering recollection of some invisible voodoo spirit in cyberspace, but that I firmly put out my mind. No, whatever the origins of my present condition, they weren't that improbable.

But maybe I'd been in an accident. Banged my head on something.

I felt through my hair, searching for bumps or a sore spot, but could find neither. That didn't really prove anything. It could have been a while ago. Or it could be some recurring medical problem. Perhaps there was someone coming to check up on me—I just couldn't remember who, or when they'd come.

Or I could be crazy.

I took the long way back to my apartment, circling the block that the grocery store was on. When I saw a homeless man sitting in the doorway of an abandoned store, I dug into my pocket for a dollar. I dropped it in his hat and smiled down at him, ready for a repeat of the reactions I'd already gotten from the other people I'd met so far today.

But he only returned my smile.

"Thanks, lady," he said. "You have a good day."

I couldn't tell his age—it could have been anywhere between thirty and sixty—but he had kind eyes. They were deep blue, clear and alert, which seemed a little at odds with his shabby clothes and weather-beaten skin. They were the eyes of someone at peace with the world, not someone living on the street and barely able to eke out a living.

"I'll try," I told him. "So far it's sucked big-time."

He nodded, eyeing me in a way that put me on edge again.

"Maybe you should try and turn down that shine of yours a watt or two," he said before I could go. "My guess is that's what's making people so uncomfortable around you."

I just stared at him, not really sure what I was hearing.

"What did you say?" I asked.

"Come on," he said. "Don't tell me you don't know. You've been touched by something—call it whatever you want. A mystery, the spirits, some kind of otherness. It's left a shine on you that most people aren't going to see, but they'll feel it and it's going to make them feel edgy and weird. It's like the world's shifting under their feet and no one likes that feeling."

"And it doesn't bother you?"

He shrugged. "I know what it is. I also know it's not going to hurt me. So why would I be bothered?"

"How do you know all this?" I asked.

"Hey," he said. "I wasn't always a bum, you know. I used to run a New Age head shop and while we sold a lot of let's pretend, some of our customers were the real thing and I learned a thing or two from them. Reading auras is pretty basic stuff."

"What happened?"

"I wasn't paying attention. That's the big lesson life teaches you: You always have to pay attention. Your marriage broke up? You weren't paying attention. Your partner cleans out your bank account and sells all your store's assets, leaving you bankrupt?"

He gave me an expectant look.

"You weren't paying attention," I said.

He nodded approvingly. "Exactly. I lost everything when the creditors came calling."

I crouched down, sitting on my haunches, so that our heads were level with each other.

"I'm sorry," I said.

"Yeah, me, too. But it's all water under the bridge now. Life goes on and most of us, we're just along for the ride."

A bus came by, making conversation impossible for a moment.

"So how do I turn down this . . . shine thing?" I asked when it was gone.

"Beats me. But the good news is, the longer you're away from the source of whatever put it on you, the weaker it'll get."

"And if it doesn't go away?"

"Then you'll only be comfortable with people like me who already believe. Who accept that there's something else out there and it's just as much a part of this world as you or me. The only difference is, it's in some hidden part that most people don't get to see. Hell, that most people don't want to see."

"Which is why I make them uncomfortable."

He nodded. "What was it that you experienced?"

"I have no idea," I told him.

I didn't really want to get into how weird my life had become in the past two days—not with a complete stranger, no matter how helpful he might be.

"Can I do anything for you?" I asked instead.

"Hey," he said. "You gave me a dollar and treated me like a human being—that's more that ninety-nine percent of the people I run into would do. So no. I'm good."

"But—"

"Just say hello the next time you see me," he said. "Let me know how you're doing."

"I will. What's your name?"

"Marc—with a 'C.' "

"I'm Saskia," I said, offering him my hand.

He cocked his head as he shook.

"Saskia Madding?" he asked.

I nodded. "How would you know that?"

"I've read some of your pieces in Street Times. No wonder you took the time to talk to me."

"Why—" I started, then stopped myself.

He'd already told me how he'd ended up on the street. It was none of my business what kept him there.

"Why do I live like I do?" he finished for me.

I shrugged. "I know it's not like you'd be doing it by choice."

"I suppose. But the truth is, I'm damned if I know. I guess I just gave up. Got tired of trying to find a job. I'm forty-eight and my back's shot. So I can't do heavy work, and nobody wants to hire an old man when he can get some bright-eyed kid with twice the energy and all the office smarts."

"Forty-eight's not old."

"It is in the work force. It's ancient. And it doesn't help that I'm a little too familiar with the bottle."

I paused for a moment, then asked, "Do you have someplace to stay?"

He smiled. "Come on now, Saskia. Don't go all caseworker on me. Let's just be friends."

"I wasn't trying to . . ."

"I know. It's just that your heart's too big. I already got that out of those pieces you wrote. But you don't want to be bringing home strays— not unless you've got a mansion on a hill and more money than you know what to do with. If you're not careful, you could end up with a mob of street people taking advantage of your goodwill and . . ." He gave me a toothy grin. "They wouldn't all be as pretty as me."

"But—"

"It's okay. I'm sharing a room with a guy in a boardinghouse off Palm. I make do. And who knows, one of these days I might actually get it together and try to rebuild my life. Next time I see you, maybe we'll go for a coffee and I'll share all these great plans I've got for fixing the world— starting with yours truly."

"All right," I said. "I'll hold you to that."

"Thanks for stopping by," he said.

I smiled and stood up. "No, thank you for helping me figure out my problems. Maybe you should consider becoming a counselor."

He laughed. "Yeah, I'm just chock-full of good advice, even if I don't put it into practice for myself."

"See you, Marc," I said.

"You know something?" he said as I started to walk away.

I paused to look back at him.

"If it was me, I wouldn't be in such a hurry to get rid of that shine of yours."

"Why not?"

"Well," he said. "It seems to me that everything's got a spirit, a mystery that most of us can't see. But invisible or not, that doesn't stop these secret spirits from being the heart of the world—sort of what keeps it beating. Are you with me so far?"

I nodded.

"Then tell me this: Why would you want to hang around people that get uncomfortable, or even scared, about that kind of thing?"

"Maybe just to feel normal," I said.

He laughed. "Normal's not all it's cracked up to be."

"You think?"

"Hell, I know."

I don't know if I could have taken Marc's advice even if I'd wanted to. So far as I could see, whatever was different about me came from inside. How do you avoid yourself?

But he made a good point about normalcy. Except I don't think it was so much that I wanted to be normal. It was more how nobody likes to be the brunt of other people's ill will—especially when you've done nothing to earn it.

I think the bigger question for me was that I needed to know *what* I was, and not even the voice in the back of my head seemed to have an answer to that.

In the weeks that followed I made a point of getting out and seeing people. It was hard. Most of the time I got the same kind of reaction as I had from my neighbour across the hall, or the woman with her dog outside the Chinese grocery store. I'd go to music shows, art openings, poetry readings— any place that a person could go by herself to meet other people. Invariably some guy would start to hit on me—especially in a club—only to back off as though he'd suddenly realized that I had a third eye, or a forked tongue, or who knows what? I'd stay for awhile, but eventually the general level of barbed comments and ill will directed toward me would get to be too much and I'd have to go.

Later, when I got to know Jilly and her crowd, I discovered that I'd been going to the wrong sorts of events—or the right events, only attended by the wrong sorts of people. But at the time, I didn't know and there were a lot of nights that I left hardly able to keep my tears in check until I was safe in my apartment with no one to see my despair.

I didn't have the same problem when people weren't actually in my presence. I was able to submit pieces to *Street Times, In the City, The Crowsea Times,* and some of the daily papers—soliciting commissions over the phone and submitting the finished pieces by e-mail. I developed a number of friendships that way, though I made sure to maintain them at a distance. The one time I didn't was a complete disaster.

Aaran Goldstein was the book editor for *The Daily Journal* at the time—still is, actually. I'd done a few reviews for him and we'd talked on the phone a number of times when he asked me if I wanted to get together for a drink before a book reading that he had to cover that night. Against my better judgment, because, logically, I knew it wouldn't work out—why should this be any different from all those openings and shows I'd attended?—I said yes.

We made plans to meet at Huxley's—not somewhere I'd have chosen on my own. It's that bar on Stanton across from Fitzhenry Park where the young execs on their way up congregate after work. Lots of chrome and leather and black glass. Lots of big exotic plants and various flavours of ambient techno music on the sound system. Lots of people who want nothing to do with mysteries or myths or magic, so you know how they'd react to me.

I started to tell him I was blonde, but he stopped me and assured me we'd have no trouble finding each other.

"Descriptions are for peons," he said. "But you and I . . . fate has already decided that we should meet."

The weird thing is, he was right. Not about fate—at least not so far as I know—but about our not needing descriptions. I stepped in through the front door of Huxley's at a little past seven that evening and immediately saw him standing at the bar. I've no idea why I recognized him. I guess he just looked like his voice.

He lifted his head and turned in my direction, smiled, and came to meet me.

"You see?" he said, taking my arm and steering me back to the bar where a pair of martinis were already waiting for us.

He clinked his glass against mine.

"To radiance," he said. "By which I mean you."

Aaran was a good-looking, confident man in his thirties—very trendy with his goatee, his dark hair cut short on the top and sides, drawn back into a small ponytail at the nape of his neck. One ear lobe sported two earrings, the other was unadorned. Pinky ring on each hand. He was wearing Armani jeans, a white T-shirt, and a tailored sports jacket that night. Shoes of Italian leather.

But the best thing about him—what let me overlook his overly suave mannerisms, what meant more to me than his appearance or his sense of fashion—was that he didn't get the look in his eyes.

Five minutes went by. Ten. Fifteen.

Not once did he seem to get creeped out by me. We just talked—or at least he talked. Mostly I sat on my stool, leaning one arm on the bar top, and listened. But it wasn't hard. He was well-spoken and had a story about anything and everybody: droll, ironic, sometimes serious.

We had two drinks at Huxley's. We went to the reading—Summer Brooks had a new book out, *So I'm a Bitch,* a collection of her weekly columns from *In the City*—and it was just as entertaining as you might imagine, if you follow the columns. We had a lovely dinner at Antonio's, this little Italian place in the Market. We went down the street to the Scene for another drink and danced awhile. Finally we ended up back at my place for a nightcap.

We'd been getting along so well, it seemed inevitable to me that we would end up in bed the way we did. I remember thinking I was glad I'd worn some sexy black lace underwear instead of the cotton panties and bra I'd almost put on when I'd been getting dressed earlier in the evening.

Sex had definitely been one of the things I'd wanted to experience as soon as I could. My own recollections of it seemed to have come out of books, and like everything else in my life, I couldn't find one real tactile memory of it in mind. From what I did know about it, it was supposed to be totally amazing, so it was disappointing to have it all be over as quickly as it was.

Later, I realized it was only because Aaran wasn't a particularly good lover, but at the time I just felt let down. Not so much by him, as by the whole build-up about the act of making love.

"Is that it?" I let slip out as he rolled over onto his back.

I hadn't meant to say it aloud and when I saw the dark look on his face, I really wished I hadn't.

He sat up. "What do you mean?"

"Nothing."

"Wasn't it good for you?"

"Of course. It's just . . . I thought . . ."

I stopped myself before I made it worse, even though what I wanted to say was, no, it was disappointing. I thought it would be more tender, and also more abandoned. That it would last longer. That the world would turn under me. That everything would stretch into this long moment of unbelievable bliss before finally releasing in long, slow waves that would leave me breathless. The way I could make it feel with my own fingers.

Yes, I stopped myself from saying any of that, but it was already too late.

"Jesus, I can't believe you," he said.

He swung his feet to the floor and stood up.

"I mean, it's not like I didn't know there was something weird about you," he added as he put on his briefs. "But I was willing to overlook it— you know, that twitch you put in people that just makes them want to back away?"

I stared at him, speechless. He found his T-shirt and pulled it on over his head, stopping to smooth back his hair.

"It's not like I'm alone in this," he said. "Sure, you look hot, but everybody who's spent any kind of time with you talks about how you've got this thing about you that just rubs them the wrong way."

"You've *talked* to people about me?"

"Well, sure. It's a small world. When a good-looking woman like yourself turns out to be such a cold fish, of course it's going to get around. What did you think? But I thought, 'I'll do her a favour. Show her a good time. Teach her how to loosen up a little and enjoy life.' "

"Get out," I told him.

"Right, like you're the one who should be pissed."

I got out of bed and gave him a shove toward the doorway.

"Now you just wait a—" he started, but I pushed him again.

He was still off-balance from the first push and stumbled backward, out into the main room. I collected the rest of his clothes and followed after him. There was a moment right there when I thought he was going to hit me, or at least try to, but I dumped the clothes and shoes into his arms and he instinctively grabbed hold of them. That gave me time to slip around him and open the front door of the apartment.

"Out," I told him, pointing to the hall.

"Jesus, would you let me put my pants—"

"Out," I repeated.

I grabbed my umbrella from where it was leaning by the door and held it like it was a baseball bat. He took one look at my face and went out into the hall. God, I wish I'd had a camera to capture that sorry image of him standing there, as good as bare-assed, skinny legs coming out from under his T-shirt, the rest of his clothes all bundled in his arms.

"This isn't the end of this," he told me.

"It is for me."

He shook his head, his face flushed with anger.

"Nobody treats me like this," he said. "I'll make you sorry you ever—"

"I already am," I said and shut the door in his face, engaged the lock.

I cried for a long time after he was gone. It wasn't because of what had happened with him—or at least not *only* because of that. Mostly it was because I felt so bereft and alone, abandoned in this unfair world where my only intimate human contact so far had been with such a sorry excuse of a loser. Now that the happy blush of just being accepted for once had been swept away, I realized that he was completely self-centered. He was full of words, but empty of anything meaningful. Our evening together had been for him, not for me, or even to be with me.

If Aaran Goldstein was an example of what it meant to be human, I wasn't so sure that I wanted to be one anymore.

I had my flying dream again that night, soaring over an endless landscape of circuit boards, their vast expanse cut with rivers of cruel electricity. . . .

I had gained some useful experience from my evening with Aaran, but otherwise not a lot had changed. Everything was still new and fresh. I knew what things were—and if I didn't, the voice in my head could give me its history—but not how they tasted, or felt, or sounded. Not how their essence reverberated under my skin.

I didn't stay away from readings or openings or clubs after that—I was too stubborn to give Aaran that small victory—but I didn't look to find acceptance or kindness at them anymore, and didn't find it either. Turns out, what honest friendships I came to make, I made on the street.

There was Marc, of course. I'd see him from time to time, always in some different doorway, panhandling on a street corner, dozing on a park bench. He carried a constant undercurrent of bitterness inside him—

directed at what he saw as his own personal failures, as much as at the uncaring world he was in, a world that had no time or place for those such as himself who, for one reason or another, had fallen through the cracks.

But most of the time, he kept that bitterness locked behind a cheerful front. I think what he liked best about me was that, no matter which face he showed me, I accepted him as he was and made no judgments. I also didn't hand out advice, or try to change him. I'd just buy him a meal or a coffee, and share it with him as though we were simply friends out to enjoy each other's company.

Charity didn't enter into it. He knew I'd give him a place to stay, or money, if he asked. But he didn't. And I didn't offer.

Then there was the woman that everyone called Malicorne whom I met on the edge of the Tombs one day, that part of the city that the citizens have abandoned, leaving I don't know how many blocks of empty lots, rubble-choked streets and fallen-down, deserted buildings. Factories, tenements, stores. The only legally-inhabited building was the old county jail, an imposing stone structure that stood on the western border of the Tombs, overlooking the Kickaha River, just north of the corner of Lee and Mac-Neil, but you couldn't call what the prisoners in there did as living. They were just marking time.

Malicorne was tall and horsy-faced, her eyes so dark they seemed to be all pupil. Her long chestnut hair was thick and matted, hanging past her shoulders like dreadlocks. But the thing about her—the strange thing, I mean—is how she had this white horn curling up into a point coming right out of the middle of her forehead. Now that's unusual enough, but even stranger is how nobody really seems to notice it.

"People don't pay attention to things that don't make sense to them," she said when I asked her about it.

Now I had a maybe strange origin, if my dreams and the voice in my head were anything to go by. She had one for certain. So why didn't people treat her the way they treated me?

She laughed. "Look at me," she said. "I'm living in a squat here in the Tombs, sharing meals and drinks with hobos and bums. Regular citizens don't even see me. I'm just one more street person to them. And if they don't see me—if I don't even register on their radar—how would they ever notice anything strange about me?"

"So why do you stay on the streets?" I asked.

"You mean, why don't I become a citizen?"

"I guess."

"Because the only stories that matter to me are the ones that are told here—on street corners, under an overpass, standing around an oil drum fire. It wouldn't be the same for someone else, but I'm not someone else, and they're not me."

I liked talking to her. She didn't just absorb stories other people told; she had countless ones of her own to tell. Stories about strange places and stranger people, of gods living as mortals, and mortals living with the extravagance of gods. I often wondered what my own story would sound like, coming from her lips. But I supposed first I'd have to figure out what it was for myself.

She left town before I could. One day she just wandered off and out of our lives the way street people do, but before she left, she introduced me to William.

He was living on the street at the time, too. There was a whole family of them that got together at night around the oil drums. Jack, Casey, William, and just before Malicorne left, a slip of a girl named Staley Cross who played a blue fiddle.

William was in his fifties, a genial alcoholic—as opposed to a mean drunk—with weather-beaten features and rheumy eyes. Something about Malicorne's going motivated most of them to get off the street. In William's case, he started attending AA meetings and got a job as a custodian in a Kelly Street tenement, just up from the Harp. He's still there today, surviving on the money he gets from odd jobs and tips.

I go to the AA meetings with him sometimes, to keep him company. He's been off the wagon for a few years now, but he's still addicted to one thing they don't have meetings for: magic. I don't mean that he's a conjuror himself, or has this need to take in magic shows. Or even that he's some kind of groupie of the supernatural and strange. He just knows a lot of what he calls "special people."

"I'm drawn to people like that," he told me one afternoon when we were sitting on the steps of the Crowsea Public Library. "Don't ask me why. I guess thinking about them, listening to them talk, just being with them, makes the world feel like a better place. Like it's not all cement and steel and glass and the kind of people who pretty much only fit into that kind of environment."

"People like Malicorne," I said.

He nodded. "And like you. You've all got this shine. You and Malicorne and Staley with that blue spirit fiddle of hers. There's lots of you, if you look around and pay attention. You remember Paperjack?"

I shook my head.

"He had it, too. Used to give you a glimpse of the future with these Chinese fortune-tellers of his that he made out of folded paper. He was the real thing—like Bones and Cassie are."

"So we've all got this shine," I said, remembering how Marc had told me he could see mine that day I first met him.

William gave me a smile. "I know it makes some people uncomfortable, but not me. I guess maybe I don't have a whole lot else left in my life, but at least I've got that. At least I know there's more to the world than what we see here."

"I suppose," I said. "Still, I wouldn't mind learning how to turn it down a notch or two."

"Why?"

"I don't know, exactly. So that I can fit in better when I want to fit in, I suppose. It's hard walking into a room and after five minutes or so, pretty much everybody's making it clear that it'd all be so much more pleasant if you'd just leave."

"That's important to you?" he asked. "Fitting in?"

"Maybe. Sometimes. I guess it's mostly wanting to do it on my own terms."

"Well, I know a guy who might be able to help you."

We tracked Robert Lonnie down at the Dear Mouse Diner, just around the corner from the library. He was sitting in a back booth, a handsome young black man in a pinstripe suit with wavy hair brushed back from his forehead. There was a cup of coffee on the table in front of him, a small-bodied old Gibson guitar standing up on the bench beside him.

"Hey, Robert," William said as he slid into the other side of the booth. I sat down next to William.

"Hey yourself, Sweet William," Robert said. "You still keeping your devil at bay?"

"I'm trying. I just take it day by day. How about you?"

"I just keep out of his way."

"This is my friend, Saskia," William said.

Robert turned his gaze to me and I realized then that he was another of William's special people. Those eyes of his were dark and old. When they looked at you, his gaze sank right under your skin, all the way down to where your bones held your spirit in place.

"Saskia," he repeated with a smile, then glanced at William. "If this isn't proof positive we're living in the modern world, I don't know what is."

I gave him a puzzled look when his dark gaze returned to me.

"Well, you see," he said. "I know that machines have always had spirits, but I look at you and see that now they're making babies, too."

I suppose that was one way of putting it.

"That's why we're here," William said. "We're looking for some advice on how to turn down her shine."

Robert pulled his guitar down onto his lap and began to pluck a melody on its strings, playing so soft, you'd have to strain to hear it. But the odd thing was, while I couldn't hear them clearly, I could *feel* those notes, resonating deep down inside me.

"Turn down your shine," he said.

I nodded. "It makes it hard to fit in."

"You should try being black," he said.

He improvised softly around a minor chord, waking an eerie feeling in the nape of my neck.

"I know it's not the same thing," I started, but his smile stopped me.

"We all know that," he said. "Don't worry. I'm not about to go all Black Panther on you."

His fingers did a funny little crab-walk up the neck of the guitar that took away the strange feeling the minor chord had called up.

"So can you help her?" William asked.

Robert smiled. "Turn down a shine? Sure." He looked at me. "That's an easy one. You've just got to stop being so aware of it yourself, that's all. Have you got any hard questions?"

"But . . . that's it?"

"Pretty much. Oh, it won't happen overnight, but if you can stop yourself from remembering, or believing, or what it is that you're doing inside that head of yours, soon enough everybody else will be seeing it your way, too. It'll be like you'll all start to agree that this is the way things are. Or should be."

"Making a consensual reality," William said. "Like the professor's always talking about."

Robert nodded. "Of course, you've got to ask yourself," he said to me, "why would you want to turn down a shine?"

Now it was my turn to smile.

"I've already been through that with William," I said. "Like I told him, I want the option of fitting in if I want to."

"Curious, isn't it?" Robert said. "All the magic people want to be normal, and all the normal people want magic. Nobody ever wants what they've already got and that's the story of the world."

He started a twelve-bar blues, humming a soft accompaniment to the aching music his fingers pulled from the guitar.

William and I sat there for a long time, just listening to him play before we finally left the diner.

I don't know if this happens to you, but it's a funny thing. There's this synchronicity with street people. Doesn't matter how unusual they might be, like Tinfoil Annie making her animals with aluminum foil that she then sets free in the gutters, or talented, like Robert Lonnie and the way he can play a guitar. See them once and suddenly you're seeing them all the time and you have to wonder, how was it that you never noticed them before?

After that afternoon in the diner, I started seeing Robert everywhere, playing that old Gibson of his. He was so good that I asked William once why Robert wasn't playing out, doing real gigs instead of sitting in the back of clubs, after-hours, or all the other places you might find him making music: on park benches, in diners, on street corners, in the subway.

"The story is," William said, "that he traded his soul to the devil to be able to make the kind of music he does. But it wasn't a fair trade. Turned out, Robert had that music in him all along—he just hadn't been patient enough to take the long way of getting it out. Anyway, he's supposed to have figured out a way he can live forever—just to spite the devil, he says—but he likes to keep a low profile anyway. Seems the devil will let you get away with a thing or two, just so long as you don't rub him in the face with it."

"Do you believe that?"

William shrugged. "I've seen enough things in this world that I'll keep an open mind about anything. And I like the idea of somebody putting one over on old Nick." Then he smiled. " 'Course there's others say Robert just ages well and has a natural talent."

Not everybody I met on the street actually lived on the street, even when, at first, it seemed as if they did. I guess some people were like I came to be— they just felt more comfortable carrying on their business on the edges of society.

I thought Geordie was homeless when I first met him—busking with his fiddle for people's spare change instead of panhandling. But once I got to know him, I realized that he just liked playing on the street. He played in clubs, too—had an apartment on Lee Street and all—but busking, he said, kept him honest. He was one of the first street musicians you'd hear in the spring—standing on some corner, all bundled up, fingerless gloves on his hands—and one of the last to give it up in the fall.

Geordie and I hit it off right away. I suppose we could have become more than friends, but I could tell he was carrying a torch for someone else and that kind of thing always gets in the way of developing a meaningful relationship. One or the other of you ends up settling for what's in front of you, but you're always remembering the something you couldn't have.

At first I thought that something was Sam, this old girlfriend of Geordie's who did this mysterious sidestep out of his life, but once I got to know him better, I realized he was really carrying the torch for his friend Jilly. I got the idea that neither of them was aware of it—or at least would admit it to themselves—though everyone else in their crowd seemed to be aware of it.

It's funny, considering how close he and Jilly are, that I must have known Geordie for almost half a year before I ever met Jilly and got pulled into her mad, swirling circle of friends. Geordie often talked about her and Sophie and Wendy and the rest of them, but somehow our paths never crossed. I know it's a big city, but when we finally did meet, it turned out we knew so many people in common, you'd have thought we'd have run into each other a lot sooner than we did.

Something similar happened with Christy, though in his case I'd actually seen him around before. I just hadn't known who he was.

The way we met, I was walking down Lee Street and saw Geordie at a table on the patio of the Rusty Lion with some fellow whose face I couldn't see because his back was to me. By the time I realized who it was, it was too late to retreat because Geordie'd already seen me. I made myself go up to their table to say hello.

You see, I'd already noticed Christy and been attracted to him long before we actually met. The first time was at a poetry reading. I spied him across the room and there was something about him that I liked enough to almost give up my promise of not trying to connect with people at those things. But then I saw that he was with Aaran and a woman—that I didn't get along with either—who worked for another paper. If they were his friends, I didn't want to be one myself.

I noticed him from time to time in the neighbourhood after that, usually on his own, but never put it together that this brother Geordie often talked about was the same person as this attractive stranger with his bad taste in friends.

Turns out I was wrong about the friends. Christy has impeccable taste in them, not least because he dislikes Aaran about as much as I do, though not for all the same reasons.

Once we got that out of the way, one thing led to another and . . . well, that's how I came to be where I am now, living with Christy.

I've learned to turn down my shine enough to get along in a crowd when I want to, but the price I paid for that is losing the voice in my head. And when I lost it, I lost my connection to whatever that big voodoo spirit in cyberspace might have been. I don't dream about flying over circuit boards anymore. I don't dream about pixels and streaming bands of electricity or any of that. Most of the time all those ideas just seem like some crazy notion I once had.

But I don't trust this flesh I'm wearing, either.

I don't trust the experiences that fill my head because they only date back to when I first appeared in this world. Like I said, I can follow a computer and paper trail tracing my background—where I was born, grew up, went to school—but I still can't recall any of it.

So, sometimes I still think that there used to be something else in my head, some vast world of information—or at least a connection to the spirit that people surfing on the Net can access as the Wordwood. Or perhaps it's still there, but I'm cut off from it.

I guess I'm not really sure of anything, except I know I'm in this world now. And I know I can count on Christy to stand by me.

Most days that's enough.

Christiana

It was different for me.

The first time I opened my eyes I knew exactly what I was: all the excess
baggage that Christy didn't want. How does he put it in his journal?

> . . . *at around the age of six or seven we separate and then hide away*
> *the parts of ourselves that don't seem acceptable, that don't fit in the*
> *world around us. Those unacceptable parts that we secret away*
> *become our shadow.*

I know. It sounds desperately grim. But it wasn't all bad. Because the
things that people think they don't want aren't necessarily negative.
Remember, they're just little kids at the time. Their personalities are still
only beginning to form. And all of this is happening on an instinctive,
almost cellular level. It's not like they're actually thinking any of it through.

Anyway, in my case . . .

Even as a little boy, Christy shut people out. That let me be open.

He was often so bloody serious—because he didn't trust people enough
to relax around them, I suppose—and that let me be cheerful.

He didn't make friends easily. I could and did.

But I got his dark baggage, too. A quick temper, because he held his in
check. A recklessness, because he didn't take chances—

Well, you get the picture. I was the opposite parts of him. Elsewhere in his journals he describes our physical differences:

She's short, where I'm tall. Dark-skinned, where I'm light. Red-haired, where mine's dark. A girl to my boy, and now a woman as I'm a man.

Basically, I opened my eyes to find that I was this seven-year-old girl who knew everything about being a seven-year-old boy, but nothing about being herself.

I suppose it could have been dangerous for me, trying to make my way through the big bad world all on my own at such a tender age, but it didn't quite work out that way. For one thing, when a shadow is created . . . yes, she's all the unwanted parts of the one who cast her, but she takes an equal amount of . . . I don't know . . . spirit, perhaps, or experience . . . some kind of essence from the borderlands. So right away, I was this unwanted baggage and something more.

What are the borderlands?

Once we started talking to each other, Christy was always asking, "Where do you go when you're not in this world?"

I wouldn't tell him for the longest time—as much because I like to hang on to the "woman of mystery" image he has of me as for any logical reason. But one night when he was going through one of his periodic bouts of self-questioning, I relented.

"To the fields beyond the fields," I finally told him, explaining how they lie all around us and inside us.

What I didn't explain is that they're part of the border countries, the fields that lie between this world he knows so well and the otherworld— Fairyland, the spirit world, the dreamlands, call it what you will. That otherworld is what the mystics and poets are always reaching out for, few of them ever realizing that the borderlands in between are a realm all their own and just as magical. They lie thin as gauze in some places—that's where it's the easiest to slip through from one world into the other—and broad as the largest continent elsewhere.

The beings that inhabit this place are sometimes called the Eadar. Most of them were created out of imagination, existing only so long as someone believed in them, though it's also the place where shadows like me usually go. The Eadar call it Meadhon. The Kickaha call it *àbitawehi-aki,* the halfway world. I just think of it as the middleworld. The borderlands. But I didn't get into any of that with Christy.

What I also didn't explain is what I was just telling you about how a shadow takes as much of her initial substance from something in the borderlands as it does from the one casting her. I don't know what it is. Maybe it's just from the air itself. Maybe something in the borderland casts another shadow and people like me are born where the two shadows meet. What I do know is that I had an immediate connection to that place and when I first slipped over, I met my guide.

I say "my guide," like everybody gets one, but that's not necessarily the case. I just know there was someone waiting for me when I crossed over.

Being new to everything, I simply accepted Mumbo at face value. It was only in the years to follow, as I began to acquire a personal history of experience and values, that I thought, isn't this typical? When other people get spirit guides or totems, they're mysterious power animals, maybe wise old men or women, like the grandparents you maybe never had.

I got Mumbo.

She was basically a mushroom brown sphere the size of a large beach ball with spindly little arms and legs that were folded close to her body when she wasn't using them to roll herself from one place to another. Much like those Balloon Men that Christy wrote about in his first book, *How to Make the Wind Blow,* I suppose. Today I can't imagine anything less mystical or learned, but she had a kind face and I was a newborn seven-year-old when I first met her. No doubt she was an appropriate shape to capture the interest of that child I was, and the immediate affection I had for her carries on to this day, for all that she's just so . . . so silly-looking.

But I'm getting ahead of myself.

The first time I opened my eyes, I was this scruffy little girl in a raggedy black dress, skin the colour of a frappuccino, eyes the blue of cornflowers, red hair falling in a spill of tangles and snarls to my shoulders. I was in the field behind the Riddell house. I sat up and looked at the window that was Christy and Geordie's bedroom. Paddy, their older brother, was already in juvie.

I knew who they were. I knew everything Christy knew up until the moment he cast me off. After that our lives were separate and we had our own experiences, although I still knew a lot more about him than he did of me.

He didn't even remember casting me out. That came years later, when he was reading about shadows in some book and decided to try to call his own back to him.

But I remembered. And I knew him. I'd follow him around sometimes, until I got bored. But I always came back, fascinated by this boy who once was me. Or I was once him. Whatever.

When he started keeping a journal, I pored over the various volumes, sitting at the shabby little desk beside his bed, reading and rereading what he'd written, trying to understand who he was, and how he was so different from me.

He woke once or twice to see me there. I'd look back at him, not saying a word. Closing the book, I'd return it to its drawer, turn off the desk light, and let myself fade back into the borderlands. I'd read later in his journal how he thought he'd only been dreaming.

But that first night I didn't go into the house. I was too mad at him for casting me out of the life we'd had together.

How dare he? How *dare* he just cast me off. Like he was putting out the trash. Like *I* was the trash. I'd show him what trash was.

Little fists clenched, I took a step toward the house, planning I don't know what—throw a rock through his window, maybe—but I accidentally stumbled out of this world and into the borderlands.

Where Mumbo was waiting for me.

Remember how easily distracted you could be as a kid? Oh, sorry. I guess you don't. Well, take my word for it. You can be in a high temper one moment, laughing your head off the next.

So I stood there, blinking in this twilit world that I'd suddenly found myself in, too surprised to be angry anymore. I can't tell you how I knew I'd stepped from one world to another, I just did. The air was different. The light was different. The biggest clue, I guess, was how the Riddell house at the far end of the field that I'd been walking toward wasn't there anymore.

I suppose I might have gotten scared, though I've never scared easily, except that was when Mumbo showed up.

I watched this brown ball come bouncing across the meadow toward me. When she stopped herself with her little spindly limbs and I saw her face, the big kind eyes twinkling, the easy smile so welcoming, I clapped my hands and grinned back.

"Hello, little girl," the brown ball said.

"You can talk."

"Of course I can talk."

"I've never heard a ball talk before."

"There are a thousand things and more that you have yet to experience," she said. "If you spend less time being surprised by them, you'll have more time to appreciate them."

"Are you going to be my friend?" I asked.

"I hope so. And your teacher, too, if you'd like. My name's Mumbo."

"I'm Christy," I said, then realized that wasn't true anymore, so I quickly amended it to "Anna," taking the first name that popped into my head.

Anna was a girl in Christy's class at school that he was sweet on at the time. Actually, Christy was always sweet on some girl or another—a serial romantic, that boy of ours. Or at least he was until he met you. But he'd never do much. Just give them moony looks and write poems that he never gave to them.

"It's nice to meet you, Christiana," Mumbo said.

I almost corrected her, but then I decided I liked the way it sounded. It was a new name, but it still had history.

"What kind of things are you going to teach me?" I asked.

I was a little nervous. Seven years of being part of Christy had taught me not to trust grown-ups. I knew Mumbo was a ball, and all of this was like out of some storybook, but she still had a bit of the sound of a grown-up about her when she spoke.

"Whatever you want to learn," she said. "We could start with my showing you how to move back and forth between the worlds. That's a very handy trick for a shadow."

"What's a shadow?" I asked.

I could tell from the way she said the word that she meant something different from what a light casts. But as soon as she started to explain, I realized I already knew. It was me. Cast out of Christy.

Not everybody has a shadow the way Christy describes it in his journal. Wait. That's not right. What I meant to say was that while everybody has a shadow, not everyone has access to the person that shadow might become.

First you have to call the shadow to you.

Some children do this naturally and never recognize these invisible companions and friends as ever having been a part of them. And most of those children put aside their shadows once they grow up so the poor creatures are rejected twice. Those that do remember, or learn about us somehow, are often surprised at who they find. I know Christy was.

At first he thought he might be going mad because I only came to him as a voice. I'm not sure why I did that. I think it was probably nervousness on my part. I wanted him to like me—I was a sort of twin, after all, and I'd long since gotten over being mad at him for casting me out of him—but I wasn't sure he would since, after all, I *was* all those parts of himself that he'd put aside.

Being born from the cast-off bits of someone else's personality isn't necessarily a bad thing. Because just like the people we echo, we go on after the split. We have the same capacity for growth and change as they do. We may begin life as evil, or clumsy, or outgoing, but we can learn to become good, or agile, or shy.

And I shouldn't have worried about Christy's reaction to me when we finally met in the flesh. He proved to be quite taken with me, half in love at first, though I've learned that isn't so surprising in situations such as this. It's also why shadows are drawn to those who cast them off, no matter what the difference is between them: You're meeting your other half, your missing half. In many cases, the changes you go through make you more alike, rather than less. Perhaps we teach each other the best parts of ourselves.

After his initial infatuation, Christy and I settled into more of a sibling relationship. He treats me as the older and wiser of the two of us, the one who understands Mystery because I live in it, because my very origins are so extraordinary. I don't feel that way. I learn as much from him, but I let him keep his misconceptions. Let's face it, a girl likes to be mysterious, doesn't matter if she's human or a shadow.

What's life like for a shadow? I don't need to eat or drink, but I love good food and a fine wine. I don't need to sleep either, but I still enjoy luxuriating under the sheets or spending the whole morning just lying in bed when the rest of the world is up and about its business.

And sometimes when I close my eyes and pretend to sleep, I actually dream.

I'm not doing such a good job of this. I should be explaining things in a more linear fashion—the way you did—but my brain doesn't work that way. Another difference between Christy and me, I guess. He's so logical, working everything through from start to expected finish, while I flit about like a moth attracted to any light with a strong enough flicker.

So where was I?

Right. Growing up as a shadow.

I grew more quickly than Christy. It wasn't just a matter of girls maturing sooner. Shadows can choose their age. We can't change our specific looks—I mean, I can't suddenly appear in front of you as a cat or a dog—but we can appear to be whatever age we want to be and that's a handy thing.

But I did mature mentally and emotionally much more quickly than he did.

That can't be helped when you spend most of your time in the borderlands where there's always something to learn. Not to mention that the spirit world lies just beyond the borderlands, and in the spirit world, anything you can possibly imagine and then some exists in one corner or another.

I also think that—remember I told you how some piece of the borderlands helps give a shadow her substance? I think it also allows you to acquire and understand knowledge more readily. It's not that you're smarter. That connection just allows you to assimilate things more easily. And you have access to more information and experience than the one that casts you off does, because you have three worlds to explore, instead of only one.

Plus, in some parts of the spirit world, time moves differently than it does here. Strictly speaking, I suppose I'm a lot older than Christy anyway because of living in some of the Rip Van Winkle folds of the spirit world, where the passing of a year is no more than the length of a day here.

And I was certainly sexually active a lot earlier than him. Truth to tell, by the time I was in what would have passed for my teens, I was pretty much an incorrigible wanton. I wanted to try everything.

I'm way more choosy about who I sleep with now.

"Why were you waiting for me?" I asked Mumbo one day after we'd known each other for a few years.

She was showing me how to braid sweetgrass into a strong, sweet-smelling rope. I don't know why. She was forever telling me about stuff and teaching me how to do things that seemed to have no relevance at the time, but proved to be useful later. So maybe at some point in the future, knowing how to make a grass rope was going to come in handy.

"You know," I added. "That first time I crossed over."

"It's what I do," was all she said. "I teach shadows."

Like that was all there was to it. But you know me—well, I suppose you don't, or we wouldn't be here talking. But I'll worry at a thing forever until

I figure out what it is or how it works. Someone told me once, "Curiosity may have killed the cat, but I'll bet she had a really interesting life up until then." I'm like that cat. I do have a really interesting life.

Still do, because I'm not dead yet.

There's always something going on in the borderlands. Between storybook characters, faerie, spirits and shadows, there's no time to be bored. Instead, you just appreciate any time you might get on your own.

You'd like the place I have there. I should take you sometime.

It's this little meadow the size of a loft apartment that I plucked out of a summer day—that's a trick Mumbo showed me. You choose it like you'd call up a memory snapshot, except it's got a physical presence that you can store away in a fold of space where the borderlands meet this world. You can visit it whenever you want and it just stays there, hidden away, forever unchanging.

I've got this meadow decked out like an apartment. I have a dresser and a wardrobe at one end where the birch trees lean up against a stand of cedars. Sofa and easy chairs, with a Turkish carpet between them, at the other end, under the apple tree. A coffee table and a floor lamp, though I don't need it because it's always light there—morning light, when the day's still fresh and anything's possible.

There are chests and bookcases all over the place because I'm a serious packrat and collect any and everything. My bed's tucked away in a shaded hollow under the cedars. I hang things from the branches of all the trees—ribbons and pictures and prisms. Whatever catches my fancy.

Christy wonders what my life is like when I'm not with him. He says, "Isn't that what we always wonder about those close to us? What are they doing when we're not together? What are they thinking?"

I know it bothers him that I don't appear to have the same curiosity about him—he doesn't know that I still go walkabout in his journals at night when he's sleeping.

But as you can see, I don't live a life seeped in ancient mystery and wonder the way he thinks I do. I have an adventurous life, a lively one, and I certainly rub elbows with all sorts of amazing people and beings, but I'm just an ordinary girl. Oh, don't smile. I am. An ordinary girl in extraordinary circumstances.

I was at a party once, in Hinterdale—that's this place on the far side of
wherever. In the otherworld, you know?

You'd have to see this place to believe it. Imagine one of those old fairy
tale castles, up on a mountaintop, deep forests spilling from near the base
of its stone walls all the way down into the valley below. It doesn't have a
moat, but it has the towers like spires and a grand hall as big as a football
field. Or at least it feels that way. But the best thing about it is that there's
this enormous tree growing right in the middle of that field-sized hall—an
ancient oak that's I don't know how many hundreds of years old.

I guess what I like the most about it is the fact that it's indoors. Like my
meadow apartment's outdoors. They're just off-kilter enough to make me
feel comfortable.

I can't remember whose party it was—the castle's sort of a communal
place with people coming and going all the time—but there must have been
at least a thousand people still there after midnight, every kind of person
you can imagine. Faeries, shadows, Eadar, ordinary folks who've learned
how to stray over into the borderlands. Everybody was in costume.

What was I? A blue-masked highwayman—highwaylady? Whatever. I
had the three-cornered hat, the knee-high boots, breeches and ruffled shirt
under a riding jacket, a pistol as long as my forearm except it wasn't real.

Anyway, I was sitting with Maxie Rose in a window seat that overlooked the courtyard outside and we got to talking about the meaning of
life—which, let me tell you, is an even bigger question in the borderlands
than it is here—and all the other sorts of things you find yourself talking
about at that time of night.

"What I don't get," Maxie was saying, "is how people keep trying to
come up with these theories to unify all the various myths and folk tales
you find in the world. I mean, I know there are correlations between the
folklore of different cultures, but really. Half the point of mystery and mag-
ics is their inconsistent and often contradictory nature. We live in a world of
arbitrary satisfactions and mayhem. Why should Faerie be any different?"

"People just need to make sense of things," I said.

"Oh, please. Sense is the last thing most of us need, though I suppose it
does keep me pretty and alive."

"What do you mean?" I asked.

She shrugged. "It's how Eadar stay potent. You know *here*. We teach
sense to the shadows."

Maxie was an old friend of mine, a green-eyed, pink-haired gamine, not quite as tall as me, with a penchant for bright-coloured clothes, clunky boots and endless conversation. Tonight she was dressed as a punk ballerina. Her tutu was the same shocking pink as her hair and her leggings were fishnets that looked as though they'd lost an argument with a shark, they were so torn and tattered. Big black Doc Martens on her feet. Truth is, her costume wasn't much of a stretch from her usual wear, except normally she didn't wear the Zorro mask—a black scarf with eyeholes cut in it.

She was always full of life, always so *present* that it was easy to forget that she'd been born as a minor character in an obscure chapbook that had been mostly unread in its author's lifetime and forgotten thereafter. Since Eadar—such as she was—depend on their existence by the potency of the belief in their existence, it never made any sense to me that she would continue to be as vibrant and lively as she was. From all I know of them, she should have faded away a long time ago.

"Teaching," I repeated, my mind going back to that day I'd asked Mumbo why she'd been waiting for me the first time I'd crossed over. "Like Mumbo did with me?"

Maxie nodded.

"And doing that makes you stay real?"

Maxie grinned. "I always said you were a quick study."

"Are there a lot of you doing that?"

"Oh, sure. Mumbo and Clarey Wise. Fenritty. Jason Truelad. Me. Whenever you see an Eadar who's *particularly* present, it's either because they were born in a story that was really popular—so lots of people believe in them and keep them real—or they're connecting with shadows."

"So Mumbo wasn't there to help me. She was only there to help herself."

"No, no, no," Maxie said. "It doesn't work like that. You really have to care about your shadows. Lots of Eadar don't even like them. I mean, think about it. You shadows show up in the borderlands, snotty little toddlers full of new life but without a clue, most of you with a chip on your shoulder and the last thing you want is advice from anybody."

"I wasn't snotty," I told her.

She grinned. "Says you. Regardless, it can be so frustrating teaching some of you how to get along. I can't imagine anyone getting into it unless they really, truly loved the work. The fact that it keeps us real is a side-benefit. Or at least it is now. I can't answer for the first Eadar who figured out that the relationship benefits them as much as the shadows under their care."

"I never knew."

"Lots of people don't. Lots of *Eadar* don't, which, when you think about it, is being really dumb. They just piss and moan and fade away. But like I said, if it's not something you feel comfortable doing, it's better that you don't try."

"But why shadows? What makes us so important to you?"

Maxie shrugged. "I don't know. For some reason your belief is really potent. All it takes is one of you to keep us *here*."

Isn't that a kick? One shadow, cast off and all, is equal, at least in this particular case, to all the readers of some bestseller.

The first time I met Christy?

I can't remember the exact when of it, but I remember the where. And the look on his face. He can be so cute, don't you think? You know, when something really catches him off-guard.

So what I did was, when I saw him out on one of those late night rambles of his, I followed along until I got a sense of where he was going then slipped on ahead of him. By the time he stepped onto the Kelly Street Bridge, I was already there, leaning on the stone balustrade and gazing down into the water. It was a lovely night, late summer, the sky clear above and full of stars. There was a bit of a wind and the moon was just coming up over the Tombs.

I listened to his footsteps, timing it so that I looked up just when he was getting close.

He started to give me a nod, the way you do when you meet someone out on a walk like this, but then he stopped and gave me a confused look. You know—he thought he knew me, but he didn't.

"Need some directions?" I asked.

I knew that my voice was just going to add to the off-kilter sense of familiarity he was feeling.

"No," he said. "You . . . I feel like I should know you."

"I'll bet you use that line on all the girls," I said, smiling when it called up a blush.

"No . . . I mean . . ."

I relented. "I know what you meant. You should know me. I'm the voice in the shadows."

I saw understanding dawn in his eyes and he got that look I was talking about, so cute.

"But . . . how can you be real?"

"Who says I'm real?"

Okay, so I was being a little mean. But I guess I still had some issues with him at that time, like how he cast me off when we were only seven years old.

He leaned against the balustrade, looking like he really needed its support.

"Relax," I said. "You're not going crazy."

"Easy for you to say."

I was going to reach out and touch his arm, just to reassure him, but something made me stop, I'm not sure what.

"I just thought we should meet," I said instead. "Rather than you sitting in your reading chair and me talking to you from the shadows. That's starting to get really old."

He was studying my features as I spoke.

"I've seen you before," he said. "How can I have seen you before?"

"Remember when you first started to keep your journals?"

He nodded. "And sometimes I dreamed that I woke and there was this red-haired girl sitting at my desk, reading them."

"That was moi."

"You've been around *that* long?"

"I've been around since you were seven and cast me off."

"I didn't know I was casting you off," he said. "I didn't even know about shadows until a couple of years ago when I came across that reference to them in a book about Jung."

"I know."

A cab went by, slowing as it neared us to see if we might be a fare, then accelerating again when we looked away.

"Did it hurt?" he asked.

"Did what hurt?"

"When you were cast off."

"Not physically."

He gave a slow nod. "Are you okay now?"

"What do you think?"

"I don't know. You seem very self-assured. I got that from our conversations. You don't seem unhappy. Actually, you seem nice."

"I am nice."

"I didn't mean—"

"I know," I said. "You just figured that all the cast-off bits of you would make some dark and evil psycho twin."

"Not exactly that."

"But someone the opposite of who you are."

He nodded.

"But you cast me off when you were only seven," I said. "Lots of what you got rid of were positive traits. And we've both grown since then. We're probably more alike than you'd expect, considering my origins."

"So . . . where do you live? What do you do?"

I smiled. "You know how you like to write about mysterious things?"

He gave another nod.

"Well, I live them," I said.

"And you won't tell me about them because—"

"Then they wouldn't be mysterious, would they?"

We both laughed.

"But seriously," he said.

"Seriously," I told him, "I live in between."

"In between what?"

"Whatever you can be in between of."

He gave a slow nod. "Where magic happens."

"Something like that."

"So why are you here now?" he asked.

"I already told you. The whole speaking from the shadows bit was getting old for me. Besides, I thought you'd be interested in us finally meeting."

"I am. It's just . . ."

I waited, but I guess for all the words he puts down on paper, he didn't have any to use right now.

"Disconcerting," I said.

"That's putting it mildly."

"Tell you what," I said. "Why don't I just let you deal with this for awhile."

He grabbed my arm as I started to turn away and an odd . . . I don't know . . . something went through me. Bigger than a tingle, not quite a shock. He let go so quickly that I knew he'd felt it, too.

"Do you have to go?" he asked.

I shook my head. "But I'm going to all the same. It's not like we won't meet again."

"When? Where? Here? On this bridge?"

"Wherever," I told him. "Whenever. Don't worry. I can always find you."

"But . . ."

I let myself fade back into the borderlands.

I'd been as interested meeting him as he'd appeared to be meeting me, but I felt a little strange, too, and suddenly felt like I needed some space between us. That strange spark that had leapt between us hadn't been the only indication that there was something going on—just the most apparent.

"It's good to keep some distance between yourself and the one who cast you," Mumbo told me when I asked her about it later.

We were on the roof of an abandoned factory in the Tombs, looking out at the lights of the city across the Kickaha River. Below us on the rubble-strewn streets, the night people who made this lost part of the city their home were going about their business. Junkies were shooting up. Homeless kids and tramps, even whole families, were picking their squats for the night and settling in. Small packs of teenagers from the suburbs and better parts of town were travelling in small packs, avoiding the bikers and such, while looking for weaker prey they could harass. Business as usual for the Tombs.

"I kind of felt that I should," I said. "Except I don't really know why."

Mumbo went into her lecture mode. "The attraction between a shadow and the one who cast her is understandably strong. You were once the same person, so it's no wonder that you'd be drawn to each other. But spend too much time with him, get too close, and you could be drawn back into him again."

"What do you mean back into him?"

"He will absorb you and it will be like you never were. It's happened before. It can happen again."

Sometimes I'd get curious about the Eadar I met, and I'd go haunting libraries and sneaking into bookstores when they were closed to see what I could find. I was probably most curious about Mumbo and Maxie Rose. It took me awhile, but I finally tracked down the books that they'd first appeared in.

Maxie's was particularly hard. There were only fifty made and it was so dreadfully written that their original owners tended to throw them away.

Oddly enough, the copy I eventually found was in Christy's library. It was a thirty-page, saddle-stitched chapbook called *The Jargon Tripper* by Hans Wunschmann and though I managed to read it all the way through twice, I never could figure out what it was supposed to be about. The only character he brought to any semblance of real life in its pages was Maxie and, in the context of the abysmal prose that made up the greater portion of the text, that seemed more by accident.

I never did find out who the "jargon tripper" of the title was, or what it meant.

"Did you ever figure out what Wunschmann was trying to say?" I asked Maxie the next time I saw her. "You know, in that story he wrote that you were in."

Maxie laughed. "Sure. He was saying, 'Look at me. I'm pathetic and I can't write a word, but that's not going to stop me from being published.' Though he didn't say it in so few words." She grinned at me. "He didn't have to. All you had to do was try to read it."

"That's a little harsh."

"You *did* read it, right?"

"Yeah. But I'm sure he must have been trying to do something good. There must have been something in what he was writing that meant a lot to him if he'd spend all that time writing it and then self-publishing it."

"You wish."

"Come on, Maxie. At least allow that he gave it his best shot."

"Did he?" Maxie said. "And don't get me wrong. I've nothing against self-published books, so it's not because of that. I just don't like crap."

"But—"

"And I guess it particularly ticks me off because *that's* the story I got born in. It couldn't be a good book. Oh, no. I had to get born in the literary equivalent of an outhouse."

"But he made you," I said. "You were good in the story. And you're still here, so there must have been something in what he was doing."

Maxie shook her head. "The only reason I'm here is because I'm tenacious and I was damned if I was going to fade away just because I had the bad luck to be born on the pages of some no-talent's story. I don't know what I'd have done if I hadn't discovered I have a gift for teaching shadows. But I would have done something."

Some days I really feel bad for the Eadar. It must be so hard to be at the whim of someone else's muse.

I also asked Christy about Wunschmann.

"I still have that?" he said when I showed him the chapbook. "I thought I'd thrown it out years ago."

"Did you know him?"

"Unfortunately. He was this little pissant who was in some of the classes I was taking when I was in Butler U.—always talking, full of big ideas and pronouncements, super critical of everybody. But that little chapbook's all he ever produced. I remember he used to really be down on me and anyone else who was actually getting stories published."

"So you didn't like him."

Christy laughed. "No. Not much."

"And the story?"

"Well, I liked this one character—Mixie, Marsha . . . ?"

"Maxie Rose."

He nodded. "Yeah. She deserved a better writer to tell her story."

"Maybe," I said. "Or maybe she figured out a way to do it herself."

He gave me a funny look, but I didn't elaborate.

Mumbo's was a sweeter story. Or perhaps I should say it was bittersweet. It was certainly better written.

The only edition was a little hardcover children's picture book called *The Midnight Toyroom* that I found in the Crowsea Public Library. The author was a man named Thomas Brigley. The watercolours, done in that turn-of-the-century style of children's book illustrators like Rackham or Dulac, were by Mary Lamb.

The book was published in Newford in the late nineteen-twenties to some local success but never really made much of a mark outside of the city. I looked Brigley up in a biographical dictionary, but he didn't even get a mention. I did find him in *The Butler University Guide to Literature in Newford*, where he got a fairly lengthy entry. He was a life-long bachelor who worked for a printing company, writing and publishing his books in his spare time, which I guess he had a lot of. Of the thirty-seven books that were published under his by-line, only one was for adults—a nonfiction history of the tram system called *Cobblestone Jack,* named after a fictional conductor he had telling the history.

Mary Lamb, his collaborator on all the books, was a librarian who, like Brigley, worked on the books in her spare time. She never married either, which made me figure there was a story in there somewhere, but I couldn't find anything about them ever having been an item—or what might have stopped them from becoming one—in any of the library's reference books. I did find pictures of them, including one of the two of them together. They made an attractive couple in that shot, and there was an obvious attraction between them from the way they were looking at each other, so it didn't make much sense to me.

I tried tracking Cobblestone Jack down, but unlike Mumbo, he'd faded away a long time ago the way most of Brigley's other characters had.

Mumbo only survived because of her connection to shadows like me, but after reading her story, I didn't understand why she'd needed us.

The Midnight Toyroom is about this girl who loves a boy so much that she has the Toy Fairy change her into a ball so that she can be with him. See, he was from this rich family and her parents were servants, so there was no way they could be together. Weren't things weird in those days?

Anyway, he loved the ball and called it Mumbo. Played with it all the time. Only when he got older, he left it out in the woods one day and never thought about it again and there she would have stayed, except the Toy Fairy had allowed her to come alive when no human was watching, so she was able to make her way back to the house. The trouble was, once she got there, she was found by the housekeeper who was packing up all of the boy's old toys to send to an orphanage, and she put Mumbo in with them. The last picture in the book is of Mumbo sitting on the top of a pile of toys in a cart as it slowly draws away from the boy's house.

It was sweet and sad, really well written, and the pictures were beautiful. So I couldn't understand why it hadn't been more of a success. Maybe it was the downbeat ending, but it's not like Hans Christian Andersen didn't write some downers that were still popular. I mean, have you ever read "The Little Match-Girl" or "The Little Mermaid"?

When I found Mumbo's book in the library, it wasn't even on the shelves anymore. I had to dig it out of the stacks because it hadn't been taken out in years. No surprise, I suppose, hidden in the back the way it was. But it was still listed on the card index, so if anybody had wanted it, they could have requested it.

It's just that nobody did.

Have I ever had a meaningful relationship? You mean like what you and Christy have? Not really. Like I said, I had a lot of . . . let's be poetic and call them dalliances, but nothing long-term. Friendships, yes. Lots of them, some I've maintained for years. But to be more intimate . . .

I've never met anyone in the borderlands or beyond that did it for me, and it's way too complicated for me to even think about it in this world. I mean, I'd either end up being this oddball curiosity—after I've told them what I really am—or I'd have to lie and make up a career, where I live, that kind of thing. It just gets too complicated.

Although I just got a cell phone that even works in the borderlands—works better there, actually, than it does here, since Maxie showed me how to rewire it so that we tap into the essence of the borderlands to make our calls, instead of having to worry about satellites and phone companies. So I suppose I could give out a number now if I wanted to and just be all mysterious about where I live and how I make a living.

Oh, don't smile. So I have this thing about being mysterious. You can blame Christy and his journals for that.

Sure, I can give you the number. But you have to promise not to give it to Christy.

No, it's not just books. Eadar are created out of the imagination, period. It doesn't have to be words on paper. It can be anything from a painting to a passing daydream, but they're not like Isabelle's numena. Eadar depend on belief to exist whereas numena are bound to their painting. The less invested in an Eadar's creation, and therefore the less belief in it, the quicker they fade. It's really sad how ephemeral some of them are, no more than ghosts, barely here and then gone. There are parts of the borderlands—those that are closest to the big cities, usually—where Eadar ghosts are as thick as midges on a summer's day.

But while they can be sad little sorry creatures, that's not always the case. Some have so much belief in them that just glow with energy. For me—probably because of Christy's influence—the really interesting ones come from mythologies.

In the borderlands, faerie are making a big comeback. And so are earth spirits—you know, earth mothers and antlered men. On the down side, so are vampires and other less pleasant creatures. And then there are new ones.

You know why you keep hearing about Elvis sightings? So many people believe he's still alive, that he actually is, except now he exists as a very potent Eadar. As more than one, actually. There's a young, kind of tough one from the early years—though he's still polite as all get-out. But there are also a couple of others: the smoother one from the films and a kind of pudgy one from the Vegas years.

You should see it when the three of them get together. You've never heard such arguments. But then you've never heard such music, either.

Anyway, you get the picture. Maybe I started my life as the cast-off bits of somebody else, but I've made my own way ever since. I grew. I changed. I became somebody that no one else is, or can be, because they don't have my life. They don't know the things I know. They don't know what I've felt, what I've experienced.

See, that's what I figure being real means. If you're able to adapt, to mature, to become something other than what it seemed you were supposed to be, then you're real. You've got a soul. Because something that's just a fictional construct, it can't do that. It can only be what its maker says it is. That's what's so sad about the Eadar. They can be as fiercely independent as Maxie Rose, but if Hans Wunschmann decided to write another story about her and changed her personality, or her history, or whatever, those changes would reflect on the Eadar that she's become and all her personal history as an Eadar wouldn't matter.

Continuity's another big topic of discussion in the borderlands and the lack of it's why so many Eadar suffer from various personality disorders. If they don't fade away first. Longevity's not exactly a big part of most of their lives.

But that's not something you or I have to worry about. Our origins might have been outside the norm, but we've grown into the skins and souls of real people. We can't be changed by a few brushstrokes, or bits of new description, or keystrokes.

And I'd like to see someone try to tell me what I'm supposed to be. Anyone does, they'd better have quick reflexes. Why? Because I'd smack 'em so hard they'd be sitting flat on their asses before they ever knew what hit them.

Oh yes. I can be fierce when I need to be. That's one of the first things you have to learn if you want to survive in any world.

And Here We Are

*It's not
the words you use;
it's what
they make you see.*
—SASKIA MADDING,
"Poems" (*Spirits and Ghosts,* 2000)

Christiana

"So I guess we're both misfits," I say.

It's funny. I can't remember the last time I've talked this much. I guess I'm like Christy in that—I like to sit back and listen, just take things in. Mind you, he's always been quiet. I had to learn to be that way.

Saskia nods. "I suppose we are."

I meant it as a joke, but she seems to take it seriously. I study her for a moment, her gaze going past me, out the window, but she's not looking at anything. She's gone someplace deep inside herself and I'm not here anymore. Not for her. Everything's gone—the café and everybody else in it.

After a moment I get up and get us each another drink—chai tea for her, black coffee for myself. Saskia's back when I return, her gaze focused, tracking me as I approach where we're sitting.

I set her tea on the table in front of her and she smiles her thanks.

"I was reading this science fiction book about A.I.s," Saskia says when I've settled back into my chair. "You know, machines with artificial intelligence?"

"Mmm."

"That's what's got me thinking about all of this. Life's not that much different than that book, really. If they knew what we were, humans really would hate us—just the way they do androids and A.I.s in fiction."

I shake my head. "We're as real as humans."

"But they're flesh and blood."

I lean forward and pinch Saskia's arm.

"So are we," I say.

"Maybe now we are, but—"

"When . . . how—what's the difference? We have spirits. We have souls. How we got them isn't important."

"It is to humans."

I smile. "Screw humans."

But she doesn't smile back.

"And maybe it's important to me, too," she says. "I guess you're okay with what you know about where you came from, but I don't even know that. I start to think back and I've got ahead full of memories, but they only go so far before I hit a wall. Did I come out of nothing? Can I still have a soul?"

"Well, there's an easy way to find out," I say.

She gives me a puzzled look.

"We'll go back to where you came from—you and me. I'll take you back into the Wordwood. The answers might not be here, but they've got to be there."

"I . . . I don't know."

"What are you worried about?"

"What if once I get there, I can't come back? What if I'm only a piece of whatever the Wordwood is and once I get there, it just absorbs me again? What if it absorbs you, too?"

I shrug. "That's just the chance we'll have to take, I guess. I mean, it all depends on how badly you need to know this thing."

Saskia gives me a considering look.

"Are you really this tough?" she asks.

"Don't forget fierce, too," I say, adding a smile.

"I wish I was. Tough and fierce. Sure of myself."

"It takes work," I tell her. "And it doesn't mean you don't get scared anymore. It just means you don't let the fear stop you from doing what you want, or need, to do. That's where the work part comes in."

She gives me a slow nod.

"And how do you plan for us to get there?" she asks.

"I'll take you by way of the borderlands."

"We can get to the Wordwood through these borderlands?"

"You can get anywhere from the borderlands," I tell her. "And if you're right, if there is some great big voodoo spirit running that Wordwood program, he or she probably lives in the otherworld."

"The otherworld . . ."

I nod. "Mind you, I can only bring you across—you'll have to figure out where we're going once we're over there. Depending on how good your homing instincts are, it could take awhile, so we should probably go sooner than later. At least that's what I would do. I mean, why wait?" I have a sip of my coffee and raise my eyebrows. "Hell, we can go right now."

"No, I'd have to talk to Christy first. I couldn't just leave him hanging."

"And he so hates change."

"He's not that bad."

"We could bring him with us," I say, though I know that could be problematic. I can't spend too much time with him or who knows what might happen.

Saskia shakes her head.

"Oh, come on," I say. "He's not that stodgy. He'd jump at the chance to visit the otherworld."

"Probably," she says. "But I think this is something I should be doing on my own. For myself. And because . . ." She hesitates, that far distance filling those blue eyes of hers again for a long moment. "Who knows what I'm going to find."

"Nothing you could find could make him feel any different about you. Those Riddell boys are so true blue loyal they make dogs seem unreliable."

"I know. But still . . ."

I wait to see if she's going to finish her sentence.

"But still," I agree when she doesn't. "I understand. How about if I come by to pick you up midmorning, then? That'll give you a chance to talk to him and get ready."

She gives me a nervous look.

"It's funny," she says. "This is something I've been thinking about for ages. But now that you're offering me this easy way to actually do it, suddenly I don't feel even remotely ready."

"That's okay, too," I say. "Why don't you think about it, talk it over with Christy, and decide in the morning. I'll come by and you can tell me what you've decided."

Now it's her turn to smile. "And you'll knock on the door like a regular visitor?"

"Maybe. We'll have to see how I'm feeling. I do like the look on Christy's face when I just step out of nowhere."

"You're incorrigible, aren't you?"

"I try to be."

We both have some more of our drinks, silence lying easily between us.

"Why do you want to do this?" Saskia asks after a few moments.

"Maybe I'm just the helpful type," I say.

"Okay."

I can tell she doesn't believe that.

"Or maybe I just like the adventure of doing something new," I add. "I've never been inside a computer program before. It's got all the promise of an interesting experience."

"And the danger doesn't worry you?"

"Tough," I remind her. "Fierce."

"Foolhardy," she adds.

"Probably that, too."

The World Wide Web Blues

The puppet thinks:
It's not so much
what they make me do
as their hands inside me.
—Saskia Madding,
"Puppet" (*Mirrors,* 1995)

Aaran Goldstein

One week before Christiana and Saskia met in the Beanery Café and shared their life histories with each other, Aaran Goldstein was in Jackson Hart's apartment, having a conversation with the young computer wizard.

"This is really strange," Jackson said, leaning forward to study his monitor more closely.

Aaran nodded. "I already know it's a weird site," he told Jackson, making an effort to keep the irritation he was feeling out of his voice. "The question is, can you hack into it?"

Jackson was one of the paper's programmers and computer troubleshooters. Younger than *The Daily Journal*'s book editor and probably twice as smart, he was in his early twenties and lived on a diet of soda and junk food, but his coffee-coloured skin remained clear and he never put on any weight—all facts that annoyed Aaran to no end since it had taken him a strict regime of proper diets and exercise to finally get rid of the acne and flab that had plagued him all through his high school years. But while Jackson's metabolism and higher intelligence annoyed Aaran, it didn't stop him from taking advantage of Jackson's expertise. Using people was second nature to Aaran at this point in his life.

They were sitting in Jackson's home office, a room that held more computer equipment than Aaran had ever seen before outside of a computer store's showroom. He didn't know what half of it did, but that didn't matter. All that mattered was that Jackson did.

"I really don't know," Jackson said in response to Aaran's question. "This is a new one on me. Here, take a look at this."

Using his mouse, he brought the arrow on his screen up to the menu bar, clicked on "View," then on "Source."

"See?" he said. "There's no code."

"And that means?"

"I don't know what it means. It's impossible. There's always code. You can't have a Web page without code. Without code, there's no way for your computer's browser to translate what's stored on the site's ISP into something you can see on your computer. What we should have here is HTML text all over the screen."

"Except it's blank," Aaran said.

Jackson wheel his chair back from the desk to look at him. "Exactly. So what's really going on here?"

Aaran shrugged.

"Because I've heard of these ghost sites before," Jackson said. "They're like the big voodoo mystery of the Internet. This is the first time I've run across one of them, but I've heard enough to know that they're trouble."

"What kind of trouble?"

Jackson's gaze returned to the screen. There was a white box in the center of the screen that doubled as a search engine and a kind of message board. Behind the box a video of a forest was displayed—very smooth streaming. You could see the leaves moving in a breeze and there was nothing jerky about their shivering movement. The resolution was crystal clear. The sound of the breeze came out of his speakers—soft and soothing. Occasionally there was movement in a tree branch—little birds and animals, though sometimes they looked like people. Or animals wearing clothes.

"I don't know," he said. "Just trouble."

"But it's interesting, isn't it?"

Jackson regarded him. "I suppose." He waited a beat, then asked, "What exactly is it that you want me to do if I can hack into this site— which, I'm telling you now, I don't see happening."

Aaran leaned back in his own chair.

"It means a lot to someone who fucked me over," he said. "So I want to mess around with it, let her know that it may take awhile, but Aaran Goldstein always pays you back."

"Well, I hate to rain on your parade," Jackson told him, "but it's not going to happen with this site."

"Okay. New plan, then. Can you shut it down?"

Jackson took another look at the screen. "Probably. If I can get who-ever's on the other side of its firewall to open an attachment."

"You're going to use a virus?"

Jackson nodded.

"That works for me," Aaran said. "The site gets shut down and you get to add another notch to your joystick, or however it is you guys keep score." He smiled. "So I guess I'm doing you a favor, really. Now you'll get to brag to your buddies about how you just took down another big bad site."

Jackson gave him a cold look.

"No," he said. "All that's happening here is you're blackmailing me into fucking up somebody's life and destroying a lot of hard work."

"Blackmail's such a harsh word," Aaran said.

"Oh, yeah? Then what would you call it?"

"An exchange of favors."

"You're not doing me a favor. I don't get any kick out of what you're asking me to do."

"That's a good line. Remember to use it when the cops come knocking at your door."

Jackson glared at him, but Aaran only smiled. It was too late for Jackson to get out of this now. If he'd wanted to stay safe, he shouldn't have gotten drunk and spilled all his secrets.

It had happened a few weeks ago. Aaran was returning from a club on Gracie Street where yet another hot babe had shut him down—something that been happening on an increasingly regular basis ever since that night Saskia Madding had thrown him out of her apartment, leaving him stand-ing there in her hallway with his clothes in his arms and anger churning like a hot cauldron in his stomach.

An anomaly, he'd told himself. She was the loser, not him.

But it had brought back all the lonely years of being the fat, pimple-faced reject with glasses he'd been in high school. Brought them back in an instant, just like that, as though they'd never gone away. He went in a flash from the guy with the cool to the loser getting turned down for the school dance by Betty Langford, who was more of a loser herself, but still thought she was too good to go out with the likes of him.

He'd been doing so well at forgetting those days, at reinventing his childhood.

Me? he projected. Hell, I've always been cool.

All he had to do was look in a mirror. That poor fat little kid with the zits and glasses was gone as though he'd never been. People he'd gone to school with weren't able to see the kid he'd been in the man he'd become. Maybe that wasn't such a surprise. That kid hadn't even registered for most of them.

But every so often something came along to remind him. Like tonight. The woman he'd been hitting on had given him such a look of disdain that when he looked away from her, his gaze locked on the mirror behind the bar where, for one painful moment, his own reflection was replaced with that of a sorry-assed little kid with a spray of zits across his face, staring back at him, hurt puppy-dog eyes bewildered behind their glasses.

He didn't know how he knew. He just knew it was Madding's fault. There was something spooky about her, always had been. Not spooky enough for him to forgo taking advantage of her the way he had. But certainly enough so that in retrospect, he realized maybe he should have stayed clear of her. Maybe then she wouldn't have cursed him, or done whatever it was she'd done to put this hex on him.

Because ever since that night it was as though the sorry vapors of his high school days had risen up and were clinging to him once again—a clear warning to any woman with her loser-radar turned on, which these days was every one of them. And the more times he got turned down, the worse it seemed to get.

He left the club, staring at the ground, walking aimlessly down Gracie Street, not ready to give the courting game another try, certainly not ready to go home. Another night shot and no way for him to get back at Madding for bewitching him, or at her little crowd of boho friends for making fun of him every chance they could.

Except fate smiled on him.

Stepping into Lobo's for a last drink before he headed home, tail between his legs, who should he see but Jackson Hart, one of *The Daily Journal*'s computer nerd squad, deep in his cups and obviously bumming, big time.

There was nothing like somebody else's misery to make you feel better about your own sorry little life.

He slid into a stool beside Jackson, ordered a beer from the bartender, then turned to his coworker.

"Having a bad night?" he asked.

Jackson lifted his gaze from where it had been locked on the empty shot glass in front him and turned to Aaran. He seemed to have a moment's trouble focusing. When he did, he gave a slow nod.

"Woman trouble?" Aaran said. "Because let me tell you, I've been there."

"I wish."

This wasn't good, Aaran thought. Come on. I want details. I want something to make me feel better.

"Well, you've got a good job," he said, "and if it's not woman trouble, then I can't think of a single reason for a successful fellow like yourself to be so depressed. Unless it's a health issue?"

"Even that'd be better," Jackson said.

Now Aaran was intrigued. He got the bartender's attention and ordered a refill for Jackson. He was drinking sipping whiskey, but he wasn't sipping it.

"Well, you know," he said. "My grandfather was always full of good advice and one of the best pieces he gave me was this: trouble shared, is trouble halved."

Actually, he'd read that in one of the endless flood of self-help books that came to the paper. This one had annoyed him so much, he'd actually taken the time to trash it in a quarter-page review.

"So if you need a sympathetic listener," he added, "I'm here."

Jackson swallowed his drink in one shot, looked blearily at the glass for a moment, then set it down on the bar top with exaggerated care.

"I screwed up," he said. "Big, big time."

Aaran waited. He had a sip of his beer. The reporters at the paper were always saying that if you kept quiet, people'd feel obliged to fill the hole, saying more, perhaps, than they meant to. And sure enough, patience paid off.

"I just wanted to see if I could get inside," Jackson said finally. He spoke slowly and carefully, a drunk trying to sound sober. "To see if I could, you know? I mean, these banks . . . it's like they think they're doing *us* some big favor by letting us pay them to keep our money, not to mention shelling out a few bucks for every little transaction that comes along. I wasn't really going to do anything once I got inside. Maybe leave a message for the manager—you know, thumb my nose at him. Here's one for the little people.

"I didn't mean to mess everything up."

He fell silent for long enough that Aaran realized he'd better offer some input.

"Nobody ever plans to mess things up," he said.

Jackson nodded. "I guess. But most people's mistakes don't have money machines spitting out twenties all over town until they run out of money."

"That was *you*?"

"It was an accident."

"Hey, I believe you," Aaran assured him. "Who cares anyway? That kind of a loss is no more to the banks than you or me getting short-changed at the grocery store. Screw them."

"I suppose. Though they aren't going to see it that way. And neither are the cops."

"First they'd have to catch you," Aaran said. "Did you leave any kind of a trail?"

Jackson shook his head. "Nothing that'd be of any use to them unless they were already looking in my direction."

"Any chance of that?"

"I guess not. I'm nobody to them."

"So like I said," Aaran told him. "Screw them all."

He ordered another round for them from the bartender. When their drinks came, he tapped the lip of his beer mug against Jackson's shot glass.

"Here's to thumbing our noses at the moneymen," he said.

"I guess," Jackson said and swallowed his shot in one gulp.

And that had been that. Jackson felt better getting the burden of guilt off his chest and Aaran came away with informational leverage that he knew would come in useful at some point in the future. He didn't know where or when—not until he'd found himself logging onto the Wordwood this morning and remembering how Madding had waxed so enthusiastic about the site that one night they'd had together. Before she tossed him out on his ear. Before she put the hex on him that had turned his love life into no life.

"Maybe I *should* tell the cops," Jackson said now, still glaring at Aaran. "Just to get you off my back."

No, that was a bad idea, Aaran thought.

"Hey, come on," he said, turning on the charm. "I was just being an asshole. You do this for me and we're square. I don't want to see you rotting away in a jail cell, turning into some big-ass biker's girlfriend, anymore than you want to be there."

Jackson wouldn't look at him. His gaze rested on his computer screen, his face giving away nothing of what he was thinking.

This was no good, Aaran thought. Time to shift gears. Get the kid talking so that he can show off his smarts and stop thinking about how I'm making him jump through hoops.

"So how come you don't hear more about these sites?" Aaran asked. "You know, like in the press?"

For a moment he thought Jackson was going to continue to ignore him, but he finally looked away from the screen and back at Aaran.

"That's just more of their weirdness," he said. "It's like you can't talk about it—at least not publicly. You can send the URL to someone, but you can't seem to write about it."

"I don't understand."

"There's no point in trying to figure it out," Jackson said. "I knew a guy who was doing a piece on another site like this for *Wired* and he just couldn't submit it. When he tried to e-mail it to his editor, it came back as undeliverable. But here's the really weird part: It was also erased from his hard drive. After that, whenever he tried to write about it, the files would disappear from his hard drive—like someone was sitting inside his machine, keeping tabs on what he was doing. Finally he wrote it out by hand, but that doesn't do you much good."

"Why not?"

"Everything's on-line these days. Everything's connected. The same computer a publisher uses to lay out an issue is hooked up to the Internet. And if his isn't, the printer's is. Somewhere along the line these things always just disappear. The only pieces I've ever seen on sites like this are what somebody photocopied."

"So you *can* get the information out."

Jackson shrugged. "I guess. But who reads hardcopy anymore?"

"Hopefully *The Daily Journal*'s readers."

"You know what I mean. Everybody's getting their information off the Net these days. It just makes more sense."

"I can't argue about the convenience."

Hell, he cribbed half the stuff he used in his own pieces from on-line reviews and articles—suitably rephrased and given his own spin, of course.

"Look," he said, figuring Jackson was calmed down enough by now to get back to the business at hand. "We've gotten off on the wrong foot here. I know it seems like an unfriendly thing that I'm asking you to do, but this woman's just been asking for it. I've let it slide for a few years—truth is, she burned me good, but I was willing to let it go if she would. But lately she and her little circle of friends have been making my life hell. Every time there's the smallest mistake in the book section, they're all over it with letters to the editor, badmouthing me to publishers' reps and in the bookstores. It's gotten to the point where my boss is on my case about it."

He took a breath.

"See, it's never anything big," he went on, "but if you get enough people complaining, it looks worse than it is. My boss doesn't know a book from a coaster, but he understands negative feedback and he doesn't like it. Which means it comes down on me and . . ."

He let his voice trail off when he realized that he was beginning to rant. Just thinking about Madding and her friends these days was enough to get him going. But from the look on Jackson's face, Jackson couldn't care less, and he wasn't here to air his own dirty laundry. He was just here to get a service done.

"So I take the site down," Jackson said, "and we're good? You won't be coming around asking for another favor two weeks down the road?"

Aaran shook his head and put his hand up in a Boy Scout's salute.

"Scout's honour," he said.

Which would mean something if he'd ever been a Scout.

Jackson studied him for a long moment, then finally sighed.

"Okay," he said. "I'll get on it."

"Any idea how long it'll take?"

"Two, three days. By the weekend, for sure. Unless . . ."

"Unless what?"

"Whoever put that site up is smarter than me."

Jackson Hart

True to his word, Jackson started working on the problem as soon as Aaran left the apartment. The first thing he did was write a simple virus program—nothing fancy. Simple was as capable of shutting down a computer as complicated. Maybe it wasn't as impressive, but it usually had a better chance of slipping in and getting the job done.

The virus he wrote now would worm into the ISP's computer that housed the Wordwood's site, dig through every file stored on it, and erase any HTML links it found, replacing them with random gibberish. Any site hosted by that ISP would immediately be rendered useless.

It wasn't a permanent meltdown. But it would require anyone using that ISP as the host for their site to send clean files to replace the ones his virus had damaged. That could take anywhere from a few hours to a few days, depending on how much material they had to transfer back onto the site. Considering the size and complexity of the Wordwood site, it should be enough of an inconvenience and take them long enough to satisfy Aaran's need for revenge.

All Jackson had to do was get somebody at the Wordwood end to open an attachment, but he didn't think that would be too hard. Since they seemed to collect texts of books, he'd simply hide the virus as a macro inside a file purporting to be a book with a trigger that would make the macro run as soon as the file was opened. Then the next time the Webmaster updated his site, the virus would piggyback along with whatever he sent and the server would go down.

Piece of cake, really.

He hummed as he worked on the program, then tested it. The programming soothed his anger the way it always did. That was half the reason he'd gotten into computers in the first place. Mostly, he loved the clean logic of programming. Computers were so much better than people. They were straightforward, doing only what they were programmed to do. They didn't lie to you, or make fun of you. Or blackmail you.

He was ready to send the virus by two A.M., only a few hours after Aaran had left.

Now, he thought, we'll see how tight the Wordwood's security is.

Logging back onto the Internet, he established his protocols through a confusing labyrinth of false trails and dummy ISPs that left no way to trace him back to the computer he was actually using. He aimed his browser at the Wordwood's site. When the forest background appeared on his screen, he began to type into the white box floating in the center of the screen.

Love your site. How do I submit a book to add to your library?
An eager reader

He'd barely finished typing when a response appeared, replacing his own text:

Hello eager reader.
Simply send the document file as an attachment addressed to:
webmaster@thewordwood.com

Whatever you say, he thought.

He opened Eudora, typed "a book from an eager reader" as a subject heading, attached his file, and hit "queue." When he closed the e-mail software, he got a prompt telling him he had an unsent message. He chose "send and close" and watched the progress bar until the file had been sent. Eudora closed and he was looking at the Wordwood site once more.

He stretched his arms over his head, then got up and went into the kitchen, returning with a can of soda and a bag of chips. He doubted that anything was going to happen immediately. If the Webmaster at the Wordwood was anything like every other Webmaster Jackson knew, he'd be so overworked that he probably wouldn't get to the e-mail for a few days. And then he'd have to actually update the site before the virus could even start to do its thing.

He had a sip of his soda to wash down a mouthful of chips.

This really was an amazing site. The video and audio of the background alone were enough to mesmerize him. No matter how long he studied it, he couldn't detect a loop in either. Then there was the swiftness of response time to messages and the sheer volume of material on the site itself.

He did another check for code, but there was still none available to view.

Whoever had done this really knew his stuff. How did you make code invisible, but still readable to the viewer's browser?

Magic.

Voodoo.

His mouth went dry, and not because of the chips. He had another sip of his soda, remembering what he'd been telling Aaran.

He wasn't entirely ready to believe that the Internet was spawning A.I.s somewhere out there in its pixelated reaches, but there was no denying that there were some brilliant programmers. If the Webmaster of the Wordwood was as good as he appeared to be, he might just detect the virus before it ever did any damage. Worse, he might be able to track it back to this computer.

You didn't need magic for that. You just needed good hacking skills.

And maybe, once the Webmaster had Jackson's I.D., he might want to deliver some payback. Do a little walkabout through, oh say, Jackson's bank accounts and set all the balances to zero.

Jackson stared at his monitor and began to regret sending the virus. He hadn't wanted to do it in the first place—who got pleasure out of trashing somebody's hard work except for emotional misers like Aaran Goldstein? There was something creepy about this whole business. The site. Aaran's need for revenge. The blackmail.

The forest on his screen was starting to give him the willies just the way a real-world forest did. The few times he'd been out in the country in the past few years, he'd always gotten the feeling that something was hidden in among the trees, watching him.

It hadn't been like that when he was a kid. As a kid, he used to spend all his spare time in the wood lots behind the housing development where he'd grown up. At least he had until a bunch of kids had taken to lying in wait for him, chasing him through the trees and beating him up whenever they could. That was when he'd first started to spend so much time in front of a computer.

Maybe that was why forests still creeped him out. Why he always felt like he was being watched. Logically, he knew it wasn't true anymore. Just like there was nothing hidden in the branches and leaves of the Wordwood's index page, watching him now.

But it *felt* like there was.

He started to reach for his mouse to click himself off-line, when his screen flickered and went blank. A moment later, a familiar message appeared along the left side of his browser window:

This page cannot be displayed.
The page you are looking for is currently unavailable. The Web site might be experiencing technical difficulties, or you may need to adjust your browser settings . . .

Followed by a list of the things he could try to reconnect with the site. Yadda, yadda, yadda.

He watched, unable to move, expecting he didn't know what. But finally, he reached forward again and disconnected his computer from the Internet.

What do you know. His virus had worked. And quickly, too.

He didn't feel any sense of accomplishment—not like when he'd finally gotten past the bank's firewalls and realized he was actually in. He just felt kind of dirty.

I should take a shower, he thought. But first . . .

He picked up his phone and dialed the number that Aaran had left him. He got an answering machine on the first ring. It was going on three A.M. He supposed not everybody was up at this time of the morning.

"I don't know how long it'll last," he said into the receiver, "but the site's down for now. They'll be able to get it back up again, but it'll probably be a few days." He paused, then added, "So we're square now, right?"

He looked across the room, the receiver still at his ear, but he had nothing else to say, so he hung up.

He took his shower and went to bed, but lay in the dark, staring at what he could see of the ceiling above his bed for a long time. He found he could still hear the breeze of the Wordwood's site. When he closed his eyes, the forest was there, as though the streaming video was playing across his eyelids.

Neither left him as the rest of the week went slowly by.

He had the breeze in his ears. It was like what you heard after a loud concert—a faint, steady ringing. Because he was always focused on it, it seemed louder than it really was, a constant soundtrack to the routine of his life. Sometimes it was just static.

The forest lived on the inside of his eyelids like a video tattoo. He caught glimpses of it every time he blinked. When he closed his eyes for longer periods of time, the breeze in his ears grew louder and he felt swept away someplace. Then he'd start, look around, check his watch. He'd lost a minute or two. By the end of the week, sometimes the pieces of lost time stretched into half an hour.

He didn't see Aaran again until two days after the Wordwood went down. Walking down a hallway in the offices of *The Daily Journal,* he came around the corner, and there was Aaran. Jackson hadn't been avoiding the paper's book editor, but also hadn't gone out of his way to contact him again after he'd left the phone message the other night.

"Jackson," Aaran said, smiling. "My man. I got your message. Excellent job. Fast service and the sucker's still down."

"I guess."

"You don't look too happy about this."

"I don't see anything to feel happy about."

Aaran shrugged. "Yeah, well, that's because you don't have the personal stake in it like I do. Man, I can't wait to see one of Madding's crew. Drop a little hint. Let them know who they're screwing around with."

Don't, Jackson wanted to say. But what was the point? Sensitivity and discretion weren't exactly among Aaran's personality traits.

"And we're good now?" he asked instead. "You know. About the bank . . . ?"

"What bank?" Aaran said. He gave Jackson a light punch on the shoulder. "Gotta run. Editorial meeting."

Jackson nodded. "Sure."

He closed his eyes for a moment as Aaran turned away. The forest reared up on the backs of his eyelids, something still watching him from within the foliage. When he opened his eyes again, Aaran was long gone and he stood alone in the hallway.

He kept checking the Wordwood site through the rest of the week, but it remained down.

On the night that Saskia and Christiana met at the Beanery Café, Jackson was in his apartment. After heating up a frozen burrito in the microwave, he sat down in the living room to eat it while he watched some TV. He never noticed when he'd dropped off, but when he snapped back into himself, he realized that he'd lost four hours this time.

Four hours.

The half-eaten burrito was sitting cold on a plate on the coffee table. He picked up his can of soda and had a drink. The soda was warm and flat. He looked around the clutter of his living room. There seemed to be a space between himself and everything familiar. The TV caught his eye as whatever show had been on went into a commercial.

He picked up the remote. Pointing it at the TV, he hit the off button.

He remembered . . .

Trees . . . branches . . . leaves . . . an endless forest . . .

But not a real forest, not even a video pretending to be a real forest like at the Wordwood site. Instead it was like someone had gone into a stretch of woods and sprayed a thin sheen of metallic paint onto everything. All around him the leaves and branches, the undergrowth, every blade, every leaf of every plant, was metal and ore. Gold and silver and steel. Copper and iron. Burnished and gleaming, but also rusty and black. When a branch brushed a wafer-thin leaf, sparks flew. Thousands of tiny firework displays were discharged whenever a breeze came sighing through the trees.

Underfoot, when he kicked at the metallic plants and dirt, the ground was made of circuit boards and wires.

And there was the voice.

He remembered hearing a voice, a quiet, murmuring voice, talking to him, but either he was just out of range, or it was speaking in a language he didn't understand, because he hadn't been able to make out a word of what it was saying.

No, that wasn't true. In amongst the gibberish he could distinguish two words, repeated so often they might have been on a loop.

Find . . . can't find . . . can't . . . can't find . . . find . . .

And though the volume of that voice had never risen, he remembered an urgency in it.

What couldn't be found?

He rubbed at his face. His eyes felt gritty, his mouth too dry. He had another drink of the flat soda, then got up and went into the washroom. He ran the water until it was cold, then bent over the sink, splashing it on his face.

The metal forest flickered on the back of his eyelids every time he closed his eyes or blinked. The breeze remained constant in his ears, like radio static now. The sense of being watched by whatever was in among those trees was stronger than ever, as though the watcher was looking for something.

Can't find . . . can't . . .

He stared at his face in the mirror, wondering, what couldn't be found? Was the thing in the forest looking for him? Or was he just going crazy?

He turned away and went over to his computer work station, turned the computer on.

He knew when all of this had started. When he'd sent that e-mail to the Wordwood site. Maybe he could stop it by sending another. He couldn't think of anything else. He just knew, if he didn't do something soon, he really would go crazy.

The e-mail he composed was short and to the point. He confessed to the virus he'd sent and included instructions on how to remedy the damage it had caused. When he was finished, he queued the e-mail and called up his dial-up window. Once he was on-line, he pressed send.

He knew that it would take hours, if not days, for the Wordwood's Webmaster to be able to fix the damage that his virus had done, but he opened his browser and aimed it at the Wordwood site anyway. The "This page cannot be displayed" message appeared almost immediately.

As he started to close his browser, the page on his screen shivered. He held his hand still on his mouse. The browser page shivered again, then a ripple ran from one side of the screen to the other and a small black dot appeared in the center. When the dot began to expand, Jackson let go of the mouse and pushed back from his computer station.

It reminded him of a pupil. As though his monitor was an eye, and the expanding dot was its dilating pupil. Looking at him. Directly at him.

The static breeze in his ears grew louder. He wanted to shut off the computer—at least go off-line—but the truth was, he was scared to even touch the machine now. It was all just too weird. His hacker's paranoia was operating at full throttle—who's watching me, who knows, what will they do? He remembered all the supernatural voodoo talk about spirits in the Net that got talked about in newsgroups and when he got together with his computer friends.

What if those spirits weren't locked into the Net? What if they *could* get out? What if they were *already* out?

Something was screwing around with his hearing.

Something was making him hallucinate—flashes during the day, dreams of metallic forests.

He didn't want to think about it. Don't articulate your fears, he'd heard once, or you might make them true. But he couldn't help it. How could he help *not* thinking about it?

Something *was* watching him.

He could feel its presence, even if he couldn't see where it was hidden. He didn't know what it was. He couldn't say if it was in his computer, or somewhere in the room with him, but it existed. The animal part of his brain, the part that operated on pure instinct, could sense its interest in him. It woke a pin prickle of warning at the nape of his neck that made the little hairs stand up and sent nervous twinges snaking down his spine.

And something *was* exerting a physical effect upon him.

The static breeze grew louder in his ears. Every time he blinked, the forest tattooed on his eyelids left a residue of its presence in his vision. The expanding eye, staring at him from his monitor, filled the screen until his monitor went black. Then something else started to happen.

He rolled his chair closer to his desk, leaning in to look at it.

Condensation appeared to be forming on the outside of the screen—dark drops of some sort of oily liquid was beading on the glass, then running down the surface of the monitor in trails to drip from the bottom onto his desk. Jackson reached a finger to touch one of the drops. Before he could, the static in his ears swelled into a roar. His monitor changed from a machine with a glass screen to an open window and a flood of the thick liquid came gushing out. It was as though his monitor had become the portal of a sinking ship already under the surface of the ocean.

He jumped up and back, sending his chair skidding, then lost his footing in the black pool that had already formed around his desk. He went down, flailing his arms.

Impossible. None of this was possible.

He mind refused to accept what was happening, but his animal brain fully believed and was in a blind panic.

When he tried to get back on his feet, the liquid was too slippery for him to find purchase. He fell again, face first into the liquid, and came up spluttering. He turned and caught a face-full of the oily liquid as it continued to gush out of the monitor.

Down he went again.

The force of the liquid pushed him in a tumble toward the door. He felt as helpless as he once had as a child, falling into a stretch of rapids while fishing with his father. His father had plucked him out of the water then, but there was no one to do that here.

He hit the door with enough to force to take the wind out of him and fell face forward into the goopy liquid again. It was almost a foot and a half deep now and showed no sign of letting up.

The static breeze in his ears had grown into a dull roar. Dimly, beneath its static rasp, he heard the voice from his dreams.

Find . . . can't find . . . can't . . .

He managed to grab hold of the door handle and haul himself up above the surface of the liquid, his feet still skidding from under him as he tried to stand. He spat to clear his mouth, but the goop clung to his gums and his teeth and the roof of his mouth. Getting a good grip of the door handle with one hand, he used the other to wipe at his face.

He froze when his hand came in front of his eyes. With numb fascination, he realized that he could see right through it as though he were fading. Or coming apart.

High school science classes came back to him, some teacher droning on about how everything was made up of molecules, constantly vibrating. Linked to each other to form matter.

Linked . . .

It was like the links that held him together were dissolving as surely as had the ones on the Wordwood Web site when he'd infected it with his virus.

This couldn't be happening.

Except he could see right through his hand. He could—

His other hand lost its grip of the door handle. Or did it simply go *through* the door handle?

It didn't matter anymore.

As he sank into the liquid, he could feel himself being absorbed by the black goop, molecule by molecule, all the links that held him together fading away, no longer able to do the job they were meant to do.

The last thing he thought was, if a Web site has a spirit, this must be what it feels like when a virus takes it down . . .

Holly Rue

To: "holly rue" <hollyl@cybercare.com>
Date: Sat, 26 Aug 2000 22:38:19 -0700
From: "thomas irwin pace" <tip@lunaloca.com>
Subject: WW down?

Hey Holly

Quick question: Have you been able to log on to the Wordwood site lately? I haven't been able to connect to it all week long, and it's not just me. Everybody I've talked to says the same thing. I don't think it's been on-line since Monday—at least that's the last time I was able to connect. Wasn't a great connection either. Pages took forever to refresh. No real-time dialogue with whoever's running the site these days. All the streaming video and sounds were down.

Any ideas?

Tip

P.S. Aiden says you'll really like Monkey Beach by Eden Robinson. She wrote that collection Traplines a few years ago, remember?

Holly hadn't been able to connect to the Wordwood all week either, but she hadn't considered that the site itself might be down. She'd simply assumed it was yet one more problem with her own service provider. CyberCare had been great when she'd first signed up with them a few years ago, but the ISP's service had been getting dodgier ever since, especially over the past couple of months. She was seriously considering switching ISPs, for all the hassle that would entail in terms of having to move her store's Web site and change its Internet address.

After rereading Tip's e-mail, she tried to log on to the Wordwood again herself and received the same message she'd been getting all week:

This page cannot be displayed.

She stared at the useless screen, wishing her partner Dick was as good at solving computer problems as he was at keeping the bookstore tidy. She was hopeless with either. She used to think she was pretty good at keeping the store neat and running smoothly all on her own, but that was before she discovered she had a hob living behind the furnace in her basement. A real hob, mind you, like in a fairy tale. Not some little man pretending to be one.

Dick Bobbins wasn't much more than two feet tall with curly brown hair, large dark eyes and a broad face creased with laugh lines. He now lived in her spare bedroom. He was the one who kept the store so shipshape, spending his evenings dusting and filing new arrivals, organizing and straightening the books on the shelves, and generally being more efficient in one day than Holly could be in a week. Though he'd share a cup of tea and meals with her, he really seemed to get his sustenance from the books he read.

Holly had no idea how that was even possible, but she supposed when it came to logic, magic marched to its own drum.

She hadn't even realized that beings such as Dick existed until she first met him a year or so ago. He'd been her own secret fairy-tale housekeeper—so secret, even she hadn't known he lived with her. And when she did find out, it seemed that real life followed the fairy tales when it came to hob lore—thank them, or give them a gift, and off they'd go. Dick had his bags all packed and was sneaking out the door until she made him an offer of partnership in the store. Ever since, she'd felt guilty because Dick worked so hard while she continued with her usual slow-mo puttering. But it was hard to *make* Dick relax. He loved to read, of course, and he read prodigious amounts of books. Which is why he'd chosen her store as a residence in the first place. But his idea of relaxing was endlessly dusting, sweeping, tidying, cleaning . . .

Fairy-tale being or not, Dick was definitely suffering from an obsessive-compulsive disorder.

She'd given him a book on the subject, but after reading it, all he said was, "Yes, Mistress Holly, that's me all right," and kept right on doing it. She guessed that breaking him of the habit of leaving a place after he'd been thanked was at least a good start—she'd just have to work on this compulsive need to be constantly cleaning. Though, really. If it was left up to her own haphazard approach to store maintenance, she didn't want to think what the place would look like.

"What do you think, Snippet?" Holly asked, turning to look at her Jack Russell terrier. "Am I taking advantage of him the way Christy says I am?"

Snippet regarded her with one eye and gave a desultory kick at the air with a hind leg. All it would require was the smallest hint of encouragement and she would bound up from the front display window where she was lying and into Holly's lap. When Holly returned her attention back to the computer, Snippet gave a heavy sigh.

"Oh, I'm not forgetting your walk," Holly said over her shoulder. "Just let me answer Tip's e-mail."

What could have happened to the Wordwood?

Anything, she realized. Almost from the first—when she and Tip, Sarah, Benjamin and Claudette had first started it up—the site had been one anomaly after another.

They'd all attended Butler University together, going their separate ways after graduating. Still, they'd stayed in touch—with e-mail it was easy—and got together whenever they could, which usually worked out to be once or twice a year since they all still had family in Newford. It was at one such get-together a number of years ago that they hit upon the idea of putting together a site specializing in literature—which had quickly gone on to encompass writing of all kinds as they couldn't agree on what should or shouldn't be considered literature.

The initial vision was to collect as many bibliographies, biographies, and public domain texts as they could, sharing the storage space on their various servers, linking to other sites such as Project Gutenberg and First

Chapters to save themselves from having to input information that already existed elsewhere on the Net.

They soon had an enormous surge in enthusiastic help from e-mail correspondents across the globe, making suggestions, pointing out errors, e-mailing new links and material. The Wordwood quickly grew from a hodge-podge of a Web site—a personal vision brought to life and existing on five separate servers—to something else again. Something they couldn't have predicted and still didn't understand.

For the site took on a life of its own.

It didn't happen overnight—or at least they didn't realize it overnight.

First they began to find texts on one or another's servers that none of them had put up. This shouldn't have been possible since, like most Web sites, theirs was password-protected and only the site owners were supposed to have access. Initially, they treated it as an anomaly, something that the more computer literate among their number tried to figure out in their spare time, but nothing they actually felt they needed to worry about.

"Strange things happen on the Net," Sarah, the real computer guru of the site's original founders, liked to say. "There's all kinds of voodoo in cyberspace. Ghosts and spirits, haunting the wires."

The unauthorized text additions didn't become a real problem until copyrighted material began to show up. Not wanting to be sued—and besides they had a healthy respect for the rights of authors, two of their number making their living as writers—they removed this material as soon as they became aware of it. But to no avail. It would simply reappear.

And then the storage sites disappeared from their servers.

You could still access the material by pointing your browser at www.thewordwood.com, but the Wordwood site itself now existed in some impossible limbo in between computers.

That's where magic happens, Christy had explained to her. Not here or there, but in between the two.

Holly was uncomfortable with the word magic, but there was no other word to explain what had happened with the Wordwood. It was now possible to have real-time conversations through the site with somebody who always seemed to be on-line, no matter what time of day or night you accessed it. More curiously, this somebody's style of communicating often echoed the voice and conversational mannerisms of someone the user had known. In Holly's case it was her grandmother, five years dead.

The Wordwood grew in enormous leaps and bounds, bibliographies and texts appearing on it at a prodigious rate. The copyrighted material all had some sort of complex protection on it so that while you could access it on-line, you couldn't read a work in its entirety, and you certainly couldn't download it.

If you tried, the Wordwood cut off your access to it. A message of explanation appeared on your screen:

> You have attempted to access copyrighted material beyond what is considered fair use. For that reason your privileges on this site have been terminated.

You lost a week's access for a first offence. A subsequent attempt to download copyrighted material barred you from the site permanently. And there was no getting around it. Logging on with a different user name, or even from someone else's computer using their I.D. and protocols, made no difference.

Sarah was unable to explain it.

It wasn't simply a text-based site anymore, either. The opening splash page had a background of what appeared to be real-time video now. It depicted an impossible forest, inhabited by the sorts of things you'd expect to find in the woods—squirrels and mice, songbirds and insects—but there were odder creatures in it as well. Sometimes you caught glimpses of hybrid beings—an owl with a man's face, a chipmunk with tiny human hands and fingers, a woman with moth wings. Or there were people that, when you saw them in context with a robin or a red squirrel, say, appeared to be no more than six or seven inches high.

The trees in the forest weren't of any species anyone could recognize— a simple enough feat if they'd simply been created on a computer and then animated. But Sarah said their details were too complex and random for animation—even with today's CGI technologies—and swore there were no loops in the video streaming. What they saw in the Wordwood's opening screen was real-time video—although real-time video of what forest, or where, she couldn't say.

And now it was gone.

Holly turned away from the computer and looked out the store's front window. She should be putting out the stock that had come in today— before Dick took it upon himself to do it for her—but she couldn't seem to muster the energy. Saturday was always a busy day in the store and today had been no exception. Helpful though Dick was behind the scenes, he left it to her to deal with the public. There were times today when it had gotten almost frantic, there were so many people in the store, each with a question, or wanting their purchase rung through, or change for the bus, or wanting her to go through their want list and recommend where they could get this or that title if she didn't have it in stock.

Many customers didn't seem to understand that in the secondary book market, she could only carry what people brought in to sell or trade. She couldn't simply order a book for them from Ingrams. Well, she could, but it would be a new book and they'd expect to buy it at a used price, and that wasn't going to happen in this lifetime. At least not in her store.

Most of the time, the book they were looking for was long out of print. "How can it be out of print? I love this book."

She heard variations on that at least once a week, if not more, and wasn't unsympathetic. There were times when she, too, felt that a particular book being out of print was a personal affront. Still, there was nothing she could do about it except to explain the vagaries of the secondary book business and do a search for the book if the customer wanted her to, both of which took up time.

Dick didn't help with the on-line customers either, though he was happy to package the books to get them ready for Holly to take to the post office. Though that still left Holly working into the evening answering e-mail on days like today, when it had been too busy to get on the computer during store hours.

But she was almost finished now. She patted her lap and Snippet rose from her bed in the front display window and jumped onto her.

"Hey, you," she said, scratching the little dog behind the ear. "Just let me send these e-mails and we'll go for that walk."

The browser window explaining that the Wordwood site wasn't available was still open when she turned back to her computer.

Maybe the pixies were causing this current problem, Holly thought. They were certainly the reason that Dick wouldn't go near the store's computer. He was too afraid that they'd come bursting out of the screen once more to wreak havoc and mischief up and down the blocks neighbouring the store as they had the last time.

If Holly hadn't seen them with her own eyes, she might not have believed that they could exist. But she had. And they did. Though she didn't know why she should be so surprised. After all, she had a hob for a business partner. And then there was the whole mystery of the Wordwood . . .

Send the e-mail, she told herself. Go for a walk and then to bed.

She started to reach for her mouse, to bring the window with her e-mail program back on screen, then stopped. Something was happening in her browser window. Right in the middle of the screen, a small black dot had appeared. As she watched, it began to expand like the eye of a camera. On her lap, Snippet lifted her head. Whining, she returned to the window seat. An inexplicable uneasiness came over Holly.

She set Snippet back in her bed in the front display window and looked around for Dick—not directly, but out of the corner of her eye. Dick had this trick where he could sit so still, he as much as became invisible to people. Even Holly wasn't completely immune to it and she'd known him for ages now, though once she caught a glimpse of him from the corner of her eye, she could hold him in sight thereafter. Strangers simply didn't register his presence.

This time she found him curled up in the club chair that stood at the end of one of the bookcases, reading, of course.

"Dick," she said. "Come and look at this."

He put down his book and joined her behind the desk—as usual, making it obvious how reluctant he was to be this close to the computer. Holly took off her glasses and gave them a quick cleaning on her shirt tails. Making room for Dick in front of the monitor, she put them on again and looked over his shoulder. The dot on her screen was still growing bigger.

Dick appeared to be mesmerized by it. He started to reach a hand toward the monitor.

"What do you think it is?" Holly asked. "Because I'll tell you, it's giving me the creeps and I don't know why."

Her voice made him start and he pulled his hand away from the screen as though he'd been about to put it on a hot stove burner.

"Dick?"

He gave her a worried look that made her uneasiness grow.

"Oh, this is bad, Mistress Holly," he said.

He dropped to the floor, scrabbling around in the nest of wires that were clustered around the power bar under the desk. Behind them, Holly could hear Snippet growling from her bed in the window.

"Which cord is it?" Dick muttered.

"Which cord is what?"

Holly glanced at the monitor to see that the black dot filled almost two thirds of the screen now. When Dick looked up and followed her gaze, he grabbed the power bar itself and gave it a wild yank. The computer went dead. The monitor, now blank, tottered on the edge of the desk—pulled off-balance because its power cord was still plugged into the bar in Dick's hand. Holly made a grab for the monitor, but she was too late. It fell to the floor, its cheap plastic casing exploding on impact.

Snippet bounded out of the window and circled the broken monitor, barking and growling at it.

Dick stood up again, still holding the power bar. His big eyes had gone bigger than ever, his lips forming an "O." He turned to Holly with such a woebegone look on his face that she wanted to bend down and give him a hug. But though Dick was small, she knew better than to try to comfort him as she might a child. He was older than her. A lot older. How much, she couldn't begin to guess. Yet there was still a childlike innocence about him, especially in moments such as this.

"I . . . I didn't mean . . ."

"It's okay," she told him.

The monitor was broken now and its tumble off the desk couldn't be taken back. There was no point in making Dick feel worse about it.

"What was happening?" she asked. "Why did you have to kill the power to the computer so quickly?"

Dick let the power bar drop to the floor.

"There . . . there was something trying to get out," he explained.

"What kind of something?"

Having once had that gang of pixies come flooding out of her monitor, Holly wasn't about to argue the impossibility of something else trying to get out as well.

"I don't know for sure," Dick said. "Not exactly bad. But wild. And hungry for . . . something."

"Like the pixies."

He shook his head. "Whatever this was, it was far bigger and stronger than a pixie." He turned to her. "It had me charmed as sure as a snake can charm a bird, Mistress Holly. If you hadn't spoken up and broken the spell . . . I don't know what would have happened. But nothing good. I can tell you that."

"But it's gone now?"

"I think so. I don't feel it anymore—do you?"

Holly shook her head. "But I didn't feel anything in the first place. Just a kind of uneasiness. Snippet, come here!" she added, calling to where the dog was still growling at the monitor.

"I think maybe you shouldn't use your computer for awhile," Dick said.

Holly nodded, not bothering to mention that, without a monitor, she couldn't anyway. Dick was only just starting to look a little less distraught about having broken it in the first place.

Snippet stood expectantly at her feet. Sitting down, Holly patted her lap and the little dog jumped up.

"This something you're talking about," she said to Dick, soothing Snippet with a scratch behind the ear. "It's loose in the Net, isn't it? Like the pixies were."

"Except if it gets free . . ."

"We're in bigger trouble than we were then. Okay. So we stay off the Net. What about phone lines? Do you think it'd be safe to make a call?"

"You could try."

Holly reached for the phone. She felt nervous picking up the receiver, then stupid for feeling nervous, but that didn't stop the uneasiness. She held the receiver so that both she and Dick could listen to the dial tone.

"What do you think?" she asked.

"I don't sense anything—not like I did when the computer was on-line."

"Okay, then," Holly said and she began to punch in a number. "Time to call in an exorcist—or at least the closest to one that I know."

Christy Riddell

I've really been caught up with a new book these days that's got me doing research into the mysteries inhabiting the World Wide Web: everything from spirits and ghosts to the new urban legends that have grown up around the use of computers—especially when they're connected to each other through the Internet and e-mail.

Jilly says I should call it *Spirits in the Wires*, but that doesn't strike me as accurate enough for my purposes. I don't see spirits haunting the hardware—the circuits and wiring, the actual technology—so much as using the hardware to get around. They ride the software, cables, and telephone lines, and make homes for themselves in the spaces that lie in between the various computers that the technology connects. Science fiction writers call those territories cyberspace, but I think of it all as a kind of voodoo. *Les invisibles* finding a more contemporary host to ride.

For these aren't new spirits—at least not from what I can tell. They're the same magical beings of the woods and fields and waters wild that first made a journey from their rural origins to more urban settings, and have now moved into the technologies of the future. They'll probably follow us into space.

Not all of them, of course. Just the more adventurous, the strongest—those with the same characteristics that human explorers need when they leave the safety of the Fields We Know to strike out into unknown territories.

I first started keeping notes on these more recent phenomena after I became aware of the anomalies surrounding the Wordwood and Saskia's connection to it. Holly's adventure with the pixies only served to convince me I was on the track of something new and worthwhile of my interest.

It's funny. The more computer literate among my friends have been telling me odd stories about the Internet and new technologies for years, but it's only in past few months that I'm paying attention to them. I almost feel like I'm coming too late into the game, since any number of urban legends have already grown up on the Internet, spreading as quickly as wildfire viruses. Or at least warnings about viruses. But people studied fairies and ghosts for centuries before I took it up and I'm still finding new things to write about. Better late than never.

Considering how much I've always loved legends—urban or ancient— I don't know why I didn't clue into these contemporary changes in folklore and myth sooner. Even when I was a kid I was drawn to this sort of thing. For a long time, cataloguing and tracking the stories that slip between the cracks of fact and history was my only real escape from a boyhood that was otherwise filled with unhappiness and discouragement.

But I guess I have a bit of a Luddite's aversion to technology. When I finally start to use something new, it's already old hat for everybody else. Or at least everybody on the cutting edge. By the time I got a fax machine, everybody else was using e-mail. My tech friends all have cell phones and handheld computers like Palms and iPAQs. I still prefer to use a phone booth if I'm away from home and write in the hardback journal that goes everywhere I do.

But now that I've found the connection to my earlier, more traditional studies of the odd, curious, and just plain strange, I've become completely absorbed by technology and its own particular take on the paranormal. It's all I want to think about and research. So, of course, just as I'm starting to get some real leads on new avenues to explore, a set of galleys shows up from Alan that he says he needs back last week.

Probably the worst thing about the business of being a writer is correcting galleys. These are the typeset page proofs the publisher sends to you for final corrections that are supposed to incorporate all of the corrections and changes that were made during the various editing and copyediting processes. At least it's the worst part for me. I like everything else, from researching and tracking down sources, through the actual writing and editing, to finally sitting in some bookstore and chatting with my readers. But the galleys . . .

By the time I'm at this point in the procedure, I've seen the words too many times and find myself wanting to change things simply for the sake of having something different to look at. You can't of course. Instead you sit there, bored stiff while you go through the mind-numbing task, trying not to get too cranky.

I'm not very good at the not getting too cranky part. Which, I guess, explains why Saskia's "I'm just dropping by the café for an hour or so" earlier in the evening was actually code for "I'm going out for the night; I hope you've finished this by the time I get back."

I wish I could be, but no such luck. I may not enjoy correcting galleys, but I take the time to do the job right. I'll be at this through next week. So when she gets back to the apartment—close on midnight, by the clock on my bookshelf—I've only got another couple of chapters done.

"How's it coming?" she asks from the door of my study.

"Swimmingly," I tell her.

"That bad?"

"No, it's just tedious. You know what it's like."

She nods, having gone through this with her poetry collections and the freelance writing she does.

"But I'm done for today," I say.

I straighten the stack of loose galley pages I've been working on, tapping them on the top of the desk to get them all aligned, then set them down in a neat stack. I'm terrible about that sort of thing, which is probably why Jilly got me that T-shirt that reads "Is there a hyphen in anal-retentive?" I don't wear it. I keep it folded up with all the other joke T-shirts people give me that I'll probably never wear. And yes, I see the irony in that. But I've always been somewhat of a compulsive tidier. I might have all sorts of books lying around, waiting to be read or put away on the bookshelves, but they're all stacked in orderly piles, often sorted by category and in alphabetical order.

Saskia settles in one of the two club chairs by the bookcases and puts her feet up on the ottoman. I turn off the light on my desk and join her, sitting in the other chair, sharing the ottoman with my own feet.

"So how was your evening?" I ask, tapping a foot against hers.

"Interesting. I met your shadow at the Beanery Café."

"Really? That seems like an odd place to run into her."

Though when it comes to my shadow, odd is usually the norm. She's the sort of person that you can never figure out what she's thinking, what she'll say, or where you'll meet her next. Even when she's forthcoming, I still usually come away from our conversations wearing a cloud of confusion. It's part of the reason I call her Mystery.

"I know," Saskia says. "It's weird to think of her hanging out in such a mundane place, isn't it? Though of course she fit right in."

I have to smile. "She fits in wherever she goes. I think environments adjust themselves to suit her rather than the other way around."

"I wish I could do that," Saskia says. "I feel like it's just the other way for me."

I give her a puzzled look.

She sighs. "Your shadow and I got talking about where we came from and that reminded me of that first morning I woke up in this world and how hard it was for me to fit in."

I nod. We've talked about this before.

"And it started me thinking again about who I am and where I came from. If I'm even real."

"It doesn't matter where you came from," I tell her. "You're real now."

"Am I? Isn't part of being real knowing where you came from? I'm like an adopted kid. It doesn't matter how happy your life is, if you don't know your parents—if you don't know *anything* about your origin—you're living with this black hole underlying who you are. And not all the platitudes in the world can make it go away."

"But you know your origin. You've said you were born in the Word-wood."

She nods. "And how weird is *that*? How *real* is that? How can a real person be born in a Web site?"

"I don't know. But you're here now." I touch her arm. "You feel real."

"Your shadow thinks I should go to the source with my questions," she says.

"You mean to the Wordwood?"

"Where else?"

"I guess. It seems to answer any question you put to it." I put my feet down from the ottoman. Sitting up, I look at my computer over on the desk. "I suppose we can see if it's come back on-line again."

"What do you mean?"

"The site's been down all week."

Saskia shakes her head wearily. "And I never even knew. What does that say about my so-called connection to it?"

"You said it cut you loose."

"Or I cut myself loose. But going on-line wasn't exactly what I had in mind. Your shadow says she can take me into the otherworld. That we can find the Wordwood on its own ground."

"Wait a minute. The Wordwood exists in the otherworld?"

"She seems to think it does."

"As what? A place? A person?"

Saskia shrugs. "Who knows? Maybe as some combination of both."

"This is getting too weird."

"And me being born in a Web site isn't?"

"You know what I mean. The Wordwood's a human construct—the product of software and HTML language. How can it exist in the other-world?"

Saskia just looks at me. "Maybe it doesn't—at least not most of the time. But if it has spirit, then the spiritworld would seem to be the easiest place to find it."

"Yes, but . . ."

"It's just a kind of magic," Saskia says. "The same magic that allowed me to walk in the world, clothed in flesh and bone."

"I guess . . ."

Truth is, I'm never one hundred percent certain that Saskia's origin is quite so exotic as she accepts it is. I know that she believes it. And there are days when I believe it, too. All I have to do is to remember how it was when I first met her. She used to be like a walking encyclopedia, able to quote amazing references at the drop of a hat, but not seeming to have had first-hand experience with something so simple as hot chocolate.

But for my all normally ready acceptance that there's more to this world than we can see—than we *expect* to see—I have a cynic living in my head as well as the believer. He's the one who insists that ghosts and spirits are delusions. That what we have here, is all there is. There's more? he asks. Then prove it. Show me.

When I listen to him, I can't imagine a Web site giving birth to a living, breathing human being. For that matter, there are times when Saskia's as much a skeptic as the cynic in my head. But this, apparently, isn't one of them.

"Okay," I say after a moment. "But let's at least check out the source by more conventional means first."

I get up and cross the room to my desk, starting up the computer. The machine's up and running by the time Saskia joins me. She stands behind my chair, hands on my shoulders. I click on my dial-up icon, the modem dials the number, and soon we're listening to the familiar squawk and buzz of the computer connecting to my ISP.

After I open Explorer and enter the Wordwood's URL, the error message I've been getting all week comes up in my browser window. I start to close my connection.

"What's that?" Saskia says.

She leans over my shoulder, the point of her index finger going to a small black dot that's appeared in the middle of my browser window. I have this flash of premonition, but before I can stop her, her fingertip touches the screen.

Have you ever seen a firecracker fuse burn? That's what it's like with her, except the detonation comes first. There's this flash of—I don't know what. Like an electrical discharge. It blows me off my chair, against the wall, and knocks the breath out of me. But I can still see what's happening to her from where I'm lying.

A flare of white hot light runs up her finger, her hand, her arm, her shoulder, travelling the length of her body. Like a fuse. But instead of leaving behind a string of ash, it leaves behind a pixelated version of her, like she's no longer solid and I can see all the molecules of her body. It's like the difference in seeing a painting, then seeing a photo of it in a newspaper where it's made up of thousands of little dots of colour.

I try to scramble to my feet, but my limbs are numbed and jellied and they won't hold me.

Saskia gives me a look—a haunting, desperate look. Then the computer just shatters and collapses into itself. One moment the monitor and keyboard are on my desk, the tower on the floor beside it, the next they're just the heaps of broken plastic, circuitry, and wiring.

Saskia reaches for me. But it isn't Saskia anymore. It's this human shape made up of thousands of flickering tiny pellets of shadow and light.

I call her name, try again to get to my feet. I hear a telephone dialing, as though somewhere in the wreckage of my computer the modem's trying to reconnect to my ISP. Then Saskia's gone and the room is so still the silence hurts.

I manage to crawl to where she'd been standing, stupidly patting the floor as though she's hidden on the carpet like a fallen pin or paperclip. But there's nothing there. She's gone. Swallowed back into the Internet from which I'd only half-believed she'd been born. Swallowed back into the Wordwood, and I don't have the slightest idea how to get her back.

The loss of her swells through me like a tsunami, threatening to tear me apart, and all I can do is press my forehead against the carpet where, only a moment ago, she was standing.

Christiana

I'm pretending to sleep when the phone rings.

I suppose that sounds odd—not the phone ringing, but my pretending to sleep. The thing is, I don't need to sleep, or even eat, but I do both anyway. It's one of the first things Mumbo taught me when I strayed over into the borderlands.

"It will help make you feel normal," she told me. "And if you feel normal—if you act and appear normal—then other people won't treat you differently."

I didn't think it was so important then, but being treated like a freak gets old fast. So I learned to eat and drink. And while I don't need the sustenance, I love the flavours that tickle across my taste buds when I do partake. A basil and tomato sandwich. Hot Mexican salsa. Squash soup. Strong coffee. A glass of red wine.

And more rarely, I sleep.

When I do, I think I actually *am* sleeping, because sometimes when I close my eyes, I go away. Time vanishes into the same black hole it does for people whose bodies require them to sleep. And sometimes, when I'm in that black hole of sleep, I dream.

That's what's happening when the phone starts to ring. I feel thick-headed and confused as the beep-beep of the cell phone pulls me out of a confusing mélange of images and sensations. Traces linger in my head as I look for the phone. Something to do with monkeys having a high tea and the Vegas Elvis, sweaters being worn backwards and flying—no I can't fly, though I'd dearly love to be able to. Even the talent to shapechange into a bird would be welcome.

The monkeys were humming an off-key rendition of a Beatles song— "Strawberry Fields," I think—and Elvis was ignoring them as he dipped a deep-fried scone into his tea. I remember being fascinated by the oily film that formed on the surface of his tea and trying to figure out why. When he took the scone out, it made this sound like a truck backing up.

But it was only the phone.

I finally spot it across the meadow, lying on the fat arm of the club chair where I tossed my clothes before going to sleep. Getting out of bed, I shuffle barefoot across the grass to the chair, wondering who it could possibly be. I hardly ever get calls on it because only a handful of people know the number. Maxie. Tom Stone—the only lover I ever managed to stay good friends with. Mumbo—though she never calls. And now Saskia.

I pick the phone up, find the "on" button, and lift the phone to my ear. It takes me a moment to recognize the odd sound I'm hearing. It's like a bad recording of wind blowing through the topmost branches of a forest—rasping and harsh, full of pops and crackling.

"Hello?" I say.

" . . . "

The response is so faint I'm not sure I actually heard anything.

"Hello?" I try again. "Is anybody there?"

The voice comes to me as though from a radio station that's not quite tuned in. Raspy, unrecognizable.

"Please . . ."

I press the phone more closely to my ear, as though that's going to make the voice louder.

"Let . . . me . . . in . . ."

I know enough about the hidden worlds beyond the World As It Is to know that it's not only vampires that need permission to enter a safe place. And though I also know better, I still find myself saying, "Yes."

There's this one dark moment where everything feels wrong. I find myself remembering a conversation I had with Christy once about the odd motivations of the characters in fairy tales, when there even is a motivation.

"Why do they do these things?" I said. "Why does the third son go on what he believes is a doomed quest? Why does the farmer boy want to marry the princess? What could they possibly have in common?"

"Who says they have a choice?" he told me.

That's what my saying "yes" feels like. Like I had no choice. Like some enchantment came through the phone's receiver and I had to welcome it into me.

I have time to think of all of that, with the underpinning impression that something's very wrong. It's like an accident, where everything's speeding up and slowing down at the same time. It's going so slow that you're aware of every nuance. You have time to replay a conversation, look across the meadow that carpets your living room floor to the fields beyond. But it's also happening so fast that you can't even begin to stop it.

There's no time for me to drop the phone. I can't take the word back.

Something like an electric shock erupts from the receiver and flashes into my ear. My hair stands upright—all my hair, from the tangle on my head to the tiny ones on my arms. My head fills with the radio static, amplified to such a volume that it's a hurricane of white noise.

Then everything goes away, me included.

Holly

Dick was miserable.

Holly had tried to cheer him up. She'd taken him with her when she went out to let Snippet do her business and even let him do the honours with the plastic bag after said business was done in the empty lot at the end of the block. When they got back, she let him clean up the mess that the monitor had made when it crashed to the floor. But not even cleaning and tidying seemed to help. So she made him a mug of tea, English Breakfast with a splash of whiskey in it, just the way he liked it. That didn't seem to help either.

He was convinced the whole business was his fault—though how that could be, he couldn't explain.

"You saved the day," she told him for about the tenth time.

They were sitting behind the desk in the store, drinking their tea.

"If it hadn't been for you," she went on, "whatever that thing was would have come right out of the monitor and swallowed us both."

She wasn't sure if that was exactly the case. She just knew that magical beings were able to step out of the Internet into the real world, as witness their invasion by a gang of vandalizing pixies a year or so ago. So if something dark and scary had been about to pounce forth this evening, Dick really had saved the day. The trouble was, Dick found any number of things dark and scary—from television shows and certain kinds of pies, to the customers that patronized the store. Considering some of the odd birds that came in, Holly could sympathize with the latter.

"But I broke your monitor, Mistress Holly," Dick said.

"Thereby saving us."

"But it's all broken and now you can't do your work on the computer."

"Hello? I can't do any work on it anyway because of creepy things that are just a modem dial-up away, waiting to pounce on us."

"But still—"

"But still, nothing. You're a veritable hero and I wish you'd stop feeling otherwise."

Dick only gave his head a mournful shake and stared into the inch or so of liquid left at the bottom of his cup. Holly sighed. She gave the phone a look, willing it to ring, but it was obstinately silent.

Dick had lent a hand when it came to figuring out a way to get the pixies out of Holly's neighbourhood and back into the Internet, but he hadn't been Holly's main source of help. That had come from a woman named Meran Kelledy, one half of a musical husband-and-wife duo who had been playing for years around the city, when they weren't touring further afield. Holly had met her the same week that all the trouble with the pixies began, and they'd become friends since then.

She was a lovely woman, attractive and smart. The sort of woman who turned heads as much for her charisma as for her trim figure, dark, wise eyes, and her waterfall of brown hair with its surprising green streaks. Dick seemed to think of her as some sort of faerie royalty and was in awe of her whenever she came by the store, but Holly didn't see her that way at all. Meran was simply good company, easy to talk to and as normal as anyone else, except she seemed to know an inordinate amount about things magical and folkloric, and how they were presently colliding with the modern technological age.

So it was Meran that Holly called from the store after the computer monitor had smashed on the floor, but no one had picked up at the other end of the line. She'd had to leave a message on the Kelledys' answering machine.

"What will we do?" Dick said, still not lifting his gaze from the bottom of his mug, although Holly noted that it was now completely empty.

"Replenish our drinks?" she asked. "Or go to bed and see if everything looks the same in the morning?"

"The monitor will still be broken."

"Yes, I know. I just meant perhaps things will feel different in the morning. We can call some other people and—"

Holly broke off as someone rapped on the glass of the door behind them. Turning, she expected to see Meran. It was something Meran would do—come directly by, rather than return Holly's earlier phone call. But a stranger stood there under the outdoor light on the other side of the store's front door. A wonderfully handsome stranger. He looked like Holly's romantic notions of a Gypsy: dark-eyed, with a tangle of shoulder-length, crow-black hair pushed back from his brow and small gold hoop earrings in each lobe. His baggy white cotton shirt added to the Romany look, even if it was tucked into a pair of ordinary blue jeans.

When he caught her gaze, he gave her a rakish smile and lifted his hand in greeting. Holly felt like melting. She wasn't the sort to be swayed so easily by a handsome face—she saw at least one good-looking man every day, operating a store that was open to the general public as she did—but something about this stranger had her all flustered and warm. She brought a hand to her hair, all too aware of how the red strands were spilling out every which way from where they'd been gathered in a loose bun at the nape of her neck this morning. She wasn't wearing any make-up—not even lipstick. And why in god's name had she changed into a pair of old cut-off jeans and her oldest flannel shirt after the store had closed?

Because, common sense said, as it did its best to quiet the sudden jump in her pulse, she wasn't expecting visitors. It was late at night. And handsome though the man was, he was still a stranger and it was long past store hours. He could be anyone. He could be dangerous.

Holly was aware of that and more. Still, she put her glasses down on the desk, got up and went to the door all the same.

"Yes?" she asked through the glass. "Can I help you?"

She couldn't hear a word he said in response, but then she doubted he'd heard her either. It was more a matter of them reading each other's lips. When she saw his—very full for a man, but not remotely effete, and oh, just look at the lashes above those gorgeous eyes—shape Meran's name, she happily threw caution to the winds and unlocked the door. Opening it just enough to pop her head out, she caught a strong whiff of apples and cinnamon. God, he even smelled good.

"What were you saying?" she asked.

"I'm taking care of Meran's place," the stranger said. "While she and Cerin are out of town."

"And that brings you here because . . . ?"

"The message you left on their machine. You sounded pretty upset so I thought I'd come by to see if you needed a hand."

His voice was perfect, too, warm and resonant. Then she realized what he'd said. Oh god. He'd heard her babbling about pixies and something weird trying to come out of her monitor?

"Are you all right?" he asked.

Only mortified, she thought. But she gave a quick nod.

"So everything's under control now?"

"Yes. I mean, no. I mean . . ." She sighed. "How do you know Meran?"

"We're sort of distant cousins."

"Sort of?"

"On her husband's side."

"So then you're not really related."

"Well, in a way I am. To Cerin's Aunt Jen. But I'm not really blood kin to any of them." He gave her another one of those rakish smiles. "It's more of a tribal thing."

Holly regarded him for a long moment. The only way he could have heard her message was if he was in the Kelledy's house. And if he was in their house, she supposed he must be trustworthy. Burglars and serial killers didn't take the time to listen to their victims' answering machines, did they?

She stepped aside and held the door open for him.

"You might as well come in," she said. "The least I can do is offer you a cup of tea after coming out all this way at such a late hour."

"Thank you," he said.

He looked past her to where Snippet was sitting up, alert, but showing no signs of alarm at the stranger coming in. That he passed whatever test it was that the Jack Russell had for strangers boded well. Snippet was good during the day—you never heard a peep out of her. But once the store was closed for business she became fiercely territorial to anyone she didn't like, or at least didn't recognize.

"Hello, dog," the stranger said.

Holly was surprised to see Snippet's tail begin to wag. Then she was surprised even more when the stranger's gaze continued to where Dick was sitting.

"And good evening to you, Master Hob," he added.

Dick gave him a small nervous nod in response.

"You can see him?" Holly said.

The stranger turned to look at her, eyebrows lifting. "You can't?"

"Of course I can. It's just that most people . . ."

She let her voice trail off and covered up the increased awkwardness she was feeling by closing and locking the door once more.

"We're having tea with whiskey in it," she said when she turned back to him.

"Sounds perfect," the stranger said. "Although perhaps I'll forgo the tea part, if I may. Tea usually keeps me up all night."

Holly smiled. "I'm Holly," she said and offered her hand. "Though I guess you already know that from the phone call."

"Borrible Jones," he told her.

His grip was firm, his hand callused, both distracting Holly until she realized what he'd said. She couldn't have heard that right.

"I'm sorry?" she said.

He grinned. "I am, too. But what can you do? My friends call me Bojo."

"But—"

"The name. I know. There are any number of theories as to its origin. One is that my father was a poet who didn't like children so he named me to have something to rhyme with 'horrible.' Another is that he was too fond of Michael de Larrabeiti's books."

Holly gave him a blank look.

"You know," Bojo said. "The author of the Borrible books? Borribles were these fictional residents of London? Sort of like little feral Peter Pans?"

Holly nodded. "I knew that."

"Of course you would. You own a bookstore."

"So you don't know who your father is?"

"Never met the man," Bojo said.

"That seems very sad." Holly'd had a wonderful relationship with her own father until he'd passed away a few years ago. "I'm sorry."

"Me, too. I'd love to have known what he was thinking."

"And your mother . . . ?"

"Would rarely speak of him."

Holly didn't know what to say. Finally she settled on, "Let me get you that whiskey."

She felt she needed a whole tumbler of it herself.

There wasn't room for all of them behind the desk, so they took their drinks and went upstairs to Holly and Dick's apartment above the store. There were as many books on shelves, in piles and boxes and hidden under furniture, up here in her living room as there were downstairs. The difference was, these weren't for sale. At least not yet.

Bojo settled into an easy sprawl on the sofa, reminding Holly of a cat, the way he could so quickly look as though he'd been relaxing there for hours. Dick perched on the other end of the sofa, holding his mug in both hands. Though he appeared to be using it to warm himself, it hadn't been refilled yet. Holly made some more tea, then pulled a chair over from the dining room table and sat down herself. Snippet, after following Holly from room to room as she made the tea, settled now under Holly's chair, curling up in a ball with her head turned so that she could watch Bojo.

"So you're having pixie trouble," Bojo said.

Holly shook her head. "Had. Do you know much about pixies?"

"Well, that depends. They're like a kind of bodach, aren't they? But malicious rather than tricksey."

Holly had no idea what a bodach was, but Dick was nodding in agreement.

"All their fun's mean," he said. "I've never heard of one with a kind thought or doing a kind deed."

"Whereas a bodach can be quite friendly—like a brownie or you hobs. At least that's what they're like where I'm from."

Holly was good at picking things up out of context and felt she was safe in assuming that a bodach was yet another kind of little fairy man. But the conversation between Dick and the stranger made her wonder where it was that such knowledge was so common.

"Where exactly are you from?" she asked.

"Where? Everywhere and nowhere. We were always travelling, and I still do. We Kelledys have always been a travelling people."

"You're tinkers, aren't you?" Dick said. "Like in Ireland."

Bojo shook his head. "We're tinkers, but of an older tribe than the Irish."

"But you said your name was Jones," Holly said.

"It is. Kelledy's a tribal name, used by most of us. But my mam was a Jones when Aunt Jen adopted us, and I stay a Jones in her memory."

Holly had a hundred more questions. Even the normally shy Dick appeared to be bubbling with curiosity for a change. But before either of them could speak, Bojo sat up a little straighter. He took a sip of his whiskey, regarded the pair of them for a long moment, then said, "Tell me about the pixies."

So Holly did, with Dick filling in the bits she left out. And when they were done with that story, they moved on to what had happened earlier in the evening.

"I guess we just got spooked," Holly said when they got to the end of that story. "After the business with the pixies and all, I mean. You wouldn't believe the havoc they created around here in just one night."

"Oh, I can imagine," Bojo said.

"So you *have* seen them before."

He shook his head. "Only the messes they've left behind. And I've heard the stories, of course."

Like that was the sort of thing that ordinary people talked about around the water cooler. The weather, the stock market, pixies . . . Not that she could ever imagine Bojo standing around a water cooler or holding any sort of a regular job. Though she supposed he must. Everybody had to do something for a living.

"I think you were wise to be careful," Bojo said, making Holly bring her thoughts back to the matter at hand. "I smelled the otherworld as soon as I stepped into the store, and it wasn't because of you, Master Hob."

"Oh, it was a spirit, all right," Dick said. "All set to come popping out of the screen. Old and dark and powerful."

Bojo shook his head. "Powerful, yes. But I sensed something young. Something new. Something the world has never seen before."

"Is that good or bad?" Holly asked.

"I don't know that it's either. Most spirits are like the weather, neither good nor bad. They simply are. They live their lives without concern for us. We're the ones to complain about a storm blowing down our barn, a drought ruining our crops."

So, Holly thought, still looking for clues about her visitor. If he was using farms as analogies, maybe he was from a rural background.

"But they're not all like that," Dick said.

"No," Bojo agreed. "There are also a number that delight to interfere in the lives of the likes of you and me. And unfortunately, they're usually . . . the less pleasant of their kind."

"But what do they want?" Holly asked.

Bojo shrugged. "Who can tell? Sometimes we're simply in the way, and they deal with us the way we would a gnat—brushing us away, squishing us between their fingers. Sometimes they're hungry."

Holly didn't like the sound of that at all.

"They want to *eat* us?"

"It's more a matter of the spirit," Bojo said. "You know, our life energy. Some spirits consider it sustenance."

This was getting worse by the minute.

"Can you help us?" she asked. "Is there anything we can do to get it out of the Internet and back to wherever it came from?"

Bojo had some more of his whiskey.

"I know next to nothing about computers," he said. "But I do know spirits. The first question we need to ask ourselves is, did it, in fact, come from somewhere else, or is it native to the Internet?"

"What do you mean?" Holly said.

She glanced at Dick and saw her own confusion mirrored in his face.

"Well, from what I understand," Bojo said, "the Internet is much like a realm unto itself. Would that be a fair assessment?"

"I guess . . ."

"Then it would seem logical that it would have its own life forms and spirits."

"But we're talking about a place that doesn't exist except as code in the files of a service provider's computers. Bits and bytes. It's nothing tangible."

"And yet the pixies have managed to find a way to travel in that realm. And then there's the whole matter of the Wordwood and the spirit you said had come to inhabit it."

Holly gave a slow nod. "I guess that's what makes me feel I have to do something. We—my friends and I—created the Wordwood. If it somehow gained sentience through what we did, then we're responsible for that as well."

"So the other question we need to answer is this," Bojo said. "Has the Wordwood gone feral, or is it under attack itself?"

"When you put it like that . . . it sounds so insane."

Bojo nodded. "It's a long way from anything I understand, too. But we'll just have to do what we can. There are people who should be able to help us. It's only a matter of tracking them down and seeing what they know."

"And I'll do the same with Sarah and the others that were in on the Wordwood from the start." She paused for a moment, then added, "I'm really glad you came along. My friends might know a lot about computers, but when it comes to the other stuff, we're in way over our heads. This sort of thing is too weird to deal with on our own and with Meran out of town . . . I guess I just want to say thanks. Really."

"I couldn't very well walk away, leaving the friend of my cousin to face this on her own." He held up his glass and added, "You wouldn't have any more of this lovely whiskey, would you?"

Holly went to fetch the bottle and poured a splash into each of their cups, this time forgoing the tea in hers and Dick's.

"I feel good about this," she said. "Like we have a real chance to beat this thing."

Bojo smiled. "We can only try."

They clinked their glasses together in a toast.

Holly was still smiling when she came back upstairs from letting Bojo out. She said goodnight to a somewhat bleary-eyed Dick and scooping up Snippet, went into her room. She paused for a moment, then went and unplugged her phone. She doubted anything would come across an ordinary phone line—and after all, she'd used it without any problem earlier to leave the message on Meran's machine—but why take chances?

Christy

There's nothing in the research I've been doing on the Web to explain what's happened to Saskia. That's not so surprising, I suppose, since there's also nothing to explain the mystery of her origin—something I'm not even remotely questioning now. The only big question for me now is, how do I get her back?

I still can't believe she's gone.

I've spent the past hour torn between despair and determination and not really able to do a lot about either. All my notes were on the computer that's now lying in pieces all over my desk and on the floor below it—a war zone, in miniature. I have backups of everything on Zip discs—multiple backups, since I'm as organized about that as I am about everything, especially after the time Sophie managed to crash my computer and I did lose a few weeks of work. But I don't have a computer to access the discs.

I need another computer.

I need Saskia back.

I need help.

But it's almost three A.M. Who am I going to call at this hour—especially with the story I've got to tell? Where are the Ghostbusters when you really need them?

I've got a long list of like-minded colleagues and friends, but their expertise lies mostly in the more traditional forms of the paranormal and folklore, and many of them have less access to modern conveniences—like a phone—than I do. There's also my new network of research sources on the Web—folks I've only met electronically through newsgroups—but I need a working computer to contact any of them. The worst thing is that, at this point in time, I'm the only one I know who's pulled together so many disparate threads of techno rumour, folklore, and gossip, and tried to find a correlation between them all.

I'm my own best expert and I don't have a clue what to do next.

I could call Jilly. She's been playing with the professor's computer since her accident, poking around with her usual intuitive sense that lets her home in on things strange and different, but I hate to bother her while she's still recovering. It's been over a year now since the accident, but she still tires quickly and needs her rest. And besides, much as I love her, she's a bit too scattershot for the kind of focus I need right now. Not to mention that she's even less technologically inclined than I was before I got into this current research. She knows how to turn the computer on and go on-line. She can use a Web browser and e-mail. She's been playing with a paint program that Wendy installed on the machine for her. But she hasn't a clue how any of it actually works. So she's out, too.

Anybody else is just going to think I'm crazy.

I decide on my brother Geordie. He'll still think I'm crazy, but at least he'll listen because of Saskia. Not only did he first introduce her to me, but he knows as well as I do that it's because of her that he and I have been a lot more successful at keeping the lines of communication open between us.

It's not that we didn't talk before Saskia came into my life. We just didn't talk about anything important. We were going through the motions of being brothers, desperate to not have our relationship be as screwed up as it is with the rest of our family, but not having the first clue how to go about it with any real success. Honesty was missing from the equation. Along with an inability to express the fact that, even after all we've been through—or maybe because of it, since we at least came out of our messed up childhoods relatively intact—we really cared about each other.

That's something we never got to do with our older brother Paddy. He died in prison. They say he hung himself, and all the evidence points towards it, but all these years later, it's still hard to believe. Of the three of us, I always thought he was the most resilient. The one who'd carry on and make something of himself. Instead he ended up in jail and died there. Just goes to show how little you can know about someone supposedly so close to you.

I'm still a wreck when Geordie arrives at my door. In the time between calling him and his arrival, I've been to the corner store and bought a pack of
smokes. He gives the smoldering cigarette in my hand a look, but to his
credit, he doesn't say anything. He knows I'd given quitting another shot—
six months and counting this time. He also knows I have to be pretty
messed up to have started up again.

"So what happened?" he asks as he comes in.

I close the door behind him and follow him into the kitchen. I've
already got a pot of coffee brewing. That's what the Riddells do when
there's a crisis. Head for the kitchen and make coffee.

I don't know how to start, so I pour us each a mug of the coffee and
bring them over to the table where he's already sitting. I light a new cigarette from the stub of the old one and grind the butt out in the saucer I'm
using for an ashtray.

"Did you have a fight?" Geordie asks.

All I told him over the phone was that Saskia was gone and I didn't
know if she'd ever be back. He didn't ask any questions. He just said, "I'll
be right over." But I know what he's thinking.

My therapist used to call the way our relationships fall apart a self-
fulfilling prophecy that was rooted in low self-esteem—yet one more
holdover from our childhood, where nothing we could do was right, or
good enough. Geordie and I both have this problem with women: We set
our sights too high—or at least on women we perceive as too good for us.
It's like we need the pedestals and can only yearn after the impossible
women. In school it was the prom queens and cheerleaders who had no time
for kids like us, hicks bussed in from the country. And we just carried that
misconception along with us after high school.

We weren't completely pathetic. But even when we did find some special
woman who wanted to be with us, in the end, they always left—often under
weird circumstances.

For Geordie there was Sam, pure cheerleader material, but also smart
and hip. She fell into the past one day—literally. She got swallowed into the
early part of the century so that we weren't even born by the time she died
in her new life. Then there was Tanya, a movie star with a one-time drug
problem. Geordie was there for her when she could have slipped back into
her old junkie ways, got her on her feet and back doing what she loved to

do: making movies. He even moved to L.A. to be with her, but in the end, she wasn't there for him.

Of course everybody knows he should be with Jilly, he's been carrying a torch for her forever and they'd be a perfect couple, but he waited too long on that and now she's with Daniel.

Before Saskia, I wasn't doing much better. The archetypal Christy Riddell romance was with a woman named Tallulah. I called her Tally. Everything was perfect, except she turned out to be the literal spirit of the city. She left me because she said the city was getting to be too hard, so she needed to be hard, too, to survive. Loving me was making her too soft.

Of the three of us, only Paddy had normal relationships—at least so far as we could tell. "Yeah, and look where that got him," I said to the therapist when she brought that up. She just shook her head and asked me, did I want to talk about that?

"No, it was nothing like that," I tell Geordie now. "We don't fight."

"Then what? There has to be some reason that she just up and left you."

"I don't know how to tell you this," I say. "You're going to think I'm putting you on."

The way I did when we were kids, always talking about fairies and the Wolfman and what-have-you like they were real—because I knew it'd get a rise out of him. It only got worse when I came to understand that there really *is* more to the world than what we can normally see. Not that he hasn't had a few brushes with the inexplicable himself, but that kind of thing always seems to wash off of him the way water does from a bird's wing.

"Just tell me," he says.

So I clear my throat and do as he asks.

I don't look at him while I'm talking. I don't want to see his reaction. I just want to get through it—get it all said before I have to deal with the disbelief that'll be plain on his face.

I wish I could be writing this down. That's what my writing really is— therapy. Doesn't matter if it's my journals, my occasional forays into fiction, or the volumes of case studies and oral collections bound for the "Isn't life strange?" section of the bookstore. When I write something down, it starts to make sense for me. It doesn't solve my problems. But at least I start to understand them.

"Jesus," he says when I'm done.

"Look," I start, but he gets up and leaves the table.

I think he's heading for the apartment door, that he's walking out on me and my weird take on life, once and for all. But he heads for my study instead. He stands there in the doorway and looks at the wreckage of my computer. I wait in the hall behind him, smoking yet another cigarette, staring at the back of his head, the set of his shoulders.

"She told me about that connection she had with the Wordwood," he says, not turning around. "I can't remember where we were, but it was after the two of you had moved in together. She said the same thing you did tonight—that I wouldn't believe her."

"And did you?"

Geordie shakes his head. He moves over to the desk, touches the wreckage of the computer with trailing fingers. Finally he turns to me.

"She didn't seem completely convinced herself," he adds.

"You don't have to explain," I say. "The further she got from being 'born,' the less real that connection felt to her as well."

"It was just so weird."

"I know."

I look around for somewhere to put the long ash at the end of my cigarette and settle on tapping it into my free hand.

"And now?" I ask.

He sighs. "What possible reason could you have to lie to me about something like that?"

"I wish I *was* making it up."

I return to the kitchen to butt out my cigarette and get another. When I return to the study, I bring the saucer with me. Geordie's sitting in the chair Saskia occupied a couple of hours ago. I take the other one, but we don't tap our feet against each other on the ottoman like I did with her.

"So what do we do?" he asks.

"I don't know where to start."

"You could talk to Joe."

Joseph Crazy Dog's a friend of Jilly's who, by Jilly's accounts, spends most of his time in the spirit lands that lie just beyond the borders of the world that the rest of us live in. According to her, that's where he's originally from—not the Kickaha rez like everybody thinks.

"He's not exactly a techno kind of guy," I say.

"What about the professor?"

Ah, the professor. Bramley Dapple. Taught at Butler U. for years, retired now. My compadre in exploring the mysteries of the world—Don Juan to my Castaneda. He was the first adult I met that took this interest of

mine seriously. He used to teach art history, but his heart was always in
mythology and folklore. "They should teach Mystery 101," he used to say.
"The real things. Fairies and spirits, ghosts and hobgoblins and all. It's a
parallel history to what's actually taught, but no less pertinent."

"He's even less computer literate than I am," I say. "I mean, he writes
on a computer, uses the Internet for research and belongs to god knows
how many obscure and arcane discussion groups, but he doesn't understand
the hardware any better than I do. And don't get me started on him and
software. I've never met anyone so incapable of doing a simple install the
way he is. Anyway, according to him, computers and the Internet are a necessary evil that he's only using by sufferance."

"But what about the stuff you've been researching lately? Doesn't that
intrigue him?"

"He doesn't believe it's relevant. Or . . . real. Or at least not as real as
the oral tradition of folklore and stories."

I've been trying to avoid paying any attention to my desk and the computer lying in pieces on top of it. Whenever I do, the loss just hits me so
hard that my chest gets tight and feels like it's going to implode. But I
glance at it now, then back to Geordie.

"I guess what I need is access to another computer. Maybe someone in
one of my newsgroups can help me."

"I've got that laptop that Amy lent me," Geordie says.

"Does it have a modem?"

He nods. "But I don't know how fast it is. I only use it for e-mail."

"It'll do. Is it at the loft?"

He gives me another nod.

Geordie's apartment is actually our friend Jilly's old studio. He's sublet-
ting it from her because the crash that left her in a wheelchair also makes it
impossible for her to navigate the stairs. The building has no elevator.

It's funny. He's been staying at Jilly's loft for almost a year now, but
none of us think of it as his place. It's still "Jilly's," or "the loft"—even
though she's been staying at the professor's house for all this time. She's a
long way from being able to navigate stairs, so Geordie moved in when he
got back from L.A. When you step inside, you can hardly tell that he's been
living there as long as he has. There are a few instruments scattered around,
some of his books and clothes, but otherwise it's pretty much the same as
when Jilly was living there. Except it's neater. And the fairy paintings are all
gone.

"Do you want to come over and use it?" he asks.

My gaze tracks back to the part of the room where Saskia disappeared and the vise closes in on my chest again. I know she's not going to simply pop back into existence. I can *feel* her absence and it's total. But at the same time, I don't know that she isn't going to pop back, either. Once you entered the world of the impossible, how can you say anything's unequivocally this or that?

Geordie stands up.

"Let me get the laptop and bring it back here," he says.

I give him a grateful look. He's gone before I can even get out of the chair. I stand by the front door for a moment, feeling completely adrift in the waves of loneliness and despair that wash over me, then slowly make my way back into the kitchen. I pour myself some more coffee. I light another cigarette. I try to empty my mind of everything, but that doesn't work so well. Worries and fears and half-made plans bounce around in my head until it feels like a pinball machine.

Mostly I just wait.

Christiana

I'm not aware of falling. Of losing my grip on the phone. Of how long I lie there in the grass that carpets my little meadow apartment, my mind a blank slate. Big time *tabula rasa*. Like all I really am is a shadow— a shadow cast on the ground and you can make anything of me you want, depending on how and where you shine the light.

<Christiana.>

The sound of my name pulls me back from the empty place into which I fell. It goes echoing and echoing through this black void where I'm floating until I finally make the connection.

Christiana. That's me.

I use my name like a line to pull myself out of the dark.

The sunlight is harsh on my eyes, making them water, and it seems to take forever to sit up, twice that for the world to stop spinning.

I've never fainted before. Somehow I thought it'd be different. You see it in the movies, the damsel swoons and someone's there to catch her. People flit about and fuss and finally she opens her eyes with a becoming flutter of long lashes and gives the male lead a dreamy look. It's all so romantic.

In my case, the ground caught me—luckily the grass is soft and I didn't whack my head on the end of the bed or something. Coming out of it, I'm disoriented and sweaty. There's a bad taste in my mouth and my head feels fuzzy, like it's too full, if that makes any sense. There's a pressure in between my temples, as though something is shifting or stretching inside my head.

You know how the first time you sleep with someone new in your bed—doesn't matter if you've made love or you're just lying there together—you're very aware of the other person's presence in what's normally a solitary place? Every movement they make is exaggerated. Every sound is magnified.

That's what this is like.

And as for romantic feelings, I feel more like crawling into bed and pulling the blankets over my head than making goo-goo eyes at some guy, just saying there was anybody around in the first place.

<Christiana.>

Scratch that. Somebody's here. And now I remember how hearing my name brought me out of the dark.

This time I look around, but there's no one here. At least no one that I can see. Whoever it is has to be hiding in the trees that border my meadow.

"Who's there?" I say.

But as the words leave my lips, I've already matched the voice against the catalogue in my memory. I know who's speaking to me.

"Where are you, Saskia?" I ask. "How come I can't see you?"

My gaze stops on the cell phone lying in the grass nearby. I remember the phone call that pulled me out of sleep. I remember the blast of white noise that came from the speaker. I remember falling. Nothing else.

I pick up the phone and bring the speaker to my ear, thinking Saskia's on the other end of the line. But the phone's dead. I turn it on and get a dial tone.

<Don't freak out on me.>

I don't like this at all. Nobody knows how to get to this place. Hardly anybody even *knows* about it.

I turn off the phone and look around some more. Wherever Saskia is, she's doing a good job of hiding.

<I didn't mean to do this, but I didn't seem to have a choice. It was either this, or oblivion.>

I'm starting to get a really creepy feeling. I realize that I'm not hearing her voice the way I should be. It's not coming to me through my ears.

<I did ask before I came in.>

The voice is in my head.

<You said yes.>

"Get out of my head," I tell her.

<But you said—>

"This isn't funny."

I want to bang my head against the end of my bed or a tree. I can't physically feel her inside me—there's just her voice, and the impression of something else, something foreign in my head—but it's giving me the major willies having her inside my skin the way she is.

"I don't know how you did this, but you'd better just get out."

<I can't.>

"I'm serious."

<I am, too. I can't get out. I didn't even know I could get in until it actually happened.>

"So what? This is some science experiment?"

<No. I had to hide in somebody.>

"Why didn't you just go into Christy's head?"

<I tried that first, but I couldn't get in. There was no . . . I don't know what to call it. Conduit, I suppose.>

"And there is with me?"

<There was with the phone line. I can't explain how it happened. It all went so fast—this expanding dot appearing on Christy's computer screen, me touching it. It was like something shorted out inside me. Like I've been an illusion all along and whatever was growing on the screen made it come apart.>

"You were never an illusion."

<Then how come I'm here in your head? This doesn't happen to real people.>

I didn't know what to say to that. There's a long pause, then she continues.

<But at the same time everything was happening in such a rush, I felt the way . . . I guess a computer would feel if it could feel. I could do a hundred things at the same time. Try to hold myself together. Try to use Christy as an anchor. Try to fight whatever it was that was taking me apart, pixel by pixel.>

"You're not made of pixels," I say.

<Molecule by molecule, then.>

"Whatever."

<And some part of me reached for you, but the only way I knew to contact you was from the phone number you left me.>

"But how did you come across the phone lines and into me?"

<I don't know. Like data, I suppose. The way you send data. Because

that's all I am. Some data that the Wordwood gussied up into a simulation of a human being.>

"Stop saying that," I tell her.

Except then I start to wonder, maybe she is just data. Maybe that's all she's ever been. Data that got more real as it began to accumulate its own life experiences. Just like a shadow does . . .

Even with my own origin in mind, even with all the strange beings I've met in the borderlands and beyond, this still feels too crazy. She was too real for that.

But then I think of myself as real, too, don't I? What's the difference between a being created out of shadows, and one created out of data?

I need to think, but I don't know where to start. It's too mondo, big-time bizarre, having her inside me. What's she doing in me? Going through my memories? Does she have control over my body? Are we sharing it in more ways than one?

"This is totally freaking me out," I tell her.

<I'm not exactly comfortable with it myself.>

"What can you see . . . you know, inside me?"

<Nothing.>

"What do you mean, 'nothing'?"

<I have no sense of a body whatsoever—at least not of my own. I can see what you see, hear what you hear, but it's like a movie with smell and taste and tactile senses thrown in for good measure. There's no sense of immediacy—of my actually being able to experience this on my own. It's all secondhand.>

"You can't read my mind? You can't access my memories?"

<No.>

Can you hear me if I specifically aim a thought at you like this?

<Yes. But it feels very strange. Like there's a ghost in my head.>

"Welcome to the club."

<Christiana . . . I'm sorry. I was desperate, grabbing at anything I could. And you . . . you said I could come in.>

"I did."

And I don't know why.

"What are we going to do?" I ask her.

Saskia's silence is all the reply I get. I understand. I don't have a clue either. How do you fix something like this? Where do you even start? It would sure help to have somebody step up and offer some advice right about now. I mean anything from "I know a good systems analyst who also happens to be a working magician," to "You must take the cursed ring across the perilous lands and cast it back into the fire from which it was forged," would put us further ahead than we are at this point.

It doesn't have to be easy. Just *some* direction.

I sigh and look off across my friendly little meadow apartment. I remember coming home last night and how comfortable I was, puttering around, reading a little bit, finally going to bed. Now everything feels different. Well, duh. I've got somebody else living in my head. But it's more than that.

<It's starting to get dark,> Saskia says.

"Yeah."

I'm too caught up in all of this to really pay attention to what she's saying. But then it registers. I realize that it *is* getting dark.

"This isn't possible," I say.

Like so much else about today is.

<What do you mean?>

"I told you how I made this place. I grabbed a perfect memory and stuck it away in this nook of the borderlands. It only has two faces—a sunny day and a twilight evening, depending on how much light I want. It doesn't have weather. It can't change."

<Well, it looks to me like there's a storm coming.>

It does to me, too. From the west. I walk toward the western edge of the meadow and step into the trees. There's really nothing past them. Walk far enough and you'll simply pop out somewhere else—into whatever place happens to be in your mind at the time, even if it's only in your subconscious. The only rule seems to be that you have to have been there before, or have a really good image of it from a photograph.

That's how most people build their memory holes. There's a clear demarcation between your private place and all the other places you can access from it. When I made mine, I added views that you'd expect to see from a meadow—rolling hills, forests, some distant mountains. But they're not really there. And they're completely static. Like a painting. Like a photo.

So it's particularly weird to see storm clouds gathering in the western skies. It'd be like you looking at a landscape on a wall in your home—some beautiful sunny hillside, say—and as you look at it, a storm starts to form in one corner of the picture. It shouldn't be able to happen.

But it does. It's happening here.

Why am I so surprised? People aren't supposed to take up residence inside your head, either.

"I'm getting a bad feeling about this," I say.

I feel like I'm reading from the script for some B-movie—a tacky horror flick or an action piece.

There's no reply for a long moment, then I hear Saskia say softly in my head, <I think it's the Wordwood.>

"What makes you say that?"

<I'm getting the same worrisome feeling from that build-up of dark clouds as I got from the expanding black dot that showed up on Christy's computer screen. I didn't know what it was then, but I recognize it now.>

"What makes you so sure it's the Wordwood?"

<I . . . I don't know. I'm not. Christy said something about the Wordwood site having been down all week. So maybe this isn't the Wordwood. Maybe it's whatever took it off-line.>

"You mean like a virus?"

<I guess.>

"How could a computer virus show up like a storm in the borderlands?"

<I don't know. How can data show up in the World As It Is and take human form the way I did?>

"Don't start in on that again," I say, but my heart's not really in it.

Maybe she was just data. Maybe she was never real. Maybe I'm not either. It would make sense. Why else would Mumbo always be showing me things to help me pass for normal among real people? The key word here is "pass." You have to pass for human when you're not.

I start to feel a little sick again, and I guess I finally understand why this has all been such a concern for Saskia. I haven't thought about this—really thought about it—in a long, long time. I wish I wasn't thinking about it now.

<We should get out of here,> Saskia says.

It's so hard to get used to this voice in my head.

"Why?" I ask her.

<Look what happened to me when I came into contact with that thing earlier tonight.>

"But I'm not made of data. It's not going to be able to affect me the way it did you."

<We don't know that.>

"No. We don't know much about anything. And we're not going to find out by running away. If this storm is an aspect of whatever it was that took away your body, then it's the very thing we have to face to get it back."

<And if it does something worse?>

"What could be worse?"

There's a pause before Saskia replies. <Are you really this brave?>

I laugh. "Maybe I just don't know any better."

But I do. The thing is, when I get into a situation like this, I almost always go forward, into the darkness. I don't think of it as being brave or foolhardy. It's just what I do. Because I don't like hiding. I get scared just like anybody else does. But I refuse to let my fear make me back away. When you do that, the darkness wins.

I take a step forward, expecting Saskia to try to pull me back. She doesn't. So she was telling the truth about that. Because I know that she wouldn't let me do this if she could stop me. But all she's got is words.

<Christiana,> she says, her nervousness plain in her voice.

"Don't worry," I tell her. "I'm the queen of getting out of trouble."

Big words. I'm good with words. Not as good as Christy, but I've always got something to say. Trouble is, words aren't really much of a help right now.

I keep walking. We're well past the border of my little memory hole. We should be somewhere else now—in the borderlands, the otherworld, even what the professor calls the World As It Is—except we're continuing across a field that lies on the other side of the line of trees demarking my memory hole. A field that shouldn't exist because it's only an image. But I can feel the grass brush against the bottoms of my jeans. The wind in my face. That invisible crackle in the air of the gathering storm that's just about upon me.

<It's getting closer.>

"I can see that."

I can *feel* it. All the little hairs on my arms and at the nape of my neck are standing straight up.

The dark clouds are rolling in fast, turning what was already twilight into something that's even closer to night. The wind's picking up and there's a sound under its bluster. It takes me a moment to figure out what it reminds me of. Then I have it. Static. Like there was on the telephone line just before Saskia came into my head. Except this time it's not coming to me through the phone. It's all around us. We're in the middle of it.

I lift my gaze to the horizon where the clouds are darkest. The light's poor, making details hard to pick out, but I find if I look hard, the landscape flickers. Distant mountains, clouds, the horizon. One moment they're in sharp focus, the next they're a pulsing storm of pixels, then they firm up again.

Maybe Saskia's right, I find myself thinking. Maybe this really is the

Wordwood. Or maybe we've been pulled into some cyber realm where the Wordwood exists and everything has different rules from the ones we know.

Maybe coming out here wasn't such a good idea.

I see a sheet of rain coming across the fields toward us, darker than any water I've seen before. I consider a hasty retreat. I know, I know. I said I like to face the darkness. But there's a right time and a wrong time to make a stand. Like if someone's got a gun in your face, it's not a good time to crack wise. And if the world falls apart and you find yourself in a place like this—real, not real, can't make up its mind—it only makes sense to fall back to firmer ground and rethink the situation.

I start to turn. Too late.

The wall of rain's right on us. Not water. Something else. Heavier, thicker. Like oil.

It hits me and pounds me into the ground.

I try to stand. I can't even get to my knees.

The impact of the black rain drives me down and keeps me there.

I feel myself losing my grip on consciousness again. I find myself thinking that I'm beginning to make a real habit of this fainting business, but then—

Saskia

I thought that losing my body the way I did was the most awful thing I could experience. I was wrong. This is worse. Way worse. I can't bear to be so helpless—an ineffectual spirit locked in Christiana's head, while my faceless enemy pounds her into the ground.

And there's nothing I can do to stop it.

It's my fault this is happening to her. All my fault.

She's gone now. I can't find even a spark of her consciousness anywhere inside this body we're sharing. The black rain continues to beat on her limp body and I can only pray that it's battered her into unconsciousness. That she's not dead.

But if she's not already dead, she soon will be. The rain turns to an oily goop on the ground, forming puddles around her that rapidly grow into a small pond of the thick liquid. When she collapsed, it was into a small hollow in the field. It's shallow, but deep enough for her to drown if the level of the goop rises much more.

I try to take control of her slack limbs, but it doesn't seem to matter that she's unconscious and unable to use them herself. I'm still just a passenger and nothing will move for me. Not even an eyelid. I focus on the task like I've never focused on anything before, but all my effort is of no more use than trying to stop a river overflowing its banks with only your hands.

The rain keeps pouring down and the little pond around Christiana continues to rise. If this keeps up . . .

I don't want to think about it, but it's all I can think about.

Until, through the oily film that covers her eyes, I see a blur of movement.

There are shapes moving in the black rain. Human figures, but they're like Spielberg aliens—all smooth, without edges.

I redouble my efforts to take control of Christiana's limbs with about as much success as before, which is none.

The oily water keeps rising. It comes up to her mouth. Her nose. The figures are all around us now, leaning closer with strange blurred features. I scream in Christiana's mind, trying to rouse her. Trying to move her. But it's no use. She won't wake and I can't move her. There's nothing I can do except sit inside her head while she drowns.

The liquid pours into her nostrils, into her mouth, down her throat, filling her lungs.

And then I go into the same black space I guess she did.

Christy

It's only been three-quarters of an hour, but it feels like a week before Geordie finally returns with Amy's laptop. He doesn't have a carrying case for it, so he brings it in his backpack.

"The battery's kind of wonky," he says as he sets the old machine on my desk. "So you have to run it off the power cord."

Which, happily, he remembered to bring along. I give the machine a quick look-over. It's a 386—still running Windows 3.1, Geordie tells me—but it has a PCMCIA modem card so that I can get on the Internet and the processor should be plenty fast enough for what I need it to do. All I want to do is send some e-mail.

While Geordie was gone, I smoked I don't know how many more cigarettes. But I also cleaned up the mess in the study, picking up all the various bits and pieces of my computer and stowing them in a cardboard box that I grabbed from the recycling container on the back balcony. I wasn't able to do much with the top of the desk. The scratches and burn marks needed more than a sponge or cloth to clean up, but they were the least of my worries.

As I worked, all I could think about was Saskia. She's all I can think about.

I didn't know what to do with the debris from the computer so I put the box beside my desk. I realized that I couldn't throw it out just yet. I have this weird idea that since Saskia disappeared into the machine just before it exploded, she's still tied to it somehow. If I throw it out, it'll be like throwing her out. I know. It makes no sense. But nothing about the night makes any sense.

"Thanks for going to get this," I tell my brother.

"No problem."

He sits in the extra straight-backed chair near my desk, watching as I finish setting up the laptop and plug it in. I pick up the phone cord that I used with my own computer, but the end got melted, so I go looking for a fresh one. Finally I give up and take the cord off the phone in the bedroom.

"It's kind of weird out there," Geordie says as I make the final connection. "On the streets, I mean."

I lift my head to look at him. "What do you mean 'weird'?"

He shrugs. "I don't know. There's just a feeling in the air. Like the shadows are too dark and . . ." He gives me an uneasy smile. "And maybe there's things moving in them."

"What did you see?"

"I didn't see anything. It was just a feeling. Like this is about more than Saskia."

I'd never took that into account. Considering Saskia's claims concerning her origin, I simply assumed this was about her.

"Why don't you check the news," I say, "while I try to get a couple of messages out."

"As if it'd be on CNN."

"So try the local stations first."

"Christy," he says. "I can't count the number of weird things that happen in this city, but when was the last time you saw a mention of any of them on the news?"

I just give him a look.

"Okay," he says. "I guess it can't hurt to check it out."

I go back to what I'm doing. Now that the hardware's all connected, I boot up the laptop and wait forever for this old version of Windows to load and give me the Desktop screen. Then I go searching for Geordie's e-mail program. Once I find it, I make a note of his sending and receiving protocols. I replace them with my own and I'm ready to go.

I don't remember the e-mail addresses of all my regular correspondents—it's like putting numbers into the automatic dial-up directory of your telephone. You get so used to simply pushing a button that your memory doesn't retain the actual numbers anymore. But I do remember the addresses of the newsgroups. The hard part is figuring out just what to say. I start typing.

I don't really know where to begin . . .

I keep it simple and don't get too specific. I don't mention Saskia's origins or how she got swallowed by the computer. Instead I talk about the Wordwood and ask if anyone's experienced any oddities with the Web site. I hesitate, then clarify that by adding:

. . . oddities with the Web site that cause actual physical anomalies in your real world environment.

I finish up by asking anyone who might have experienced anything along those lines to contact me and put my phone number under my name at the end of the message. Lighting up yet another cigarette, I read it back to myself. There's so much more I could say, but I want to leave this clear enough that someone with a genuine experience will contact me, yet vague enough that I don't get inundated with calls from the cranks on those same newsgroups. Satisfied, I queue it up.

Now comes the part that I've been worrying about ever since Geordie went out to get the laptop: connecting to the Internet again. I don't know what to expect, but I'll tell you this. The first hint of anything weird and I'm just pulling the phone jack out of the computer, never mind shutting down the connection.

But I needn't have worried. Everything acts the way it's supposed to. Dial-up, connect. I hit send and watch the progress bar as the e-mails go off into the pixelated ether.

I'm shutting down the e-mail and Internet connection when Geordie comes back into the room with an expression on his face that I can't read.

"You have to come see this," he says.

"See what?"

"It's on CNN. Saskia's not the only one that's disappeared into a computer."

"What?"

"Just come look at this," he says and leaves the room again.

I turn off the laptop and follow him into the living room. We sit side-by-side on the sofa watching the calm, perfectly-coifed anchorperson coordinate her own commentary with cuts to correspondents in various parts of

North America and abroad. There's live footage, of course, but it consists mostly of the exteriors of various houses and apartment buildings that look perfectly normal except for the police cars and emergency vehicles parked outside.

While all the incidents happened at approximately the same time—and also, not coincidentally, I'm sure, at the same time that Saskia disappeared—it took the authorities a while to realize that the rash of 911 calls were connected.

"The count of those missing now stands at one hundred eighty-six," the blonde anchorperson is saying. "Authorities believe that the final figure will be much higher, as the information they have to date doesn't take into account those living alone with no one to report their disappearance."

There's no actual mention of www.thewordwood.com. I can't decide if they're keeping that under wraps, or if they simply don't know. From the footage of the interior of one of the disappeared's homes, it must be the latter. There's a camera pan across a study and the brief glimpse I get of the computer shows that it's a mess. Not shattered like mine did, but it's dripping some kind of black oily goop. The emergency workers in the room are wearing bio-hazard containment suits, giving the video an even more surreal quality.

The reportage cuts to a woman being interviewed outside of her home. As she starts talking about this flood of thick black oil pouring out of her husband's computer screen, I turn to Geordie.

"That's not what happened to Saskia," I say.

He nods. "But there's no way it's not connected."

"No question," I agree.

"So we should tell someone," he adds.

"What for?"

"So that it doesn't happen to anyone else who tries to log on to the Wordwood."

I shake my head. "I'm pretty sure we don't have to worry about that."

"But—"

"Weren't you listening to what they were saying?" I ask, nodding at the TV. "It all happened around the same time. I'm guessing it was a spike of . . . I don't know, some kind of energy or whatever. It happened, now it's done."

"We don't know that. If we can save other lives by—"

"Nobody's dead," I tell him, needing to believe it myself. "They were taken away to . . . well, I don't know that either. Someplace else. And if we

let the 'proper authorities' deal with it, we'll never get Saskia or any of them
back. They'll just screw it up."

"We can't take that chance."

I sigh. "Okay, I'll prove it," I tell him.

I get up and go back into the study where I boot up the laptop again.

"What are you doing?" Geordie asks.

"We're going to run a test. If nothing happens, we keep the Wordwood
connection to ourselves. If it looks like there's going to be a problem, I'll
pull the plug and we phone the police or whoever will listen to us."

When the Desktop shows up on the screen, I double-click on the Internet connection icon.

"Wait a minute," Geordie says. "Amy only loaned that to me. If you
blow it up she's going to kill me."

"Nothing's going to get blown up."

The connection's made and I start up the Internet browser, an old version of Netscape.

"This is just being stupid," Geordie says. "It's too dangerous."

"I know what I'm doing," I tell him as I type in the Wordwood's URL.
"If that dot shows up, I'll unplug it so fast it'll make your head spin."

"My head's already spinning."

I hit return and the browser goes searching for the Wordwood.

"We're going to end up sucked away into wherever along with the rest
of them," Geordie says.

I think about that. Think about how Saskia was stolen away. I've gone
over it a million times, how I could have forestalled all of it if I just hadn't
suggested we go on-line to check with the Wordwood. But no. I had all the
answers.

Turns out I didn't have any.

"Maybe that wouldn't be such a bad thing," I say.

"What?"

"Nothing."

"We can't just—"

"Too late," I tell him. "We're already there."

The familiar "This page cannot be displayed" dialogue comes up on
the screen. I realize I'm holding my breath as I wait for the black dot to
reappear, but the seconds tick away into a minute, two, three. Nothing
changes.

I close the page and take the computer off-line.

"You see?" I say as I shut it down. "It's just a dead link again."

"You really think you can figure this thing out?" Geordie asks.

"Not by myself. But with the right input from some of the others in my newsgroups, we've got a fighting chance."

"And if that doesn't work?"

"I don't want to think about that right now," I say. "Let's try to keep a positive spin on things."

"But—"

"Please?"

He nods and we go back into the living room. I light another cigarette. Geordie makes some more coffee and we watch the TV, where all the experts fumble to make sense of what's going on. What I find most interesting is how everybody avoids any consideration of the supernatural being involved. Reporters, police and government spokespeople, the experts. None of them bring it up. They're postulating terrorist biological attacks, bizarre cult conspiracies, anything but what actually happened.

We're still watching TV when the phone rings. Geordie lowers the sound with the remote.

"Is this Christy Riddell?" a woman's voice asks after I say hello.

"Yes. And you are . . . ?"

"It's Estie. From the alt-mythology-computers newsgroup. Is your computer still on-line?"

"No, but I don't think it matters. I figure it was a one-time anomaly. I've been back on-line since . . . since the incident and all I get is the dead link."

There's a moment of silence, then I hear her take a steadying breath.

"Okay," she says finally. "Do you want me to go first or do you want to tell me what happened to you?"

"Have you got your TV on?" I ask.

"No. Why?"

"Maybe you should have a look at what's on CNN."

I figure she's on a roam phone as I can hear her moving around, probably from one room to another. I hear her TV come on—it sounds like a commercial until she punches in the channel number for CNN, and I get a tinny echo through the phone's receiver of what's playing on low volume on the TV set in my living room.

"Oh my god," she says after a minute or so. "This is worse than I thought."

I give her a moment to digest what she's seeing, though a moment isn't going to be nearly enough. At least it hasn't been for me.

"Tell me what happened," I say.

There's a long pause, where all I can hear from the receiver is the sound of her TV set coming over the line.

"My name's Sarah Taylor," she says finally.

I know that name and say as much, though I can't remember where I know it from.

"We have a mutual friend," she says. "Holly Rue."

"Wait a minute." I start to make the connections. "Does that mean you're—"

"Yes. I'm one of the original founders of the Wordwood."

I get this immediate sense of relief. She'll know what to do. We're going to get Saskia and all those other people back.

But my relief is fleeting.

"But that doesn't mean I have the first clue as to what's going on," she adds.

The grin that was starting to pull at my lips dies.

"So what do we do?" I say.

I pull another cigarette out of the pack and frown. It's almost empty.

"Well, to start with," she says, "we can compare our stories. I was on-line with Benny—Benjamin Davis. Do you know who he is?"

Now that Estie's made the connection to Holly for me, various conversations Holly and I have had about the Wordwood are coming back to me.

"He's another of the cofounders," I say.

"Right. I keep in touch with him more than the others. No real reason. Maybe just because I've known him the longest, or because he's like me: more of a techie than the rest."

"I know how that goes."

"Anyway," she says. "We were just trying out some new software for our Web cameras, chatting to each other through instant messaging while we screwed around with the settings. Then we got sidetracked by this e-mail we got from Tip about the Wordwood."

She doesn't stop to explain who Tip is, but I remember Holly talking about him. She means Tom Pace, another of the founders.

"Neither Benny nor I have much to do with it anymore . . . not since, you know."

"It became sentient."

She gives a nervous laugh. "I guess that's one way of putting it. Anyway, we didn't even know that the site had been down, so Benny decides to go have a look. He aims his browser at the Wordwood, but we still have our Web cameras on."

She goes on to describe the images the Web camera put on her monitor's screen, how he has this puzzled look and leans closer to the screen then suddenly jumps back. She gets a glimpse of this gush of black liquid issuing from something in front of him. Sees him fall into it. He goes down, out of camera range, and then nothing. He doesn't get back up. Frantically, she sends him an instant message, then an e-mail. No answer. Finally she phones him and gets his boyfriend Raul on the line.

Raul's in a total panic. The story she manages to get out of him, and that she now relates to me, is pretty much the same as what Geordie and I have been hearing on CNN from the few eyewitnesses that reporters have managed to track down: black goop pouring out of the monitor in an impossible flood, enveloping the victim, then slowly dissolving away to leave not a trace.

I don't want to get into Saskia's origins—not even with one of the Wordwood's founders. Maybe especially not with one. So I make like it happened pretty much the same way for Saskia as it did for Estie's friend Benny.

"How's something like that even possible?" Estie says. I can hear the strain in her voice. She's feeling the same shock I did when Saskia was taken away. "What could that stuff be?"

"I think it must be a kind of ectoplasm," I say.

"You know, I've heard that term before, but when I think about it, I really have no idea what it means."

"In spiritualist terms, it's this thick, sticky substance that supposedly flows out of the body of a medium to produce . . . I guess you could say manifestations. Living forms that usually have some relationship to the spirit being called up."

There's a pause and then she says, "Do you buy this?"

"I've seen stranger things."

She gives that nervous laugh again. "Yeah, I keep forgetting who I'm talking to. We were all surprised to have a celebrity like you show up on our newsgroup."

"I'm no celebrity," I say.

"Well, you've got a higher public profile that all the rest of us put together." There's another pause. "So who was having the séance?"

"What do you mean?"

"Well, isn't that where you'd find a medium?"

"I suppose the medium could be the computer," I tell her. "Or perhaps even the Internet."

"And the spirit that got called up is whatever took over the Wordwood way back when?"

"Who knows? Until we can get more information, it's all just specula-tion."

"So what happens to the people that get taken?" she asks.

"I don't know. I figure that what happened was a flare-up of some sort, though what could have caused it is anybody's guess. Whoever happened to be trying to log onto the Wordwood at that instant got caught up in it and taken away."

"Taken where?"

I'm slow in responding. It's just now occurring to me that the flare-up could well have been caused by Saskia's trying to get in touch with the spirit of the Wordwood. Something as simple as a spiritual short-out brought about when creation and creator come into unexpected contact. Like when wires cross, except here it was spirits in the wires.

"I don't know that either," I finally tell her. "I'd say the spiritworld, but I don't know that technological spirits would exist in the same world as fairies and goblins."

Now it's her turn to be quiet.

"Are you still there?" I ask after a few moments.

"Yeah. I was just thinking. Growing up, I was never much of a one for fairy tales and such. But ever since that business with the Wordwood taking on a life of its own, I've just known that there's something lurking in cyber-space. Not just whatever took over the Wordwood site, but other spirits, too. Maybe lots of them. Which is weird, when you think about it. Because cyberspace doesn't really exist. It's more just a concept that we created. A label for us to put on what goes on when the vast nets of data crisscross over the wires and in the computers that house Web sites.

"It's something we made up. So I guess we made up these spirits, too."

"Maybe," I say. "There's certainly a line of thinking that believes that gods and fairies and the things that go bump in the night exist only because we believe in them. That we created them to explain the confusing mystery of the world."

"But you don't," she says.

"Not entirely, no. I think some of the mysteries of the world can be explained that way, but not all of them. Not even most of them."

"This is so frigging weird."

"Uh-huh." I wait a heartbeat, then ask, "How come you never talk about this kind of thing in the newsgroup?"

"Have you ever noticed how you *can't* really talk about it on-line?" she says. "I know people who have tried. They've written articles, or even just done like you said. Talked about it in newsgroups, or tried to start new ones. But those spirits are jealous of their privacy. You watch. By six or seven this morning, CNN's coverage isn't going to even talk about the computer connection anymore."

"You're probably right. The human mind is very good at forgetting what it can't explain."

"I'm not saying it will be people, forgetting in order to hang onto their sanity," she says. "Those spirits don't let it happen."

"But—"

"It's something all the hackers know. There are things you just don't talk about on-line. Hell, you can't talk about it on any medium that's connected to computers, which is pretty much every medium we have, except for word-of-mouth or handwriting. Come at it from any other way—anything that touches a computer—and the words, the videos, the whatever you used to try to get the message out just gets erased. I can tell you about chapters disappearing from books. Scenes from documentaries. It's been going on for years."

"I've come across some of that in my research," I say.

"But only face-to-face research, right?"

I light yet another cigarette and think about that for a long moment before agreeing with her.

"So where do we go from here?" I ask.

"I've got a flight booked," she says, "that'll bring me into Newford midmorning tomorrow. Before I leave, I'll try to get Tip and Claudette to fly in as well and meet me at Holly's store. Raul told me he's coming, too. He's enough of a techie that he'll be useful and I know he needs something to get his mind off of what happened to Benny. To feel like he's doing something to bring him back."

"I know exactly how he feels," I tell her.

"We could use your help, too. You know more about the whole spirit side of this than any of us."

"You've got it," I say. "But what is it that you're planning to do?"

"I don't know exactly. Brainstorm, I guess. I've got this idea that maybe we can start over again with the Wordwood, see if we can't make another connection with the spirit that stepped into it, except this time show that we're benevolent. That we don't mean it any harm. I figured if we do that, we should use Holly's old 386—the one we used to make the Wordwood in the first place."

"I'd think you'd want to use a faster machine."

"But what if the magic's in that particular machine?"

I think about all the times I've hung around in Holly's store, sitting behind the desk with her and yakking about books, the computer monitor casting its light on the various papers, magazines, and books scattered about on the surface of the desk.

"She doesn't use that computer any more," I tell Estie.

"I know that. But I'm pretty sure she's still got the old one stashed away in her basement. You know Holly. When does she throw anything away?"

"Have you checked that she still has it?"

"I was hoping you would. I haven't been able to get in touch with her. I've tried calling her a number of times in the last hour or so, but there doesn't seem to be any phone service at her apartment, and downstairs in the store, the machine just picks up."

"You don't think something's happened to her?"

"No. Her computer's in the store. If something had happened to her like it did Benny or your friend Saskia, it would've fried the phone wires the way it did at Benny's place. The only reason I was able to get through to Raul was because they have a second line in the house for Raul's business. He imports clothing and furniture from Mexico and wholesales it to stores."

"I'll go by Holly's as soon as I get off the phone," I tell her.

I'm starting to feel a little worried about Holly now. Because the thing is, while the one phone cord got wrecked in my study when Saskia disappeared, I didn't lose my phone service. All I had to do was replace the cord to get back on-line and the phone was never out. But to bring that up now with Estie means I'd have to explain about Saskia and why I didn't tell her earlier. I'm still not ready to get into that.

"Great," Estie says. "I'll see you sometime in the morning—noon at the latest."

"I'll be there." I hesitate a moment, then add, "Have you talked to the authorities yet?"

"And tell them what? They'd think I was insane. And if they didn't, they might just lock me away for being one the people who started up the Wordwood in the first place. I won't be able to do anything to stop it from a jail cell."

"Good point," I say, as though it hadn't occurred to me.

"And you?" she asks.

"I'll follow your lead in this."

When I hang up, Geordie gives me a quizzical look so I take him through a much shortened rundown of Estie's side of the conversation.

"I notice you didn't tell her much about what really happened with Saskia," he says.

"I couldn't."

"Why not?"

"Because I've got this bad feeling that maybe Saskia was the catalyst for all these disappearances."

"Oh, come on now," he says. "Saskia'd never do anything like that."

"I didn't say she'd do it on purpose. I'm thinking it was more like . . . I don't know, the computer version of a chemical reaction. Or the way a pin can burst a balloon."

Geordie's still shaking his head.

"You know the Wordwood was already down before any of this happened?" I say.

"Yeah, but—"

"So something happened to it. Something *changed* it. That being the case, her contacting it could easily have set off a chain reaction."

"You don't know that."

I shake my head. "No. But until we *do* know more, what really happened to Saskia's going to stay between you and me. It has to, Geordie."

"Okay."

I start to get up, but he grabs my arm.

"Wait a sec'," he says. "You need to see this."

He turns up the sound as CNN replays some of the interview footage from one of the witnesses.

"All I know," the middle-aged woman on the screen is saying to the reporter, "is that he was down in the rec room. I don't pay any attention when he's down there, but then I hear this strange burbling sound coming up the stairs. So I get up to go have a—"

Geordie thumbs the "Mute" on the remote, cutting her of in mid-sentence.

"Estie was right," he says. "It's already starting to happen."

"I'm not following you."

"That woman's quote," Geordie says. "I've heard it a few times now. The first couple of times she said, 'He was down in the rec room messing around on that stupid computer of his.' But the part about the computer's been cut out now."

"Are you sure?"

Geordie nods.

I give the TV a worried look.

"Jesus," I say. "I wish I knew whether this really is the doing of spirits like Estie said, or if the authorities have caused a blackout because they've decided to sit on that information."

"Well, you could give the police a call," Geordie says. "Tell them you're this expert on computer myths . . ."

His voice trails off when he sees the joke's not going anywhere.

"Come on, Christy," he says. "You can't seriously believe that these spirits can be monitoring all broadcasts, the Internet, satellite feeds, cable . . ."

"What are computers better at than we are?" I ask. When he shakes his head, I say, "Multitasking and crunching data. They do it as easily, and probably with about as much attention, as you or I breathe."

"But to believe they're eavesdropping—"

"I know."

Probably the biggest bullshit paranoia dealing with computers is the myth that people—the government, aliens, your neighbours, it doesn't matter who—can watch what you're doing through the screen of your monitor. It's not even a new idea. I've heard it applied to TVs, as well. It's something you laugh off when you hear it, but now, thinking that perhaps there really are spirits in the wires—jealous of their privacy, as Estie put it—I'm wondering if maybe it's not such a farfetched notion after all.

Considering what happened to Saskia, and now this business with how the spirits are able to protect themselves by erasing any mention of them in electronic media, who's to say they *aren't* watching us from the screens of our computer monitors and TV sets? Maybe they're not simply inhabiting cyberspace. Maybe they can move through any technology that uses electricity or phone lines.

And how about satellite feeds? They could be listening and watching us from the skies, from our household appliances, from anything that's plugged in or utilizes power . . .

I should call Estie back, I think. Warn her that the spirits could have been listening to us over the phone lines. But I don't have her number. And—

I give my head a shake and force myself to stop thinking about this kind of thing before I drive myself crazy.

"You want to take a ride up to Holly's store with me?" I ask Geordie.

"Sure. It's not like I'm going to be able to sleep."

Borrible Jones

Bojo stood alone in the library of the Kelledys' house, feeling over-whelmed. The ceiling was almost fourteen feet high, as befit an old mansion such as this, but such heights also gave a room far too much wall space, so far as Bojo was concerned. He stood looking at floor-to-ceiling book cases that lined each wall except for the doorway where he stood, and a space across from him on the west wall, where the bookcases were broken up by a lead-paned bay window that had a seat underneath large enough to hold two people comfortably.

There were simply too many books. He walked slowly around the room, reading the spines. It was an eclectic selection—music books, fiction, histories, biographies, fairy tales, and esoteric texts, some of the latter writ-ten in languages so obscure that Bojo couldn't even recognize the alphabet they used. He wondered if the cursive marks and ideograms were, in fact, languages and not some sort of arcane code like the *patteran* of his own people—the ideographic marks they left on the sides of buildings and on roadsides as messages for each other.

It didn't help, either, that the books appeared to be filed in haphazard order. Nor that, when it came down to brass tacks, as his Aunt Jen would say, Bojo didn't really have a clear idea as to what he was looking for.

He wasn't really a book person—that was the main problem here. Bojo came from an oral tradition where advice was taken from tribal elders, or found in the tribe's stories and histories that had been handed down through the years. He knew how to read, but had rarely opened a book since learning to do so. Books, subsequently, had acquired a somewhat mystical connotation in his mind, this library being a perfect example.

He knew they were divided into two basic categories: those you read for entertainment, and those used for reference. Over the years of visiting the Kelledy house, he'd often seen either Meran or Cerin come into the library with a problem, take down a book, and there, as magically as he might read trail signs in the wild hills, they would have the solution.

But they knew what they were looking for, or at least where to look. And to further complicate matters, they as often found what they needed in the fictional books as they did in those that were more obviously kept for reference.

Sighing, Bojo stood in the middle of the room for a while longer, hands in the pockets of his jeans, gaze scanning the bewildering array of titles. Finally, he decided that whatever gift the Kelledys had for finding just the right needed book lay in them, not the library, and he called it quits. He would have to find what he needed in his own way.

He left the library, left the Kelledys' house with its gables and tower, and walked under the oaks in the front yard until he reached the sidewalk. There he looked up and down Stanton Street before lifting his gaze skyward, eyes half-closed. For a long moment, he stood, quiet and attentive, silently sifting through an overabundance of impressions.

Anyone without his understanding of the steady traffic between this world and those it bordered would be unaware of the greater percentage of whom and what Bojo sensed. He was looking for magic, and there was plenty to be detected in this rambling city, but he was also looking for wisdom, and that wasn't as readily found.

He was conscious of any number of bodachs and spirits, shadowmen and border folk, faerie and ghosts, all going about their business. They were under the trees behind him and up in the boughs of those same oaks. They wandered along the streets, keeping to the shadows. They slept in gardens, poked through dumpsters. They scurried about in the sewers and alleyways, crept along rooftops or along windowsills, peering into people's apartments.

Bojo wasn't particularly surprised to sense them out and about the way they were. The hidden people were always present—as much at the height of noon as in the middle of the night. But it was easier to spy them now, when the streets were quiet. Glimpses caught from the corner of the eye, rustles heard from an apparently empty corner.

Tonight the streets seemed very busy, as though this was a holy day when the bone fires burned high in the parks and empty lots. Beltane. Or All Hallows' Eve. Nights when the hidden folk ran in packs and troops, full of mischief and song. But though they were out in large numbers, they were subdued.

And there was a sense of something unfamiliar in the air, as well. As though the shadows in alleyways and along the sides of buildings were casting loose from their moorings. The power lines hummed louder than usual, and there was a scent like an electrical fire when wires short out—faint, but present. Bojo's curiosity itched, but whatever this new thing might be, abroad tonight, he didn't have time to investigate it.

He forced himself to concentrate on the inquiry at hand. He cast the scope of his search farther and wider and finally brushed up against an indication of the sort of magical sage he required—a faint and flickering spark that came from a good distance away.

Closing his eyes, he focused on that spark, trying to get a better impression of who or what it represented. All that came back to him was a whisper of old power and shadows. And that it was a man—or at least male. He couldn't get much more than that. It was as though a cloak of darkness lay upon the man, and it was impossible to tell if the shadows it cast grew from the one he was looking for, or were pressing in upon him.

It didn't matter. Whoever he was, he was the only presence Bojo could find tonight who might be strong enough for their purposes. For better or worse, the tinker knew he would have to find this man or go back to Holly empty-handed, and that, he was unwilling to do.

Thinking of Holly made him smile. Don't get involved, the uncles and the aunts were always telling him. That isn't your world. But how could he not be attracted to someone like Holly? She was so pretty and smart, and that red hair.

Bojo had a weakness for red-haired women. Especially when they rode a motorcycle. He wondered if Holly had one stowed away in a shed behind her shop. A Norton or an Indian. Perhaps a Vincent Black Lightning.

Concentrate on the task at hand, he told himself. Fail in this and he wouldn't be able to show his face back at the bookstore to find out. Women liked men who kept their word. He said he'd help, so first he'd help, then he'd determine how she felt about motorcycles.

Like the hidden folk with whom he shared the night, he kept to the shadows. His route took him east on Stanton where the estates became steadily more rundown before finally giving over to brownstones and storefronts. He ducked into doorways or alleys whenever he saw a vehicle approaching, or—more rarely—another pedestrian. He carried no papers, nothing to identify himself at all, so he was wary of being stopped by one of the city's authorities and having to answer questions about what he was doing out so late at night. Keeping a low profile was almost second nature by now.

It didn't matter what world one was in, tinkers were used to unwanted altercations with the law. The sheriffs and police of any place—village, town, or city—could never make up their minds if they wanted to lock you up or move you along, but they were united in their dislike of the rambling men and women of the tinker clans. That was no longer news for Bojo.

Once he reached Palm Street, he didn't need to be so cautious anymore. He passed more than one parked police cruiser, engine idling, the officers inside barely giving him a glance. They had far more to interest them here than one footloose tinker.

Palm was the main through street of the Combat Zone, this less reputable part of the city, the streets lined with pool halls, diners, strip joints, nightclubs, hotels, the Men's Mission, and innumerable small stores specializing in discount merchandise that were locked up so tightly at this time of night with graffiti-festooned metal sheeting that one might be forgiven in thinking they actually had something valuable to sell.

Even at this hour, cars drifted slowly by, drivers and passengers checking out the lively assortment of bikers, transients, drug dealers, prostitutes of both sexes, not to mention the slumming regular citizens drawn by curiosity or, more likely, the hope of conducting a transaction. The developers hadn't yet cleaned up the Zone the way that they'd Disney-fied Times Square in New York City, but that was only because no one had yet stepped up with enough cash in hand. Still, that time was coming and the gentrification had already begun at the south end of Palm, where it ran along Fitzhenry Park.

Bojo liked this part of town. He felt he could relax here where identification papers or one's station in life were of far less concern than how much money you had in your pocket. He'd spent time in some of the jazz clubs and pool halls and even sat in on a few back room card games, never drawing too much attention to himself, but still able to be himself.

But he didn't have time for amusements tonight.

The spark grew steadily stronger. It led him north on Palm, up to Grasso Street where he took a right, until he finally stood across the street from a diner that was obviously closed for the night. If it wasn't for the spark, he would have walked right by. He stood watching the darkened windows for a long time, but saw no movement, no indication at all that there might be anyone inside.

He waited a little longer before he finally crossed the street. He tapped on the glass door. There was no response. But when he pressed his hand against the cool pane, the door moved under the pressure.

He pushed it open, just enough to poke his head in.

"Hello?" he called, his voice pitched low, but loud enough to carry. "Is anybody here?"

Still no response.

He pushed a little harder, widening the opening until he could step inside.

"Hello?" he called again.

The pull of the spark towed his gaze to left side of the diner. There, in the middle of a row of booths, was a silent figure, a man sitting so quietly that he would have remained invisible except that his aura of potent energy drew Bojo's attention to him as surely as movement might have.

Walking slowly to show he meant no harm, he approached the man's booth. It was hard to make out his features in the poor streetlight coming in from the windows, but Bojo put him in his early twenties, a slender black man in a pinstriped suit, small-boned and handsome, with long delicate fingers and wavy hair brushed back from his forehead. An old Gibson guitar stood upright on the seat on the other side of the booth, as though the two of them were having a visit, sharing confidences.

Bojo opened his mouth to speak. Before he could, the black man's hand lifted from where it had been hidden under the table and Bojo found himself looking into the muzzle of what appeared to be a very large revolver.

"So you found me," the man said. "Don't think I haven't felt you sniffing me out for the past couple of hours. But the question you've got to answer is, now that you're here, what am I going to do with you?"

Christy

When we step outside, I see what Geordie meant about there being an odd feeling in the air tonight.

Tonight? What am I saying?

I shake my head as we walk down the block. It's almost dawn and the night's pretty much gone. Though it's still dark here in the narrow canyons between the brownstones, the skies are already lightening in the east. But the dawn's not quite here yet and there's a *mood* on the streets that I can't quite put my finger on. I walk around a lot at night—a habit I first picked up from Jilly—and I'm used to the otherworldly air that the city streets can take on at this early hour when there's hardly anybody about. At least not in Crowsea. Other parts of downtown—like Palm Street, or up on Grasso— it's busy twenty-four/seven. But in Crowsea, the buildings themselves seem to drift off some time after midnight.

Here, you get a breathing space between when the last stragglers from the clubs have gone home and the morning rush hour starts, with its first trickles of commuters passing through on their way downtown. Movement in the corner of your eye could be an alley cat, could be some little man, hauling his goods to a goblin market. It doesn't matter. Everything just feels open and deep and . . . possible.

But tonight it's different. I spy flickering hints of electric foxfire along the edges of roofs and around distant manhole covers, blue-white and crackling. The transformers on the power and telephone poles are humming louder than usual, and I keep catching an echo of that same smell that filled my study when the computer imploded.

There's definitely something in the air and it's not something I recognize from other late night excursions on the streets. I don't know whether it's because my mood's been coloured by what happened to Saskia, or if there really is something new in the shadows, something dark and maybe a little hungry. But I can feel a warning prickle at the nape of my neck that's usually not there. It's like someone—*something*—is watching us.

My car's parked a couple of blocks away in a garage I rent from the owner of a dollar store over on Williamson Street—what we used to call dime stores back when Geordie and I were kids. There's a sign of inflation that I never thought of before. The car's an old Dodge stationwagon. Give me a North American car any day. These K-cars might not look like much when you've put the years on them like I have this battered old beast, but they just won't die. Stick the key in, winter or summer, and the engine turns over, pretty much every time.

I don't drive it often—maybe once or twice a week—and my apartment building doesn't have parking, but I don't like leaving it on the street, even if it's only the rust that's keeping it together. Sure, it's too beat-up to get stolen, but it would definitely get ticketed during the day, and it's a royal pain to have to keep moving it around every few hours, just to stay ahead of the parking control officers. I know people who do it, people who can easily afford the cost of renting a parking place, but they'd rather play the parking spot game. Takes all kinds.

We finally reach Mr. Li's building. I unlock the garage door and roll it up, metal sheets rattling loudly as they fold away. The Dodge starts right up and I pull it out, idling by the curb while Geordie shuts the garage door behind us.

"So what do you really think about all of this?" he asks as I pull away and turn onto Williamson Street. "This idea of Estie's, I mean. Trying to make a new connection to the Wordwood seems like clutching at straws."

"I don't know what to think."

"Well, I think we should call in someone like Joe, who can walk between the worlds. I mean, this whole cyberspace thing—it's like another world, right? A variation on *manidò-ak*—Joe's spiritworld."

I give him a quick glance before returning my gaze to the street.

"I still can't get used to hearing you say something like that," I tell him.

"I mean, considering how hard you've always fought the idea of there being anything more than what we can see and feel in the World As It Is."

"I've seen too much not to believe anymore, starting with how these days we've got Wendy and Sophie happily crossing over whenever the fancy takes them." He gives a small laugh that holds more discomfort than humour. "I've actually gotten used to seeing someone step into a doorway and disappear instead of going on into the room the way logic says they should."

"You've never been tempted to go over yourself?" I ask.

He nods. "But I'm waiting for Jilly to get better so that I can do it with her. It doesn't seem fair to go on my own—not when it's something she's always dreamed of doing."

I think about how sad it is that the two people in this world that couldn't be more perfect for each other, always seem to have something keeping them apart from being more than friends. Before Jilly was with Daniel, it was Geordie with Tanya. They never seem to get it right.

"What about you?" he asks.

I take the time to light a cigarette before responding, cracking the window open on my side to let the smoke out.

"I've thought about it," I say. "You know, asking Wendy or Sophie, or even Joe, to walk me over, but something always stops me. I think it's because everything that interests me about these kinds of phenomena centers around how they interact with the World As It Is, and how those of us living here react to these intrusions. To just cross those borders and be someplace where everything's magical, where anything can happen . . ." I shake my head. "I suppose I'll go one of these days, if only to have the experience. But I'm not in any hurry."

Geordie nods. "It's funny. I always thought you'd be over there in a flash. That you were like Jilly and this was something you'd spent your whole life looking for."

"I thought the same thing," I tell him. "Until suddenly it was possible. Now I worry that if I do go over, this world will pale too much and it won't satisfy me anymore."

"You think it's that much better?"

I shake my head. "That much more intense. I like this world too much to take the chance lightly."

"You just don't like change."

I smile. "That, too."

"But what if we have to do it now?" Geordie asks. "To get Saskia."

"I'd cross over in a flash."

We fall silent for a couple of blocks, Geordie looking out the passenger's side window, while I keep my attention on the road ahead. There's next to no traffic. A few cabs and delivery vans. A police cruiser that followed us for a couple of blocks before it turned off onto Gellar Street.

"Do you really think we'll get them back?" Geordie asks. "These . . ." He hesitates, then uses the term CNN coined for their coverage. "The disappeared."

I nod, light another cigarette. "Of course we will."

"I don't see how," he says. "What are we supposed to do? Download them from a Web site?"

"If they were able to vanish into their computers, then there's a way to pull them out again. Remember those pixies that caused all that trouble for Holly a couple of years ago? They stepped in and out of her computer."

From the corner of my eye I can see Geordie just shaking his head. I suppose that even with all he's seen, Holly's pixel pixies are still too much like a storybook for him.

"Okay," I say. "Think of the computers as portals—you know, doors to the otherworld—no different from the ones that Wendy steps through."

"She has to hold some little red stone that this Cody guy gave her."

"You know what I mean. It's a similar principle. Something has to act as a catalyst to open these hidden doors. In Wendy's case it's a magic stone. With the disappeared, it's something else—something to do with the Wordwood. We just have to figure out what."

I don't know who I'm trying to convince more—him or me—and we fall quiet again as we cross Gracie Street and head into the Tombs, what the runaways call Squatland.

This part of town just depresses the hell out of me. I can't believe the city council ever let it get this bad. Or that after it had, they haven't done something to make it right. It's a whole condemned section of the city, block after block of abandoned buildings and empty lots. Except for a few through streets, mostly running north/south, the side streets are all blocked with rubble from collapsed buildings, the wrecks of rusting cars and trucks, and other, often less identifiable, debris. The rats grow as big as cats here, hunted by small packs of wild dogs that were originally family pets before they were cast aside and went feral.

It's not just an eyesore, it's dangerous. The wild dogs aren't the only things running feral in Squatland. This is where the bikers have their parties, where the dealers and outlaws hide out, because once you make your way into the Tombs, you disappear from the cops' radar. It's where the lost and the hopeless go to make their last stand—the runaways, the homeless, the junkies and winos.

I believe that everything has a spirit—people, animals, plants, minerals, water. Everything. Even places, like parts of a city. The one that hangs like a cloud over these streets is despair. When I'm as close to it as we are now, I can feel my own old depressions start to press against the walls of my chest. Maybe that's what starts me talking again—anything to distract myself, even if it's to tell Geordie things I've probably told him before. But we didn't really talk to each other for years and I can never remember what I have or haven't shared with him.

"But getting back to the otherworld for a moment," I say, "I guess maybe the real reason I hold back from visiting it is that I have this feeling that once I cross over, that'll be it. This journey I've been on for my whole life will be over."

Geordie gives me a puzzled look.

"The thing people chasing magic forget," I tell him, "is that catching the magic isn't what it's all about. It's how you conduct yourself while you're along the way."

"Like with Tao," he says. "It's the journey that's important."

"It's like everything, if you stop and consider it. I can't think of one process that an individual might undertake where it wouldn't hold true."

Geordie nods. "It's why I don't really care about making the big time. I just want to make music."

I'm surprised—here's more of what we don't know about each other. And I never thought of it like that . . . how his single-minded pursuit of his music might be the same as my chasing magic. That they're just different ghosts wearing the same coat.

We leave the Tombs behind and get back onto more civilized territory, though now Williamson is increasingly lined with fast-food outlets, muffler and body work shops, discount retail outlets. The older buildings still have apartments above them. The newer ones sport parking lots in various shapes and sizes. But they all back onto older parts of the city: tenements, and clapboard and brick houses set snug against one another with the odd driveway in between. We're still a few miles from the suburbs with their scrubbed houses and lawns.

I light another cigarette and find myself thinking about my shadow, that elusive piece of my childhood self, part Nimue, part Huckleberry Finn, who went walkabout when she was separated from me. They don't come any more free-spirited than her. I wonder if Geordie's ever met his shadow, and if he has, what she's like. Or maybe he doesn't even know that he has one. Most people don't. If they do interact with their shadow, it's in dreams, or they're unaware of it.

Then I realize that in a lot of ways, Jilly could fit the bill for him. She could easily be his shadow. Maybe that's why they connect so well as friends, but it never goes any further. I almost bring it up, but then we're turning onto Holly's street and the moment's gone.

"Holly's probably not going to appreciate this," Geordie says.

I pull into a parking spot right in front of the store. There's no jockeying for a good spot at this time of the morning. I look at the darkened store. The apartment upstairs shows the same lack of lights.

"I don't know if appreciate's the right word," I say. "But she'll want to know. They were all really tight in university."

"Only one way to find out," he says.

I step out of the car and up to the front door, Geordie trailing along behind me. I reach up to about a third of the way down from the top of the doorframe and move aside a false brick that's on a hinge. There's a buzzer hidden in the alcove that was behind the brick. I give it a couple of jabs, then cover it over again with the brick.

"Cute," Geordie says.

"Holly got tired of customers ringing the apartment at all hours of the night and day, looking for a particular book that they needed *right now*. This is so her friends can buzz her. The other one—" I point to the regular buzzer on the exterior that's a foot or so below the hidden one. "—only rings in the store."

"Having worked in retail," Geordie says, "it makes sense to me. I can't believe the things that customers will assume."

I'm peering through the door as we talk.

"Here she comes," I say.

We both step back while Holly unlocks the door and opens it wide enough to look out at us. She's barefoot, dressed in a fluffy coral terrycloth robe held closed at the neck with one hand, her hair mussed, her eyes sleepy behind her glasses as she peers at us through the crack.

"Christy," she says, looking from me to my brother. "Geordie."

Geordie nods. "Hi, Holly."

"What do you get when you've got double the Riddells?" she asks.

I smile. "I'll bite. What do you get?"

She blinks then shrugs. "I thought I had a joke going somewhere but I'm too sleepy to find the punch line. What time is it anyway?"

"Going on six."

"And *what* are you doing here?"

"We need to talk and your phone seems to be out of order."

"I unplugged it earlier." She gives me a considering look, the sleepiness in her eyes starting to fade. "So what couldn't wait until a decent hour?"

"It's about Benny," I say.

"Benny . . . ? *My* Benny?"

I nod. "There's been some trouble with him and the Wordwood."

I don't recognize the look that crosses her face—not until later when she tells me about her own evening's adventures. For now, she opens the door wider and steps back.

"You'd better come in," she says.

Saskia

If Christiana's in this place, I can't find her.

First I fall into a black void—it's like that moment between when I lost my body and got into the phone lines, just before I willed myself to the number that Christiana gave me when I first met her in the Beanery Café. It was only last night, but it already feels like a lifetime ago.

That void seemed to draw every molecule of my essence toward . . . something. I'm not sure what. A cage, a trap, a place from which there would be no escape. I didn't know what it was, only what it would do to me. It manifested itself as a tiny, invisible maelstrom that I could sense was no bigger than a pinpoint, but it had the inexorable tow that lies at the heart of a black hole. Those dense remnants of a supernova can swallow millions of tons of matter every second. If I'd let myself go, I would have immediately vanished into that maelstrom and been lost forever.

This void is the exact opposite. It's just as overwhelming, but here every piece and particle that makes me who I am is being pulled in a hundred thousand different directions. If I let myself go here, I'll never be able to find all those pieces and put myself together again.

Maybe I'm in the heart of that black hole this time. Maybe I'm already lost.

I can't accept that.

I won't accept that.

I do what I did the last time. I search for a pulse, a wave, some kind of energy in motion that I can latch onto. Something I can focus on that will get me out of here, though that's not the only reason I focus with such determination. I need to escape this place, but I also know that the very act of concentrating so intensely upon release will help keep me in one piece, giving my efforts a two-fold purpose.

There are no clues to time's passage so I've no idea how long I'm lost in this utter darkness, searching for a way out, fighting the tearing pull that yanks at me from every direction. Maybe there is no way out. Maybe this is what death means for someone like me, born in pixels and data. Maybe I should stop fighting; just let myself go and return to the anonymity where the spirit that inhabits the Wordwood site found me before it brought me into physical existence.

There's no pain involved in my struggle. How can I feel pain when I don't have a body? There's only this mental panic that doesn't even feel real because there are no physical symptoms to back it up. But the strain on my spirit is slowly eroding my will to survive.

I'm so tired.

I'm so close to letting go.

But then I hear—no, what am I saying? I don't have ears. I can't hear anything. I become *aware* of this humming. It's long and narrow, like a thin wire of sound, cutting though the darkness.

It's there.

No, there.

No, *there.*

I fling a net of my thoughts towards it, wrapping myself around the invisible drone of its passage through this place.

And suddenly there's motion. I realize that there must be air here, because sound couldn't exist without it. The droning sound wave is putting pressure on the air, like ripples in water, and I'm riding the rise and fall of its passage. I'm a part of the variations it causes in the atmosphere, staying with it as it turns into an electrical sound signal where the voltage varies at the same rate that the original drone created its ripples in the air. And I'm still a part of it as voltage converts into binary numbers, a bewildering flicker of on-off electrical pulses that change so quickly it's impossible to focus on a string of them, never mind one.

Each measurement is changed into a 16-bit number.

Coded into digital sound.

And now I know where I am.

No, not *where* I am, but *what* I'm in. I'm somewhere in a computer processor. Or I'm a part of a signal travelling between processors. I'm back in the digital womb where I was born, except this time I'm aware of being here. I know who I am. I don't know what I am, but I know who.

And now I have hope of finding a way out. It won't be easy. The digital domain is immense. The bits that make it up aren't simply patterns stored in one computer any more. With Internet connections, they can cross vast distances, lodging in distant processors and memory stores. Millions of computers communicate with each other throughout the world. I could be anywhere.

But machines operate on logic. I may be lost, but if I can figure out how to access HyperText Transfer Protocol, I can direct this signal I'm hitching a ride on to take me where I need to go.

I visualize the URL in my mind.

www.thewordwood.com

That's where all of this started—my trying to contact the pixelated spirit that brought me into this world. That's where *I* started, in the domain it carved out for itself from the World Wide Web. So that's where I need to return. I don't just need answers anymore. I need my body back. The spirit gave it to me once. I'll have to convince it to give it to me again.

I put all my concentration into the Wordwood's site.

I can't be sure, but I think I detect a slight variation in the signal's passage. I concentrate harder.

Time passes—in a confusing blur now, I'm moving so fast. But it's no easier to judge how long I'm riding on the back of this digital signal than it was trying to measure how long I was floating in the earlier darkness.

Then suddenly my awareness explodes with a dazzling array of strings of blue-white light. I'm flying at immeasurable speeds over a bewildering grid work of crisscrossing lines. It's circuitry, I realize, only viewed not from a physical viewpoint, but in terms of the energy it emits.

The signal takes me faster. Faster.

I focus harder on the Wordwood's URL, but I can't muster the strength to hold onto it anymore. I can't hold onto anything. No matter how much I try, how determined I am, everything slips away and my consciousness is gone again. . . .

Bojo

"Wait a minute," Bojo said.

Staring into the muzzle of the enormous handgun pointed at his face, all Bojo seemed able to do was hold his hands out in front of him, palms forward. He wasn't sure if it would look like he was hoping to stop a bullet with his hands, or showing that he was unarmed and presented no danger. It didn't matter. Just so long as the man didn't shoot.

It was hot in the diner, with a close smell in the air—a mix of old grease from the kitchen and whatever had been used to clean the countertop, tables and floor. But under that was a faint, pleasant scent, like a fruity cologne smelling of apples and roses. Or maybe lilacs with a hint of citrus. Whenever Bojo thought he recognized it, the scent shifted into something else.

He tried to muster up a smile, but it was hard. His mouth was dry and he swallowed hard as he considered the best way to frame an explanation of what he was doing here. It turned out he didn't need to.

"You're no hellhound," the man said, lowering his arm.

"No," Bojo agreed. Whatever a hellhound was. "I'm just a simple tinker who's come looking for advice."

The man smiled. "Advice. I should see about getting myself a column, maybe have it syndicated."

He got up from his booth and shifted the revolver from his right hand to his left.

"I'm Robert Lonnie," he added, offering his free hand.

Bojo shook hands with him, noting that for all his slender frame and his long, delicate fingers, Robert had a firm grip—more like that of a man who worked with his hands, than the besuited gangster dandy he appeared to be.

"Pleased to meet you," he said. "I'm Borrible Jones, but most people call me Bojo."

Robert's eyebrows lifted. "Unusual name to give a kid."

"Well, the story is that when the midwife lifted me up, my father took one look at this bloody baby, wailing its lungs out and dripping all over the floor, and he said, 'That's horrible.' Except he had a speech impediment, so it came out, 'Bat's borrible.' For some reason, the name stuck. I suppose it didn't help that I wasn't a very well-behaved child."

Robert regarded him for a long moment, amusement flickering in his eyes.

"Have a seat," he finally said, motioning to the side of the booth he'd just vacated.

He sat down beside the guitar, laying his revolver on the table between them.

"They call it a Peacemaker," he said when he saw Bojo's gaze settle on the large handgun. "A single-action Colt, .44 caliber. But the only peace it makes is if you shoot the person that's troubling you. My daddy took it from a dead man who'd been considering a lynching before his own premature demise."

Bojo wasn't sure he'd heard that right.

"They still lynch people around here?" he asked.

"Oh, that was a long time ago—another part of history that folks'd sooner forget, though it's hard when it's your own people that were hanging like strange fruit from trees and lampposts."

Bojo's gaze had adjusted enough to the bad lighting in the diner that he was able to see the something in Robert's eyes that said he'd been around for generations—not the way tinkers circumvented time, by stepping through worlds, but simply by living through the years, ageless.

As the knowledge came to Bojo, he saw a smile pull at one corner of Robert's mouth, as though the bluesman could read his mind. Robert picked up the Gibson and began to pluck a slow walking blues from its strings, right-hand thumb keeping the bass rhythm, those long fingers of his left hand travelling the fingerboard like the legs of a spider.

"So what's this advice you need?" he asked.

"It's kind of a long story."

"One thing I've got plenty of is time," Robert assured him.

"I guess you would," Bojo said.

That crooked smile stayed on Robert's lips. He didn't speak, but a simple hammer-on on the bass string, followed by a bluesy slide of notes on the high E, seemed to say, Why don't you tell me this story of yours?

So Bojo started in, beginning with the telephone message that had brought him around to Holly's store and finishing with what he'd sensed on the streets on his way to finding Robert here in this diner. The guitar laid a counterpoint rhythm to the cadence of his voice, making Bojo feel as though he was delivering a talking blues rather than simply telling a story.

"And the advice you need is . . . ?" Robert asked when Bojo's voice trailed off.

He made the high strings call a quizzical note while the bass line continued, faint but keeping the rhythm.

"Because I've got to tell you," Robert said, "I don't know the first thing about computers or the spirits that might be sitting there somewhere inside them. What do they call those places—virtual worlds?"

Bojo shook his head. "No, those are the ones that aren't real."

"Depends where you stand, I suppose. Probably real to those living in them."

"I suppose."

"The way I see it," Robert went on, the guitar continuing to play a counter rhythm to the flow of his voice, "is maybe what you've got here is more like the Native take on things. See, with my people there's always a lot of trading going on when it comes to the spirits. Baptist minister or gris-gris man, everybody's trying to cut themselves a bargain, doesn't matter if they're figuring out how to get into heaven or working on some piece of hoodoo. But for the Indians it's more like a tree. You see the trunk and foliage, but all the important stuff's going on underground, out of sight."

"A tree."

Robert smiled. "I just mean things are hidden. That there's more sitting in front of you than you can see. It's not like an onion where you've got to peel back layers to see what's going on. Or even like those Russian dolls where each one's got itself a smaller one inside. It's more you see the one thing, but there's a whole invisible world going on behind it. One you don't even know is there, never mind being able to see it."

Bojo nodded to show he understood.

"'Course maybe we're talking words here," Robert went on. "They have to use words to tell the computers what to do, right?"

"I think they call it code," Bojo said, remembering what Holly had told him about it. "Programming languages."

"Which is still words and words . . . well, words are an old magic that goes right back to the first days. The ones they're using for their computers are just that old magic dressed up in some new technological jacket." He paused for a moment, the guitar still playing. "There's a lot of people believe that the universe was created with just a word, but I guess you know that."

"Like the Word of God in the Bible," Bojo said.

It was something he'd heard about, but he was hazy on the details.

"Right," Robert said. "Logos. Though Christianity's not the first religion, and I doubt it's going to be the last, to slip that bit of old history into its stories about how we all came to be. You know how it usually goes?"

Robert didn't wait for an answer. The music from his guitar shifted into a minor key.

"Way I heard it," Robert says, "is that this one word that jump-started the world became a language and that language started up a conversation that gives everything its shape and meaning—a conversation that's still going on to this day. The trouble is, over time, that original language went and fragmented into a thousand thousand variations and dialects. Before you know it, none of us can really speak to each other anymore. Animals, plants, people, the dirt under our feet—everything has a different language now. Hell, these days we can't even be sure that some word we use is even close to what it means to the person we're talking to.

"But bits and pieces of that original language still remain. Some of those old words. And we're talking powerful mojo here."

Bojo nodded. "I remember Meran talking to me about that. I think she even knows some of those old words."

"Everybody's got a few of them floating around in the old parts of their minds—the places inside them where instincts still work and the soul spends its time. Most of them just don't know it, which is probably a good thing. You speak one of those words and things . . . change."

"You know any of those words?" Bojo asked.

"Only one. It's what keeps the hellhounds circling around, but they never can quite find me."

Bojo nodded. He wanted to ask about these hellhounds Robert kept mentioning, but his years on the road had taught him that you didn't ask after personal information, you only took it when it was offered. So instead he sat there on the other side of the booth and listened to the music his companion pulled out of that old Gibson. It had shifted back into a major key, but when exactly that had happened, Bojo hadn't noticed.

"So I take it you like this girl," Robert said after a few moments.

His fingers never stopped their spiderwalk up and down the neck of his guitar, his right hand pulling the notes.

"What do you mean?"

Robert smiled. "Well, for someone you just up and met, you seem pretty fixed on wanting to make a good impression. You know, save the day, have her in your arms when the story's done."

"It's not like that."

"Every time a mention of her comes up, your heartbeat tells me different."

Bojo shrugged. "Can you help us?" he asked, wanting to steer the conversation back to something that might be useful.

"Don't know that you want my help, exactly," Robert said.

"Why's that?"

Robert shrugged. "Trouble's always got an eye out for me—it's why I keep a low profile. I come along to your friend's store and I could be bringing more problems than we're trying to solve."

"You mean these helldogs you keep talking about."

"Hellhounds," Robert said. "And they're not necessarily dogs. They come in all shapes and sizes. The only thing they have in common is their interest in me."

Since Robert had started the personal questions by asking how he felt about Holly, Bojo thought maybe he could satisfy some of his own curiosity without appearing impolite.

"Why are they chasing you?" he asked.

Robert smiled. "You might say we had us an altercation. That was a time ago, but there's some that don't know the meaning of either forgive or forget."

"Old spirits."

Robert nodded.

"Well," Bojo said, "I think the ones we're talking about here are new ones. Technological spirits, I suppose we could call them."

"Unless it's old spirits wearing new clothes." Before Bojo could comment, Robert added, "But you're right. It doesn't feel like it, does it? Because that's the thing about spirits—they get more set in their ways than we do."

"Maybe because they've been at it a lot longer."

"Could be," Robert agreed.

"So will you help?"

"How about if the most I promise is that I'll come along and have a look-see?"

They took a cab up to Holly's store, the two of them sitting in the back with the guitar in its case on the seat between them. Bojo hadn't seen where the handgun had gone. One moment it was on the table in the diner, the next it wasn't, and the classic cut of Robert's suit didn't sport any new bulges to show where it might have been hidden. For all Bojo knew, it could be under the fedora that Robert had put on before they left the diner, locking the door behind them.

"I know this store your friend owns," Robert said as the cab took them north. "Though I don't think I ever went in. I'm not much of a book reader."

"Me, neither."

"But there used to be a coffee shop I liked a few doors down. I spent many a morning sitting in there, drinking my coffee and looking out the window. I'd read the papers, play a few tunes."

"What made you stop?"

Robert shrugged. "It got to be a pattern and I try to keep patterns out of my life."

"Because of the hellhounds."

"Partly. Partly I just don't like to acquire habits. And then that coffee shop went all upscale on me. I don't blame Joe—Joe Lapegna, the guy who owns the place. He saw which way the wind was blowing and had to stay competitive, what with all the high-end cafés coming into town and all."

He looked out the window as the cab turned onto Holly's street.

"Guess what I'm trying to say," he said, "is that I miss the place."

Holly

"She really just . . . disappeared into your computer?" Holly asked when Christy finished his story.

The part about Saskia's disappearance had come early on, but Holly was still trying to get her head around the idea of it. Even with the pixie infestation that she and Dick had experienced, not to mention living with the hob for the past two years since then, what had happened to Saskia and Benny still seemed impossible.

But Christy nodded. "Like she never existed."

Holly heard the catch in his voice and reached out across the table to put her hand on his.

"We'll get her back," she said. "Saskia and Benny and all of them."

She knew they were just words, but sometimes people needed words, even when the promise held in them couldn't necessarily be fulfilled.

They were sitting around in her apartment—just as she'd sat with Dick and Bojo earlier, except the tinker had been replaced by the Riddell brothers, and they were in the kitchen rather than the living room. She got up now to make a second pot of coffee and pulled out a tin of day-old, home-made scones that were still fresh enough to serve to company if you slathered them with jam. The coffee went quickly, but no one seemed to have much appetite.

There was a restlessness in the air—a need to be doing something, *anything,* but no one knew what. The only one who appeared to be immune was Geordie, but Geordie was always able to put a calm face on things. As Jilly would say, "It's just this gift he has." But Christy kept opening the screen door and standing out on the fire escape to have a cigarette, and Dick was wearing a path in the floor between the kitchen and the front room windows that overlooked the street, though what he was expecting or looking for he didn't say.

Holly was feeling a bit jittery herself. It looked like she and Dick had come *so* close to getting pulled into the computer themselves. If Dick hadn't accidentally broken their Internet connection, not to mention her monitor . . .

Don't think about it, she told herself and poured herself another half-cup of coffee.

"So they're all coming?" she asked. "Estie and Tip and all?"

"Apparently," Geordie said. "Do you still have that old computer stored away somewhere?"

Holly looked to Dick, but he was in the front room again.

"I think so," she said. "Dick'd know better."

Geordie stirred at the sound of the hob's name and looked around. Holly knew exactly what was happening to him: magical being that Dick was, his existence kept slipping Geordie's mind, the way it did for most people. You'd forget, then you'd hear his name or see him again and you'd wonder how you'd ever forgotten.

"It's okay," she told him. "Dick has that effect on pretty much everybody until you get to really know him."

Geordie nodded. "That's what Christy keeps telling me. But it's still disconcerting when it's actually happening to you. Makes you wonder what else you're missing."

"Who's missing what?" Christy asked, coming in after having another cigarette.

Geordie shrugged. "Me. Missing all the hidden things in the world."

"It's not your fault," Christy said. "You just don't have the trick of it yet, that's all. You need to immerse yourself in—"

He broke off as Dick came running back into the room.

"The tinker's back," Dick said. "And he's brought a friend."

"Tinker?" Christy asked.

"He's that fellow taking care of Meran's place," Holly said. "I told you about him."

They heard the buzzer ring in the store downstairs, followed by a knock on the door. Holly stood up.

"I'll get that," she said.

She was happy that none of the others had come down with her because she immediately started to blush at the warm smile Bojo gave her when she unlocked the door and let them in. His companion was a dapper black man with a relaxed look about him, belied only by his penetrating eyes. He was easily as striking as Bojo, though his neat suit and fedora were a far cry from the tinker's more Bohemian look, and he carried a battered guitar case in his left hand. He took off his hat, tucking it under his arm when he came into the store.

"You'll be Holly," he said, offering her his hand. "I'm Robert Lonnie."

They shook hands, then Holly stepped aside to let them by. She closed the door behind them and locked it again. When she turned, Bojo laid a hand on her shoulder and gave it a squeeze.

Be still my heart, Holly thought.

"I told you I'd be back," Bojo said. "With help in tow and all. Robert here—"

"Doesn't know much about anything when it comes to computers," Robert broke in, "but he's seen a thing or two that doesn't make sense in this world." He paused, then smiled. "He also hates it when people talk in the third person about themselves, so I'm going to stop right about now."

"There've been some complications since you left," Holly told Bojo.

"You and Dick are okay?"

Holly nodded. "We're fine. But—well, you should just come upstairs and I'll let the others fill you in."

She started for the stairs to her apartment, pausing when only Bojo followed.

"Aren't you coming, Mr. Lonnie?"

"It's Robert," he said, looking up briefly before his gaze tracked through the store, settling on the desk again.

"Are you looking for something?" Holly asked.

Robert shook his head. He continued to study the desk for a long moment, then finally turned and joined them at the foot of the stairs.

"I was just taking in a sense of this place," he said. "Getting a feel for things. Something almost came through here tonight—from the other side, I mean."

Holly nodded. "If Dick hadn't been as quick as he was, we could've been sucked away just like all those other people."

"What other people?" Bojo asked.

The question was repeated in Robert's eyes.

"That's what I was trying to tell you," Holly said. "It's not just me and my weird little computer woes anymore. But Christy can tell you more."

"Lead on," Robert told her at the same time as Bojo asked, "Who's Christy?"

"Christy Riddell," Holly said over her shoulder as she started up the stairs. "He and his brother Geordie lost someone to a computer last night and there have been other disappearances, too. Apparently it's been on the news and everything. Christy thinks it's all tied to the Wordwood site."

"Wordwood," Robert said, repeating it as though he was tasting the way the two words came together into one.

Before Holly could explain more, they were upstairs and she was too busy introducing everybody. Geordie and Robert had already met, though only in passing. Everybody else needed an introduction. Robert appeared to be particularly delighted to meet Dick.

"I've never met one of the little people before," he said, then paused. "Do you mind being called that?"

Dick shook his head. "Oh, no, sir. You've been calling us that for hundreds of years now, just like we've been calling you big folk, or tall folk."

"Well, I'm very pleased to make your acquaintance," Robert told him.

"Borrible," Christy said to Bojo. "That's an unusual name. I'm a bit of a collector of names and I've never come across it before. Is it a given name?"

Bojo nodded. "It comes from the time before we became a travelling people. We lived in a mountainous area of our homeland and when the traders first came to our villages, they referred to us as aboriginals. Later, when relationships became more acrimonious between us, they started to call us borribles instead. My father, apparently, decided that we should reclaim the term and replace its negative associations with positive ones. So he changed his name to Borrible and named me the same. I'm told he hoped that I'd name my firstborn son the same, but I don't have a cruel streak in me."

Holly shot him a hurt look, disappointed to find out that he'd lied to her, but Robert only laughed.

"Sounds like you've got a different story for everyone you meet," he said.

Bojo shrugged. "Depends on how you look at it. Somewhere, some-when, each of those stories is true."

"I don't understand," Holly said.

"It's how the tinkers circumvent time," Robert explained. "Travelling in and out of worlds, they have many lives, rather than just one. It makes it hard for the years to catch up with them."

"Is this true?" Holly asked.

"My Aunt Meran notwithstanding, we're a restless people. Few of us settle down the way she and Cerin have."

"Though," Geordie put in, "the pair of them are still away touring for half the year or more."

Bojo gave a slow nod. "I hadn't thought of it like that."

There was a brief lull in the conversation then. Christy went out onto the fire escape for another cigarette. Dick got up as well.

"What do you keep looking for out there?" Holly asked him.

This time he had an answer.

"Pixies," he said over his shoulder.

Bojo poured himself and Robert another coffee, the others declining when he offered the pot to them. Robert took his mug and returned to the chair in the corner. He slipped his guitar out of its case and began to noodle on the strings, the unconnected notes finally falling into a simple twelve-bar blues.

"From the residue I sensed downstairs," Robert said when Christy and Dick had both returned to the kitchen, his voice following the rhythm of the music, "and with what I've been hearing now, I think Bojo is right. This is a deep magic, but it's not an old one."

"Does that mean there's nothing we can do?" Holly asked.

The bluesman shook his head. "On the contrary, the fact that it's not an old spirit works in our favour. It'll be less experienced and that means we'll have a better chance to get it to do what we want—so long as we do it right. But we're going to need some way to start up a conversation with it."

"Without a monitor, the store's computer isn't going to be much use," Holly said. "But if we can find my old one . . ."

This time when she looked at Dick, he was still in the room.

"It's still in the basement," he said. "Behind all those boxes of *National Geographic*."

"So, should we set it up?" Holly asked.

Robert nodded. "But since it doesn't seem like any of us is particularly computer-adept, we should probably wait for your friends before we try to use it. When you're working a mojo like this, you pretty much only have the one chance to get it right. Spirits learn fast. We won't get a second shot."

"But we do have a chance?" Christy said.

"Oh, yeah," Robert told him. "People always have a chance. Only trouble is, once we get that thing we need so bad, it doesn't always work out the way we thought it would."

"What's that supposed to mean?"

Robert slipped from the E♭ blues pattern he was playing into a minor key.

"Come on now," he said, his gaze mild as it lifted from the Gibson's strings and settled on Christy's features. "I know who you are. You've studied on this for years. Don't tell me you can't be surprised anymore."

"I don't understand," Holly said.

"What he means," Bojo explained, "is that some spirits just have it in their nature to play unfair. Maybe you asked for wealth. So you find you've got a cave full of treasure stashed away somewhere safe. Except you're sitting on Death Row and there's nothing you can do to get to it."

Holly glanced at Dick and the hob gave her an unhappy nod.

"It's true, Mistress Holly," he said. "Some of the old ones delight in thinking up new ways to keep their word but at the same time make it impossible for you to benefit."

"I've still got to try," Christy said.

" 'Course we've got to try," Robert said. "We've just got to step up to this with our thinking caps on. Figure out what the spirit wants. Figure out how we can guarantee we get what *we* want with no strings attached."

"But you're telling us it'll be hard," Geordie said.

Robert nodded. "Oh, yeah. It'll be hard. But hard doesn't mean impossible."

Aaran

One of the great side benefits of being the newspaper's book editor, so far as Aaran was concerned, was that he got an endless supply of freebies. And it wasn't only books and galleys that got packed away in his briefcase every day to be taken home. Because he made a point of writing reviews for other parts of the entertainment section, he got to cherry pick all the various promotional items that arrived at the paper. Prereleases of new CDs, videos, and DVDs. T-shirts, stickers, mugs, shooter glasses, watches, posters . . . whatever a company might use to promote their product.

It was a running joke at the office that Aaran would take home anything. What they didn't know was that he made a tidy little profit on the side, selling the various items on eBay, or to a few select record and book shops in Crowsea. Like he'd actually ever wear an Eminem T-shirt, or put a signed poster of Mariah Carey up in his living room. Or drink his morning coffee from a mug with the characters from *The Simpsons* printed on the side.

He also got to snap up tickets to concerts, films, and shows, which was what had brought him out to the Standish Hall last night for a concert by the Australian country singer Kasey Chambers. She was obviously a huge success with the sold-out crowd that had filled the 3000-seat concert hall, though Aaran couldn't understand why. He just didn't like this kind of music—alt-country, Americana, whatever you wanted to call it. But attend-

ing the odd dud concert such as this—or at least the first twenty minutes or
so of the headliner's set, which was invariably enough for him to write a
review—was the price he paid for also being able to score front-row Elton
John tickets.

He sat now in his study, face and hands tinted blue from the glow of
his computer screen as he composed his review of the show. He restrained
himself from being too nasty—the entertainment editor had a different philosophy from Aaran's own in the book pages and preferred her reviewers to
focus on the positive elements of what was being covered—but he couldn't
resist slipping in a few digs about Australia, a country he'd never visited
but instinctively disliked, and the idea that Chambers could have any sort
of real experience on which to base her songs of heartbreak and country
life.

And really, what was with the twang in her voice? Chambers should
take a page from real country artists like Shania Twain, or Faith Hill's more
recent work.

Melissa Lawrence, the entertainment editor, would probably edit out
the digs, since she was a fan of Australia in general and Chambers's music
in particular, but at least Aaran got the satisfaction of bringing her blood
pressure up a notch or two. Especially since she hadn't been able to attend
the show last night, which was how he got the job. It was never a bad thing
to have people owe you favours.

The real highlight of last night's concert hadn't been the music, but a
conversation he'd overheard while waiting in line to get into the Standish
Hall. He'd recognized the pair standing ahead of him to be a couple of
Saskia's friends and couldn't hold back a grin as he listened to them lament
the fact that the Wordwood site was still down. He'd been very tempted to
tap them on the shoulder and brag about the part he'd played in bringing its
collapse, but common sense prevailed.

There was no point in making a scene.

Some of the people in that crowd of Saskia's were very high-strung and
argumentative. It seemed to be one of the prerequisites of being an artist.
That celebrated creative temperament.

When he was finished writing the review, he saved it on a disk then shut
down his machine. Pocketing the disk, he set off for the newspaper's offices.
He could as easily have e-mailed it to Melissa, but this was Sunday, when
the Arts & Living offices would be pretty much empty, which made it a perfect time to go rooting about in the week's new promotional arrivals to see
if there was anything he might have missed.

The office was a hubbub of conversation when Aaran stepped out of the elevator. Clusters of the newspaper's employees gathered around various desks, caught up in animated conversations, or sat in front of their monitors, fingers tapping on their keyboards. CNN was on the television set in the corner, but from where he stood, Aaran couldn't make out what its earnest news anchors were discussing. Either some big story had broken, or something had happened to one of the staff. His coworkers never got this interested in much else.

Big story, he decided when he spied a few of the hard news guys working at their terminals. Chuck Tremaine. Barbara Haley. Rob Watley. You never saw any of them in the office on a weekend unless there was a story well worth their time. And then, as though to confirm his suspicions, his gaze went to the glass windows of Kathleen Winter's office. There was a meeting underway in the news editor's office with a half-dozen production people sitting or standing around her desk. Which probably meant she was shooting for an extra edition and needed to work out the logistics.

"What's going on?" Aaran asked of the three reporters talking around the desk closest to the elevator doors.

Harold Cole turned to him. "Christ, Goldstein," he said. "Are you living in a cave? CNN's been running the story for hours."

Aaran shrugged. "I was out late last night and didn't turn on the TV this morning."

"So was she good?"

That was Mark Sakers, fresh out of journalism school and always eager to hear Aaran's stories of sexual conquest. Aaran never disappointed him, even if he had to make the stories up.

"They're always good," he told Mark, before turning back to Harold. "Seriously, what's up?"

"CNN's calling them 'the disappeared'—which should piss off anyone who lost relatives to South American dictators. But I suppose it's as descriptive a term as any, seeing how a few hundred people just up and vanished from their homes last night."

"What do you mean 'vanished'?"

"As in gone without a trace," George Hooper said. He was the third of the reporters standing around Harold's desk, an old hippie with his grey hair tied back in a ponytail. "There one moment, gone the next."

"But . . . how's that even possible?"

George smiled. "It's not—hence the big story."

"How many people are we talking about here?" Aaran asked.

When Harold turned to look at the television set, Aaran's gaze followed, but he couldn't make anything out beyond the blonde anchor looking into the camera with her patented serious expression.

"I think it was just tipping three-fifty," Harold said. "The last time I looked."

"All from the city?" Aaran asked.

George shook his head. "From all over the country, and abroad, too."

"We lost one of the nerd squad," Mark put in. "Disappeared right out of his apartment last night. Very *X-Files*."

Aaran got an eerie feeling in the pit of his stomach.

"Who was it?" he asked, though he was pretty sure he already knew. It just came to him in a flash, the way a good phrase did when he was writing a review.

"Jackson Hart," Mark said. "Did you know him?"

Aaran shook his head. "Just to see him around the office. What did you mean about it being very *X-Files*?"

"This is where it gets good," George said. "Apparently his landlady heard something dripping outside her apartment door. When she looked in the hall, there was this black goop dripping down the stairs, coming out of the crack under Hart's door. She stepped around it and banged on his door—no answer. So she uses her master key, opens the door, and this flood of the crap comes flowing out."

"Black goop?"

George shrugged. "Who knows? Anyway, she beats a hasty retreat and calls the cops. No sign of Hart inside—though she swears she heard him up there a few minutes before and he never went out. And then, get this, over the next fifteen minutes or so the goop just fades away like it never was. Now you tell me. If that isn't weird, what is?"

"No kidding," Aaran said. "I'm still trying to take it all in."

Not to mention trying to figure out how he'd known it was Jackson that had disappeared. And why he also knew—as clearly, if as inexplicably—that it had something to do with the little blackmail task he'd set Jackson. What, he didn't know. But somehow the disappearances were connected.

"Thing like this," Harold said. "I'll bet it makes you wish you were a real reporter."

Aaran gave a slow, distracted nod, not rising to the bait.

"You guys all have assignments?" he asked.

George shook his head. "We're waiting for Winter to finish with the production people to have our meeting with her."

"Well, good luck with it," Aaran told them.

He went into Melissa's office. Pulling the disk with the Chambers review out of his pocket, he dropped it on the entertainment editor's desk, then left the office without even bothering to go through the promotional materials that were on the bookcase behind her desk, or piled up in boxes along one wall.

After leaving the paper, Aaran went straight home and switched on his TV. He sat down on the couch, punched in CNN on his remote, and watched the story unfold. To anybody who'd been tuned in to the channel for awhile, this would be the umpteenth repeat of their coverage, but it was all new to Aaran as he watched in disbelief.

The truth was, back at the office, he hadn't really taken his coworkers seriously. While he'd known that there was something major going on— that was obvious—he hadn't really believed it to be some massive disappearance of people, figuring that Harold and the others had just been having him on. All he'd known for sure was that it had something to do with Jackson Hart, and therefore it could possibly be connected to him. How, he wasn't sure. What exactly it was, he hadn't known either, but was willing to wait until he got home rather than make a fool of himself by asking someone else in the office.

But there it was on the screen, and unless CNN had taken a page from Orson Welles and was doing their own version of *The War of the Worlds,* this had really happened.

The disappeared.

According to a little box in the corner of the screen, the number of people confirmed to be missing stood at eight hundred sixty-three, worldwide. Half that number had disappeared from North America.

At least there was nothing about computers, he thought, as the anchor woman completed her update. Nothing to connect any of this to me. It was just coincidence that Jackson Hart was involved. That little frisson of alarm that had made him think it had anything to do with blackmailing Jackson was obviously wrong.

But he still couldn't completely quell the uneasiness that had gripped him ever since he'd heard the news back at the paper. And questions kept rising to jangle his nerves.

Like, what if the authorities were merely withholding the fact that computers had been involved?

That was exactly the kind of thing they'd do, hoping some schmuck would trip himself up by showing he knew more than what was reported in the media. Just asking about it could get you into trouble.

But Aaran still had to know.

He sat awhile longer, staring at the TV but no longer hearing the anchor's voice or seeing what played out on the screen. Finally he shut it off, got his coat and went out again.

Don't do this, Aaran told himself as he made his way to Jackson's apartment.

But he went all the same.

"I've already talked to someone from the *Journal*," Jackson's landlady said.

She started to hand Aaran back his press I.D., then gave it another look.

"I know you," she said. "Jackson's talked about you."

The hand of fear tightened its grip inside Aaran.

"Did he now?" he said, managing to keep his face far calmer than he was feeling.

The landlady nodded. Although he put her age at not much more than his own thirty-eight, she gave him the impression of being older, like someone from his parents' generation rather than his own. It was something in the cut of her skirt and blouse, and those sensible brown shoes. Her make-up and the nondescript styling of her short, already greying hair only added to the impression.

"Nothing bad, I hope," Aaran said.

"Oh, no. He seemed to quite admire you. All the books you read and how you're able to write about them in a manner that's both intelligent, yet accessible to the lay person."

"Really?"

Jesus, Aaran thought. No wonder Jackson had opened up to him in the bar that night. And what had he done? Turned around and blackmailed him.

The landlady was nodding again. "Yes. Though he hasn't spoken of you in a while. I take it yours was more of an office friendship."

"The truth is, I didn't really know him all that well."

"Then it's all the more commendable for you to have come by to see about him now."

Aaran blinked in surprise. He felt as though he'd stepped into some surreal alternate dimension where dowdy tenement landladies turned out to be well-spoken and people only seemed to have nice things to say about him. That didn't normally happen. He wanted to be liked, but he also knew that he sabotaged any relationships—romantic or otherwise—with his constant need for control. To be the one on top.

Occasionally, he even made an effort to change, but it never lasted.

"Well, I just hope nothing bad's happened to him," he managed to say.

"So do I," the landlady said. "Jackson's a good man. He worked hard to make a success of himself. Most people with his unfortunate background don't."

Aaran had no idea what she was talking about. But while he was curious about what she meant, right now all he wanted to do was get away.

"If—*when* he comes back," he said. "Will you tell him I was by?"

The landlady nodded. "Keep him in your prayers, Mr. Goldstein."

"I will. Thank you for your time."

"The pleasure was mine."

Aaran backed away. He lifted a hand by way of goodbye and made his retreat through the front door of the building, feeling the weight of the landlady's eyes upon his back with every step he took.

Halfway down the block, he stopped and turned around to have another long look at the building. He wasn't really sure what had happened back there, or even why he'd come in the first place. What had he expected to find out? Yellow police tape had sealed the door to Jackson's apartment and it wasn't as though the landlady would have let him in anyway. Nor could he have asked about a computer connection to Jackson's disappearance, or what Jackson might have said about the Wordwood site.

He hadn't learned anything about the strange fluid that the landlady had noticed before Jackson's disappearance. Hadn't learned anything at all, except for what he already knew on nights when he was sitting in his own apartment with nowhere to go, no one to call: He was a heel.

Sighing, he turned his back on the building and continued on his way. God, but it was turning into a miserable day. And with not much improvement to look forward to, either. You'd think that he could just—

"Spare change?"

Aaran hadn't even seen the panhandler, tucked away in the doorway of the store he was walking by.

No, but I've got some spare saliva, he wanted to tell her, and then maybe he'd spit in her hand. Or at least tell her off.

Street people just annoyed him, from the big scary drunks trying to browbeat a few dollars out of you, to whiny runaways who left perfectly good homes and then expected people like him to support them.

But when he turned to look at her, his displeasure got swallowed by a rather earthy curiosity. Behind her dirty face, this ragged gamine with her short spiky blonde hair was actually pretty good-looking. And she also had what looked like a fine body under her baggy T-shirt and skateboarder's cargo pants—a little on the thin side, maybe, but an excellent lung capacity all the same.

His attraction to her was instant, but it was tempered with a vague uneasiness that he couldn't quite identify. He supposed it had to do with her age, which was hard to tell. She might be in late teens or early twenties, which would put her at about half his age.

He'd have to be careful here; she could be underage. But he'd long carried around a fantasy of picking up one of these little street girls, bringing her home and cleaning her up. . . .

Play this right and he could just get lucky.

Looking for an opening, his gaze went to the face of the native man on her T-shirt. Under it a slogan read, "Remember Dudley George." It took Aaran a moment, but then his eidetic memory kicked in and he connected the face to the relevant news story: Thirty-five natives peacefully protesting land seized during the Second World War—native land that contained an ancient burial ground—were confronted by two hundred and fifty heavily armed policemen. The resulting clash left George dead and ruined the career of the cop that had shot him. It had happened over five years ago, but the civil lawsuit was just going to court now.

"You think his family will win their lawsuit?" he asked.

Her look of surprise and the sudden interest in her eyes told him he had the hook in. Gently now, he told himself.

"What?" she said. "And ruin the government's record of successfully screwing indigenous people?"

Aaran nodded. "There's that. I've never understood why they don't just bite the bullet and do what's right."

"Money," she said, rubbing the pad of her thumb against her index and middle fingers. "Someone's making a buck, or we'd see a change." She smiled at him. "So what are you, an activist?"

"Not really," Aaran said. "I just believe we have to stand up against injustice."

And he supposed he really did believe that, so long as it didn't interfere with his own quality of life.

He let a pause hang for a moment between them, then turned the conversation to more personal concerns.

"I guess you've hit some rough times?" he asked.

She shrugged. "They say there's no recession, but . . ."

"Tell that to the people who can't get a job," Aaran filled in for her. "Not to mention how they make it so hard to collect welfare that a lot of people don't even try anymore."

She gave him a considering look.

"So what are you?" she asked. "A social worker?"

Aaran laughed. "No, I'm a book editor for a newspaper. My name's Aaran."

She shook the hand he offered her. Her hand was small in his, but her grip was firm.

"I'm Suzi."

"Pleased to meet you, Suzi," Aaran told her, "though I wish it was under better circumstances—for you, I mean."

"Oh, I get by."

"You been on the street a while?"

"Long enough to know the score."

"What do you mean?"

"Well, you're hitting on me, aren't you? Except you're going easy 'cause you're thinking I just might be jailbait."

Aaran shook his head. "No, I'm not—"

"Well, I'm not jailbait," she went on, "but I don't fuck for money, or whatever else you're offering."

"You've got me mixed up with someone who did you a bad turn," Aaran said. "I just stopped for some conversation, though I can't help but wonder how you got into your present situation. And I can't help feeling bad about it."

She studied him again. "So you weren't trying to figure how to get into my pants? Maybe offer me a shower and a meal back at your place in exchange for a fuck and a blowjob?"

She was turning him on, but he didn't let it show.

"I'll admit the thought crossed my mind," he said. "I mean the part about giving you the chance to clean up and have a good meal."

"Well, you can just—"

"But I wasn't going to," he went on, cutting her off, "because as soon as the thought came to mind, I realized exactly what it would sound like, and I didn't want to insult you or make you feel bad. I figure you've got it tough enough as it is without having to worry about my intentions."

"Yeah, right. As if—"

"I would have just given you some money," he lied, "but I don't think I've even got a quarter in my pocket at the moment." He added in a rueful smile. "Spent a bit too much last night and I haven't had the chance to hit a bank machine."

She shook her head. "Man, you sound almost genuine."

"Look," Aaran said. "I should just go."

But she put a hand on his arm as he was turning away. If she hadn't, he would have found another excuse to dawdle.

"So you're a book editor," she said, dropping her hand.

He nodded. "For *The Daily Journal*. Though I actually edit the book pages—you know, reviews, author features, that sort of thing. Not the books themselves."

"And you're not some old guy with a thing for young little street girls?"

"Hey, I'm not that old."

She nodded. "Yeah, I guess you're not."

"I should go," he said. "If I've got some money the next time I see you, I'll—"

"Wait," she said. "Look, it's rough. I've been fighting off straight guys with hard-ons for the past few months that I've been on the street. And all the classy businesswomen just sneer at me—when I even register at all."

He nodded to show he was listening.

"Thing is," she went on, "I haven't had a decent meal in ages and I'm dying for a shower. I'd go to the shelter, but the last time I was there I almost got my face cut by some butch top thinking I was hitting on her sweet young thing. So . . ."

Aaran waited.

"So you're on the level? You're really just offering me a chance to clean up and get something to eat?"

"Nothing's going to happen that you don't want to have happen," Aaran assured her. "You can even get a good night's sleep—though I'm really going to insist that you have that shower first. But I'll make up a bed for you on the sofa."

She gave a short laugh. "Yeah, I guess I'm not exactly debutante material right now."

"You're fine," Aaran said. "You've just had a few bad breaks."

"So . . ." She had to swallow, before going on. "If your offer's still open . . ."

"Of course it is."

She hesitated a moment longer, then turned to pick up her duffel bag from where it was lying against the door.

"Let me get that for you," Aaran said.

He knew she was nervous. He knew she wanted to take this at face value and was determined not to have to pay for it with her body. But he had faith in his ability to sweet-talk anybody into anything. He could maintain a charming face for an evening. It was the long-term that always undermined his relationships. Like anything longer than a weekend.

The only thing that worried him was that flash of disquiet he'd felt when he'd first seen her. Because it hadn't gone away. Though it hadn't gotten any stronger, either, which he couldn't say for his hunger to hold her, to feel her hands on him . . .

He figured he had a right to feel on edge. The last time he'd felt this combination of intense attraction and vague unease had been with Saskia, and look where that had gotten him. But he'd be cool this time. Besides, it was probably just nerves from this business with Jackson. Or the worry about her age.

"So, are you from the city?" he asked as they walked along. He carried her duffel bag slung over a shoulder and maintained a body's distance between her and himself.

She shook her head. "I don't think I'm from anywhere, we moved around so much when I was a kid. . . ."

Holly

Holly woke with a start to find that she'd dozed off right there at the kitchen table. She wondered if anyone had noticed.

Dick had gone to his room earlier—to lie down, he'd said, but Holly knew he was reading. Reading and tidying were the two things that sustained the hob, especially when he was feeling stressed. Christy was gone as well—probably out onto the fire escape for another cigarette. Bojo smiled at her when she looked in his direction. *He*'d noticed that she'd dropped off there for a moment and that made her blush again, pleased that he paid attention, but annoyed with herself for acting like some young schoolgirl around him. Robert and Geordie hadn't, however, and she tuned in to what they were saying.

". . . are true?" Geordie asked.

"How many?" Robert shrugged. "Depends on which stories you're talking about. I'd say not so many." He smiled. "But enough to keep some people's lips flapping."

Holly liked the cadence of his voice. Set against the soft melody he seemed to draw without thinking from his guitar, it lent the air of an old ballad or blues song to everything he said. She looked over the top of her glasses at the clock on the wall above the stove. It was almost nine. They'd already set up her old computer on the dining room table, after first clearing away tottering piles of books and magazines. She and Dick invariably took their meals in the kitchen.

Almost nine. In a few hours, Estie and the others would be here. For now, all they could do was worry and wait.

"But you know," Robert went on, "if you stick around long enough, there's always bound to be stories. Trick for someone like me who doesn't care for the limelight is to keep to the shadows. When you're not easy to see, and harder to find, people tend to forget there was some puzzle about you."

"Out of sight, out of mind," Holly said, joining the conversation. Maybe it would keep her awake.

Robert nodded. "Though it's more than that. We've all got something in our heads, like a dial on an old radio set, that lets us turn down the memories of things we see that don't make sense. Some of us turn them down and only remember them at times when we're alone. Maybe it's in the quiet of the night, when we're lying in bed, looking for sleep, and we hear a creak we can't place. Or maybe it's when we're walking by a boneyard. Others are so good with that, they can dial those memories right out of their heads."

"So the story about the crossroads . . . ?" Geordie began.

Robert's smile widened. "Is one that just won't go away."

"But *was* it you who—"

"Oh, I've been to a crossroads or two in my time," Robert said. "I'd say they were overrated. Mysteries often are."

"Except when they're not," Bojo said.

Robert just laughed.

"So, have you ever run into anything like this before?" Geordie asked.

Both Robert and Bojo shook their heads.

"But there's a thousand things I've never heard of in this world," Robert said. "And a thousand more for each and every one of them. Some days just about everything can surprise me."

Geordie nodded. "But this still seems new. I've listened to Christy and Jilly and the prof go on and on about stuff like this. But not *like* this, if you know what I mean."

"I suppose I do. So let me put it this way: Whatever spirit we're dealing with here is unfamiliar, but the disappearances aren't."

"They're not?"

"Nope. You go back through history and you'll find a long list of large groups of people disappearing overnight. Armies in China. The Aztec civilizations. Ships in the Bermuda Triangle. Indian tribes in the American southwest. A village in New England. Another in Scotland."

They were all staring at him now. Robert laid his hand upon the strings of his Gibson, stilling its sound.

"See," he said, "the thing is this, spirits—certain spirits—thrive on attention. Some swell up with prayers and rituals. Others have to find more dramatic ways to get us to be mindful to them. I don't have an explanation for where the people they take go, or even why the spirits take them, but it's happened before."

Geordie glanced at the kitchen door. They could see Christy leaning on the railing, still smoking.

"Do they ever come back?" he asked.

Robert hesitated a moment, then shook his head. He waited a few beats, then began another twelve-bar blues progression, fingers so light on the strings that they didn't so much hear the music as sense its presence.

The bluesman's final words lay heavy on all of them.

Holly sighed, closing her eyes again, head propped by her arms. Why couldn't he just have lied? Left them some hope.

As though he'd read her mind, Robert added, "But like I told Christy earlier, that doesn't mean we shouldn't do our best to find them and bring them back."

"But—"

"Just because something's never been done before, doesn't mean it can't be done. There's always got to be a first time."

Suzanne Chancey

Coming back to some stranger's apartment to have a shower wasn't high on Suzi's list of things she would do. But so far, this wasn't so bad. Aaran was easy to talk to. He might be a little flirty—she could see his interest every time he looked at her—but he hadn't actually hit on her yet. And god, she'd needed a shower.

She came out of the bathroom now, hair tousled and still wet, wearing an oversized Heather Nova T-shirt under a terrycloth bathrobe. Aaran told her she could keep the T-shirt—"you wouldn't believe how much merchandise shows up in the office every week." The dirty clothes she'd been wearing and that were in her duffel bag were all in Aaran's washing machine.

It was a little bit like heaven.

Aaran came out of the kitchen with a cup of tea for her. "I thought we'd eat in, considering you don't have anything to wear."

"That's cool," she told him.

"An omelet sound good?"

She smiled. "You guys and your bachelor food. I think cooking eggs is hardwired into you from birth."

"We could have something else."

"No, I love eggs." She took a sip of her tea. "Say, would you mind if I checked my e-mail while you're cooking?"

He gave her a look of surprise.

"Yes," she said. "Street people have e-mail. All we need is a Hotmail account and a couple of bucks for one of the Internet cafés. Hell, some public libraries even offer access for free."

"Of course. The machine's over in the corner there."

Suzi turned and saw the slim notebook computer sitting closed on a beautiful antique writing desk in a corner of the room. The desk appeared to be mahogany, with turned legs and little slots for envelopes at the back of the desk's surface.

"Would you mind connecting to the Net for me?" she asked. "I don't want to screw anything up on your machine. Don't worry," she added when she saw him looking a little anxious. "I'll be fine once I'm in a browser. It's just that every machine seems to be a little different in how it connects."

"No problem," he said.

She followed him over to the desk and watched as he went through the protocols. Finally he double-clicked on the Explorer icon and the browser window came up to fill the screen.

"There you go," he said, standing up.

She took the seat. "Thanks."

She typed in the Hotmail URL and Aaran went back into the kitchen. While she was waiting for the page to come up, she glanced at the kitchen door, then quickly checked the "Favorites" drop-down menu, scanning the sites he'd bookmarked.

Okay, she thought. This was another good sign. No porn or weird sex sites. No "My Favorite Serial Killers" Web sites bookmarked.

Maybe he really was on the level. That'd be a first. But she'd been so dirty and was still so hungry, that she'd had to take the chance. People just didn't much care in this city, and Sundays were the worst for panhandling.

She'd actually been looking forward to this weekend. The week had been rough, but she'd done well in the Market on Saturday, cadging enough money to splurge on two nights at the hostel with enough left over for a laundry and a couple of decent meals. If she stuck to the soup and sandwich specials at the donut shop, that is. It would have left her nothing to start out the week, but at least she'd have been clean, well-rested, and fed. She would have been able to spend most of Monday applying for jobs before she'd have to start panhandling again.

Everything would have been fine except her good fortune hadn't gone unnoticed. On her way to the donut shop, a couple of guys dragged her into an alleyway. The knife one of them stuck in her face had her digging in her pocket and handing over the handful of small bills and change she'd managed to collect through the day. The one without the knife took the money. The one with the knife gave her an ugly little grin, then punched her in the stomach with his free hand.

She stumbled back into some garbage cans, lost her balance, and fell to the ground. By the time she got up, they were gone.

She supposed she was lucky they hadn't done worse. Really beat the crap out of her, say. Or even raped her. But she didn't feel lucky last night, huddled in a doorway, stomach sore and growling with hunger. And she hadn't felt lucky this morning, either.

So she'd taken the chance with Aaran and it looked like it was paying off. Hell, she might even take him up on the offer of his sofa for the night.

She took another sip of her tea as she logged onto her Yahoo account. There were a handful of new messages, but they were all spam. Still nothing from Marie.

Suzi sighed. She'd been so hoping to be able to open the lines of communication with her little sister again, but it had been almost three months now since that terrible day, and Marie still wouldn't respond to either phone calls or e-mail. Suzi wondered if they'd ever talk again.

She could understand Marie being upset. Traumatized even. The two of them had been sitting around the kitchen in the house Suzi had shared with her husband—so far as she was concerned, her ex-husband—Darryl. Darryl had been drinking that evening. Nothing hard, but he'd gone through the six-pack that had been in the fridge. When he came in looking for another beer and found they were all gone, he'd flown into a rage.

That had been new. Not his anger, but the fact that he wasn't controlling it in front of Marie. He was usually so careful when there was anyone else around and he knew Marie adored him, so he seemed to take special care when she was present. But not that day. That day he'd backhanded Suzi so hard, he knocked her off her chair. When she started to get up, he hit her again. Swore at her. Swore at Marie when she started to cry. Told her she'd get the same if she didn't shut up, which only made Marie cry harder.

He took a step toward her, hand lifted, but Suzi'd managed to get in between him and her little sister. She took the blow. And something snapped inside her. Her fear and weakness shattered, and she was surprised to find courage waiting for her. Or maybe he'd just pushed her so far that she was past being afraid or feeling weak. She just didn't care anymore. Or maybe it was for Marie, to protect her little sister from the monster that her husband had become.

Whatever it was, he read something in her face that made him back away. He gave her one long look, the promise of pain to come lying in his eyes, then he stormed out the front door, slamming it behind him.

Suzi had turned to Marie then, wanting to comfort her. But Marie pushed her away.

"How could you?" she'd cried. "What did you do to him?"

And then she fled herself. Out the back door.

Suzi had stood for a long time in the kitchen, leaning heavily against the kitchen counter before she'd finally picked up the phone. She started to dial 911, but then slowly cradled the receiver. She made her way into the bedroom. Every breath she took made her wince. She'd taken the old duffel bag that had accompanied her on many a camping trip and stuffed it with a few essentials. Took the grocery money. Then she left, too.

It wasn't the first time she'd left her husband. But it was the first time it stuck. The first time the old love she'd felt for him hadn't managed to smooth over her hurts and anger. The love was finally gone.

But so was any support she should have received. She didn't know what Darryl had told their friends and her parents—or maybe it was Marie who had talked to Mom and Dad—but overnight she seemed to have become a pariah in their eyes.

So she set aside enough money for meals and a couple of nights in a motel, then took a bus as far as what was left would take her. Which is how she ended up in Newford, basically broke and all too soon living on the streets. Funny how fast that could happen. Funny how prospective employers could read your desperation no matter how well you thought you'd hidden it.

Pimps tried to recruit her, but she'd managed to keep them at bay. She could have worked in a strip club, but she preferred the indignity of panhandling to dancing naked to a room full of Darryls.

She rubbed her face, then pinched the bridge of her nose with her forefingers.

Her gaze remained on the computer screen, but she hadn't really seen it for quite a few minutes now. She was focused on some far-off, unseen summation of her life that scrolled by in her mind's eye.

It was odd, how distanced she felt from it all. Had three months on the street already made her that hard? It seemed so easy to look at the story of her life as though it belonged to someone else, as though she was hearing about it, rather than having lived it herself. Is this what she had to pay to be strong enough to be free? She was happy that she'd proved resilient enough to make it on her own—even just living hand-to-mouth the way she did at the moment—but had to wonder at the cost.

She used to *feel* things so intensely. And she supposed she still did. But what she felt was *now*. The relief of being clean again. The warmth of the tea. The chance to relax for a moment, instead of having to be focused on her safety in dangerous surroundings.

She couldn't feel her past in the same way.

She didn't like Darryl, but she didn't experience that residue flash of anger or hatred when she thought about him. She didn't even feel the fear anymore. She believed that her parents and Marie had treated her unfairly, but the hurt she felt was intellectual, not in her gut.

How could all of that have just faded?

Sighing again, Suzi tried to put all of this out of her mind and focused on the computer screen in front of her. She deleted the spam unread, then composed her usual message for her sister.

I miss you, Marie. Please write.

She sent it and was about to close the browser when a small window popped up in the middle of the screen. She expected an ad and was already moving the cursor to click on the little "X" in its corner when the image registered.

It was a grainy, black-and-white photo of a young, good-looking black man standing in some kind of forest that looked like it had been built out of old circuit boards, wire, and other electronic litter. His face was tilted up so that she felt as though she was looking down at him from a higher perspective.

She waited to see if anything was going to happen, finger hesitating on the mouse button that would make the window disappear. But the message, when it started to scroll across the bottom of the window, wasn't an ad.

. . . aaran . . . help . . . me . . . aaran . . . help . . . me . . .

For a long moment she stared at the words as they continued to scroll across the bottom of the small window. Finally she raised her gaze to the kitchen door.

"Aaran," she called.

He popped his head out the door.

"You better come see this," she said.

She got out of the chair to make room for him in front of the computer.

"What is it?" he asked as he took her place.

But then he looked at the screen, took in the picture, read the words scrolling under it. His face drained of colour. He turned to her.

"How did . . . what did you . . ."

"I didn't do anything," Suzi said. "Honest. That window just popped up."

She bit at her lower lip, trying to figure out what she'd done, why this was freaking him out so much. He looked like he was about to have a stroke.

"Do . . . do you know that guy?" she asked.

Aaran gave a slow nod, his gaze returning to the screen.

"His name's Jackson Hart," he said. "He works at the paper and . . . he's one of the disappeared."

"I don't get you. What are 'the disappeared'?"

Aaran started to answer, but then shook his head. He got out of the chair and picked up the TV remote. He switched on the TV, and CNN came up on the screen. Suzi came and sat beside him on the sofa and tried to make sense out of the bizarre story that the anchorwoman was reporting.

Christy

I've come out onto the fire escape for another smoke, but it's mostly just to get away from all the planning and conversation going on inside.

It's quiet out here, almost peaceful, if it wasn't for the anxieties pressing on my heart. The city's just beginning to wake up—Sunday mornings it always takes its time. Even most of the stores don't open until noon. I lean on the railing and look down the alley that runs behind Holly's building. Nothing's moving here, only a cat sniffing at the base of the dumpster behind Joe's café, a few buildings down.

I start to take another drag from my cigarette, but pause, my gaze caught by the red ember burning at its end. It's funny, how quickly you get back into these things. And what do you get? A momentary calm. Something to do with your hands. But mostly it leaves your mouth tasting like crap and you get to carry the stink of the smoke around with you. Lovely. I can almost see Saskia wrinkling her nose, the frown marks forming between her eyebrows.

I flick the butt away, watch as it explodes in a shower of sparks on the pavement below.

I miss Saskia so much it's a constant pain in my chest.

I've never had a lot of luck in my relationships—at least not the romantic ones. I always pick the women who are different, I mean *really* different.

Spirits and ghosts and those that are just *other*. But it's not the same with Saskia, for all her otherness. I mean, we're all mysteries to each other anyway, aren't we? So, she's a little more mysterious, that's all.

What I do know is that we've made a good life with one another, snugly fitting together the separate pieces of who we are, but remaining individual at the same time. How often do you get *that* in a relationship?

I can't bear the idea of her being gone forever.

Whoever or whatever's responsible—man, woman, or some damned spirit in the wires—they'll pay.

Funny, I'm beginning to sound like my older brother Paddy. Violence was the way he solved most of his problems. Me, I prefer to find more peaceful solutions. Usually. But right now . . .

I guess it's true that most anybody can go over the edge, if you push them far enough. If you push them hard enough. Because right now, I just want to hit something. If I had whoever took Saskia away from me in front of me right now, and there was no way to bring her back, I think I could kill them. I could . . .

I shake my head. She's not gone forever, I tell myself. We'll get her back, one way or another. We have to.

I find myself remembering a dream I once had. I was at a book signing, opening a book to sign it for a reader, and all the words slid off the page and fell onto the floor. A couple of people were standing to one side—one of them was Aaran Goldstein, *The Daily Journal*'s book editor. He turned to whoever he was with and said, "I've always said that his words don't really have any staying power."

It has nothing to do with my life right at this moment, except for the helplessness I felt in the dream.

I stand and stare down the alley, watching Joe from the café down the street step out his back door to throw a garbage bag in the dumpster. The cat that was there earlier is long gone. The door closes with a bang behind Joe as he goes back inside.

I listen to the other sounds of the city, the traffic over on Williamson, a distant siren, but it hardly registers.

I think of Saskia.

The world of hurt I carry twists inside my chest again.

Eventually, I light up another smoke.

Aaran

"So what does any of this have to do with you?" Suzi asked, finally turning away from the screen to face Aaran where he sat on the other end of the sofa.

Aaran muted the sound on the TV and regarded her for a long moment. Sometimes when he looked at her—surreptitiously, when her attention was focused on something else, rather than like this—an unaccountable feeling rose up to collide with the other, more earthy, hunger of his libido.

He didn't know exactly what it was, but he could feel it now. There was this subtle something different about her that set her apart from the other people he knew. Something that rose from her like an almost visible aura. If he had to describe what it felt like, the first word that came to mind was blue—a warm, electric blue, if that was possible with such an inherently cool colour.

Maybe it had something to do with him seeing her through this growing infatuation he had for her. Maybe it was her living the way she did. He couldn't remember ever really talking to a street person before, never mind spending this much time with one. But whatever it was, she seemed to have a different take on everything, a different way of looking at the most simple thing. Like with this business on CNN.

She didn't seem to be in the least perturbed by what she'd just seen on the TV screen. Maybe once you were homeless, events beyond the ragged borders of your street life didn't really register anymore. Or matter. But it mattered to him. And the longer he sat here thinking about it, thinking of the enormity of what he'd gotten himself involved with, the more of a need he had to talk to someone about it.

Suzi was here. She was also so divorced from any other part of his life, that talking with her felt like it would be easier than with someone he actually knew. And it wasn't like there was anyone else he could turn to. But he *had* to talk about it.

"It's all my fault," he said.

"I don't get it."

"That guy in the computer," Aaran said, jerking his head to the desk. "I got him to run a virus to bring down this Web site called the Wordwood."

"I still don't follow you."

"Something must have gone wrong. Don't you see? All those people got sucked into their computers. I knew this was connected to the virus the first time I heard about it. I just *knew* it. Jackson sitting there in my notebook only confirms it."

"That's not a person," Suzi said. "It's just an image—and not a very good one, either."

"No. He's in there. Maybe not in my notebook, per se, but somewhere in the Internet. They all are. Jackson told me about these, I don't know, things that live in the wires. They're like voodoo gods or spirits or something. And they don't like people messing around with them. They don't even like people talking about them."

He could see what she was thinking, how she thought he was crazy. She was probably seriously regretting that her clothes were still in the dryer and she couldn't just bolt from the apartment. He didn't blame her. He felt a little crazy himself.

"Hold on a minute," Suzi said. "First of all, nothing *lives* on the Internet. That's just impossible. And secondly—" She pointed to the muted TV screen. "Nobody's saying anything about computers on the news. When you cut through all the bullshit, they're not really saying much of anything."

"And you know what makes me feel the worst about all of this?" Aaran went on as though she hadn't spoken. "His landlady told me that he used to admire me. I'm such a shit."

"Listen to me," Suzi said. "Computers don't swallow people."

"Then where did they go?"

"I have no idea. But they're not on the Internet."

"But these spirits . . ."

"Web sites are set up by people," Suzi said. "Living, breathing people, no different from you or me."

Aaran shook his head. "I don't know . . ."

Neither of them said anything for a time. They sat on the sofa, watching the talking heads on the silent TV screen. The dryer stopped its cycle in the laundry room and Suzi got up. She took her clean, dry clothes into the bedroom and closed the door. A few minutes later she came back out again. Aaran noted that she was still wearing the T-shirt he'd give her under a zippered fleece jersey.

"Okay," Suzi said as she sat down beside him again. "Let's not talk about where these people have gone or spooky Web sites because we're never going to agree on that. Instead, let's deal with where you're at. You feel responsible. So what are you going to do?"

"What *can* I do?"

"Well . . . you could go the police and tell them what you've told me."

Aaran nodded. "And they'd believe me as much as you do. I know how crazy it sounds. To tell you the truth, I don't know if *I* even believe what I've been saying."

"No," Suzi said. "You don't talk about boogiemen on the Internet. You talk about the site. How this guy—"

"Jackson Hart."

"How Jackson Hart brought it down with a virus. How maybe the people running the site have found some weird way to take their revenge on him."

"Not to mention how many hundreds of other people."

She shook her head. "No, just stay focused with this. Talk about what you do know. Nothing more. Let them make connections and try to sort it out."

"I'll probably spend the rest of my life in jail by admitting to any kind of involvement. This is a big deal now. Way bigger than anything I was really trying to do."

"But all those people . . ."

Aaran bent over, his hands against his face.

"I know," he said, his voice muffled.

How had it come to this? It had seemed so simple a week or so ago— just a way to get back at Saskia and her too-cool crowd.

"Well," Suzi said. "I guess the other thing you could do is contact the people who run the site. Do you know who they are?"

"Not really . . ."

"You must know something about them to have enough of a grudge to have your friend write a virus that would take down their Web site."

Aaran sighed. He really didn't want to get into any of this. But he felt committed now, having told Suzi as much as he had. Besides, what would it matter? It wasn't like they knew anybody in common. What made him hesitate was that he didn't just want to get into her pants anymore. However improbable it might seem to anyone who knew him—including himself— he was beginning to care about what she thought of him. But he was into this too far to hold back now.

"It wasn't with them, per se," he said. "There's just this woman. She treated me like shit and then she got all her friends to do the same."

Suzi gave him a funny look. "I know how that feels."

"You do?"

"Maybe we'll have time to exchange war stories later, seeing how we're sharing all these confidences. Right now let's focus on the problem at hand."

Aaran sighed again. "God, I feel like such a shit. When I think of all those people . . . it makes me feel like a monster."

"Did you ever hit a woman or a kid?" Suzi asked. "Did you ever beat on someone not as strong as you? Someone you should have been protecting?"

He shook his head.

"Then you're not so bad." She smiled. "Or at least not entirely bad. So tell me what this ex-girlfriend of yours—I'm assuming she's an ex?—"

Aaran nodded.

"What do she and her friends have to do with what's happening now?"

"They were all really into this Wordwood site," Aaran explained. "So I thought a way to get back at them would be to have Jackson take the site down with a virus. I wasn't planning anything permanent—and certainly not on this scale. It was just supposed to be an inconvenience."

"But you don't know any of the people who actually own the site?"

"I'm not sure who's running it now, but one of the people who started it up lives here in town."

"Then start with him."

"It's a her. She owns a bookstore up on the north side."

"Then we should start with her."

"I guess . . ."

Suzi stood up. "So come on."

"What, now?"

"Why put it off? Is it okay if I leave my stuff here till we get back?"

Aaran pushed himself up from the sofa and gave her a puzzled look.

"You're coming with me?" he asked.

"Sure."

"Why?"

She smiled. "I've got a bunch of reasons. The first is, well, you seem to be a pretty good guy. I know you'd like to jump my bones—oh, don't deny it. You don't think I can tell from the way you've been looking at me? But the thing is, you've been polite and you haven't pushed or anything. After what my life's been like for the past few months, I appreciate that."

Aaran was going to protest, but then he simply shrugged. He'd started out with the truth when they started talking about Jackson. He might as well stick with it.

"Secondly," Suzi went on, "I get the feeling you don't have a whole lot of friends, and I know what *that's* like, as well. Especially when people you thought were your friends turn on you."

Aaran caught something, not so much in her voice, as passing over her features, that told him there was more to it than that. A world of more. He wanted to ask her about it. He wanted to know why this whole conversation, why *everything* about Suzi was making him the feel the way he did. He'd never talked to anyone the way he was talking to her.

"I wasn't all that nice to her, either," he said instead. "To Saskia, I mean. The woman I was trying to get back at when I started all of this."

"But we've already established that you weren't hitting her or anything, right?"

"Words can be almost as hurtful," Aaran said.

Suzi's eyes clouded. "Yeah, don't I know that. But you regret it now, don't you?"

Aaran nodded. Surprisingly, he actually did. Not because of the trouble it had ended up getting him into, but because it had been wrong.

"Who are you anyway?" he said. "You've got me saying things and feeling things no one else ever has."

She smiled. "Maybe I'm your guardian angel. I mean, we're all supposed to have them, right? But who says they have to be these celestial beings floating around with harps and halos? Maybe they're just someone you happen to meet by chance and that meeting changes your life. Hell, if that's the case, maybe you're *my* guardian angel because I'm sure feeling a lot more human than I have in a long time. You know, being able to have a conversation like this where the other person doesn't think you're just some loser or freak."

Aaran could only shake his head.

"Which brings me to my last reason," she said. "I've been living on the streets for three months now. I know that's not a long time in the overall scheme of things, but when you're actually *doing* it, it feels like forever. Every damn *day* feels like forever. And the worst of it is how you just feel so worthless. But I don't feel like that right now. I feel like I'm helping you, that you appreciate my support, and that makes me feel like maybe I'm not as useless as people make me feel when I'm trying to get a job or panhandling."

She paused. "I'm talking too much, aren't I?"

"No. And you're right on all accounts. But let's eat first and then I'll call a cab."

"Let's take the bus. Does it go as far as we need to go?"

Aaran nodded. "We can take the subway up as far as Alicia and Moore and transfer from there. But what's wrong with a cab?"

"We'll probably still be talking about all of this and when you're in a cab, you don't think the driver's listening to every word you say?"

"But there'll be even more people on public transport."

"That's true," she said. "But only ten percent of them actually pay any attention to what the people around them are talking about. We'll just sit among the other ninety percent."

"And we'll know the difference because...?"

"I'm good at noticing that kind of thing."

Aaran laughed. "Okay. You want to make some toast while I finish cooking us brunch?"

"Love to," she said as she trailed into the kitchen behind him.

She touched his arm before he could pick up the whisk to beat the eggs.

"This'll all work out," she said. "That's why doing the right thing is always the right thing to do."

"We'll see," he told her. "But these people dislike me something fierce. And . . ." He hesitated, then added, "I guess with good cause."

"Don't be so hard on yourself."

Aaran shook his head. He couldn't believe this woman. She was living under the worst circumstances he could imagine—penniless, homeless, and apparently, though he found this hard to believe, friendless—and yet she was still so upbeat and positive.

"I'm beginning to really like you," he said.

"It's always good to be liked," Suzi told him, "but don't go getting any ideas. It could never work out between us."

"Why not?"

"Because no matter what happened, I'd always be the homeless woman you took in off the street. That simple truth would lie under everything else. You don't think it would matter, but you'd never forget it either."

Aaran started to protest.

"And neither would I," she added.

Christy

It's midmorning and we're still playing the waiting game, killing time until Estie and the rest of Holly's computer friends show up. Dick's finally come out of his room, but it's only to go downstairs and dust the already immaculate bookshelves. It's how he deals, Holly says. The rest of us sit around in the kitchen, drinking too much coffee and tea while Robert noodles on his guitar, though for me to call it noodling is a real injustice. Somehow he can take the most simple progressions and infuse them with all these layers of nuance and meaning. I know that. I know he's good. Normally I'd be captivated, but today the magic he's waking from that old Gibson of his just disappears into the background, the way everything else that doesn't concern Saskia does.

Occasionally one of us starts to talk, and somebody else joins in, but after a few moments the conversation always comes around to the problem at hand, and there's nothing new we can add to that. All we can do is speculate. Too much speculation and you begin to feel crazy.

We end up with a lot of big holes in the conversation—not the comfortable kind you have when you're together with friends, but they aren't entirely uncomfortable, either. They're just . . . periods of waiting. Stretches of silence, where time slows down until minutes feel like days and hours never seem to finish. But it's not like we can really do anything. Everything we can do has already been done. It wasn't much. We cleared all the books out of the dining room and got the old computer out of the basement and set it up on the table in there. Checked to make sure it's still working. Plugged the modem in and checked it as well, though not by logging on to the Wordwood site.

And that was it. Now there's nothing to do but wait.

I'm not good at waiting, so I keep coming out here onto the fire escape. I'm not entirely sure why. Having yet another smoke is only an excuse, it's not the reason. I don't think I'm specifically trying to avoid the people inside. After all, Geordie's my brother, Holly's a very dear friend, and I've really come to like Dick over the past year. The two strangers to me, Bojo and Robert, are the kind of people I'd normally want to listen to for hours, taking notes in my head while they talk. But right now I can't seem to spend more than ten minutes sitting with the group of them in the kitchen before I start getting all antsy and have to come out here on the fire escape again.

I hear the screen door open behind me and turn to see Geordie coming out to join me.

"How are you holding up?" he asks.

I shrug. "Okay, considering."

He leans on the railing beside me and looks off down the alley the way I've been doing for the past few hours whenever I've been out here. Mostly nothing happens except for that one scrawny alley cat making his rounds, and people from the shops that back onto the alley stepping out for a smoke, or throwing their garbage into the dumpster. Once, a couple of kids in their late teens did a furtive exchange at the far end of the alley, standing close to each other, looking about as suspicious as you can as one of them passed something to another. Probably a drug deal. But who knows? Maybe they were just trading a different kind of crack—registration codes for bootlegged software. Though you'd expect them to do that on-line.

"It's funny," Geordie says after we've been standing there awhile, "but I'm not even tired."

"I know what you mean," I tell him. "It's been a long time since I've pulled an all-nighter."

Geordie nods. "I've got that taste in my mouth and a bit of a burn behind my eyes, but that's about it. I keep expecting to crash, but I guess the adrenaline's still got me firing on all cylinders." He gives me a small humourless smile. "Even though we're all just waiting around like this, doing nothing."

I think about what I can add to that and come up empty. I consider lighting up another cigarette, but that doesn't have any immediate appeal either. The silence starts to drag out, but before it becomes uncomfortable, we hear the door open again. I turn and think there's no one there until I lower my gaze and see Dick standing in the doorway, looking anxious. It must be hard to get noticed sometimes, when you're barely two feet tall, never mind having that whole "most people can't see you" fairy thing going for you.

"Master and Master Riddell," he says. "Mistress Holly says you'd better come quick."

I squat on my haunches so that I'm not towering over him.

"What's happening?" I ask. "Is Estie here?"

I'm surprised that we hadn't heard them arrive—or at least Snippet's welcoming barks.

He shakes his head. "Other guests have come," he says. He hesitates, then adds, "Maybe not so welcome."

I don't like the sound of that at all.

When he turns, Geordie and I follow him through an empty kitchen, then down the stairs where we can hear voices ahead. I don't know who I'm expecting as we step into the store, but if I'd had to guess, Aaran Goldstein would have been the last person on the list. He's standing just inside the front door by the recent arrivals shelf with a briefcase in his hand and a pretty girl I don't recognize at his side. She's short and slender and I can't place her age. Her blonde spiky hair, the faded green cargo pants and grey hooded jersey make her look younger than I feel she is. What I do know is that she's not the kind of person I'd expect to see in Aaran's company.

Holly and Bojo are talking to them, with Snippet staring at them from around Holly's legs. I have to look around to find Robert. He's standing down one of the aisles, just out of the line of vision of Aaran and his friend.

"What the hell are you doing here?" Geordie says as we approach the group.

He's got a glare fixed on Aaran, and I can hear the anger in his voice. I give him a surprised look. Geordie's such an easygoing guy that I can't remember the last time I actually heard him raise his voice. But he's loyal almost to a fault, and I guess the way Aaran's treated both Saskia and me over the years just pushes all the wrong buttons, even for a gentle soul like my brother.

Then we find out what Aaran's been telling the others, and I have to put a hand on Geordie's arm as he takes a sudden step forward.

"Let him talk," I say. "It's not like he meant for this to get as out of hand as it has."

I'm surprised to find myself defending him. It's funny. Aaran's such an officious little prick, and I've never liked him, but I can't even seem to find the energy to get mad at him right now. And there I was, out on the fire escape a few hours ago, ready to do physical harm to whoever was responsible for this nightmare. I guess in the end I'm more like Geordie usually is than like our older brother Paddy was.

Geordie gives me a surprised look. "But—"

I shake my head. "No. This isn't about bad reviews or how much we hate to see dipstick here strutting around like he owns the world. This is about Saskia. It's her life that's at stake and I'd deal with the devil if that's what it'll take to get her back."

"Not sure I'd recommend that," Robert says stepping out of the aisle where he's been standing. "Dealing with the devil," he clarifies. "I'm behind you on every other count."

We go upstairs and crowd into the kitchen, bringing in extra chairs from the dining room so that everyone can have a seat. The woman with Aaran is Suzi Chancey, a street person he's just met today. For those of us who know Aaran—which would be Holly, Geordie and myself—the idea that Aaran would stop to talk to a street person, never mind bring them home, is almost as surprising as finding Aaran knocking on Holly's door. What doesn't surprise us is what we learn when he goes back through his whole story and we find out why he was getting this Jackson Hart fellow to sic a virus on the Wordwood site. That's the pure, mean-spirited Aaran Goldstein we know, through and through.

But I'll give him this. He seems genuinely regretful for what he's done—especially when he finds out that Saskia was one of the victims.

"Wait a minute," Suzi says to us. "Are you trying to tell me that you actually believe that people have disappeared into the Internet?"

"I know what I saw," I tell her.

"And if pixies can come out of the Internet," Holly adds, "I'm not surprised that people can get trapped in it."

That comment requires a sidebar. Neither Aaran nor Suzi seem completely convinced by Holly's story, though when Dick does his sudden "I've been here all along" pop into view, I can see the cogs of reconsideration start to turn in their heads.

Bojo, Geordie, and Robert have been quiet through all of this. Geordie still has his mad on. He sits at the table, arms crossed, obviously distrustful

210 Charles de Lint

of Aaran and his motives for coming here. Bojo's relaxed, slouched in his chair and giving the appearance that he's only barely paying attention, but I get the sense he's not missing a thing. I notice that Robert hasn't touched his guitar since we came back to the kitchen and I wonder about that, just as I wonder about why he stayed out of sight when Aaran and Suzi first arrived. I guess if the stories about him are true, he wants to be cautious about who hears his music, and whom they might tell.

At one point Aaran takes his laptop out of his briefcase and shows us the image of Jackson Hart that had appeared on his screen while Suzi had been using the machine to check her e-mail. He'd saved it as an HTML document so that he could bring it back up at any time, even when the computer's off-line.

Bojo sits up then and gives the grainy image a careful study before slouching back in his chair.

"Recognize the place?" Robert asks.

Bojo shakes his head. "But there's not much to go by from that picture."

"Why would he recognize it?" Suzi asks.

He smiles. "I travel a lot."

I can tell she feels she's missing things here, that there are undercurrents she's not getting. And let's face it, there are. When she introduced herself, telling us so forthrightly how she lives on the street, almost making it a challenge, I think she expected us all to tell her more about ourselves in return. But no one did. For my part, I just wondered, why's she with Aaran? And what's her stake in all of this?

I can accept Good Samaritanism—I wish the world had a lot more of it—but she came in a package with Aaran Goldstein, and while I'm willing to hear him out—hopefully to find something that will help us reclaim Saskia and the others—I don't particularly like or trust him now any more than I ever have. Maybe it should be different, but the sad truth is, you're always judged by the company you keep.

There's more talk and we finally start drifting into speculation again. I'm just about to make another retreat to the fire escape when we hear a banging on the front door downstairs. Snippet jumps up from under Holly's chair and goes to the head of the stairs, ears twitching, a small growl rumbling in her chest. I glance at the wall clock. It's a quarter to twelve.

"Maybe this'll be Estie," Holly says as she gets up to go have a look.

Snippet goes down the stairs, claws clattering on the wood, with Holly right behind her. Bojo waits a beat, then seems to not so much rise as drift out of his chair to follow them. The rest of us wait in the kitchen. From the happy sounds that come from downstairs, it's obvious that the welcome the new arrivals are getting is far different from Aaran and Suzi's. Bojo reappears and returns to his chair, dropping back into his slouch as though he'd never gotten up in the first place. Moments later, Holly leads her friends into the kitchen and for a few minutes chaos reigns as introductions are made all around.

Sarah Taylor—Estie—turns out to be a tall, dark-haired woman with grave eyes and an air of quiet grace. Her girlish voice on the phone last night had put such a different image in my head that I wouldn't have come close to recognizing her today without an introduction. She gives me a warm, sympathetic smile when we shake hands.

"Have you heard anything from your friend?" she asks.

I shake my head. "But we've got some new leads."

The dark-haired Hispanic man standing beside her perks up at that. I've already heard him introduced as Raul Flores, which would make him Benny Davis's boyfriend, Benny being the one of the Wordwood founders who disappeared while on-line with Estie.

"What have you heard?" he asks.

I start to answer, but then Holly's introducing me to someone else. I see Estie put her hand on Raul's arm. She leans over to him and murmurs something in his ear, and he nods, but with obvious reluctance. I don't blame him. If someone had even a scrap of information about Saskia, I'd say be damned to politeness and want to know right away as well.

But Holly's introducing me to Tom Pace—the one they call Tip—and I don't have the chance to tell Raul what we've found out so far. Tip's taller than me, a lean and lanky throwback to the old hippie days with his ponytail hanging past his shoulders and long, wispy beard. His eyes are serious, peering at me from behind wire-framed glasses, and his features are thoughtful, but I can tell by the laugh lines around his eyes that he's not always like this.

The last of the newcomers is Claudette Saint-Martin, a full-figured black woman in a business suit with a delightful French accent. Apparently she was on her way to work when she got the call from Estie and simply had the cab she was in take her to the airport instead of the office where she'd originally been bound.

There's not nearly enough room in the kitchen, so we take what chairs we need and set up command central in the dining room where the computer's waiting for us. The newcomers are startled when Dick seems to appear out of nowhere, but while they're plainly intrigued, they're too

212 Charles de Lint

polite to ask about him. Holly and Bojo bring in a new round of coffee, tea, and soft drinks as we get settled. There's a lot of cross-conversation, different people talking at once, but somehow everybody gets brought up to date.

An awkward silence follows the revelation that Aaran was responsible for the virus that started all of this, and all heads turn in his direction. I actually feel sorry for him, but Suzi's the one who speaks up for him.

"Okay," she says. "So he messed up. Didn't any of you ever mess up? And at least he's had the balls to come here to try and make amends."

I notice that Holly's friends aren't particularly impressed with that. They don't seem too taken with Suzi herself, either, but I don't have to wonder about that. She seems very nice—too nice to be in Aaran's company, and that's the problem. Aaran's not exactly on anybody's favorite people list that I know, though I have to say he's doing a very good job of acting like a normal person today. Maybe he really is sorry about what he's done and genuinely wants to make up for how badly he's messed things up.

Then the conversation turns to the mechanics of how they set up the original Wordwood site and speculations on how they might be able to recapture those original configurations. Estie reaches into her purse and pulls out a stack of floppy disks held together with a rubber band.

"I managed to dig out my copy of the first back-up we did," she says.

"That's good," Tip says. "I couldn't find mine. But the thing is, if there *is* an actual spirit in the Wordwood, won't it have evolved since it was first created? I'm not sure there's any point in starting at the beginning again."

"What we really need to do," Claudette puts in, "is establish some sort of communication with whomever or whatever is running the show on the other end of that URL."

"You don't have to play coy," Estie says. "Not with anybody that's here. We all know we're dealing with the spirit that lives in the Wordwood."

"But we don't know *what* it is," Holly says.

Claudette nods. "That's true. But we still have to find some way to contact it."

"Except basics is still the best place to start," Raul says. "You strip away all the fancy flash and plug-ins, and everything's still built on that original HTML you guys wrote way back when."

I listen to them brainstorm, but even with all the research I've been doing lately, they soon get so esoteric that they lose me. After a while I turn to Holly who's sitting beside me, Snippet asleep on her lap.

"Are you following any of this?" I ask.

She shakes her head. "Even though we used my computer to initially set up the site, I was always just one of the content people. Back in those days, all I did was collect the material and pass it on to one of the others to format. I've since learned to do HTML, but I don't really understand it."

On the other side of Holly, Claudette turns around and grins.

"That's because you never tried," she says. "And besides—"

"I had you all to do it for me," Holly finishes.

It's obviously an old joke between them.

I listen awhile longer, then go out onto the fire escape for another smoke. When I return, the conversation's in another lull. Raul and Tip are studying the picture of Jackson Hart on Aaran's laptop. Estie's loading the data from her floppy discs onto Holly's old 386. Everybody else is just sitting around, looking tired.

I try not to let my frustration show, but none of this seems to be getting us anywhere. I want to say, let's just get *on* with it. Hook the damn computer up to the Internet and let's go.

Except I don't know where to go any more than the others do.

That's when Bojo clears his throat.

"I don't know much about computers," he says, when he's got everybody's attention, "so correct me if I'm heading down the wrong road here. But this virus that got sent to the Wordwood site—does it work the same way that a virus you or I could get would work?"

There's a moment's silence, then Estie shakes her head.

"Not really," she says. "This is something that only affects computers."

"The software, to be precise," Tip adds. "You know, the protocols that tell the hardware how to work and where to look for information. It doesn't physically affect the hardware, except that your operating system doesn't know where to find it anymore—depending on how the virus was set up, of course."

Bojo nods. "I was just thinking, when someone gets sick among my people, we use herbs and cures . . . the way your doctors will prescribe antibiotics. So I thought if a computer virus worked in the same way, maybe there might be some sort of an antivirus we could send to the Wordwood site to combat the virus that Hart created to bring it down."

The computer experts among us exchange glances.

"Maybe," Estie says slowly. "If we knew *what* the virus was . . ."

"We'd need to get into Hart's computer," Claudette says. "But what are the chances of that? The police have probably impounded it by now."

Raul nods. "Or at least sealed off his apartment because it's a crime scene. We'd never be able to get in."

"I think I can help with that," Aaran says.

Everybody turns to look at him.

"I mean, so long as the police really haven't taken it away."

"I thought you hardly knew him," I say.

"I don't. But his landlady seems to like me, and if I told her it would help us bring him back, I think she'd let us in."

I look at Estie. "What do you think?"

"It's hard to say without actually seeing what he's written," she says. "But I like this a lot better than trying to sort out mystical mumbo jumbo. At least I understand programming languages."

"So some of us can work on that," I say, "while the rest of us can work on trying to set up some kind of communication with the spirit that runs the site."

"And if we can't get it to come to us," Robert says, speaking up for the first time, "maybe we can go to it."

His words hang at the table for a long moment, and everybody just looks at him.

"You're talking about a place, right?" Robert asks. "Am I hearing this right? You're saying that this spirit's got its own place, out there in the wires somewhere?"

"I suppose . . ." Estie says. "I mean, there's the Wordwood site."

"And that's on the Internet? Or at least it's in some computer connected to the Internet?"

"Well, logically . . ." Tip begins, but then he laughs. "What am I saying? There's nothing logical about this. You're right. The files that make up the Wordwood site *should* be housed in a computer somewhere. But that's where the site got really strange. Not only did it develop this personality of its own, but it also disappeared from the computers where we were storing it."

"And took up residence out on the Internet somewhere?" Robert asks.

"I don't see how that's possible," Claudette says. "It's got to be housed in a physical computer. There's no physical *place* for it in the wires or satellite feeds or however people access the Web."

"Tell that to the people that have disappeared," Estie says.

Claudette nods. "Point taken. Not understood, but taken."

Something starts niggling at the back of my mind. A conversation I had, maybe. I'm not sure what. I start to think out loud, hoping to catch the memory unaware.

"The way I see it," I say, "is that these spirits might use the Internet as a means of getting from one place to another—travelling pretty much the same as the data we send—but they *exist* somewhere else. And if I had to guess, I'd say it was *between*."

That's not quite it, but I can almost taste myself coming up on that elusive memory.

"I don't follow that," Estie says.

"*Between* is where magic is strongest," I explain. "The spaces between one thing and another. Not day or night, but dusk or dawn. Not the land on either side of a river, but the bridge that connects them. The boat that will take you from one side to the other."

"So you're saying that the Wordwood site exists someplace in between the routes we use to connect our computers to the ISPs housing Web sites?"

I nod. And now I've got the memory that had just been out of reach.

"And what's more magical than the spiritworld?" I say. "Just before Saskia disappeared, she was telling me about a conversation she had with . . . with a friend of ours. It doesn't matter who. But this friend believes that the Wordwood site exists in the spiritworld. Or at least that it can be accessed through the spiritworld. I don't know how I could have forgotten that."

"The spiritworld," Claudette repeats.

I see Geordie giving me a puzzled look. I want to tell him that Saskia was talking to my shadow, but that's something I don't even want to start to get into with this group. They're all looking at me with varying levels of confusion.

"Not the spiritworld, Master Riddell," Dick says. He blushes when everyone looks at him, but gamely goes on. "The spiritworld isn't *between*. But the borderlands are."

Bojo nods. "And the borderlands can take you anywhere—so long as you know what you're looking for."

"These are actual places?" Estie asks.

"Oh, yeah," Robert tells her. "You don't get more actual. Some people will even tell you that this world we're living in is just one echo of what you'll find across the borders."

After telling his own story, Aaran's been sitting quietly through all of the various conversations we've been having around the table. But he leans forward now, his gaze fixed on me.

"And is that a place you can take us?" he asks. "We can go there and get these people back?"

"I can't," I say. "But I know people who can cross over. The big problem's going to be figuring out *where* to go once we do cross over. You can't begin to imagine how vast the spiritworld is."

Suzi laughs. "I can't even imagine *it*."

That wakes smiles from many sitting around the table.

"You don't have to go looking for more people to bring into this," Robert says. "What you're talking about now is pretty much my own take on the problem. I can't see people disappearing into a machine. But if that machine's a gate into the otherworld? Oh, yeah. That's more than possible." He looks from me to Bojo, to Dick. "And it makes sense, doesn't it?"

"Now wait a minute," Claudette starts. "I can't believe any of you are taking this fairy-tale nonsense seriously. What we need is a real solution to—"

But Raul puts his hand on her arm.

"Let's hear this out," he says. "I'm willing to listen to anything that offers up a chance of getting Benny back." He turns his attention to Robert. "You can do this? You can get us into this place?"

Robert nods. "Like Bojo said. I don't know much about computers either. But I know the spiritworld. I figure between those of us who've got some familiarity with the place, we won't be shooting completely blind."

He looks to Dick who gives a sad, negative shake of his head.

"Not me," he says. "I've no sense of direction and I've never gone very far into the borderlands." He shoots Holly an apologetic look. "Hobs hardly ever do."

Robert's gaze travels on to Bojo.

"I'd need more to go on than guesswork," he says. "Christy wasn't exaggerating," he adds, looking up and down the dining room table. "It's a big place. Anything you've ever imagined, exists somewhere in there. And that goes for everyone who's ever lived—they might die and travel on, but the places and people they imagined stay behind. There are worlds upon worlds upon worlds in there. They're not all hospitable. And they're mostly dangerous. And the borderlands are even more confusing for those who don't know exactly where they're going."

"I might be able to call up the right door," Robert says. "Everything's got its own signature, and I've been hearing enough about this place that I figure I can find a piece of music that'll get us close, if not right to where we want to go. Though it's not something I care to work on for too long."

"Why's that?" Estie asks.

Robert shrugs. "Let's just say that there are all kinds of spirits over there on the other side of the veil separating this world from the otherworld and not all of them have taken a liking to me. They know the sound of my Gibson. They know *my* signature—the way I pull a tune from its strings. I play too long and they'll come sniffing around. And when they come, we'll be in a whole mess of new trouble."

"You get us close," Bojo says, "And I'll take us the rest of the way. I don't need music."

"Just like that," Claudette says. "We're just going to up and step into Never-Never Land, following you like you're the Pied Piper."

"You're mixing up your fairy tales," Holly says.

"You know what I mean."

"Once we get there," Tip asks. "Can you bring us back again?"

Bojo hesitates, but he nods. "Like someone once said, there and back again. But only so long as you do what I say and stick to the paths I take you on. Take even one step off the way I lay out for you, just to look at a flower or pick up some bauble that catches your eye, and I might never be able to find you again."

"Though something else might," Robert says.

"Why are you trying to scare us?" Tip asks.

"Because it's *dangerous,*" Robert tells him. "Truth is, I'd just as soon none of you go, but once we get there, we're going to need at least one person that's familiar with this spirit."

"But none of us are really familiar with it," Estie says. "None of us know what it really is. I'm not trying to back out of this," she adds. "It's just . . . we know computers. We know *this* world." She looks at her friends. "None of us know about spirits and . . . you know, magic."

"You've talked to it," Robert says.

He's not asking a question, but Estie and the others nod in response all the same.

"So that'll be a job for one of you," Robert tells them. "To recognize the spirit and put your case to it. The others are going to go to Hart's apartment to see if they can figure out a way to undo his virus."

"What about Saskia?" I ask. "And the other disappeared?"

"If we're right," Robert says, "and this spirit's made a hidey-hole for the Wordwood site on the other side, then I don't figure it takes much guesswork to expect we'll find them there, as well."

"You said none of the people from these other mass disappearances ever came back," Holly says.

"That's right. I did say that. But I also said that shouldn't stop us from trying. And who knows? Maybe some folks did escape before, but they just didn't want to go around talking about it after. Time was that every big story didn't have to end up on the news. Some people like to keep things to themselves."

"Or maybe they turned the radio dials in their heads *way* down," Holly says, "and just made themselves forget."

Robert smiles. "Maybe so." He looks around the table. "So now you need to decide. Who's coming with us, who's going to Hart's apartment, who's staying to hold the fort. Those of you who are going, you're going to need travelling gear: good footwear and at least a couple of pairs of socks. Clothes that can take some hard living. Bedding. Water. Food. Don't forget a hat."

"What about weapons?" Raul asks.

"Bring what you want. But I'll warn you, keep it simple. A lot of things made in this world don't work the same on the other side. It's iffy in the borderlands, but if we have to go into the spiritworld itself, you'll find no use for a compass, or a walkie-talkie, and you can just plain forget about your fancy automatic pistols and the like."

"You really think we can do this?" Geordie asks.

"I don't know," Robert tells him. "But at least you'll be doing something. The way it stands now, you don't know how to bring all these people back from wherever they've been taken—at least not from this end. But maybe, if we can get you to the right place, you can work it out from the other end."

I stand up.

"What time is it?" I ask.

Raul looks at his watch. "Almost four-thirty."

I didn't realize we'd been talking that long. No one says anything for another long moment and then I realize something.

"Why's everybody looking at me?" I ask.

Robert smiles. "The troops need a general."

"I'd think you'd be better suited than me."

He shakes his head. "I'm not good with people."

"What makes you think I am?"

"You can be," Geordie puts in. "I'm with Robert on this."

Holly agrees, which has Bojo and Dick nodding their assent. Then one by one the others agree as well, even Aaran.

I sigh. I don't feel prepared for this. It's not like I've got a military mindset or have ever coordinated anything more than a book signing before. But then I think of Saskia. Lost somewhere. Counting on me.

"Okay," I say. "Here's how we'll do it."

I divide us up into teams.

Dick's too nervous to come across into the spiritworld—that's easy enough to tell. I know he'd come if Holly was going, but with Bojo and Robert, I figure we already have the experts we need for the trip, so I have him stay at the store with Holly and Geordie. Geordie protests until I tell him that I'm counting on him to be our backup.

"If anything goes wrong," I say, "you know people to contact."

"Like Joe."

I nod. "Just don't go borrowing that stone Wendy uses to cross over. You won't know where to start looking for us."

For the trip into the otherworld, no one argues when I say that Bojo and Robert will be coming with me. It's only when I include Raul that the questions arise.

"But he wasn't part of the original group," Claudette says. "Not that I'm saying I want to go. But don't we need one of the founders?"

"I don't think we'd be able to stop him from coming," I say.

"You've got that right," Raul says. Then he looks at the others. "And maybe I wasn't in at the beginning, but at this point I've logged as much or more time on the site than any of you."

I see something in his eyes and I guess Estie does, too.

"Whose voice does it use to talk to you?" she asks.

"My grandfather's."

She nods. "I hear my cousin Jane's inflections." She looks around the table. "She died in a car crash when she was eighteen. Drunken driver."

"Abuelo—my grandfather," Raul says. "He's dead, too."

"Why do you think the Wordwood uses the voices of dead people to talk to us?" Tip asks.

"It's not using those voices," Robert says. "That's just the way you're hearing them. Spirits like to make a quick personal connection to you. I don't know how they do it, but they're good at sounding like someone you once knew—especially someone you had feelings for."

The rest of them I send off to accompany Aaran. Estie's the real computer expert—so I don't doubt that she'll be doing most of the work—but I wanted her people to outnumber Aaran and his new sidekick Suzi, just in case Aaran has a change of heart. Naturally, I don't say that. But I don't have to. Estie's group leaves first and as soon as they're out the door, Holly turns to me.

"Do you really trust him?" she asks.

"You mean Aaran?"

She nods.

I shrug. "Yes and no. I think he's genuinely appalled at what he's done."

"Yeah, but how long's that going to last?" Geordie says.

"I don't know. He's never been one to sustain any one thing for very long. But I don't think he's actually evil. He's just what he's always been: self-centered and more than a little mean-spirited."

"And this Suzi?"

I shake my head. "I really don't know about her."

I find my gaze going to Robert, who's finally taken his guitar out again and started to play.

"There's something about her," he says, "though I couldn't tell you what. She's just *more* here than most people you meet. That doesn't mean she's dangerous or supernatural or anything," he adds when he sees our worried looks. "Just means she's living *now* instead of carrying around the baggage that most of us do."

"But she could be trouble?" Holly asks.

Robert just smiles. "Anybody can be trouble. You haven't figured that out yet?"

"Well, we've got enough to do with the trouble we already have," I say as I get up from the table again. "I'm not going to go looking for more."

"Good advice to remember," Robert says. "Though not always so easy to put into practice. The world has a habit of deciding that kind of thing for us."

I nod, then look at Geordie. "Do you want to come back to the apartment while I pick up some gear?"

"Sure," he says, rising from his seat.

I know him well enough to see he's still got something worrying at him.

"What're you thinking about?" I ask.

He shrugs. "I was just wondering who told Saskia that the Wordwood site might be in the spiritworld."

I hesitate for a moment, then say, "My shadow."

"Your shadow."

A world of unspoken commentary wakes in his eyes. We've been through this before. It's just another trip down all those roads where I believe things and he doesn't. But he doesn't say anything. Maybe he's finally coming around to actually believing the things that so many of our circle of friends have experienced, himself included.

"Now that's interesting," Robert says. "You don't meet many folks that have a working relationship with their shadow."

"I wouldn't call it a working relationship," I tell him. "She pretty much comes and goes as she pleases."

"Well, what do you expect, you being the one that threw her out and all?"

"*What* are you talking about?" Holly asks.

"I'll tell you later," Geordie says.

I study Robert for a moment. There's something in the way he was defending my shadow that tells me he's had his own experiences with the phenomenon. I'm curious about it, naturally—truth is, I'm curious about everything to do with the bluesman—but now's not the time to get into any of it.

"You guys need anything in the way of gear?" I ask instead.

Bojo shakes his head. "I travel light."

"I don't go anywhere without my girl," Robert says, running a hand down the neck of his Gibson. "Otherwise, you could say the same for me."

"Does she have a name?" Bojo asks. "Your guitar?"

"Everything's got a name," Robert replies, "but she's never told me hers and I haven't asked."

Bojo nodded. "Among my people, the instruments all have names. But I think they're given to them by their players."

"I don't go around handing out names. Things have got enough personality of their own without my hanging another tag on them that they've got to live up to."

"How about you?" I ask Raul. "Anything we can get for you?"

"I've got everything I need except for food and water," he says, "and Holly says we can get that at a grocery store down the street while you're gone. But I wouldn't mind a knapsack to carry my stuff in. All I brought was a carry-on for the plane."

"I've got a spare," I tell him, then I turn to Geordie. "We should get going."

"We'll be ready to go when you get back," Bojo says.

I nod. I know why he's with us—it's obvious that he's got a thing for Holly. But Robert's still a mystery.

"Why are you helping us?" I find myself asking before I can leave.

Robert smiles. "I don't know. I guess it's for the same reasons that always get me into trouble. Curiosity, plain and simple. I get this need to find out what a thing is. I have to know how it all turns out."

I suppose that's as good a reason as any. I know I've stepped into a hundred situations because of my own insatiable curiosity.

"Well, I want you to know we're grateful," I say.

"Tell me that again if we survive this trip."

Aaran

"I haven't felt like that since high school," Aaran said.

He and Suzi were waiting in the lobby of the hotel while Estie and the others checked in at the front desk, then went up to their rooms to drop off their luggage and change. They sat side by side on a fat leather couch in the lobby, an island of stillness as the hotel staff and guests bustled around them.

"I can barely remember high school," Suzi said.

Aaran laughed. "That's all I *can* remember some days. It set the tone for the rest of my life."

She glanced at him. "What do you mean?"

"You remember the fat, pimply kid with the Coke bottle glasses that no one ever wanted to talk to?"

She nodded.

"I'm the grown-up version of him. You may not see him when you look at me, but he's still sitting there inside me."

Now it was her turn to laugh.

"That's funny," she said. "I was your typical popular cheerleader type—you know, most likely to succeed and all that."

"Why's that funny?"

"Well, look at us now. You're a big success and I'm living on the street." She touched his arm. "But don't take what happened back there too hard. You did the right thing and they know it."

"I suppose."

"And they didn't all hate you. What's his name—Christy. He stood up for you."

"Yeah. That really surprised me. I used to see him a fair amount before he started going out with Saskia. We got along pretty well, but I always thought he was just sucking up to me to make sure his books would get a good review. Now I'm beginning to realize that he's actually a decent guy. I mean, his girlfriend's one of these disappeared. I doubt I'd be as fair-minded about all of this if I were in his shoes."

"Hopefully, this'll all be over soon," Suzi said. "Estie and her friends seem really smart. I'm sure they'll figure it out once we get to Hart's apartment."

"*If* I can get us in."

"Think positively," she said. "It's always better to put out positive energy. Otherwise you're just going to attract bad luck."

Aaran smiled. "This from the woman who doesn't believe any of this is possible in the first place."

"You believe it's real, don't you?" Suzi asked. "I mean Web sites with spirits and other worlds and everything?"

Aaran shrugged. "The evidence has moved way over to the 'hard not to believe' side of the scale for me."

"Then I do, too."

Holly

"I feel like I'm in the middle of some Looney Toons cartoon," Holly said to Christy.

She'd come downstairs with the Riddell brothers as they left the store. Geordie had already gone ahead to the car.

"But you know this stuff is real," Christy said.

Holly gave a slow nod. She bent down and picked up Snippet as the terrier tried to slip past Christy's feet and have an impromptu solo walk.

"But that doesn't make it feel any less weird," she said. She hesitated for a moment, then added, "You were awfully nice to Aaran, all things considered."

"Don't make more of it than it was," Christy said. "I wanted to know what he could tell us, and he wasn't going to tell us anything if we treated him the way he deserves to be treated. And while it turns out it wasn't a lot, well . . ." He shrugged. "We're further ahead knowing about Jackson Hart and this virus than we were before Aaran showed up."

"And it might even be useful—if Estie and the others can figure something out." She paused for a moment, then added, "You don't think you should wait to see if they can?"

Christy shook his head. "I don't know how much time we have, but in my heart, I can feel it running out on us."

"You'll be careful."

He smiled. "You can count on it." He waited a beat, then added, "And I'll make sure Bojo is, too."

Holly couldn't stop herself from blushing.

"I hardly even know him," she managed to say.

Christy bumped a feather-light fist against her chin. "Doesn't mean you shouldn't get the chance to know him better."

He leaned over and gave her a quick peck on the cheek, then he was out the door. Holly closed it behind him and engaged the lock. Her gaze fell on what was left of the store's computer. Even if they managed to succeed at stopping the Wordwood spirit and were able to get all those missing people back, she didn't know how she was ever going to use the machine again.

Shadows in the Wordwood

Skin spun off,
stripped of
flesh and bone,
spirit singing,
free at last.

Come my turn
to take the journey,
will there be anything
left of me
to go on?
—SASKIA MADDING,
"Death Is for the Living"
(*Spirits and Ghosts,* 2000)

Christiana

I come slowly out of this second blackout of mine, drifting from complete unconsciousness into a dreamy state where I'm not fully aware of my body. I'm not sure that I even have one. Whatever I am is floating through a meadow, dotted with trees, that sits on the edge of a dark forest, but it's a confusing place because everything is made of words.

The grass and wildflowers are narrow phrases, swaying in the wind, punctuated with blossoms whose wordy petals radiate from clusters of vowels. The trees are thick paragraphs, dense with description, that lighten into shorter sentences and finally simply words as they follow the natural progression of trunk to branch to twig to leaf. Small verbs and nouns scamper along the branches or in amongst the roots of the trees. Others sit in the topmost branches, trilling sweet wordsongs, or soar by on wings of poetry.

It's all very strange, but I'm completely accepting of it, the way you are in a dream. My spirits are buoyant and light.

I don't know how long I'm in this place, but after awhile it starts to drift away—or I drift away from it. A sharp pang of disappointment goes through me. I felt safe and happy there, even with some of those darker stories I spied hiding in the shadows under the trees where the forest of legends and fairy tales began in earnest.

But then I feel a tingling in my limbs. I realize I have limbs. I have a body again. I hear one last trilling song from a small yellow-breasted verb perched high in a paragraphing oak—

Catch as catch as catch as can!

—before it's all gone and I'm waking up.

When I open my eyes, the world's spinning. I imagine all these faces crowded close, peering down at me, blurred and colourless. But when the spinning stops, the faces are still there, still blurred and leeched of colour. There's no colour anywhere, which is a real shock after the brightly-hued world of words I've just left behind.

I sit up and see that the faces are attached to bodies as ill-defined as the out-of-focus features on the heads above them. They drift away from me whenever I turn to look at a particular group, the ones not in my view taking the opportunity to crowd closer behind me.

"Back off!" I tell them.

I get to my knees, waving my hands at them. They do what I tell them and give me some space, watching me from a distance. The effort of chasing them off makes me dizzy, but I force myself to put one foot on the ground and push up until I'm standing, though swaying would be a better description of what I'm doing.

"I mean it," I say as the ghostly figures begin to move closer again.

That's when I realize that I still have my colour. I lift one hand, then the other. They're the same coppery brown they always are. I look down at my sweater and jeans. I'm far more *here* than the ghost people are. I'm far more here than the place *itself* is. The pale rose of my sweater, the faded blue of my jeans, the scuffed brown leather of my walking shoes—they all vibrate with presence and colour.

Well, I guess they would, here in this chiraoscuro world, where everything's just black and white and the shades of grey that lie in between. Standing here, I jump out like a spot of tinted colour in a black-and-white photograph.

But that's not the strangest thing about this place. The setting could be the same as my dream of the word world, except this meadow borders a forest that looks like a sculpture made out of junk metal and old electronic parts: trees, branches, leaves, undergrowth and all. It's all circuitry and wires and bits of metal and cast-off scraps of god knows what.

Everything's like that. I bend down and touch the vegetation underfoot. It looks like its made up of hundreds of tiny wires, soft and pliable like grass would be.

But I think it's the lack of colour that gets to me the most.

I've been in colourless worlds before—or ones that were as close to it to make no difference. A lot of the borderlands exist in a perpetual twilight that lays a grey hue over everything. But they're nothing like this. There's something in the air here that feels heavy. That makes me feel heavy. Maybe it's the lack of colour. Maybe it's all the metal and electronic junk. More likely, it's those ghostly figures that drift around as easily as mist.

But if this is one of the strangest places I've ever been, it does have this much going for it: it's still a place. I'm not sure where it is—somewhere in the spiritworld, I suppose—but if I'm here, that means I'm not dead.

"Is this weird or what?" I say to Saskia.

There's no reply in my head and I realize that the slight pressure of her presence is gone.

That figures. Just when I could really use someone to talk to—if only in my head—she's found somebody else to inhabit. Or maybe she got left behind when I . . . when whatever happened to bring me here.

I try to remember and it slowly comes back to me. The storm that shouldn't be able to exist. Me going out into it. The black rain beating me to the ground . . .

I guess Saskia was right. Maybe I should learn to be a little less head-strong. Can't see it happening, though. If Mumbo hasn't been able to convince me after all these years, I doubt anything can.

I study the ghosts some more, wondering what they want from me. I suppose it could just have been curiosity, the way they were all hovering around me when I was coming to. They don't seem particularly menacing. In fact, they're all keeping their distance now. Though they haven't lost interest in me—not by a long shot. I think the weight of their observation is adding to this heaviness that's settled over me.

I thought they were all the same at first, but I can see differences now. Even as out-of-focus as they are, their features are individual when you look at them long enough. Men and women of all races. Teenagers, pensioners, and all the ages in between.

Since they still haven't made any threatening moves in my direction, I decide to try open up the lines of communication between us.

"So," I call out to the nearest group of them. "What's this place called?"

That bunch immediately backs away. I hear an odd sound coming from them which sounds like radio static. It takes me a moment, but after I try another two or three times with other groups, I realize it's their voices.

Scratch communication with the natives.

I look away from them and try to get my bearings. The meadow I'm in is actually the scrub between the forest and a sweep of grasslands that goes all the way to a line of low hills that I can see on the far horizon. There are probably dips and valleys, but from where I'm standing it appears to be one big, flat expanse of open land.

That direction seems less than promising, so I turn back to the forest. I know I'm probably going to have to go into there, but I'm not looking forward to it. I don't like the idea of being in such a confined space, not with all those ghostly creatures floating about.

I fasten onto that word. Ghosts. Maybe I am in some land of the dead. Since I'm so solidly present, I guess I'm still alive. But *they* could be spirits of the dead. Or lost souls.

I immediately think of Saskia again.

Lost soul pretty much sums the state she was in the last time I—I want to say "saw her," but she had even less physical presence than the ghostly figures I've got floating around me here. Could she be one of them? Is that what I'm doing here? She got pulled into this place and I got dragged along with her?

I call her name. Once, twice, and again. I call as loud as I can, letting my voice ring, but all I succeed in doing is totally scaring off the ghosts that have been watching me. That's okay. I can live without the weight of their attention.

I listen hard, hoping for a response, but I don't get one. I realize that there's next to no sound here. No birdsong. No wind. Nothing except this faint hum that seems to come out of the ground underfoot.

I try calling for Saskia some more, keeping it up until my throat gets raspy.

There's still no response.

So I give up. I have a last look at the grasslands, then slowly turn to the forest. I can't see anything worth my attention in the grasslands, but the forest . . . the forest could be hiding anything. That's the trouble as well as a possible solution to my situation, of course. That anything waiting for me under those strange, junk metal trees could just as easily be dangerous as helpful. But I really don't see that I have a choice beyond standing here like a dummy, doing nothing.

So. I take a deep breath. I start forward the way you do any journey, big or small. You put one foot in front of the other.

I get maybe a dozen paces closer when something hits me in the head with enough force to bowl me over and send me sprawling in the wiry grass.

I scrabble quickly to one side, moving on all fours, before I turn to see what hit me.

There's no one there.

I lift a hand to my head and feel around through my hair. But there's no sore spot. There's no blood. Nothing. Only this pressure in my head. A familiar pressure . . .

"Saskia?" I say. Then I repeat it as a thought. *Saskia, are you in there?*

<Christiana?>

She sounds totally surprised.

"Are you here because I was calling you?"

<That was you?>

"I don't see anybody else here. Where've you been?"

<Lost,> she says. <Lost somewhere in cyberspace. I was trying to follow this URL, but it was just taking me in circles and—>

"Hold up there. What's an URL?"

<It's like an address. On the Internet.>

"Ohh-kay."

<It doesn't matter. I was just in this loop and until I heard something calling to me . . . my name, I guess . . . > Her voice trails off for a moment, then she adds, <The next thing I knew I was back in your head.> Another pause. <Sorry about the hard landing.>

"No problem. I'm happy to have the company."

<So I guess that's twice I owe you my life now—if you can call this living.>

"Oh, don't go all mournful on me. This place is depressing enough as it is. Speaking of which, do you have *any* idea where we might be?"

<Well, I was aiming for the Wordwood site . . . >

"I think I was there," I say and tell her about the dream I had just before I regained consciousness.

<I don't know what that place was,> she says, <but I don't think that was it. I think this is.>

"*This?* Come on. This is just a junkyard—a creative one, I'll grant you, but really. This other place was *made* of words. There were even animals and birds that were somehow both words and themselves at the same time, if that makes any sense."

<Not really. But this place *feels* right. Remember, I was born here.>

"So you recognize it?"

<No, it's just how it feels. Though obviously something's gone very wrong with it.>

"Okay, say this is the Wordwood. Any ideas where we go from here?"

<I don't know. What have you found so far?>

"Pretty much nothing," I tell her and then I fill her in on what little I've seen since I found myself waking up here in a field of grassy wires.

<These ghosts wouldn't talk to you?> she asks when I'm done.

"They seem to scare pretty easily. I think that static-y sound they were making was their language, but I couldn't make out a word."

<Probably because we're from two different operating systems.>

"Say what?"

<You know, like a Windows PC trying to talk to an iMac.>

"I don't have the first clue as to what you're talking about."

<It's like people from different countries who can't understand each other.>

"If that static I heard even was a language." I get another thought then. "Are you the only one the spirit sent out into the consensual world?"

<The what?>

"Where we met—what Christy calls the World As It Is. I was just wondering if the spirit sent others like you out into it."

<I never even thought of that. They'd be like my brothers and sisters.> She's quiet for as moment, then adds, <But if the Wordwood did send others out, I sure hope it prepared them better than it did me.>

"I guess if you were the first, it would have learned from that until you . . . what? Stopped broadcasting information back?"

<That worked two ways,> Saskia says. <I also had access to everything that was in the Wordwood. Which was strange, but useful. I could give you an historical overview of chocolate, but I had no idea how it actually tasted.>

"That would be handy right about now."

<You mean some chocolate?>

"No. Some more background info."

<Oh.>

I take another look at the forest. "Well, I say we should get a move on. Are you ready to do a little exploring?"

<I guess . . . >

I start forward, my gaze sweeping the shadows under the trees for I'm not sure what. Ghosts, I guess. Danger.

Something in here worries me.

The undergrowth isn't thick—this forest is too old and overgrown for much light to get through the thick canopy above. Then I have to laugh. I touch the bark of one of the first trees—it's like running my hand over a sculpture made up of circuit boards pasted together. Does this stuff even grow?

I'm about to ask Saskia what she thinks when, from the corner of my eye, I catch something move, like a figure ducking behind a tree. It looked like a man—still black and white, but much more substantial than the ghosts I saw earlier.

Did you see that? I ask, then I feel foolish. Of course she did. She sees everything I see.

<It looked like a person.>

If I can grab him, maybe we can convince him to tell us a little something about this place . . .

<Be careful,> Saskia says. <Remember where your last bold move got us.>

I know. Here. But now we really have nothing to lose, do we?

<But . . . >

Don't worry. This is something I'm good at.

It's true. I lead an active life, which surprises some people who only see this delicate creature the way Christy does. I've always been more tomboy than debutante. Maybe it's because I started life out as a boy.

I keep walking, as though I never noticed the figure ducking out of sight, slowly shifting my direction until I'll pass right by the tree that he's hiding behind. When I come up to its fat bole with all the circuits and wires hanging from it like bark, I dart around the opposite side from where he'd be expecting me to pass. He has his back to me, but he senses me and starts to turn. Too late. I charge at him like a defensive line back. My shoulder hits his chest and he goes tumbling down in a sprawl with me on top of him.

I'm stronger than I look, but he's bigger than me and he pushes me off, scrabbling backwards until his back comes up against another of these weird circuit board trees.

"Don't hurt me, don't hurt me!" he cries as I move toward him.

I hold my hands up, palms out.

"I'm not going to hurt you," I say. "What makes you think I want to hurt you?"

"You jumped on me, didn't you?"

"Yeah, but that was only after you started stalking me."

"I wasn't stalking you. I was just . . . observing you."

"Sounds like stalking to me."

"I was just trying to figure out who you are," he adds quickly. "To see if you're dangerous or anything."

"And?" I ask. "Am I dangerous?"

"Jesus, I don't know."

The look in his eye tells me he thinks I am, but I don't call him on it.

He's solid flesh and bone, for all that he has no colour. From his features and the darker grey tones of his skin, I figure he's of African descent. Mid-twenties and good-looking. Kind of twitchy, but I think that's more to do with me surprising him than any natural inclination on his part.

<At least we can understand him,> Saskia says.

Yeah, but did you notice that there's a bit of static when he talks? Like hearing a radio that's not quite on the station.

<Was that what it was like with the others?>

No, I couldn't make out a word they were saying—if they were saying anything. And this guy's a lot more solid.

"Who are you?" I ask out loud so that he can hear me.

"My name's Jackson. Jackson Hart."

"And do you live around here, Jack?"

"I prefer Jackson."

"Okay, Jackson it is. Do you live around here?"

He shakes his head.

"So where are you from?"

"A place called Newford. I . . ."

His voice trails off as he cocks his head to listen to something. As soon as he does, I hear it too.

<What a strange sound,> Saskia says.

No kidding.

I can't quite figure out what it is. It's not high-pitched, but it's still got that quality of a fingernail on a blackboard mixed with a dull, um, I guess I have to say wet whine, if that makes any sense. You'd have to hear it. There's also a hissing sound, like water boiling, maybe.

"Oh, Jesus," Jackson says. "It's the leeches."

I'd put a mild panic in his eyes when I knocked him over, but now they hold pure, unadulterated terror.

"Leeches?"

"That's just what I call them," he says. "Land leeches." He gives another anxious glance in the direction the strange sounds are coming from, then turns back to me. "I don't know who you are or what you're doing here, but you *don't* want to meet these creatures. And with the way you look, they're going to be all over you."

"What do you mean the way I look?"

He holds out a black and white hand, then points at my own.

"You're in Technicolor—that makes you stand out in a black-and-white world."

"Sure, but—"

"There's no time to explain. Just do what I do."

He starts to tear at the forest floor, peeling back layers of matted wires, circuitry, handfuls of what looks like thin, small pieces of sheet metal, but is far more pliable.

"I'm serious," he says when he realizes I'm still just standing there.

The sound's a lot closer now and it's starting to hurt my ears.

<Maybe we should do what he says, Christiana.>

I guess.

He's dug himself a hole and now here's something even weirder. Under all this crap we've been walking on is a mess of words—a great tangle of them, like a thick undercarpet of leaves and weed clippings. I flash back to the word world I was dreaming about before I woke up here. But these are different. They're like dirt, dark, with a smell that's a mix of ink and something metallic.

Jackson lies down on the words and starts to cover himself up.

<Christiana!>

I stir at Saskia's sharp cry.

I'm on it, I tell her.

And none too soon. I scrabble in the debris, getting I-don't-even-want-to-think-about-what under my nails as I dig my way down under the rubbish to the layer of words below. They feel odd against my skin. Warm and dry, for all that they look so damp. I feel almost cozy as I burrow down among them and cover myself over with the junk that was covering them. I leave myself a small hole to peek out of. Saskia makes a gasping sound inside my head and she doesn't even have lungs.

But I understand.

If this world is hard to describe, and the sound the approaching creatures make is even harder, I'm not sure where to begin with the creatures themselves. Imagine some weird combination of a snake and a garden slug, with a shark's fin on the hump of its back. They're solid black, fast and slick, and I see why Jackson calls them land leeches, because there's something like a leech in them as well, for all that they're flowing over the land instead of in water. They're just skimming along, but you can't see any legs and their body doesn't undulate. Electricity seems to flicker on their oily skin, running from one end to the other.

I don't know how many of them there are. I see two, three, then I look away, afraid that they'll feel the weight of my gaze.

I'm sure they know we're here. They ooze menace and have eyestalks on their front ends that are constantly in motion, checking everything out with a field of vision that encompasses a full three hundred and sixty degrees, and probably above them as well.

I burrow deeper and try not to breathe.

Nothing here, nothing here, I chant in my head. No need to stop and check this spot out.

This close, the sound they make sets my teeth on edge. And then there's their smell. Like burnt wiring and sulfuric acid. Like when an outlet fries an electric cord, along with something organic and rotting.

I don't know how long I lie there—Saskia and I don't even talk to each other—but after what feels like forever, I hear something moving in the debris around my hidey-hole. I tense up, ready to go down fighting, when I realize that the sound of the creatures has been steadily receding and the smell's not nearly so pungent any more.

What do you think? I ask Saskia.

But before she can reply, I hear Jackson's voice.

"Hey," he whispers. "Are you okay down there?"

I push up through the circuits and matted wiring and other junk and sit up.

"They're gone?" I ask.

He nods.

<Thank god,> Saskia says.

Ditto, I tell her.

"What *were* those things?" I ask Jackson.

"I think they're a manifestation of the virus."

"What virus?"

"The one that took down the site," he says. "The Wordwood site."

"So this *is* the Wordwood."

He shrugs. "I guess. I just assumed it was when I got here. The damn place was haunting me the whole week before . . . you know . . . ever since it went down."

He looked like he was going to say something else, but I don't push.

Right now he's the only one here who has even a vague clue as to what's going on, so I'll let him dole out the information in his own time. At least for now.

I look over to where the leeches went by and see they've left behind a wake of slagged debris. Some of it's still smoking the way metal will when you drop acid on it.

"How did you figure out how to hide like this?" I ask.

Though I realize even that wouldn't have helped if the creatures had come oozing by right on top of where we were hiding.

"I was desperate," he says. "The first time I heard them, I didn't know what was making that sound. I just knew it would probably be dangerous. They caught me out in the open or I would have tried to climb one of these weird trees. Instead I just dug at the grass—I guess I was going to try to cover myself with it—but when I pulled at it, I found all this code underneath."

He brushes some of the debris from the hole I'd been hiding in, and pulls out some of the words.

"Code?" I say.

He nods. "Yeah. HTML. The code you use to build Web pages. See?"

He's holding what's like a transparent ribbon with words on it. This one says:

Dickens, Charles

"Dig far enough through this stuff and it's all binary," he says. "A big mess of zeros and ones."

"I don't know what you're talking about," I tell him.

<He's means the programming languages that tell a computer how it's supposed to operate. It's what lets us talk to the machines, and to each other.>

"This place is like an old DOS program," Jackson says. "Everything's really basic and it doesn't have any of the graphics or scripts we can access today. I think the virus is what's brought it back to this primitive state."

I give a slow nod, like I know what he's talking about.

"How did you get here?" I ask.

"I don't know for sure. One moment I was sitting in front of my computer, and the next, this flood of black goop came bursting out of my monitor and I was drowning in it. Or I thought I was. I guess I just blacked out, because I woke up here." He gives me a weak smile. "Unless this is the afterlife."

The liquid black goop sounds like the storm that knocked me off my feet, back in the borderlands. Looks like I came the same way. The only difference is, I haven't lost my colour. The first explanation for that doesn't do anything to lighten my spirits: It's probably because I'm a shadow. I've been listening too much to Saskia, I guess, but I can't help feeling like there's something missing in me. And since I don't really exist in the consensual world, why should it be any different in this one?

"How long have you been here?" I ask.

Maybe it's not just me, I find myself thinking. Maybe it's something that happens over time. You lose colour, then substance, until finally you're like the ghosts I saw when I first came to.

"I don't know that either," Jackson says. "It feels like forever."

"We . . ." I begin, then correct myself. No need to let on there's more than one person inside my head. "I just got here. And there were these ghosts . . ."

"They're like us—they're not from here. Or they're like me, anyway. People that got sucked into their computers. The way it seems to work is, you're like a ghost when you first get here, and you stay like that, too, it seems, until you start to figure things out. At least the more I've explored and worked out stuff, the more solid I've become." He gives me a kind of yearning look. "But I'm still black-and-white."

So it works the opposite from the way I thought.

"Are there others like you?" I ask.

He nods. "But they all seem to keep to themselves. And here's something really weird: Some of them don't even speak English. You have to wonder. What were they doing, accessing an English language database?"

<The Wordwood's not just English,> Saskia says. <It automatically translates into whatever language you're using.>

I repeat what Saskia just said so that Jackson can hear it.

He starts shaking his head. "That's not possible."

"We're not talking about a program," I tell him. "We're talking about an entity. A spirit. Something that's alive and lives in . . . wherever we are. Cyberspace, I guess. It communicates with us through the Internet. Or at least it did."

"But—"

"Okay, maybe this is simpler. You remember your classical mythology—how there was a god or goddess for everything?"

"Vaguely," he says, but he nods at the same time.

"So the Wordwood site was the home of the god of something like electronic books. Pixelated words."

"A god."

"I'm just trying to put this in terms you might be able to relate to," I say.

"But a god."

"Maybe that's not the best analogy."

"And he'll be pissed off at me."

"Maybe it's a she," I say, thinking of Saskia. The spirit could have made her in its own image. Then I realize what he said. "Why would it be mad at you in particular?"

"You want to know the truth?"

"No, I prefer it when people lie to me."

<Christiana,> Saskia says. <Maybe we can learn something here.>

Now you're my conscience?

<I'm sorry, but—>

No, you're right. I shouldn't be taking it out on you. Or him.

"So why's the spirit of the Wordwood mad at you?" I ask, gentling my voice.

He's shaking his head again.

"You know, it figures," he says. "Forests have creeped me out for years, so naturally, if I'm going to piss off a god, it'd have to be one that lives in a forest. Even if it's a metaphorical forest. Though weird as this place is, it feels pretty real."

"Jackson," I say, trying to get him back on track. "It's not a god. It's just a spirit. Yes, they can be powerful, but they're only another kind of being, like the difference between, oh, a bear and a gnat. No, that's another bad analogy," I quickly add when I see the stricken look on his face.

Help me here, Saskia.

<Tell him they can be reasoned with.>

Yeah, right. Have you met any of the really old—

<I know,> she says, cutting me off. <But he hasn't. It'll make him feel better.>

So I tell him, and sure enough, Saskia's right. I can see him relax a little.

"Maybe I can just explain to it how it was all a mistake," he says. "Well, not exactly a mistake, but I didn't have a choice."

"I need for you to back up a little here," I say. "I don't know what you're talking about."

"This," he says, waving a hand. "It's all my fault."

"Maybe you should start at the beginning," I say.

So he tells us the whole sorry tale of hacking into this bank's computer, how Aaran Goldstein blackmailed him into sending a virus to the site. How he was haunted by visions of this forest, hearing a static-y wind. How he kept losing chunks of time until one day he lost the world and ended up here.

We listen to it pretty much without interruption, except for the first time he mentions Aaran.

Is this the same guy that—

<God, I hate him,> Saskia breaks in before I can finish my question. But it doesn't matter. She's answered me all the same. <Of *course* he'd be involved in something like this.>

"Is he here?" I ask aloud.

"Who, Aaran? I doubt it. I don't think he spends much time on the computer. And especially not the Wordwood site. I mean, why would he want me to take it down, if he did? I figure it's mostly a bookish lot that got pulled over. Librarians. Avid readers."

<I doubt Aaran Goldstein even likes books,> Saskia says.

Something had to get him started as a book editor.

<I suppose. But I don't think he likes them anymore. Christy says he hates writers because he tried to write himself, and it was a complete disaster.>

Yeah, well, Goldstein isn't exactly one of Christy's favorite people.

<Is he anybody's?>

I'm just saying there's a lot we don't know about him—you know, why he is the way he is.

<Why are you defending him?>

I'm not. I'm just trying to get a full picture.

Jackson has no idea about the conversation going on in my head, so he's just been talking away.

"What did you say?" I ask.

"I was just saying that the few people I have talked to since I got here were all on their computers, trying to access the Wordwood site when . . . whatever happened went down."

I nod and he goes on, telling us about how he sent an e-mail to the site's Webmaster—"I guess I was talking to the spirit itself, right?"—explaining what he'd done and how it could be fixed.

"But right after that . . . boom. Here we are."

<Boom,> Saskia repeats. <Though in my case, it was more like fire-
works gone awry.>

There's so much loss in her voice that I start to feel bad about the way I
was talking about Goldstein earlier. I really *wasn't* trying to defend him,
but I can see how she might take it that way.

When we get all of this sorted out, I tell her, *we'll find a way to make
him pay.*

But now it's her turn to be the voice of reason.

<I don't necessarily agree with the idea of revenge,> she says. <I think
the bad you do comes back on you, no matter how justified you might think
you were to do it.>

*We don't have to do anything ourselves. We can just tell the Wordwood
spirit where it can find him.*

<I don't know . . . >

"Jesus," Jackson says, distracting us from our own silent conversation.
"You know what's happening here?"

My sympathies are more with Jackson than Goldstein in this mess, but
after listening to his story, I'm not feeling particularly charitable to either of
them.

"Yeah," I tell him. "You were playing show-off computer nerd and you
screwed a whole bunch of people."

"No. I mean, that's true. But he forced me to do it."

"You could have said no."

"And gone to jail."

"I'm just saying you had a choice."

I see in his eyes that he knows this all too well. That it's been eating at
him ever since he got here. Not just because of what's happened to him, but
because of how many other people have been hurt as well.

"I shouldn't have said that," I say.

He shrugs. "Why not? It's true."

"Okay. It's true. But we need to move on now. You were saying something about knowing what's going on?"

It takes him a moment to shift gears, but then he nods. "It's just that, if
the Wordwood is a being rather than a Web site, then my virus hit it like a
disease. I wrote it to screw up all the HTML links in the site. But if it hit a
person—or at least a being of some sort—then what it's doing is playing
havoc with their metabolism. It's not letting the various parts of its body

communicate with each other. At the very least, it's not going to be able to form a coherent thought—or at least not one that has any correlation to anything else it happens to know."

<He's probably right.>

Probably.

"How does this helps us?" I ask.

"I don't know. But maybe if I can access a computer . . ." He looks around himself and his excitement dies. "What am I saying? We're *inside* a damn computer."

He bends down and tears up a handful of the words we burrowed in to hide from the sliders. I get a flash of that binary code he was talking about earlier—zeros and ones flashing by at an incredible rate, almost too fast to see.

"What we really need," I tell him, "is to find some of these other people. Or . . . have you seen anything that could be the place where the spirit would be staying?"

He sighs and looks deeper into the woods.

"There are the ruins," he says.

"Ruins? What kind of ruins? And where are they?"

"Deeper in the forest. It looks like the foundation of some old building, but all that's left of it is the fieldstone base on which it was built. The only weird thing there is the glass coffin with the girl in it."

"What?"

"You'd have to see it. It's like out of *Snow White and the Seven Dwarfs.* Before you, it was the only piece of colour I've seen in this whole place."

"The coffin's in colour?"

He shakes his head. "No. The dead girl inside is. Or maybe she's not dead. Maybe she's only sleeping. All I know is she doesn't move. She just lies there with her hands folded on her chest and her eyes closed. You can't get into the coffin and you can't wake her up. I've tried."

"Show us," I say.

I've no way to gauge how long we tramp through the woods. The light never changes. Actually, nothing really changes except that the land underfoot rises steadily. It's a long gentle slope, so it's not too arduous, but it's hard to get a sense of where we are, or where we're going. For all their size and the lack of real undergrowth, the circuit board trees grow too thick to allow for much of a long view.

That plays in our favor when it comes to the land leeches. We can't see them from far off, and they can't see us. But we can certainly hear them coming.

Twice on the way to the ruins we have to hide from them. The first time we hear that unmistakable sound of their approach, I don't even wait for Jackson to say a word. I just stop where I am and start digging.

I've seen a lot of strange things in my travels through the spiritworld and the borderlands, but these things are definitely the scariest. I think it's because they appear to be so utterly implacable. I can't imagine reasoning with them, or outwitting them, which are pretty much the only two tricks in my repertoire when it comes to beings that are much more powerful than me. How would you even talk to something like that in the first place?

So I follow Jackson's example. I hear them coming and I'm gone, burrowed as deep as I can get into forest floor before their arrival. I've seen the smoking slag they've left behind when they're gone. And Jackson tells me he's seen them absorb ghosts that are too slow to get out of their way. Not for me, thanks.

Anyway, it's a while before the trees start to thin out and the ground gets steeper. But finally we come out of the forest into an open field. There's more of that strange wiring here, pretending to be grass and gorse and who knows what kind of weed. As we keep climbing, I look around and see that the forest stretches as far as I can see on all sides. Here and there, other bare peaks rise from the forest.

I try to see them as a pattern, the way you'd expect inside something as logical as a computer, but their placement appears to be completely random. Here a pair close to each other. There three in a cluster. Between them a huge expanse with nothing to break up the forest.

After a good long look on my part, we continue up.

I'm a little worried about those leeches catching us here, out in the open, with nowhere to hide. But I don't see any of their trails and Jackson assures me that the grass will pull up as easily here as the carpet of metal leaves and crap does in the forest. I believe him, but I have to give it a try anyway. He's right. Under the layer of wiry grass I peel back, I find more of those dark code words that pass for soil in this place.

When we reach the summit, I take a close look at the stones that make up the ruined walls of the foundation. I can't tell what they're made of, but it's some kind of metal, discoloured and patterned just like field stones would be.

"She's in there," Jackson says.

246 Charles de Lint

The wall's too high here for me to look over, so I follow him around to an opening where I guess a window would have been. It's easy to climb over the sill and jump down onto the vegetation inside. It's spongy underfoot—like a thick bed of lichen.

The inside of the ruins is broken up into a maze of rooms. Walls marking the boundaries of the rooms and halls, with no roof, no floor or furnishings.

<I wonder who lived here?> Saskia says as we look back out through the window.

Maybe you did, I say. *Before you were born in the consensual world.*

<Maybe . . . >

Jackson leads the way through the rooms, two right turns, a left, another right, then he stops in the doorway of an enormous room and moves aside. I step by him, my gaze immediately going to the explosion of colour that's the dead girl he was talking about. Her coffin's in the center of the room.

For a moment I can't make out any detail. Seeing this much colour after all these hours of monochrome makes my eyes hurt. It's like looking directly into the sun. Spots dance in front of my eyes, but they adjust quickly.

It's right out of a fairy tale scene all right—a blonde woman lying on her back in a glass coffin, hands folded over her stomach—except she's wearing blue jeans, a white T-shirt, and running shoes, which kind of takes some of the romance out of the image. Then I focus on her face and I'm sure all the blood drains out of my own.

<That's . . . >

You, I agree.

<Me.>

Sarah "Estie" Taylor

"So what's the deal with her?" Claudette said.

Estie shrugged. The two of them walked side by side as they made their way down the block to Jackson's apartment, trailing behind Aaran and Suzi who were in the lead, with Tip in between. It reminded Estie a little of the old days when they'd go wandering through the city, sometimes two or three of them, usually all five of the original Wordwood founders. In those days, they'd been pretty much inseparable.

"Suzi?" she asked.

"Who else?"

"I've no idea," Estie said.

"There's something off about her. I don't know exactly what, there's just *something* . . . "

Estie nodded. She knew what Claudette meant, though she wouldn't have put it exactly that way. For her, Suzi's presence was more confusing than anything. She understood why she and Tip and Claudette were here—if it wasn't for them, the Wordwood wouldn't exist in the first place. And if the Wordwood hadn't developed this spirit of its own and then gone wrong, Benny and Saskia and all these hundreds of other people would still be safe in their homes, happily surfing the Internet instead of having been kidnapped into some pixelated corner of it.

She also understood Aaran's wanting to atone for the part he'd played in the recent crisis.

But Suzi had no stake in any of this. So far as Estie could tell, she was just tagging along.

"Maybe she feels grateful to Aaran," she said. "You know, for taking her off the street."

"She doesn't look like any street kid I've ever seen."

"Well, she's had a chance to get cleaned up. . . ."

"And besides," Claudette went on. "He's old enough to be her father."

Estie smiled. Trust Claudette to zoom in on that. She'd been the worst gossip, back in the old days.

"We don't know that they're sleeping together," she told Claudette. "Not that it's even any of our business."

"But still . . ."

"She could be in her mid-twenties," Estie said, "and I doubt Aaran's forty. So it might not be *that* huge an age gap."

"Well, if they're not sleeping together," Claudette said, "then what *is* she doing here? I don't buy her being all super grateful for a meal and a shower."

"Why not?"

"It's just weird. And I don't trust her. I don't trust him either, mind you, but I *really* don't trust her."

Estie nodded. "I suppose it's just—you know how sometimes you meet somebody and they're perfectly okay, but you still don't click anyway?"

"I guess . . ."

"Well, that's probably what this is. For whatever reason, we're not clicking with her. It doesn't have to mean anything more than that. There's enough weird stuff going on without us looking for more."

"But that's just it. We weren't looking. The weirdness came to us and—"

"Shh," Estie said.

The others had stopped ahead of them and were going up the stairs of a brownstone, indistinguishable from the rest of the buildings on the street, but obviously their destination. Claudette followed them up onto its stoop, but Estie paused on the sidewalk to look up at the sky. There wasn't a cloud in sight and the sun was almost directly overhead, beating down on the city's streets. She'd forgotten how hot August could get in Newford. It got hot in Boston, too, but the breezes that came in from the ocean usually kept it from getting too unbearable.

"Are you coming, Estie?" Tip called down from the top of the stairs.

Estie look up and saw that he was holding the door open for her. The others had already gone inside.

"I was just remembering why I moved from Newford. God, it's hot."

Tip grinned. "I had The Weather Channel on in my hotel room while we were changing. It's going up into the nineties today."

"Still," she said. "It's not the heat—"

Tip laughed and they finished in unison: "It's the humidity."

"But if you think this is bad," he added, "don't come down to Austin in the summer. There are days it's still this hot at midnight."

"So why do you keep inviting me?"

"Can't beat the music."

Smiling, she stepped by him and entered the foyer.

It was cooler inside the brownstone, but not by much. The relief Estie felt after first getting out of the sun quickly faded and she found herself wishing that she'd stopped to buy a bottle of water at one of the grocery stores they'd passed. She felt dehydrated and the way they were all crowded together in the narrow hallway outside the landlady's door wasn't helping. She shifted the carrying case for her laptop from one shoulder to the other while they waited for the landlady to respond to the knock on her door.

Mrs. Landis surprised her. When Aaran explained that they wanted to access Jackson's computer in hopes of finding some clues as to where he'd gone, she seemed to take it as an everyday request.

"If you think it will help," she said. "Only why does it need so many of you?"

The landlady gave Suzi a particularly searching glance as she spoke. Claudette caught Estie's eye and gave her a "you see?" look. Estie shrugged in response, then returned her attention to the conversation between Aaran and the landlady—or rather the lack thereof.

Mrs. Landis appeared to have caught Aaran off-guard with her simple question.

"We . . . um . . ." he began.

"It doesn't need all of us," Estie said, jumping in. "I'm the one who knows about computers and Aaran knows Jackson and will be the best one to sort through what we do find. The rest of us can wait outside."

The landlady shook her head. "No, that's all right. It's much too warm for anyone to be sitting out in this hot sun. It's just . . . do you really think this will help you find Jackson . . . ?"

"I sure hope so," Aaran said. "But we won't know until we see what's actually on the computer."

"Then how could I not let you have a look at it?"

Estie couldn't remember the last time she'd met someone so trusting. She realized that Mrs. Landis was worried about Jackson and only wanted to help, but Estie was happy all the same that her own landlord back in Boston was the grumpy Mr. Morello, who would barely exchange more than a couple of words with his tenants, never mind someone he didn't know. It was comforting to know that even if she ended up vanishing herself, there wouldn't be gangs of strangers traipsing through her apartment. Or at least not until the police were called in.

Mrs. Landis went into her own apartment to get her keys, then led them up the stairs to Jackson's.

"I don't know that you'll even be able to start his computer," she said as she unlocked the door to the apartment. "It's not in very good shape after . . . after what happened last night."

"It's probably not as bad as it looks," Estie said. "If the hard drive's intact, we'll be able to access his data."

"I still don't understand what you hope to find."

Estie shrugged. "We thought if we looked through his agenda and his e-mail, we might find something. Perhaps he made an appointment to see someone. Or there could be e-mail about some plans he might have made. We really won't know until we look."

"I'm surprised the police didn't think of this," Mrs. Landis said.

"I'm sure they would have eventually," Claudette said.

"And whatever we find out," Aaran added, "we'll make sure to pass along to them."

The landlady got the door open and stood aside to let them in.

"It's all so mysterious," she said.

Mysterious didn't begin to describe it, Estie thought. She wondered what the landlady would think if they explained what they really believed and why they were really here.

She'd have the police here in minutes. Or at least the men in white coats from the Zeb with their one-size-fits-all straightjackets.

Estie slipped past Mrs. Landis and walked into the middle of a familiar room. It wasn't that she'd been here before—she'd simply been in a lot of apartments much like this where bachelor computer geeks set up shop with all their computer paraphernalia, stereo equipment, oversized TV sets, and other tech toys. There was no room left over for traditional furnishings.

Though she shouldn't talk. She might keep her living room relatively geek-toy free, but the rest of her own apartment wasn't much better.

"Do you see what I mean?" Mrs. Landis said, pointing to the main desk. "I really don't see how you'll ever be able to get it up and running again."

Estie's heart sank when she turned her attention to the main computer. It really *was* a mess. It looked as though it had been through an electrical fire—much the same as Raul had described the condition of Benny's computer to be. The faint scent of burnt wiring still hung in the air. The monitor was especially scorched, the glass webbed with dozens of tiny hairline cracks, the beige casing streaked with dark burn marks.

"I thought there was some kind of oil," she said.

Mrs. Landis nodded. "There was. An awful black liquid."

"This looks like it's been in a fire."

"That's the way it was when I came in last night. I haven't touched a thing and neither did the police." Mrs. Landis paused, looking at the mess. "I suppose it's hopeless."

Estie wasn't sure they'd get anything out of this machine, but she put on a good face.

"We don't necessarily need to actually get it up and running," she said. "We just need to access the hard drive and see if the data on it is salvageable."

Mrs. Landis gave a slow nod, but though Estie could tell she had something else on her mind, the landlady didn't say anything more. If anything, she seemed nervous, even uncomfortable. Estie might have put it down to Mrs. Landis having second thoughts about letting all these strangers into one of her tenant's apartments, except she felt something, too. There was a *feeling* in the room. A sense of wrongness that appeared to originate from the area where the computer sat. It was as though the machine was casting shadows, the way a bulb casts light.

Estie stole a glance at Suzi, curious as to what her reaction would be. The small blonde woman stood very quietly beside Aaran, her gaze slightly unfocused.

"God, it really is a mess," Tip said.

Estie blinked, his voice pulling her out of her reverie. Tip had walked over behind the long desk and bent down now to look at something that was below her line of sight.

"There are two more towers down here," he said, "all connected to each other and the one on top of the desk through a cable router. Even if their hard drives are only twenty gig each, we've got our work cut out for us."

Estie joined him. She cleared a space on the desk so that she could set down her laptop's case, then studied the setup herself.

"Looks like there's an ADSL line connected to the router," she said.

Tip nodded. "Yeah, here's the modem."

Estie was happy to see the cable router. That was going to save her a lot of time. Instead of having to try to set up a dialogue between her machine and the towers with the gear she'd brought, she could just plug the cable from her network card directly into the router and access Jackson's towers the way she would any other drive connected to her laptop.

Tip leaned a little closer to the modem.

"Okay, this is weird," he said.

"What is?"

"See that little green light? The system's still on-line."

"So now we know why he's got three towers," Estie said. "He must be running a little service provider business on the side."

"Or he just does a lot of FTP exchanges."

Estie nodded.

"But when Benny got taken," Tip said. "Didn't you say that it fried all the phone lines?"

"That's what Raul said. But it didn't at Christy's place."

"Okay. Still, maybe we should unplug the modem anyway . . . just to be safe."

"I suppose."

She stood up and was about to start unpacking her laptop when she glanced at Claudette and the others. They were all standing around by the doorway, obviously unsure as to what they should be doing.

"I've just made some iced tea," Mrs. Landis said when Estie's gaze went to her. "Can I bring up a pitcher?"

Estie smiled her thanks at the offer. "We don't want to be a bother," she said, but she was only being polite. She was absolutely parched.

"It's no bother."

"Then that would be lovely," Estie told her.

"Let me help you," Claudette said.

The landlady smiled at Claudette and the two left the apartment. Now it was only Aaran and Suzi standing awkwardly by the door.

"You guys should find someplace to sit," Estie told them. "This could take awhile."

Aaran nodded. Before Estie could turn away, Suzi spoke up.

"Do you feel . . . nervous at all?" she asked.

Estie gave her a puzzled look. "Why should we be nervous?"

"I don't know. There's just something in the air. I felt it as soon as we stepped into the apartment."

"I did, too," Estie told her. "I think it's just some residual . . . I don't know. Vibes, I guess. Left over from what happened."

Suzi gave her a doubtful nod.

"Estie?"

She turned from Suzi to look at Tip. He was holding up the end of a phone cord.

"What is it?" she asked.

"The outside phone cord going into the modem. I've unplugged it."

"So?"

"So the modem's still working."

Estie bent down to see that he was right. The small green light on the modem was steadily pulsing. She started to reach for the cable connecting the modem to the router, but Tip stopped her.

"I don't know," he said. "I don't think you should be linking up with Jackson's system while it's still on-line—especially considering that it shouldn't even *be* on-line anymore."

Estie nodded. "You think it's the Wordwood."

"What else?"

"Well, we wanted to talk to it. This could be our chance."

"I don't know if that's such a good idea."

Estie smiled, trying to project a confidence she wasn't really feeling. Perhaps she was being foolhardy, and certainly she understood and felt some of Tip's nervousness, but if this was an opportunity for them to communicate with the spirit of the Wordwood, she didn't see how they could pass it up.

She took the Ethernet cable coming from her laptop and plugged it into the router, then stood up.

"Only one way to find out," she said as she turned on her laptop.

Christy

Now that we're actually ready to go, Raul seems to be getting cold feet. I don't blame him. This isn't like taking the subway downtown.

We're in the basement of Holly's store, the two of us with our backpacks and wearing more clothes than I'd normally have on in this heat: good walking shoes with thick socks, jeans, T-shirts, flannel shirts on top of that, jackets, baseball caps. Normally it'd be shorts, sandals and a T-shirt for me. But Robert told us to be prepared because we wouldn't necessarily find the same hot August weather where we were going and I took him at his word.

Mind you, neither he nor Bojo have changed, though Bojo does have a leather shoulder bag with a jacket lying on top of it. Robert's still in his suit, fedora tilted at a jaunty angle. All he's carrying when we come down to the basement is his guitar case.

"I don't know about this," Raul tells me. "I'm feeling really nervous."

"Me, too."

I'm not just saying it to make him feel better. I had a nervous prickle at the nape of my neck the whole ride from my apartment with Geordie. We had to park a couple of blocks away from the store—there's not much in the way of close parking for anyone at this time of day. Walking back to the store in the sun, even with the temperature having climbed into the nineties the way it has this afternoon, my skin goose-bumped thinking about this trip I'm about to take.

"Have you ever . . . you know, been over there before?" Raul asks.

I shake my head. "But we'll be with guides who have," I say, glancing over to where Robert's laying his guitar case down on the floor.

"Don't look at me," Robert says. "I've crossed over into the border-lands a time or two, but I like to stay clear of the spiritworld itself."

"Keeping your low profile," Bojo says with a smile.

Robert flashes him a quick grin. "Keeping myself alive."

I can feel Raul tensing up even more beside me at that. I guess Robert notices, too.

"Don't worry," he tells us. "You'll be okay. There's nothing actively hunting you."

The others have come down to see us off: Holly, with Snippet in her arms. Dick and Geordie. None of them look particularly happy to see us going. When Robert takes his old Gibson out of its case, Holly pushes her glasses back onto the bridge of her nose.

"Why do you need music to cross over?" she asks.

"It doesn't have to be music," Robert says. He adjusts the tuning on his guitar while he talks. "It's whatever you need to help you focus your will."

Holly's gaze goes to the tinker. "But I thought Bojo could just step in and out as he wanted."

"I can," Bojo says. "But only to places I've been before. If I don't have the familiarity, I have to do the same as anyone else. Make my own way by foot or whatever transportation I can find until I get to that new place."

"So that's where the music comes in," Robert explains. "Music can take you to places you've never been before. I guess any kind of art can, when you do it right. I got a good sense of the spirit we're looking for from the traces it left behind in your store. What I'm going to do now is let the music reach out and find us a way to get to wherever that spirit might have hidden itself away."

"That sounds too easy."

Robert smiles. "The world's a pretty simple place. We're the ones that make it so complicated."

I can see she's got more she wants to ask, but Robert starts to pull a twelve-bar from the Gibson, a slow bluesy number in some minor key, and then no one wants to say a word. We're caught, listening, mesmerized, just like that, no more than a couple of chords and a handful of lead notes into the tune. I may not have Geordie's ear, but I can tell right away there's something different in this music.

"Mmm-mmm-mmm."

Robert's humming. It's not a melody, more like a soft, growling counterpart to the melody that the guitar hints at, like a fragment of conversation that only he and the instrument understand. But if I can't be privy to that conversation, I am aware of a change in the air.

One moment we're in an ordinary basement under Holly's store. An old oil furnace crouches in the corner, like a hibernating bear, drowsing the season away until it can be useful once more. There are boxes floor-to-ceiling along one wall, full of books and magazines, I assume, from the black marker itemization scrawled on their side. "National Geos," one reads. I glance at some of the others. "Sci. Amers." "Hist.—pub pre-60." "Ace doubles."

Another corner holds a tall pile of cardboard flats. Under the stairs is a tidy array of snow shovels, rakes, skis, a bicycle with a flat tire and other, less readily identifiable objects. There's a long worktable set against the wall near the stairs going up to the store, with tools hanging above it. Its surface area is covered with material necessary for shipping books: more box flats, padded envelopes, shipping tape, address labels and the like.

The four of us would-be travellers are in a clear space in the middle of the floor. Dick and Holly are sitting on the stairs with Snippet on a riser between Holly's knees. Geordie leans up against the worktable.

One moment, that's all there is. The next, nothing changes physically, but suddenly the air is thick with . . . possibilities. I can't think of any other way to put it. I just know that the music has opened the potential for us to be anywhere. Perhaps Bojo and Robert are seeing these doors to the otherworld that they spoke of earlier. I don't know. I can't see anything other than what was here when we first came down the stairs. But I can *feel* the difference.

I suppose time passes, but I don't know how much. But now I begin to see flickers in the corners of my eye. Still not doors. They're more like heat mirages: ripples in the air that are gone before I can turn and give them my full attention.

"We're getting close," someone says.

I'm not sure who. Either Bojo or Robert, I assume, because who else among us would know? I turn to look at them.

"Just tell me when," Bojo says.

So it was Robert who spoke earlier.

I'm not that familiar with blues music, but this sounds darker and, at the same time, full of joy and more languid than any I've heard before. And I'm not always sure that it's just Robert playing. Sometimes I think I hear the whisper of another instrument, here one moment, gone the next. A scratchy fiddle. The soft wail of a blues harp. Another guitar. A banjo—or some banjo-like instrument playing softer, almost muffled notes. Robert isn't using a slide on the strings, but occasionally the notes he's playing ease, one into the other, the way they do on a dobro.

It's confusing and satisfying all at once. And so full of promise.

"Get ready," Robert says.

I see Bojo nod. He gives Raul and me a look and we both stand a little straighter, waiting for I don't know what. One of these invisible doors to open, I guess. I take a look behind me and see the wall has a shimmer to it, like it's not quite solid anymore.

And then we hear something else. Another faraway sound, but this one grates against the music.

For a long moment, I can't place what it is.

"You better stop," Bojo says.

Robert doesn't look up, but he shakes his head. "No, we're almost there."

"And so are they."

Then I recognize that new sound. It's the distant baying of dogs. And I know what it must mean.

Robert's hellhounds have caught his scent.

Christiana

"**Do you know this woman?**" Jackson says.

I walk slowly toward the coffin and lay my hands on the cool glass. This woman, he says, like she's some picture we've come across while flipping through a magazine. That's Saskia lying in there. Of course I know who she is.

"What makes you ask that?" I say, which is no reply at all.

It's just the kind of thing you say when you have nothing you can or want to say. I'm sure not telling him more than he needs to know.

"You had this look on your face," he says. "Like you'd seen her before."

I shrug. "It's just . . . pretty surprising."

<Does this mean . . . am I dead?> Saskia asks.

Of course not, I tell her.

But all I can give her are words. Neither of us knows anything for sure. Not anymore. Because this is beyond understanding.

I stare at the body lying there under the glass and try to figure out where we go from here. Whatever I expected to find in this cyber world, this isn't it. But I suppose it figures. The Wordwood is loaded with fairy tales, so why wouldn't it use a fairy-tale touchstone as a motif for what it's done to Saskia? Only what happens now? Do we have to find a way to get Christy into this world so that he can give her the traditional prince's magical kiss? Or am I supposed to do it?

There are no seams in the glass, at least none that I can see. The body's lying on a covering of crimson velvet. Maybe the casket opens from underneath. I wonder if we can tip it over to see.

I rap on the glass with my knuckles.

Or we could just break it open with a rock, though Jackson says he's already tried that without any luck. Obviously.

Then there's the whole question of, what if her being in this glass casket is what's keeping her alive? *If* she's even alive.

No, I tell myself. Don't even go there.

But I can't stop thinking about it. That she's already dead and I have a ghost in my head. Or that if I break into the coffin, she really will die. She'll disappear from my head and be gone forever.

Christy would never forgive me.

I don't know if I would.

I haven't known her for very long, but I like her. For a lot of reasons. And because we've both got these strange origins of ours, because of our connection to Christy, I feel as though we're family. Sisters.

<What . . . what are we going to do?> Saskia asks.

I don't know, I tell her.

I wish I did.

I turn to look at Jackson.

"There's got to be something you aren't telling me," I say, although I'm one to talk. "Something else you've seen. Something someone's told you."

He shakes his head.

"What about these other people you've met? Where can we find them?"

"I haven't seen anybody for a while," he says. "Except for the ghosts. And you."

"And there are no other buildings or ruins like this? No other . . ." I stop myself from saying bodies. ". . . mysteries you haven't told us about?"

"No. There's just the leeches."

I don't even want to think about them.

<We have to find the spirit itself.>

I'm open to suggestions.

<Maybe we could just . . . I don't know. Invoke it.>

Well, since, best case scenario, Jackson's virus has made it a little crazy,

*worst case, this whole world's steadily disintegrating right under us, I don't
know how much help it would be even if we could find the spirit.*

<Jackson's a programmer,> Saskia says. <Maybe he knows how.>

But—

<That's what we came for, right? To talk to the spirit?>

*That was the plan, I agree. At least it was until we got hijacked into
this mechanical fairy-tale wood. Now we're just trying to get back to the
status quo.*

<At least ask him.>

Okay.

When I turn from the casket, Jackson's got this strange expression on
his face which makes me wonder what I look like when I'm having these
internal conversations with Saskia. Do my features go all slack and I start
to drool?

I stop myself from lifting a finger to check. At least I can't *feel* anything
in the corners of my mouth.

"What?" I say.

"Nothing. You just looked like you'd gone away."

"Don't I wish."

"I mean gone away somewhere in your head."

"Let's focus on the other kind of going away," I say.

"Don't think I haven't tried."

I lean my hip against the glass casket, stick my hands in my pockets.

"Okay," I say. "So what exactly have you tried?"

He gives me a puzzled look.

"You know," I say. "Did you try to figure something out with the other
people you met? Have you tried to contact the spirit? Where have you
gone? What have you done?"

"I told you. Nobody seems to know anything. And I didn't even know
there was a spirit until you told me."

"So, really, you haven't done anything?"

He frowns at me. "I haven't been this solid for very long."

"I'm not getting on your case," I tell him. "I'm just trying to find a
place to start looking for some answers."

"Yeah, well, good luck."

I go down on one knee and pull at the ground, grabbing handfuls of the
wiry lichen to reveal the dark loam of words underneath.

"Let's start with this stuff," I say. "You told me it was some kind of
code."

"HTML. Yeah."

I dig through that first layer until the binary code is revealed, the ones and zeros flashing by at an incredible rate.

"And this stuff," I say. "It's what runs a computer?"

"They're binary numbers."

"Another kind of code?"

He nods. "The numerals represent bits that are read like electrical charges—'1' meaning on, '0' meaning off."

"So everything in a computer comes down to these bits?"

"It's like a basic language," he says. "But it's not that simple. I can't actually do anything with it."

"Why not? You're a programmer, right? Isn't this what you do?"

"I need to write code to manipulate the binary numbers. And I need a keyboard to write the code. This is like trying to mix the ingredients to bake a cake while you're inside the oven. I can't work directly with the binary. I can't even read it. It's going by too fast."

<I can read it,> Saskia says.

What does it say?

<It's a story. A book, I guess. But all the words are jumbled together— no punctuation or paragraphing or even spaces between the words.>

Because of the virus.

<I guess.>

I focus back on Jackson. "So all those ones and zeros we see flashing by—that's just information?"

"It's raw data, yes."

"And there's no way we can tap into it?"

He starts to shake his head, but before he can answer, we all hear it. That now-familiar, high-pitched, hissing whine. Approaching.

Jackson's face goes pale.

"Leeches," he says.

"I thought you said they didn't come up here," I say.

"I said I hadn't seen them up here before. Come on. We have to hide."

<My body,> Saskia says at the same time as I turn to the casket.

"We can't leave her here," I tell Jackson. "Unprotected."

He just looks at me.

"I don't know who she is, or why she's here," he says, "but there's nothing we can do for her now. We have to look out for ourselves."

I grab his arm. "No, we can't just—"

"Hey, for all we know she's what they've been looking for all along.

Maybe she's in charge—directing them with her dreams or thoughts or something. Who cares? We have to get out of here."

He starts to pull his arm free, but I tighten my grip. That horrible sound of the leeches is getting closer.

<Why are they all coming here?> Saskia says, the growing panic plain in her voice.

I've been wondering the same thing, and I think I have an idea.

I don't know what you being in the casket means, I say. *But I'll bet our coming here—the proximity of your spirit—has set off some kind of alarm. You're either supposed to reconnect with your body, or it's the last thing they want.*

<How do we know which it should be?>

We don't. Not until we try it.

"Help me see if we can topple it over," I say to Jackson. "Maybe we can get into the casket from the bottom."

He gives his arm another yank. This time he pulls free.

"Work it out on your own," he says.

He goes over to the far end of the room and begins to pull up the wiry lichen.

"Every time you cover yourself up," I tell him, "I'm going to pull that crap off of you. And then I'm going to wave and yell and call the leeches over."

"What, are you *nuts?*"

"Just help me here."

He glances in the direction from which the sound is coming, but it's not coming from any one direction anymore. They must be coming up the hill from all sides, zeroing in on the ruins of this house.

"Jesus, we're surrounded," he says. "We're *completely* screwed."

"So help me."

"Don't you understand? I said—"

"You're wasting time."

He glares at me with a look I've seen before. He knows I'm not going to back down, knows there's nothing he can do about it but help me. But that doesn't mean he's going to be happy about it.

"Fuck you," he says.

But his heart's not in it and he joins me by the casket. We reach underneath, fingers scrabbling for purchase, and find an edge we can actually grab. Looks like it's flat on the bottom.

"On three," I tell him.

I count it out and we put our backs to it.

Nothing.

"You see?" Jackson says. "Now can we—"

"Stop wasting your breath," I tell him. "Again. On three."

From the sound of it, the leeches are almost at the walls of this ruined building.

<God, they're getting so close,> Saskia says.

Let me concentrate on this.

<Sorry.>

I count it out again. I feel like my shoulders are going to pop out of joint, I'm straining so hard. Still nothing. But just when I'm about to give up, I feel something. A shift in the casket. So miniscule, I could have imagined it. But I'm grabbing for hope here, and refuse to believe that.

"Put. Some. Muscle. Into. It," I tell Jackson.

He doesn't bother to answer. He doesn't have to. We can both feel it now. It's like when you've got your foot stuck in thick mud and you just can't pull it out no matter how hard you tug. You get that mild panic feeling, that you're never going to get it out, but then there's that feeling, no more than the hint of a promise, and the next thing you know, there's movement. The mud gives up its death grip and suddenly you're free.

That's how it happens with the casket.

One minute we might as well be trying to shift a ten-ton rock. The next the casket pops free from whatever was holding it down. Some kind of adhesive, I guess. It sure wasn't because the casket was that heavy, because it weighs next to nothing, we find out all too soon. When the adhesive gives, it's like somebody suddenly opened a door we were pushing on. The casket goes toppling over. I get a flash of the body tumbling from its velvet bed. It slides toward the top of the casket, which is now the bottom. Jackson and I both lose our balance and fall with it, adding to the casket's momentum. When it hits the edge of the faux stone platform it was on, the glass cracks.

All along I've been hearing that wet, fingernail-on-a-chalkboard whining of the leeches. But it's drowned out now as the casket breaks open and something—air, I guess—comes rushing out. More air than could possibly be in that small enclosed space. The roar of it fills my head—like standing beside a jet that's getting ready for take-off.

Jackson and I tumble onto the wiry lichen, falling in different directions. We regain our balance at the same time and stare wide-eyed as the casket breaks apart. The glass is in five or six pieces and Saskia's body falls out of it onto the ground. I want to go to her, but the body starts to glow.

Electric blue. A deep gold. Blue again. And then a pillar of light explodes skyward, going straight up into the monochrome sky.

No. Not light. Or at least not *just* light.

Inside it are those binary numbers. The code. The flashing 1s and 0s are a part of the strobing blue and gold pillar of light.

<What . . . ?> Saskia begins, but she can't finish.

I understand. I don't have the words either. But Jackson manages to get out a whole sentence.

"What the fuck have we done?" he says.

And then, over the roar of the burning pillar as it pierces the sky like a searchlight, we hear them.

The leeches.

I turn and see the first one coming through the nearest wall, the faux stones melting away like wax from the contact of its slick black body. The stench of sulphur and hot metal fills the air.

Suzi

Suzi was nervous as soon as she set foot in the tenement building from which Jackson Hart had so mysteriously disappeared the night before. It didn't help that, except for Aaran, everyone was making it pretty clear that they didn't much like her and were suspicious of her tagging along. Even the landlady, who'd had a friendly smile for everyone else, had given her a weird look. Aaran was good, lending her some moral support by staying close to her, but she knew that even he couldn't quite figure her out.

She couldn't blame him, not being entirely sure herself why she felt so determined to stick it out. It was no longer simply to be supportive of Aaran—at the moment she was getting more from him than he was from her. And it wasn't even a need to know how this would all play out, though that was certainly a part of it.

It was more as if she was being compelled to come here, that she *had* to be a part of it, for all that she was feeling progressively more nervous the closer they got to Jackson's building.

She was edgy entering the tenement. Going up the stairs to Jackson's apartment made all the little hairs stand up on her arms and once she actually followed the others inside, all she wanted to do was turn around and walk right out again. There was something too creepy about the place. It was nothing specific, nothing that she could put her finger on. There were no visible signs that this was other than what it was supposed to be: the home of a techie, filled with all the latest computer, stereo, and video gear. But from the moment she crossed the threshold, she sensed that they were all in danger.

She listened to the others make small talk. Watched Estie and Tip decipher Jackson's computer setup. When Claudette offered to help the landlady get the iced tea, she wished she had the nerve to ask if she could accompany them, but she knew she wouldn't be welcome. Not that she was particularly welcome here in the apartment, either. But at least going with them would have got her out of this room and let her think about something other than the inexplicable foreboding that had taken root in her head.

Finally she had to say something. Estie agreed with her that there was an odd feeling in the air when Suzi expressed her concerns, but then she went right back to talking to Tip about the computer connections. Tip hadn't even looked up.

"Don't worry," Aaran said. He spoke softly so as not to disturb Estie and Tip. "They sound like they know what they're doing."

Do they? Suzi thought.

It didn't feel like it. Nothing felt right about any of this.

"I just . . . I get the sense that something's about to open," she said. "In this room. Maybe in me. Or that . . . I don't know. That something's approaching. Something big, that can't be touched or held. Something . . . dreadful."

She managed to give him a half-smile to show that she knew she was overreacting, but Aaran returned it with a worried look.

Suzi sighed. "Look, I know how stupid this must sound—especially since I was pooh-poohing the whole idea of Internet spirits just a few hours ago."

"It doesn't sound stupid," he told her. "I'm just not sure I understand what you mean. Is it like a premonition?"

"I guess."

She could hear Claudette and Jackson's landlady coming up the stairs behind them. Aaran had turned away from her to listen to what Estie and Tip were saying to each other. It took Suzi a moment to register what the words meant. They rasped inside her like glass, sharp and brittle. The air in the apartment grew more close, almost oppressive.

"No," she said. "You can't bring it here."

But it was too late. She saw that Estie had already connected her laptop to Jackson's system and turned it on.

"Bring what here?" Claudette asked from behind her.

Estie looked up. "We've got another mystery," she said. "Jackson's computer is still on-line, but as Tip's discovered, the ADSL connection is broken."

Tip held up the outside phone jack that he'd disconnected from the router.

"But that's not possible," Claudette said. "Is it?"

Estie shrugged. "Apparently it is. Tip seems to think that by my having connected my laptop to the router, the Wordwood spirit is going to come to us." Her gaze went to Suzi. "And so, it seems, does Suzi."

Tip stood up from behind the desk. Claudette came into the room, with Mrs. Landis trailing behind her. The landlady looked from Suzi to Estie, plainly confused.

"I don't understand," she said. "What do you mean about a spirit?"

"Maybe we should ask Suzi," Estie said. Her gaze stayed locked on Suzi. "What *do* you know about all of this?"

Suzi wanted to bolt. The room was suddenly too small. Too close, too confining. The air too heavy.

"I . . . I don't know anything," she said. "I can just . . . feel something. Like . . . like there are things in the corners of the room that we can't see. Waiting. Watching us . . ."

Oh, just shut up, she told herself. You're sounding like a lunatic.

Except she didn't feel crazy. She *did* feel that they were in danger. It was just that the words to explain it didn't seem to exist.

"It *is* oppressive in here," the landlady said. "We should open a window and see where Jackson keeps his fans. We need to move the air around a little."

"Suzi's not talking about the heat," Estie said. "Are you, Suzi? At least not that kind of heat."

Aaran stepped in between them. "Stop bullying her. It *is* hot in here."

"Sure, it is," Estie said. "We're all hot. But we're not all hiding something."

Suzi's gaze darted from one face to another. They were all staring at her, even Aaran, though at least in his case, it appeared to be out of concern for her. The weight of their combined attention was almost as bad as the sense she had that there was something watching them from the corners of the room.

"I'm not hiding anything," she said. "It's just . . . can't you *feel* it?"

Mrs. Landis stepped forward. "Maybe if you have some of this iced tea."

Suzi stepped back as the landlady held out her tray, offering her a glass.

Why couldn't they feel it? It reached right into her, like it was trying to pull something out of her chest.

But from their expressions, the only thing they sensed was that she was losing it. Maybe she was crazy.

Except there *was* something in the corners of the room—though not what she'd thought at first. There weren't monsters or evil spirits coming for them. It was that the room itself was . . . fraying at the edges.

There was no other way to put it.

She couldn't see the dissolution when she looked directly at any part of the room, but seen from the corners of her eyes the walls and corners were shivering. No longer solid. Unraveling.

It was like the difference between a real photo and a picture in a newspaper. The walls weren't solid like a photograph. Instead they were made of hundreds of tiny dots of colour, all pressed in tight against each other. And now all those tiny dots weren't holding together anymore.

"Suzi . . . ?" Aaran said.

She focused hard on his face. Maybe if she didn't look at anything else, it would all go away. The fraying walls. And this new sensation . . . like something was grabbing at her, reaching deep into her chest . . .

Don't look away from him, she told herself. Focus.

But a mild vertigo slid through her. She swayed and then made the mistake of looking down to keep her balance.

And saw her hands.

She lifted them up, not quite sure what she was seeing.

"Jesus," someone said.

Her hands were unraveling, just like the walls. She could see the molecules that made up her flesh and bone, except they looked more like the pixels of a Web photo with really bad resolution.

She lifted her gaze back to Aaran's face. It was like looking through gauze, as though her eyes were shivering apart, just like her hands.

"What . . ." She could hardly speak. "What's happening to me?"

No one replied. She looked at them, one by one, but they only stared back at her with incomprehension, in horror.

Her own growing panic exploded full-blown.

Her legs crumpled beneath her, but before she hit the floor, a shaft of light burst out of Estie's laptop and darted for the three computer towers around Jackson's desk. Parts of it were blue, others gold, all of it woven together like a braid. In an instant all four machines were connected by it, forming not quite a circle, not quite a square. Then the braid of light sent out a shaft, straight as a laser beam, right for her chest.

There was no time to dodge. No time at all.

At the moment of contact, there was a brief instant where nothing existed for her. The light entered her like a flashlight beam cutting through shadows. It enveloped the pixels that her flesh had become, and she was gone, lost in a soundless void, devoid of any tactile sensation. But almost before she could react to her new environment, that void was gone as suddenly as though a switch had been thrown. She was back in Jackson's apartment, floating a few feet up in the air, and everything was changed.

The flesh and blood world was gone, or if not gone, utterly transformed. This new version of it was like finding herself transported inside a Saturday morning cartoon. Or some computer game with primitive graphics that was making a valiant, though less than successful, attempt at three-dimensionality.

Almost as strange was that her panic had disappeared along with the world as it was supposed to be. Here, in this new version of the world, she was the calm eye in a storm of garish colour, bold linework, and bad animation.

The looks on the faces of her companions now seemed exaggerated, almost comical. She wanted to laugh at Estie and Tip's big round eyes, the exaggerated "O" that was Aaran's mouth. Mrs. Landis appeared to have fainted. She lay in a slapstick sprawl that made her limbs seem to be out of proportion. Claudette stood with her back pressed up against the wall, cartoon hands held defensively in front of her.

But Suzi's humour faded as she returned her attention to the braided bands of gold and blue that still connected her to Estie's computer and Jackson's three towers. The ray had changed from a laser-straight beam to an undulating tendril that felt as much a part of her as her arms and legs. And now it connected her to . . . not so much an orb of light, as a portal of some sort, in which the beams of light had broken up to become pale swirls of blue and gold. Forming in the pattern they made was the impression of a figure, indistinct, but shaped like a human. Beyond the figure she could see endless rows of what looked like bookcases, hundreds of thousands of them disappearing into an infinity point.

"Child," the figure said.

The voice was soft, but resonant. It had a mother's strength, a father's warmth, and that one word it spoke was like a key, unlocking knowledge inside her. She knew who this was, half hidden in the swirl of blues and golds.

It was the spirit of the Wordwood.

At first she thought it was addressing only her, but the same inner knowledge that let her recognize the spirit for who it was also told her that she was only one of many. In other places—she didn't know exactly where, some close, some distant—other people floated in the air just like her, connected to the Wordwood spirit through the closest electronic device and by their own undulating braids of light. They were all individual, but once they had each been a part of this being in its library of light. The life history she remembered had been constructed for her, just as each of the others had had their own life histories constructed for them. They'd been sent out . . . sent out to . . .

It took her a long moment to pull her gaze from the world inside the swirling lights to focus on Aaran's cartoonish features.

They'd been sent out to track down those responsible for the virus that had crippled the Wordwood spirit. Sent out to track them down and bring them to a place such as this, where the spirit itself could have physical access to them.

"Our enemies are found," the spirit said. "You can come home now where I will deal with them, or you may keep your new life. The choice is yours. Consider it payment for how you have helped me."

"What will you do to him?" Suzi found herself asking.

The spirit's gazed settled on her and she knew that it was seeing only her now, not all the other pieces of itself that it had given individuality to and then sent out into the world.

"That remains to be decided," it told her. It paused a moment, then added, "He was not alone."

Suzi nodded. She knew. The spirit had probably found out about both Aaran and Jackson through her.

"I think," the spirit went on, "that I will bring the tenets of the Old Testament to bear upon them. I will do to them what they did to me. Sever all the ties that link their minds to their bodies. The ties that give their thoughts coherence. That link their cells to each other."

"That will kill them," Suzi said.

"Not necessarily. It didn't kill me."

"But you're not human."

"They should have considered that before they began this."

"They didn't know. They thought you were just a Web site."

The spirit regarded her steadily. "Ignorance is a state of being, not an excuse."

A state of being for Aaran and Jackson. And also for her.

A coal of anger began to smolder and glow in her chest. The spirit of the Wordwood had used her, her and all the others it had sent out. Given them lives, identities, made them think they were real. That they had been born, had families, friends. Or in her case, a family and friends that had dissolved into ruined relationships around her. But it had still been *her* history. Her life.

Except it hadn't, had it?

The Wordwood had created perfect moles with her and the others. Spies hidden so deep under cover that even they hadn't known who or what they were until they were activated by the one who had created them and then sent them out. To do what? In her case, it was to betray others the way she'd been betrayed herself. By a violent husband. Family and friends that turned their backs on her. A sister that hated her.

No, she told herself. Those memories weren't real. She had never been betrayed—not unless you counted what the Wordwood spirit had done to her.

Aaran might have been a little shit to other people—what was she saying? Of course he had been. But he hadn't been like that with her and he hadn't betrayed her. He hadn't known what was going to happen when he got Jackson to bring down the Wordwood site. *Who* could have guessed a simple computer virus would cause so much harm? And when he found out, he'd tried to make right.

But it was obvious that the Wordwood spirit didn't see it in the same way. The part of her that was connected to the spirit knew that it wasn't some bookish, kind-hearted being, merely defending itself. It was an amoral creature, reacting to how you interacted with it. Converse with it and it would happily converse back. Use its resources for research and it would open the doors of its virtual library to you.

But attack, and it would strike back. Hard, without consideration of extenuating circumstances.

She doubted that it had ever initiated a single random act of kindness in its life.

"And the others?" she asked. "The people that were pulled into . . . into your world?"

"They are not our concern."

But they were. At least *she* felt they were.

How could that be, if she was only an errant piece of this amoral spirit? Shouldn't she feel the same as it did? Or had she truly become her own person once the Wordwood had sent her out into the world, tied to it only by this service it had needed her to perform?

They weren't questions for which she had answers. She didn't have them now. She might never have them. But she did know one thing.

"You can't have him," she told the spirit.

"How can you stop me?" it replied.

She looked down at the rippling cord of light that bound her to the Wordwood. Reaching down, she found that the braided beams of gold and blue actually had substance. It was like holding onto warm, firm gel that squirmed in her grasp.

"How about if I do this?" she asked.

Tightening her grip, she gave a hard yank.

She hadn't known what to expect. She hadn't even really thought about what she was doing. It was an action born out of frustration and anger, not reason.

The beam broke in two.

Light flared so bright she was blinded and thrown violently backward. She hit the wall behind her, hard enough to knock the breath out of her before she slid down to the floor. But the pain of that was nothing compared to what exploded inside her chest. It felt like something was being torn out of her. Her heart. Her lungs. The hurt was so intense that she blacked out for a moment.

When she opened her eyes, stars flashed in her gaze. But the cartoon world was gone. As was the portal through which she'd accessed the Wordwood spirit.

She took a breath and almost cried at the pain it woke in her chest. Her hands hurt, too—from where she'd gripped the beam of light—but looking down she could see no physical damage. Just as there wasn't a hole in her chest for all that it felt like there should be.

Aaran finally stirred and moved towards her. He still looked a little stunned, but concern for her seemed to be bringing him out of his shock.

"Get . . . we have to . . . get out . . ." she managed to say as he knelt down beside her.

She tried to get up.

"Easy," he told her. "Maybe you shouldn't try to move just yet."

She looked past him. Didn't anybody feel the urgency she did? Tip stood staring at the space where the Wordwood spirit had opened its portal into this world. Estie was white-faced as she looked at her hands, turning them up and down as though to reassure herself that they were flesh once more. Claudette was helping Mrs. Landis to her feet. They acted as though they had all the time in the world.

Suzi wasn't connected to the Wordwood anymore, but that didn't stop her from feeling the approaching storm of the spirit's wrath.

"No, we . . ." She took another painful breath. "We have to get out."

"But—"

"Now!"

Talking so sharply hurt, but at least it galvanized Aaran, if not the others. He helped her stand up and she took a faltering step towards the door. That made Aaran follow her, if only to keep her from falling down.

"Get them out of here," she told him when they reached the doorway.

He nodded. Still holding onto her, he looked back into the room.

"Suzi says we have to get out of here," he said. "Right away."

Estie looked up from her hands to frown at Suzi.

"What did you do to us?" she demanded.

"She didn't do anything," Aaran said. "You saw what happened. It was the spirit of the Wordwood. Suzi saved your ass."

"Saved *your* ass, you mean," Claudette said.

Estie nodded, her hard gaze never leaving Suzi's face. "Where did you take us? What *was* that place?"

"I . . . I didn't . . ." Suzi began.

"Like hell you didn't," Claudette said.

She was supporting Mrs. Landis, much the way Aaran was helping Suzi stay on her feet, but the landlady was in worse shape. She appeared to be shell-shocked, unable to focus on anything. Beside her, Claudette glared at Suzi, the vague animosity she'd shown earlier now full-blown.

Suzi looked away and started to move out into the hall, using the door-jamb, and then the walls, to support herself. The pain in her chest was lessening but it still hurt to breathe too sharply.

"Just . . . just get them out of there," she told Aaran over her shoulder.

"You heard her," Aaran told the others.

"Screw you," Claudette said. "If she says leave, I'm guessing the safest thing we can do is stay right here where we are."

"Suit yourself," Aaran said.

He turned to go into the hall himself.

"No," Suzi said when she saw he was abandoning the others. "We can't just leave them behind."

"We can't force—" Aaran began.

He never got to finish.

Estie's notebook exploded—not in a shower of metal and plastic and circuitry, which would have been bad enough. Instead it was like it had turned into a geyser, spewing out a towering fountain of some thick black fluid. The liquid went straight up from the laptop, moving at such velocity that when it hit the ceiling, it sprayed out over everything in the room, drenching people and furnishings alike. Estie and the others cried out in panic, frantically wiping the black goop from their faces.

Aaran stood in the doorway, dumbstruck for a long moment. Then he started forward, only to be stopped when Suzi grabbed his arm. The sudden movement made her wince with pain, but she knew she had to stop him from going in.

"It's too late," she said. "Remember what happened to the others that got caught in that stuff."

"But—"

"We've got to find higher ground," she said, pointing at how the liquid had pooled onto the floor and was now flooding in their direction.

Aaran nodded, understanding now.

"You're right," he said. "Unless that stuff can move up hill, the stairs are our best bet."

He bent slightly, lifted Suzi behind the knees so that most of her weight was on his shoulder, then staggered to the stairs. He deposited her a few steps up, just before the liquid began to pool against the first riser. They couldn't see into the apartment any more, but they could still hear the sound of the gushing liquid and the cries of those they'd had to leave behind.

Then there was only the sound of the fountaining geyser.

The liquid rose to the top of the first riser and began to flood the second one.

Without speaking, they started up the stairs, Aaran supporting Suzi as they slowly climbed one riser after the other. The light was either turned off or burned out in the halls and stairwell, so their progress was slow and further encumbered by Suzi's pain. The next flight past the third floor wasn't any better.

They didn't stop until they reached the door to the roof. The handle wouldn't move and for a moment they thought it might be locked. Aaran cranked down hard on it, putting his shoulder to the door's metal panel. On his second try, the door popped open with a squeal, and then they were outside on the gravel rooftop. Aaran waited until Suzi was through before he slammed the heavy door behind them.

Twilight had fallen while they were inside, but even its half-light seemed bright after the dark stairwell. The air was humid, still holding the heat of the day, and they both began to perspire—as much from the close air as their recent exertion.

Suzi pressed her hands against her chest. It didn't stop the sharp pain when she breathed, but it helped ease the worst of it—or at least the physical aspect of it. She didn't know if anything would quell the hopeless sense of loss she was also suffering. She bore no love for the Wordwood spirit, had no idea of the connection between them until it had told her. But now that the link had been severed, there was an ache inside that felt ready to swallow her whole.

"Are you okay?" Aaran asked.

She nodded, then led the way to the edge of roof. There was a low wall running around the building and someone had laid down some bamboo mats—for sunbathing, she supposed. She let her knees sink down on them and leaned her forearms on the wall.

"That was horrible," Aaran said. "God, I can't believe how everything's gotten so out of control."

"Things just happen," Suzi said. "You'll go crazy trying to shoulder the blame for everything."

"Except I *did* set this whole thing off."

"You didn't know."

"Like the spirit said, ignorance isn't an excuse."

She couldn't see his face, but she knew how bad he was feeling from his voice.

"It's done," she said. "We should concentrate on what we're going to do now instead of worrying about blame."

"I suppose."

She understood how he felt. After what they'd just been through, it was hard to concentrate on much of anything. For her part, she just wanted to be held for a moment. To have some human contact. To know that she *was* flesh and blood, that she could feel and be felt. But knowing how Aaran had originally felt about her when he'd met her on the street, she didn't think it was such a good idea right now. It would only complicate an already messy day.

"You really did save my life back there," Aaran said suddenly.

Suzi turned from the view to look at him. "You pretty much carried me up the stairs, so I think we're even."

"I meant in the room when . . . when the world went all strange." He paused, his gaze steady on her. "That happened, didn't it? You were floating in the air and everything was like some kind of cartoon?"

She nodded. "I think the spirit pulled the room into some part of cyberspace."

"The spirit. That's what I was talking about. It was going to kill me, wasn't it?"

"It sure looked that way."

"So, thanks."

Suzi shrugged. "You'd have done the same."

"I hope so, but I don't know if I'd have been that brave." There was another pause and she could tell he was deciding whether or not to go on. Finally he did. "What the spirit was saying about you—was all that stuff true?"

"Apparently."

"So then, what . . . ?"

This time he didn't, or couldn't, finish.

"What am I?" she said for him. "I don't know. I feel like an ordinary person. I get dirty. I get hungry. I feel the heat. I feel—" She banged her hand on the wall. "I can feel pain."

"But it's weird . . ."

"No argument there."

Neither of them said anything for awhile. Suzi slid down the side of the wall so that she could lean her back against it. She was hot and sweaty and her heart still beat too fast from their recent escape. Just sitting here, she could feel it hammering in her chest. She wondered how long it would take for that black goop to dissipate so that they could go back downstairs and leave the building.

Aaran came over and stood beside her. He had his back to the roof so that he could take in the view.

"So you never knew?" he said.

She shook her head. "I didn't even have a clue, though I suppose I should have. I mean, I have all of these memories, but except for what I've experienced since yesterday morning, none of them feel . . . immediate. They're just facts with no emotional resonance." She gave a short laugh that didn't hold any humour. "Though who's going to guess that they were only born a day or so ago and that everything they know is only there because it's been loaded into them like software. And then there's the whole physical impossibility of translating something digital into flesh and blood."

"I don't know how you deal with it."

"By trying really hard not to think about it," Suzi said. "Whenever I do, I just want to curl up in a ball in some dark corner and hide away from everything. I mean, talk about being a freak."

"I don't think you're a freak."

"Then you're the exception. Everybody else seems to dislike me the moment they meet me."

She glanced at Aaran when he didn't reply. He was still looking out at the city, but he turned and smiled.

"I was just thinking," he said. "I got a bit of that weird vibe from you—right at the first. Nothing I could put my finger on, but I just knew there was something about you that's—"

"Not human."

"I was going to say different. A kind of dissonance. Maybe it came from the transition you made from digital to flesh and blood."

Suzi gave a slow nod. That made sense. It was something people would sense on an instinctual level.

"Funny thing is," Aaran went on, "the last time I felt that vibe was when I first met Saskia. And she had the same problem you have—people just taking an immediate dislike to her."

"I got the sense that people really like her."

"They do," Aaran said. "That vibe went away after awhile."

"So you think she's like me—born in cyberspace?"

Aaran laughed. "No, I'm guessing you're unique in that."

"But I'm not alone," she said. "The Wordwood spirit created others."

"Then maybe she is like you. Maybe all of the people who disappeared originated in cyberspace and that's why they got pulled back into it so easily."

"Software recall," Suzi said, her voice soft.

Aaran had been looking away again and turned back to her.

"What did you say?" he asked.

"Nothing. What is it you keep looking at out there?"

"Just all these lights."

"Yeah, they're pretty," Suzi agreed. "When you look out across the city at night, you never think of all the mess that's hidden under that pattern of lights."

"I didn't mean the lights from the buildings and street lamps."

She got up and leaned on the wall once more to see what he was talking about. It took her a moment before she saw what he'd been referring to—flashes of blue-gold light, sparking here and there. Not many, but enough, if they were what she thought they were. She noted a half-dozen, raising her count to nine when she spotted a few others she hadn't seen the first time. They were too distant for her to be able to confirm her suspicions, but as she watched, she could see that they were steadily coming their way.

"It's some of the others," she said.

"What others?"

"Like I said, the Wordwood didn't just send me out. It sent out a whole pack of searchers."

Aaran nodded. "That's right. I remember." He looked out at the lights and added, "So are they all like you?"

"Like I was—inside, I mean." She shrugged. "I've no idea what they'll actually look like."

"They're coming for us, aren't they?"

"I'm afraid so."

Aaran turned and sat on the edge of the parapet. "So what do we do now?"

"Get away from here and then don't go near any computer—even if it's off-line."

"But if it's not on-line . . ."

"Remember what happened downstairs?"

"Yeah. But . . . how's that even possible?"

"I don't know," she said. "I think it's like the way the Wordwood spirit made me and the others—as much magic as tech."

"Voodoo spirits," Aaran said.

"Whatever. But it looks to me that the Wordwood spirit can leave pieces of itself in computers that have accessed its site, which, in turn, lets it manifest in that machine whenever it wants."

"So we stay away from computers." He jerked his chin toward the edge of the roof. "What about them?"

"We have to avoid them, obviously. I don't think they can actually track us. I don't feel a connection to either them or the Wordwood anymore, so why would they have one to me? But this is the last place we were seen, so I guess it makes sense that they'd come here."

"We should see if the hallway's clear."

Suzi nodded. "And then make our way back to Holly's store. If nothing else, we have some new information to share."

"God, they're going to hate me even more now," Aaran said.

There was no self-pity in his voice, just a stating of the facts.

"They're going to hate us both," Suzi said, "once they find out the part I played."

"You had no choice—you didn't know."

"Neither did you when you got Jackson to send the virus in the first place."

Aaran nodded. "But that was still an act of meanness. I don't think you have a mean bone in your body."

Suzi wasn't so sure about that. The anger she'd felt earlier toward the Wordwood still frightened her. It had been so intense.

"It doesn't matter what they think of us," she said. "We still have to help all those people who've gotten caught up in this through no fault of their own. And the best way we can do that at this moment is to go back to the store and see if they've had any success."

Aaran nodded. "I'll check the hallway."

Suzi took the opportunity while he was gone to lift her shirt and assess the physical damage that breaking the link to the Wordwood had done, but her abdomen was smooth, the skin not even bruised. The hurt was all inside, physical as well as psychological. She dropped her shirt when Aaran came back out the door, the squeaking hinges giving her plenty of warning.

"It's still a mess down there," he said. "That goop's a couple of inches deep and pouring down into the lobby. But there's an exit to a fire escape just down this first flight of stairs. I had a look and it'll take us right into the side alley."

Suzi looked over the wall. Two or three of the approaching lights were little more than a block away now. Aaran came over as she got to her feet.

"It's okay," she said. "I can move a little easier now."

But she let him take her arm as they walked across the roof back to the door, gravel crunching under their feet. The exit to the fire escape was through a window at the foot of the stairs. Aaran had left it open and they both climbed through, making it down to the pavement without incident.

The alley ran the length of the building, connecting the streets in front and behind the building. Without discussing it, they both headed toward the street at the rear of the building, navigating their way around garbage cans, debris, and a junked car. When they were almost at the street, Suzi took Aaran's arm and leaned her head against his shoulder.

"Just be casual," she said.

"Right."

They ambled out of the alley and looked both ways. Cars were parked along the curb on either side of the street. A van idled by the mouth of an alley across from them and other vehicles were moving on the street. Residents sat on their stoops. A bunch of kids were playing with a hacky-sack, some others were sitting on the sidewalk with their backs against a tenement, sharing what was either a cigarette or a joint. There were no people with blue-gold auras pointing straight up into the sky like searchlights.

"Let's go," Suzi said.

She chose the direction in which she'd seen the fewest approaching lights, still leaning against Aaran's shoulder like they were a couple out for a stroll. They were between stoops when she saw the telltale blue and gold glow at the far corner. Grabbing Aaran, she pushed him against the wall of the tenement.

"Kiss me," she said. "Like you mean it."

"What makes you think I wouldn't?"

She smiled. "Just do it. Now."

She liked the way he held her. She liked the firmness of his lips against hers. She had memories of making out—with old boyfriends, with her husband before he'd turned mean and started treating her like a doormat—but thinking of those occasions called up none of the immediacy of the sweet, weak-kneed sensations she was experiencing now. Because they weren't real. But this was.

She'd almost forgotten why they were kissing when she realized that one of the Wordwood's searchers was standing on the pavement studying them.

She broke off the kiss to look at him. He was of medium height and build with pleasant, if forgettable, features. Without the blue-gold aura, no one would give him a second look. But right now, up and down the street, everybody was staring at him.

She felt nothing from him—no bond, no connection. But he seemed to sense something in her. She decided to brave it out.

"What's your problem, freak?" she demanded.

Aaran had turned with her to look at the man. When she spoke, the muscles in his arm went tight.

Trust me, she wanted to tell him. I know what I'm doing.

Or at least she thought she did.

"Okay," she added when the man made no response except continuing to study them. "You've had a good look, now why don't you go find somebody's birthday cake to stand on?"

"You're not . . . surprised to see someone like me?" the man finally said. "The others—" He indicated the people on the street that were all staring at him with varying degrees of surprise and wonder.

"Jesus," she told him. "You live long enough in this city and you'll see any damn thing. So what? A freak like you with a built-in spotlight is supposed to be something special? I've seen lots weirder."

The man blinked, obviously taken aback by her attitude, which was just what Suzi was aiming for. The Wordwood spirit would have sent its searchers out looking for a man and woman on the run, trying to hide and not make waves.

"I am looking—" the man tried, but she cut him off.

"To get your face rearranged. And you know, looking at you, I don't even think I'll let my boyfriend do it. I figure I can take you all on my own." She stepped away from Aaran and made a pair of fists. "So bring it on, spotlight boy."

The man took a step back.

"That's right," Suzi told him. "Bugger on off to wherever you came from." She linked her arm in Aaran's again. "Come on, Tommy. Let's find someplace we don't have to put up with shitheads like this."

She gave him a tug and they walked off in the direction from which the searcher had come.

" 'Go find somebody's birthday cake to stand on'?" Aaran said softly.

For all his obvious nervousness, she could see a smile pulling at his lips. And they were nice lips, she remembered.

"I didn't hear you complaining back there, 'Tommy,' " she said.

"I couldn't have come close to putting on a show like that." He started to look behind them.

"Don't check him out," she said. "We have to act like we couldn't care less. In fact, let's stop right here and have another kiss—just to show how carefree and guiltless we are."

She stopped and tilted her head.

Aaran smiled. "And is that the only reason?"

She grinned back at him. "That's for me to know and you to find out."

This time when they kissed she let herself melt against him, breasts pressed tight against his chest, her pelvis rubbing against his own growing interest. She almost forgot to steal a glance back the way they'd come. When she did, it was just in time to see the blue-gold aura of the searcher disappear into the alley that ran along Jackson's apartment building.

"God," Aaran said when they came up for air. "You're a complete wanton."

"But that's a good thing, right?"

He nodded.

"So, come on," she said, taking his hand. "We've got a bookstore to visit."

"Don't remind me," Aaran said, but he fell in step beside her.

They'd walked a couple more blocks without passing another searcher. Whether someone was following them was another matter, but Suzi'd been keeping an eye out and she didn't think anyone was.

"Back there," Aaran said.

"Was really nice," Suzi broke in before he could go on. "And who knows? Maybe when this is all over, we can find the time to sneak in a little romance, but what I said before still stands. It'd never work out between us in the long-term—especially not now. When I'm, you know, not just some homeless woman you brought home, but . . . well, who knows what I am?"

"That doesn't matter to me."

"I know. At least it doesn't right now."

He shook his head. "I don't know how to explain this, but ever since I met you, I feel changed. Like I'm a different person and I can't imagine doing the things I've done—not ever again."

"So I'm, what? Your epiphany?" She smiled to take the sting out of her words.

"Is that such a bad thing?" he asked. "But, no. It's more like what you were saying before we left my apartment. How maybe we're each other's guardian angels. At least, I know that you bring out the best in me."

"Maybe it's because I'm willing to believe in you. I get the idea nobody's ever believed in you before—at least not the real you."

He nodded. "That's exactly it. And to tell you the truth, I feel redeemed. I don't mean that suddenly everything's okay," he added quickly. "I know I've got a lot to atone for. I've left behind a history of a lot of damage and we're not just talking about the current fiasco. But now I *want* to do better. I want to make up for the wrongs I've done. And I don't want to repeat them. The only thing is . . . ."

"You don't think you can do it without me?"

That earned her a smile. "No, I was going to say I don't know that I'll get the chance to make it up to a lot of people—that anybody's going to be willing to give me another shot."

"That's the hardest part," Suzi said. "Carrying on with your good intentions even when no one believes that you mean them."

Aaran nodded. "I guess it will be. But none of that's where you come in."

"Where *do* I come in?" Suzi asked.

She didn't mean to, but she couldn't help being flirty as she spoke.

"I just think we're good for each other," Aaran said. "That maybe we really can be each other's guardian angels. I don't mean or expect some lifetime commitment. I'd just like to think that as soon as this is done, you're not going to just walk out of my life and I'll never see you again. I'd like to get to know you better."

"I'm not going to make any promises."

"No promises," Aaran agreed. "But tell me you won't close the door either."

Suzi smiled. "No door closings, either."

They were so busy talking that they didn't notice that they'd reached Williamson Street until they were right upon it. A northbound bus pulled into a stop directly ahead of them. Suzi looked around, but there were no blue-gold auras in sight. Maybe they'd toned them back down again. Or maybe all the searchers were still milling around in Jackson's apartment building.

"Will this take us up to Holly's store?" she asked.

Aaran checked the bus number and nodded.

"I think we should just leave things where they stand," Suzi said. "With you and me, I mean. Right now it's time to go face the music."

But she took his hand while they waited in line to board the bus.

Christy

I've been writing about the unexplained for over half my life now. Of spirits and mysteries, hauntings and haunted places. Of ghosts and fairies and goblins. Of hidden races of curious beings that live both in the wilds and right under our noses in the city—some whimsical, some dangerous, all strange.

But I don't have much actual hands-on experience.

Sure, Tallulah, one of my first serious girlfriends, turned out to be the literal spirit of this city. And Saskia was born in a Web site—maybe the same one into which she's disappeared again. But these are only words. Anyone can *say* they're whomever or whatever. I never actually saw Tallulah do anything more inexplicable than make me feel like I was floating on air whenever we were together—and you know, that's what love does. And until Saskia vanished right before my eyes, she never exhibited any mysteries that couldn't also be explained away with a more mundane rationale.

What I'm trying to say is that I don't hobnob with the otherworldly the way my readers think I do. The first time Wendy used that little magical red stone of hers, opening a threshold into the otherworld, where a doorway leading into the professor's kitchen was supposed to be, I was so overcome with the sheer impossibility of it that I literally went numb. For a long moment, I couldn't move, couldn't even think. My head felt like it was stuffed with cotton batting.

Wendy offered me her hand and said something I couldn't hear. But I understood. She was asking me to join her as she stepped through the arch of the kitchen door into this stunning vista of red rock canyons. It took me awhile before I was finally able to reply. But the bigshot writer, as Geordie likes to call me, so rarely at a loss for words, could only shake his head.

No one could understand why I declined to cross over, except maybe for Jilly. But it's like I told Geordie last night, what interests me about these kinds of phenomena centers around how they interact with the World As It Is, and how those of us living here react to these intrusions. I don't like the idea of a mundane world, devoid of wonder or mystery. But I know I wouldn't be any happier in a world where it's all wonder and mystery.

Up to that moment, I'd always been equal parts skeptic and believer. That might also explain the success of my books. My readers see that in me: The skeptics think I agree with them, but isn't it interesting to consider anyway? And the believers just assume I'm in their camp, only more experienced than most of them.

I guess now I am.

I hear the sound of the hellhounds again. Closer.

And once again I'd just as soon decline the invitation to step into the unknown territories of the otherworld. But I've got Saskia to think about now.

"Let it go," Bojo says.

Robert shakes his head and keeps playing his guitar. That music of his could make angels swap their celestial harps for a blues harp, just to try to capture even an echo of what he's calling up. It's earthy and slinky. It's a gospel choir wrapping their voices around a twelve-bar blues. It promises and it delivers. It reaches right inside to your most private place and says, I know you. I know your pain, but I know your joy, too.

I don't doubt that he can call up any damn thing he wants with it—not just some doorway into an errant Web site, hidden away in a digital version of Never-never Land.

Trouble is, we've just discovered that we're not the only ones listening.

The hellhounds bay, closer still.

"I'm telling you," Bojo says. "You've got to let it go."

Robert doesn't even look at him. "Hell, no," he says. "We're almost there. I can pretty much taste that Wordwood spirit."

"You don't stop playing," Bojo tells him, "the only tasting that'll go on here is the hellhounds taking a bite out of you."

I glance at Raul and he's looking more nervous than I am and that's not easy, considering how I'm feeling. Over by the stairs, Dick is hiding his face in his hands. Geordie and Holly are staring wide-eyed at the shimmering wall behind me. Snippet's trying to be invisible and fierce, all at the same time, and not doing a good job of either.

"We've got time," Robert says. "You just open that door when I tell you."

"Oh, yeah, time," an unfamiliar voice says from behind me. "Funny how it works. Sometimes it moves like molasses and you've got all you might ever need to do any damn thing at all."

I turn slowly, realizing now that Geordie and Holly weren't just looking at the shimmer of the wall. Three men are standing there—having stepped right out of the wall, I guess, because they certainly didn't come down the stairs.

Up until this moment, the biggest, darkest-skinned black man I've ever seen is Lucius Portsmouth, this friend of the professor's that Jilly says is the raven uncle of the crow girls, her personal favorite of the animal people that figure in local folklore and stories.

These men are as big, but where Lucius reminds me of a serene, black Buddha, our uninvited guests are grim-faced, with a mean look in their eyes, and they're built like weightlifters or linebackers, seeming as wide across the shoulders as they are tall. Their skin isn't just black, it's pure ebony—that absence of light you find in the heart of a shadow. Like Robert, they're wearing suits, only theirs are solid black broadcloth, with white shirts, narrow black ties, and fancy, tooled leather boots.

One of them shifts his foot and I hear what sounds like the low, deep-throated growl of a hunting hound. Snippet whimpers and burrows his head against Holly's leg.

"And sometimes," says that same unfamiliar voice I first heard, but now I can see it's coming from the man standing in the center of the three, "time goes by so fast you never can catch up with anything."

Robert holds his guitar by the neck and stands up to face the men.

"This has got nothing to do with anybody but you and me," he says. "Don't you go bothering these folks."

"They're with you, aren't they?"

There's absolute menace in that voice, despite its mild tone. Another of the men shifts his feet and again I hear a low, throaty growl. That's when I realize that *these* are the hellhounds. I don't know if they're shapechangers, animal people like Jilly loves to talk about, or something else again. The only thing I'm sure of is that they're dangerous and we're in big trouble.

But Robert doesn't concede one iota of defeat. He stands there stiff-backed, radiating strength, guitar dangling from his left hand. He slips his other under the front panel of his suit coat.

"I'm only telling you this one more time," he says. "Maybe we have ourselves a difference of opinion, but don't go dragging anybody else into this business."

"Or you'll what? Pull out that old Colt of yours and try to shoot me? After all these years, do you really think something like that can stop us?"

"That your final word?" Robert asks, his voice as mild, but as full of threat as the hellhound's.

"What do you think?"

"I just need to hear you say it, plain and clear."

The hellhounds' spokesman looks left and right, grinning at his companions, before he turns back to reply.

"Then I'm saying it," he tells Robert. "All your lives are forfeit."

Robert just smiles. "I was hoping that'd be the case."

That earns him as puzzled a look from the hellhounds as I know we've got on our faces, but Robert keeps smiling. The hand that we all thought was reaching under his jacket for a weapon comes out empty. He hefts his guitar in front of him and when he pulls a chord from that old Gibson of his, I swear the brick walls shiver around us. The concrete trembles at our feet. The hellhounds make like it's no big deal, but I can tell they're running down a list of what Robert's got planned. They know he's up to something, but they can't figure out what, any more than I can.

But Robert just pulls another chord from his guitar—a minor chord, rumbling with dark promise—and turns his back on them to look at us.

"I should explain something to you," he says. "What we've got here are some of *les baka mal*, hellhound spirits who like to lay proprietary claim to *les carrefours*—or at least they will at whatever crossroads they think Legba isn't watching. These particular ones have stolen the names of the three Rada drums for themselves. Guy in the middle calls himself Maman. The other two are Bula and Seconde."

I can't believe he's taking this time-out to fill us in. I give the hellhounds a nervous look over Robert's shoulder, but they still seem confused. The two on either side of the one Robert called Maman are trying to get his attention. He ignores them, his gaze fixed on the back of Robert's head. Behind his eyes, you can tell his mind is still in overtime, trying to work out what Robert's up to.

Well, the hellhounds and me both.

"They know about this engagement I've made with Legba," Robert's saying like none of this is any big deal. "I'm not going into the whys and wherefores. All you've got to know about that part of our pact is that I can't defend myself against *les baka mal*. It's why I work so hard to keep out of their way. They're not more powerful than me. My problem is that I can't break my word to Legba and raise a hand against them. If I do, dying's the least of my worries. Legba won't just have my soul, he'll have it in pieces."

Now he finally turns back to the hellhounds.

"But what you forgot, Maman," he says to the lead hellhound, "is that Legba never said anything about me not being allowed to defend somebody else from your kind."

The understanding comes to them at the same time as I get it. Whatever this deal between Robert and Legba is, it left Robert helpless against the hellhounds—*unless* they happen to threaten someone else.

I can see their indecision. Attack, or break and make a run for it? I wonder that they even hesitate. There's three of them. We might outnumber them, but except for Bojo, not one of us looks like much of a fighter. Doesn't mean we won't try—at least I know Geordie and I will. Our brother Paddy taught us a long time ago: You may get the crap beat out of you, but it's better to go down fighting than not stand up at all. Funny thing is, once or twice, I've even come out still standing on my own two feet.

But it doesn't come down to that.

"We're not alone," Maman says. "You know how many hounds are out there on the wild roads?"

Robert nods. "But you're alone right now."

"We can have a pack on your ass so fast—"

Robert breaks in. "But you've got to be alive long enough to call them down on me."

I don't see the man on the left of Maman draw the knife. One moment his hand's empty, the next there's a length of pointed steel flashing through the air at Robert. Robert manages to pull another chord and lift the body of the guitar at the same time. The knife bites into the wood, setting up a discordant echo to an already dissonant music. Something dark starts to take shape in the space between the *les baka mal* and Robert. The hellhounds hesitate a moment longer, then they turn and make their escape through the hole in the basement wall behind them.

"I can't let them go," Robert tell us. "I do and they'll be back ten times as strong and there'll be no finessing our way out of that encounter."

Bojo takes a step forward. "But you can't just go on your—"

"That place we're looking for is close," Robert says, interrupting. "You should be able to find it."

He pulls the knife from his guitar and drops it on the floor, then starts for the hole where the hellhounds disappeared.

"Robert!" Bojo calls after him.

The bluesman stops at the edge of the hole and looks back.

"You don't understand," he says. "That was my one ace-in-the-hole—that they'd come on me when I was with someone else and they'd threaten whoever I was with. Unless I stop those three, I can't use it again."

"But—"

Robert shakes his head. "They weren't lying. They've been hunting me a long, long time and now I've gone and put them on the run. That's something they'll never forget or forgive. Give them half a chance and they really will have an army down on us. And let me tell you, they'll be wanting you as much as me, seeing as you were here to witness it all."

And then he's gone.

Silence fills the basement.

You ever have that moment when you just *know* what's going to happen? I *know* everyone's going to start talking at once. We're going to be divided on whether we follow Robert or proceed with our initial undertaking. I can feel it coming and I'm trying to decide how to forestall it when we hear a hammering on the front door of the store upstairs.

Our reaction time is still molasses slow. Finally Geordie says, "I'll go see who it is."

I nod. When he starts up the stairs, I look over to where Bojo's picking up the hellhound's knife. His gaze rises from the polished blade to meet my own.

"We can't just let Robert go after them on his own," he says as he stands up.

"I don't see that we have a choice," I tell him. "There are a lot of people trapped somewhere in the Wordwood and I get the feeling that we're their only hope of ever getting back."

"Yeah, but—"

"He looked like he thought he could take care of it. I don't know much about Robert, but if the reaction of those hellhounds is any indication, I'm guessing he's not just some snappy dresser who plays a mean guitar. Those men were . . . if not scared, certainly nervous. I didn't see them sticking around."

"I suppose."

Holly comes walking up with Snippet in her arms. I get the sense that if she put the little dog down, Snippet would be up the stairs as fast as her legs could carry her. Dick's still sitting on a riser, shoulder pressed up against the wall, eyes large. Raul stands beside me and his eyes seem almost as big. I can feel the nervousness still coming off him in waves. Or maybe it's only my own anxiety that I'm feeling.

Holly steps by us to take a closer look at the opening in the wall with its shimmering edges. There's an odd optical illusion at work because not only can you see the wall, but you can also see what's on the other side of it, the two images seeming to occupy the same space.

The other side appears innocuous. We're looking at a moonlit cross-roads, but all that are crossing here are a pair of narrow footpaths with an old oak tree towering above the spot where they meet. There's a heap of stones under the tree and a hint of forest and fields beyond.

But the hellhounds came out of that world we're looking in on, so I know it's not as innocent as it seems. And being a crossroads . . . didn't Robert say Legba hung around them?

Voudoun's not a major study of mine, but I recognize the name. Legba is one of their *loa*—the god of gates and crossroads. All the ceremonies begin with a salute to him because he embodies the principle of crossing, of communicating with the divine world. He's usually depicted with a cane and a tall hat, and his brother is Baron Samedi, the *loa* of the dead.

I don't know that I want to meet either of them.

"I can't believe this is real," Holly says.

"Welcome to the weird world," I tell her.

She turns to look at me. "I guess this is old hat for you, but I have to tell you that it's giving me the major heebie-jeebies."

I shake my head. "I just write about it. I can count my actual experiences on one hand. Bojo's the only expert we have left."

But he shakes his head. "Keep a low profile is the tinker's way. When we're in your towns, we stay clear of the sheriffs and lawmen. In the other-world, we stay away from the spirits. The more powerful they are, the less I want to do with them, and *there's* the real trick."

"What's that?" Raul asks.

"Figuring out how powerful they are. Some of the smaller, more harm-less looking ones, are actually the most powerful. The best thing is to avoid them all if you can."

"That hole . . . portal," I say, pointing to the opening in the wall with its shimmering edges. "How long is it going to be there?"

"I can keep it open," he says. "Robert's music was like a cardsharp shuffling a deck, honing in on the place we want to get to. We needed the music to find the Wordwood because I've never been there, but that's not the only way. Trial and error works, too. It just takes a lot longer. The otherworld's a big place—you can't imagine how big a place. The worlds it contains fold in on themselves so that there are places where one step can take you through three or four of them, and you won't even know it without a guide."

"So without Robert, we're screwed."

Bojo shakes his head.

"If he says we're close, we should be able to find it now on our own, without magic. It'll take longer than it might have with Robert's help, but not as long as it would have without his getting us this far."

I feel a clock ticking in my head—it's been there ever since Saskia was taken away from my study. Each passing moment without her, this world, the World As It Is as the professor likes to call it, feels emptier and emptier. And I can't shake the fear that the longer she's gone, the less chance we'll have of getting her back. Of getting any of them back.

I nod. "We've got to go on."

"We will," Bojo tells me.

He's about to say more, but then we hear footsteps at the top of the stairs. We turn to see Geordie leading Aaran and his friend Suzi down to where we're all gathered.

"Apparently we've got more problems," Geordie says.

My heart sinks as Aaran and Suzi relate what happened at Jackson's apartment. And I have to admit that my earlier suspicions about them aren't put to rest by their story. Suzi's like Saskia, a part of the Wordwood? They managed to escape while the others were taken away? Aaran's genuinely remorseful?

"So you just got away?" Geordie says, putting into words what I guess we're all feeling.

"They wouldn't listen to us," Aaran says. "To Suzi."

I can see how it wouldn't have been their fault—*if* things went the way they said they had.

"And there are more of these . . . scouts?" Bojo asks.

Geordie gives me a look, and I know what he's thinking, but I only shrug. I really don't see what talking about Saskia's origin is going to add to the discussion at this point. But I can't let it completely go. Not when I know how it was for Saskia and seeing that strong suspicion towards Suzi that's on Holly, Raul and Bojo's faces. Dick's still on the stairs, so I can't judge his reaction.

"They aren't necessarily the enemy," I find myself saying. I feel confident telling them that, because Saskia certainly isn't. "I mean, think about it. They can only operate on the information that they've been fed by the Wordwood spirit. There's a good chance that, given the whole story, they'll come over to our side. Suzi's proved that."

Suzi gives me a grateful look, which just makes me feel guilty. I'm expressing a faith in her that I don't feel—it's based on Saskia and the fact that it seems as though they have a similar origin.

But they all accept what I'm saying—one of the benefits of being considered an expert in this sort of thing, I suppose. Though with all the complications that keep cropping up on us, and none of us with a clear idea as to what they mean or what to do about them, I feel about as far from an expert as any of them.

"What can you tell us about the Wordwood?" I ask Suzi. "Do you know if the spirit has any weaknesses we can exploit?"

"I don't really know a lot about either of them," she says. "It's . . ." She gives a small nervous laugh. "It's really weird. I mean, I only just found out what I am, that all these memories I have of a life have been put in my head. When I actually stop and think about it, I feel like I'm insane."

"I understand."

She cocks her head and studies me for a moment. "You know, I think maybe you do."

"So you can't give us anything that might help?" Bojo asks.

She sighs. "The problem is, once I found out what I am, I did gain some memories of what it was like in the Wordwood. But I don't remember it as an awful place. When I think about it, I get this really strong impression of knowledge and peace. I . . ." She looks at us, one by one. "You'll probably think I'm just saying this, but I don't think the Wordwood spirit is bad. The virus is doing this to it. Instead of making plans on how to fight it, we should be trying to figure out how to heal it."

"Any ideas on that?" I ask.

She shakes her head. "And the encounter I had with it in Jackson's apartment doesn't add a whole lot of credibility to my theory. But I can't shake the feeling that what I met there wasn't all of it. It's like the thought-fulness and kindness I feel when I think of the place I came from have been buried by this new cruel and vengeful persona. That it's put the good in itself aside so that it can take its revenge without having to argue with a conscience."

I find myself thinking of the red-haired woman who visits me from time to time, the one who claims that she's all the pieces of me that I didn't want when I was a kid.

"Like a shadow," I say, and I explain Jung's theory without going into the experiences I've had with my own shadow.

Suzi's nodding as I talk.

"Isn't that possible?" She looks from me to the others. "Couldn't that be what happened to the Wordwood spirit?"

"Well, they say that spirits are much like us," Bojo says, "only the canvas of their lives is bigger."

I pick up my pack from where I placed it on the floor earlier and swing it to my back.

"We're just going to have to play it by ear," I say. "I don't want anybody to get hurt, but I'm not coming back without Saskia and as many of the others as we can find."

Bojo looks at the knife in his hand. He gets a shirt out of his own small shoulder bag. Wrapping the knife in it, he stows it away in his bag and stands up. Raul's already waiting by the portal in the wall. He doesn't look any happier than I feel, but just like me, he's got someone in there that he's not coming back without. I don't know if we're brave or stupid; I just know it's something we have to do.

"We're coming," Suzi says.

I hesitate as she and Aaran approach the wall, as well.

"I know you don't trust us," Aaran says, "or at least me, but it's something I have to do."

It's weird how his words echo my thoughts of a moment ago.

"Think of us as the spear-carriers," he goes on. "If you lose anybody on an adventure, the spear-carriers always go first. So that'll give you that much of a better chance to get out yourselves."

"If that's the case," Suzi says, "I wouldn't mind having an actual spear to bring along."

I look at Bojo and Raul and they both shrug, leaving it up to me. My gaze returns to Aaran and Suzi.

"Let's go," I tell them.

I don't want any long goodbyes. I don't want to think about what I'm doing, where we're going. So I give a quick wave of my hand to my brother, to Holly and Dick. Then I turn and step through the wall.

Christiana

I feel like we're caught between all that's good and all that can go wrong, that this ruined building in the Wordwood site stands right on some precarious border where Heaven meets Hell.

The spiraling rush of blue-gold light bursting out of Saskia's limp body pierces the sky like a searchlight, casting a shimmering glow over everything. Highlights sparkle and flicker in the wiry lichen underfoot and flash on the low metal walls of the foundations around us. It makes for an astonishing glamour, as glorious in its own way as some of the fairylands I've seen across the borders. But all its bright wonder is sharply contrasted by the virus, manifesting here in the shape of the leeches, black and slick, reeking of sulfur and burnt wiring and hot metal.

It doesn't feel right. Somehow it's worse being bathed in this amazing light as the virus is about to kill us.

As though echoing my own dismay, I hear Saskia cry in my head, a long aching wail. She was plugged back into the Wordwood when the light first burst from her—connected again, if only for a few brief moments, to that long-severed link that once bound her to the Wordwood's vast library of knowledge and the beatific spirit of the wood itself. It was as though she'd been taken back to those first few months after the spirit had created her, when she was still newly-arrived in the consensual world and could readily access the Wordwood's knowledge with no more than a thought.

The cry she makes at that brief familiar connection is involuntary. She tells me that it wasn't that she wanted to be a part of it again—surprise simply pulled it out of her—but at the same time, she can't deny a sense of regret for what's now gone.

I suppose it's like coming out of the womb a second time . . . when you want to stay where it's warm and safe, but you're longing for the world outside at the same time. I can still remember that feeling, back when I was a baby boy—or at least a part of a boy.

But Saskia says it's more like the comfort Christy knows when he's researching a project and finally has all the material on hand. He doesn't *know* it all, but he knows how and where to access it, and that's what gives him the confidence to actually start writing. When she was connected to the Wordwood, she had this unlimited access to pretty much anything she needed to know about the world, which, in the face of all the unpleasantness she faced in those first few months, was what helped give her the confidence to become who she is.

So I've got Saskia wailing in my head. There's the pillar of light, impossibly tall and bright and awesome. There's Jackson falling apart beside me, head whipping back and forth, desperately looking for some way to escape, only there's nowhere to go. And then there's the virus, slagging its way through the walls on all sides, coming right for us.

I hesitate for a moment, then reach into the light and cradle Saskia's body to my chest. That's when I discover that the light wasn't so much coming from the body, as somehow shining right through it, because the pillar of light continues to stream up just as it did before. The only difference is Saskia—or at least her body—isn't part of it anymore.

I rock the body gently and try not to think of much of anything. I know there's nothing I can do to stop the sliders, but they're still going to have to go through me first to get at her.

It's funny. I almost expected the light to burn, but it was cool to the touch. Saskia's body still is. It seems to weigh nothing—no more than a gentle thought, or a dream. She's gone quiet in my head as well, her presence like a feather.

I turn to face the nearest of the sliders. I've always said that when the time came, I'd look my death in the eye and not turn my face away. I'm a little surprised to find myself actually able to do it, now that the moment's here.

<I'm so sorry to have gotten you into all of this,> Saskia says.

I'm glad to have her back again.

It's been weird, I tell her—like having her talking in my head while her body lies limp in my arms isn't—*but I'm still glad I met you.*

And that should have been it. The virus should have been upon us and we would have come to the end of our story.

But a moment after I've taken the body in my arms, I feel a change in the light. I can't exactly explain what. It's not the temperature or brightness—more in its . . . mass, if that makes any sense. It goes from an intangible radiance to something with actual physical presence. But while that presence has no more physical weight behind it than the touch of a feather as it brushes my skin, its effect on everything around me is far different.

Glowing waves of the gold and blue light spill from the pillar, waves that undulate and wash over me before they travel on. Whatever they touch regains its normal form and colour. The lichen goes from dense fine wiring to vegetation, pale green and yellow. The stones change from metal to natural rock, mottled and patched with moss. Jackson becomes a regular black man, his dark hair tinged with highlights of red, his skin all these wonderful hues of mocha and chocolate brown.

And the river of light continues to spread out, wave after wave. A waxing tide of radiance.

The light envelopes the leeches, washing over their slick black bodies and melting the virus creatures away. The immense threat they presented only moments ago vanishes with their disappearance. And still the light continues to spread. The ruins of the building explode with colour—you never know how much colour there is in grey stone until you see it go from black and white to the way it really is. I guess you don't normally pay attention to that kind of thing, but I'm sure paying attention right now.

I lay Saskia's body gently down on the lichen and stand up. I'm about to ask Jackson to give me a hand getting her out of the building when everything shimmers, like in a heat mirage, and the building goes away, just like that. It dissipates into the ground, like it was never there. For a long moment we're still on the crest of that high hill we climbed what seems days ago. We can see the light washing over the forests on all sides, leaving wave after wave of colour in its wake.

Then, like it's all part of some stately gavotte, the hill begins to sink, its heights lowering until we're standing in a large glade that's at the same elevation as the rest of the landscape. Trees rise up out of the ground as smoothly and naturally as when the foundation of the building melted away earlier. It's like watching one of those time-lapsed nature documentaries where the bud opens into a full blossom in moments, except these are trees, growing from sprigs with a leaf or two, to what look like hundred-year-old giants in moments.

My legs have a bit of a jelly-feel to them—the way they can when you step back onto land after a long boat ride. There's a smell in the air of old forest. Mossy and a little damp, earthy. It reminds me of when I first crossed into the otherworld with Mumbo, when everything was still so marvelous and I was just a little tomboy of a girl, my ball-shaped companion rolling along at my side, propelling herself with her long spindly limbs. We spent a lot of time in that old forest in those days. Mumbo called it the Greatwood and told me it's the closest echo there is of the First Forest, that vast tract of ancient wood that Raven supposedly called up out of the darkness when he made the world.

This cyber wood feels like that forest did. It has the smells and resonance of a close echo to the First Forest, except I sense an undercurrent of something foreign running underneath what I can physically sense and feel. I suppose it's a digital pulse. The fact that I know everything I'm experiencing has its actual origin in binary code. But knowing that doesn't lessen any of the wonder I experience as this enormous forest forms around us.

<What . . . what's happening . . . ?> Saskia says.

I have no idea, I tell her.

I stand there with my mouth open for the longest time, then I finally turn to Jackson. But before I can speak to him, rooty vines come snaking from the ground to wrap themselves around our legs. They hoist Jackson up and tie him to the nearest tree, so that he's hanging there, limp. The bottoms of his feet are a couple of yards off the ground, and he's not even trying to get free. I guess he was already in shock from our escape from the leeches and the transformation of the ruined hilltop foundation into this forest.

I don't struggle either, although in my case it's because the vines can't seem to find a hold on my legs. They keep sliding off like my calves and ankles are covered with a film of grease, allowing them no purchase. But that doesn't stop me from being majorly creeped as they continue to writhe around my feet and try to crawl up my legs.

I step away from them, moving closer to Saskia's body which they're not trying to grab at all. They follow, new vines slinking their way out of the ground, but none of them can hold me.

Why can't they get a grip? I ask Saskia.

Not that I'm complaining. I don't want to suffer Jackson's fate, trussed up in a tree like a spider's prey.

<I don't know,> Saskia says.

Maybe it's because I'm not real.

<Or maybe it's because you began life as a shadow.>

Same difference, I want to say. And I'm still a shadow, no matter how much I like to pretend that my life is now my own. Considering my origin, how can I ever be anything but?

I keep my thoughts to myself. These days, neither Saskia nor I am all that strong on the self-confidence front—at least, not when it comes to what sort of beings we are. Animal, vegetable, mineral. Or just make-believe. Pick one.

So I just say, *Maybe.*

Neither of us is really feeling all that coherent either—or at least I sure don't. I've been in some strange places in the otherworld, but nothing to compare to this. It's like we've fallen down some cyber version of Alice's rabbit hole, where nothing makes sense anymore. I'm waiting on the Cheshire cat or an army of playing cards to drag us away to the Queen's court for judgment. All I get are the vines. They keep crawling up my ankles and I have to kick them away. I hate the feel of them as they crawl up under my jeans, the rough sound as they rub against the coarse fabric.

My gaze goes to where Jackson's hanging from the tree. He can't talk because his mouth is full of leaves now, but his panicked eyes are more than eloquent enough to get his message across. He reminds me of the Green Men, forest spirits I've met in the Greatwood from time to time. Root-and-leaf people like the Green Knight in his wooden armor, riding a red-flanked stag, or the Jill-in-the-Wood with her bird's-nest hair and cloak of leaves—except they're born of the green sap and they run free. They're not trapped and hanging from the trunk of some tree the way Jackson is.

His eyes plead with me to get him down.

I'm torn between staying with Saskia's body and going to see if I can help him. So far, the vines are still ignoring her limp body, but I'm not sure how long that's going to last. Do I want to risk losing her to them while I try to give Jackson a hand? It's not like I owe him anything. After all, he's the one that got us into this mess in the first place.

But he's a handsome man and I can be a sucker for a handsome man.

<We can't just leave him hanging there,> Saskia says when I put the question to her. As I expected, her heart's so big she's full of indignation that I'd even consider such an uncharitable course.

And if the vines go after your body while we're cutting him down?

<Oh, yeah . . . >

I've been standing, facing Jackson. Now that my initial surprise at the transformation of our surroundings is over, I realize that there's still a blue-gold glow on everything—cast by that pillar of light, I suppose. I turn to look at it, only to find that it's been transformed, as well.

There's a man there. Or at least the pillar has taken on the form of a man, but there's no way he's human, not radiating light the way he is.

There's only one person he can be: the spirit of the Wordwood.

I'm not sure what I expected him to look like, but it certainly wasn't this. Pressed, I'd have said an angel or a monster because, from other experiences I've had in the otherworld, that's the way these beings usually manifest. They come in all shapes and sizes, of course, but in the end they will invariably be something to either wake awe, or strike terror. Which is why I try to avoid them. Too many of them are just these big picture beings with little or no consideration for the small concerns of the likes of you and me. Unless we get in their way, and then they can be merciless.

I'm not saying they're always like that. And to be fair, most of the scary ones are more like forces of nature, so we really shouldn't try to put our own concepts of ethics and morality on them. That'd be like criticizing a tornado or the winter for being what it is. You can't, though it shouldn't make you any less cautious around them. I can understand a storm, but that doesn't mean I want to go out and tromp around in the middle of it.

But I'm getting way off the point. The real point here is that the Wordwood spirit has chosen to appear as the stereotypical image of a male librarian—you know, the lifelong bachelor—slight, a little stooped at the shoulders, wispy hair, white shirt with tweed vest and trousers, wire-frame glasses. I'd smile, but the fact is, no matter what he looks like, he's still made of blue-gold light. He's still a powerful spirit.

I find myself wondering if this is what he really looks like, or if it's just some mask he's put on—the same way that this forest around us masks the binary code lying at its heart. And if it is a mask, then what's it for? I doubt it's to put us at our ease, because he doesn't even acknowledge our presence. All of his attention is on Jackson, hanging there in the tree.

"So," the spirit says to him. "We have one of you, at least."

I look around to see if the spirit has companions, but except for the writhing roots and vines, he seems to be on his own. He must be using the royal we.

Jackson's only response to the spirit's attention is a glassy-eyed stare—that's all it can be, I guess, what with his mouth still full of leaves—but the spirit doesn't seem to care much about his captive's lack of response. And he certainly doesn't go on to acknowledge that I'm here either, standing a half-dozen yards away with Saskia's body lying at my feet and her spirit in my head.

It's probably better that he's not paying any attention to us. Unfortunately, I can't leave it at that. We have questions that need answers, and this spirit in his guise of a glowing little librarian man is all we have at hand to give them to us. Considering what happened to Jackson, I'd just as soon stay unnoticed. But I don't see it as an option. Not if we want to get Saskia back into her body and the both of us out of this place.

I take a steadying breath to gather my courage.

One thing I've learned about these otherworld spirits is, if you want them to take you seriously, you have to come to them like an equal. It's different if they're the figurehead of some religion that you follow. Then the respectful follower route is a good choice: bended knee, cast-down gaze, that sort of thing. But that isn't the case here. I like books, but I don't worship them.

"Hey," I say. "You with the glow."

It's a good thing I've never been shy. Saskia would probably add cautious and smart to that.

<Christiana!> Saskia says in my head. <Don't get him angry.>

There she is, right on cue.

Relax, I tell her. *I know what I'm doing.*

The spirit turns to me. More roots and vines burst from the ground at my feet, trying to wrap themselves around me, but they can't get any better purchase on me than the others did—the ones that were in automatic snatch-and-grab mode, I guess.

"This is curious," the spirit says.

I'm hoping he doesn't start referring to himself in the third person. I hate it when they do that, although it can be a good way to find out their name.

"You're telling me," I say. "One moment I'm home, minding my own business, and the next I find myself in this place, wherever *it* is."

"I was referring to your presence here."

"Yeah, well, it's not my idea of a good time, either. Think you can point me to the quickest route out of here?"

"What makes you think I will let you leave?"

I offer him my cockiest smile and give the vegetation still moving around at my feet a little kick.

"What makes you think you can stop me?" I ask.

I can feel Saskia vibrating in my head, just waiting for him to do something horrible to us. I have to admit, I half expect it myself. But I've got this going for me: there are a lot of different spirits in the otherworld, some, despite their appearance, far more powerful than others. No one knows them all. So even for a spirit such as the one glowing in front of me, it pays to be a little cautious. I could be just what I am, though he doesn't know it: the shadow of a seven-year-old boy grown up now in my own right. Or I could be some old creation spirit, slumming in the shape of a young woman.

You can't tell, just by looking.

The spirit's been studying me. Now his gaze drops to Saskia's body.

"I know that woman," he says.

"Wouldn't surprise me," I tell him. "I think she's from around here, originally. But right now there's nobody home."

The spirit nods. "But she is near. In the Web, if not somewhere in this particular site."

Close, but no cigar. Then I think about what he said and realize he's just confirmed that we're in the Wordwood site. I know, I know. No big surprise since we'd pretty much worked that out on our own. Still, it's good to have the corroboration. The question now is, is the Wordwood a part of the otherworld, or somewhere else again. And how do we get out of here?

But I figure since his attention's on Saskia at the moment, I might as well work on the other half of our problem.

"Have you ever seen this kind of thing before?" I ask him. "Where the spirit is gone, but the body's still alive?"

He gives me what I feel is a reluctant shake of his head and that makes me reconsider his standing. Maybe he's not such an old spirit. Maybe he just came into being when the Wordwood did. He could have been floating in whatever netherworld spirits float around in before they manifest, just waiting to attach himself to something. I remember Mumbo talking to me about that kind of thing, but she didn't seem entirely clear on the concept and I wasn't interested enough to ask her to clarify it at the time.

"I found her in a glass coffin," I say. "When this place . . ." I wave a hand around at our surroundings. "Was different."

The spirit's gaze goes to where Jackson's still hanging from the tree.

"We . . . I've been . . . ill," he says. "I don't remember a great deal of what has happened in the past little while."

I give him a sympathetic look.

"But the funny thing," I go on when he doesn't continue himself, "is that when I knocked the coffin over, that's when you showed up. Or at least, this beam of light that became you."

"I really don't remember."

"It was as though breaking her out of the coffin was . . ." I hesitate. I was about to say "what set you free," but settle for, "the catalyst for your return to health."

<You're sly,> Saskia says. <But do you really think he'll feel beholden?>

I can't remember the last time I heard that word used in a sentence.

The spirit is studying me again, a careful look in his eyes.

"There did seem to be some sense of outside intervention," he finally says. "There at the end."

I open my arms expansively and say, "Ta da. That was us."

He continues to study me.

"It's hard for me to say 'you're welcome' when you don't say 'thank you' first," I tell him.

"So you want something from me," he says.

I shake my head. "Nothing for me. But for her . . ."

He closes his eyes and it's like he goes away. It's only when he starts to talk that I realize he must have been referencing some of the texts he has stored on the site.

"You need a soulstone," he says, opening his eyes again. "To allow her to return to her body."

<I've never heard of such a thing,> Saskia says.

Me, either, I tell her.

"A soulstone," I repeat aloud.

He nods.

"Which is?"

"It looks like an ordinary pebble, smoothed by a river's current or the ocean's tide, but when you place it in the mouth of someone whose soul has become detached from her body, it creates a conduit to allow the soul's return. They're quite difficult to acquire."

"Do you know how I can get one?"

He nods. "You must find the dawn branch of the Secret Road and take it eastward through the Hills of Morning. It's a long journey, but if you keep on the road, eventually you will see the tall crags of the Brismandarian Mountains to the north. You will come in time to a path that leads off from the road—I'm not sure if it's marked, probably not. But when you find it, it will take you cross country into the foothills and then into the mountains themselves.

"Once there, you have to look for a ruined goblin tower nestled in the lower peaks. Under it is the entrance to a dragon's cave where—"

"Oh, get real," I tell him, breaking in. I feel like I'm being read the dust jacket of some high fantasy quest novel. "What book did you steal that from? How about we skip over the bullshit and you just tell it to me straight? What's a soulstone? Does it really exist? And if it does, how do I get one?"

<Christiana,> Saskia says. She's been giving me free rein so far, but I guess she really doesn't like it when I get too pushy. <This isn't helping. You're just going to make him angry.>

So? He's not exactly endearing himself to me, either.

<Please.>

The spirit's looking a little pouty, which makes me question again how powerful he really is. Or at least how young. It's the look a kid gets when you call him on something he's not really sure about himself, but has presented with great authority.

"That's how it was described in the book," he says.

I sigh and try to keep the irritation out of my voice.

"What book?" I ask.

He hesitates a long moment, then finally says, "*Her Glorious Hoard.* By Caitlin Midhir."

"Which is a novel?"

He nods.

"So really, you have no idea."

He shakes his head.

"And you can't help us at all—at least not with this detached soul business."

"Sorry."

And he looks so full of regret.

"Well, can you at least show us how we can get out of this place?" I ask.

"I don't travel beyond this site."

Don't, he says, but I'm guessing can't. This makes me think that maybe the Wordwood spirit is a *genus loci*—the tutelary spirit of a place. One that's bound to his location, rather than obliged. The obliged can leave; they simply have to return from time to time—check in like a watchman on his rounds. The bound can never leave. Which would be why he'd send some- one like Saskia out to experience the world for him. And that makes me wonder if he maybe he really does recognize her. Maybe he's being so unhelpful because he's got some other use for her body.

But I don't let any of this show on my face.

"No clues?" I ask. "Not even a hint?"

"I'd say the same way you arrived."

Great.

"I have to go now," he says. "Other business to attend to and all."

But he doesn't move. I'm guessing either he can't—either that pillar of light he was is bound to the spot where he's standing, the way the beam of a searchlight can't escape the mechanism that casts it—or he has nowhere to go, but he doesn't want us to know.

I think about that royal "we" he used when he first spoke, how he started to use it again during our conversation, but caught himself. Then there's the way he looks and his whole attitude. How he talks big, but he seems kind of weak and inexperienced.

What if he's putting up a bigger front than I am?

"You're not the Wordwood spirit," I find myself saying aloud.

I'm just trying the idea on, throwing it out to see what kind of reaction I might get. He gets this look—caught out, wanting to protest, knowing he hasn't got it in him to pull it off.

Bingo.

"So who are you?" I ask.

<Oh my god,> Saskia says in my head. <I think you're right. He must be another construct, except his job is probably something like administrating the day-to-day running of the site.>

What he says next only confirms it.

"Perhaps it's true," he says. "perhaps I am not the spirit of this place. Perhaps I am only *of* the spirit."

"So which is it?"

"When the site was still operational and we would be contacted with questions and requests, I was the one who found the information they required and furnished them with it."

<He's like a macro,> Saskia says.

Say what?

<It's a little program you can write that will handle some mundane computer task so you don't have to keep doing it over and over again yourself.>

"So you're like a macro," I say aloud, trying out the word on him.

He gets this affronted look. "I am far more than that. You could call me Librarius, the Master Librarian of the Wordwood. I am its administrator, in charge of all acquisitions and communications. Without my expertise and effort, this site would never have had any interaction at all with the myriad territories beyond its borders. It would merely be a pocket world—home to a Great One, it is true, but he would be alone. There would be no one to look after him. There would be no one to maintain the flow of and collect all the attention paid to him that he requires for his sustenance."

"Sustenance? What, you mean he eats e-mail?"

Librarius shakes his head. "Hardly. But like many gods, he requires attention. Without it, he will wither away and die."

I get it. I've heard of these spirits that buy into godhood—buy into it so much that their belief in how it works becomes fact. Eventually, they really do require the prayers and attention of their followers in order to exist. In the case of the Wordwood, all the e-mails that arrive at the site would be like prayers, sustaining him. Making him strong. Without them, cut off by the virus, he thinks he's dying.

"The virus hurt him bad," I say.

Librarius nods. "I've managed to purge the last of it from the site, but even with it gone, the Great One is still stricken."

"Can we see him?" I ask.

"Normally, I would say no," Librarius tells me. "Normally, all you see would be the Great One, for he would be part and parcel of everything that makes up this world. But now . . . ."

He does something with his hands, some kind of ritualistic motion in the air in front of him, or maybe he's just touching controls we can't see. Whatever it is that he does, our surroundings change again, only this time it's as fast as you might snap your fingers. There's no gradual change from forest to this new place we find ourselves in. We're just *here*.

<Oh my . . . > Saskia breathes in my head.

No kidding.

We're in a library, an enormous chamber filled with shelves and shelves of books, a chamber that is so vast that I can't see an end to it, no matter which way I look. Everything is lit with a diffused version of the blue-gold light I've come to associate with the Wordwood, but I can't see a source for the light. The bookshelves tower up until they disappear into shadow. The top shelves are only accessible from rolling ladders that are so tall I can't imagine climbing up one and I have a good head for heights. There's carpeting underfoot, an Oriental pattern that, if handwoven, would take centuries to make by an army of carpet-makers.

I turn to Librarius and he looks like flesh and blood now. The soft light touches him, like it touches everything, but he's no longer made of light himself. Saskia's body is still at my feet. I look to where Jackson had been hanging from that tree, but he's in a leather club chair now, his arms and legs strapped and buckled to it so that he can't get up. His mouth is no longer full of leaves, but he doesn't say anything. He just sits there, looking scared, but a little angry, too. I don't blame him.

"Where's the spirit?" I ask, turning back to Librarius.

"This way," he says.

He starts off down one of the corridors between the bookshelves, pausing when I don't immediately follow.

"What's the matter?" he asks.

"I don't want to leave my friend just lying here."

He gives a slow nod and does something with his hands again, manipulating the air. Saskia's body and the chair that Jackson's sitting in float up, hovering a few inches from the carpet. I take an experimental step and Saskia's body keeps pace, floating beside me.

Librarius turns and sets off once more and this time I follow him, Saskia's body at my side, Jackson's chair trailing along behind.

<He's not just a servant,> Saskia says, referring to the librarian. <He's got access to power.>

His own, or the spirit's?

<Does it matter?>

I suppose not.

After a number of twists and turns through the maze of bookshelves, we come out into a cavernous space—it might even *be* a cavern for all I know. It's hard to tell because the diffuse lighting doesn't really allow you to get a real sense of distance. I just know we're on the shore of something. A river. A lake. Maybe even an ocean. It's hard to tell. The water stretches away from us, disappearing into shadow.

On our left, the bookcases march up to the shore. On the right, there's a jumble of rock that goes right into the water. Then I realize it's not rock. That enormous shape is a body, its lower torso and legs submerged in the water. I hear Jackson make a soft choking sound behind me when it registers for him. I can barely breathe myself, but I try not to let it show.

Instead, I walk boldly up to the body.

<Christiana,> Saskia says in my head.

There's the usual warning in how she uses my name, but what does she think I'm going to do?

I just want a closer look, I tell her.

I walk up to the head, Librarius keeping pace with me. I can't believe the size of the body. The head alone is as big as a city bus.

I just about die when one enormous eye opens and looks at me.

Aaran

From the moment that Geordie, wearing a thin veneer of politeness over his hostility, had led them down to the basement, Aaran hadn't been able to take his gaze from the wall. That was another world he could see through the shimmer. A real, honest-to-God other world. Even after their experience in Jackson's apartment, and given the evidence of his own two eyes, it still seemed too improbable to be real. But there it was all the same. So amazing, but at the same time, so ordinary as well. As though every Newford basement had a portal to another world in one of its walls.

He almost smiled at the idea.

Maybe they did. Maybe there was one in the basement of his own building. He wouldn't know. He'd only been down there a few times, and only so far as his storage locker. Past the lockers, there could be anything.

The portal continued to distract him as they all brought each other up to date, Christy and Suzi doing most of the talking. But he did tear his attention away from it later, when the discussion arose as to what to do next. He was surprised to find Christy not only defending Suzi, but allowing the two of them to join the group going into the otherworld. That required more than a little trust on Christy's part, and Christy was the one they had to win over, because the others appeared to be following his lead.

Considering how Aaran had treated Christy over the years—more to the point, considering how he was directly responsible for Saskia's disappearance—Aaran thought it was awfully big of him. He wasn't sure if the situation were reversed, that he'd have been able to do the same. Certainly not before he met Suzi and she did whatever it was that she'd done to him to make him see himself and the world in a different light.

Once the decision to go ahead with their journey into the otherworld was made, people began lifting their packs and moving toward the portal.

We didn't bring anything, Aaran realized. No extra clothes, no food or water. Nothing.

He was about to ask Suzi if she was okay being so unprepared for the trip when Holly approached them with a pack in her hand. She offered it to them.

"What's this?" he asked.

Holly shrugged. "I kept thinking that I'd wait until the last moment and then talk Christy into letting me join them, so I packed some stuff. Nothing that'll fit you, but Suzi should find things she can wear. There's also some bottled water, a first aid kit and matches, and some food."

"You sure you don't want to come?" Suzi asked.

Holly shook her head. "After seeing those guys that came for Robert . . . nope, I don't think so. I'm happy to stay here and hold the fort."

Aaran took the pack. "Thanks."

"Just bring them back. Saskia, my friends. Everybody."

"We'll do our best."

Holly fixed him with a serious look.

"And you'd better not be playing a game here," she told him. "Because if you are and you screw things up, I will personally—"

Suzi put her hand on Holly's arm. "No games," she said. "We want this to end as much as you do."

"Right. Of course, you do. I'm sorry. It's just . . ."

"Really hard," Suzi said.

Holly nodded. "I love those guys. If they're gone for good . . . I just don't know what I'll do."

"We'll bring them back," Suzi assured her.

You can't know that, Aaran thought, so why make the promise? He saw that knowledge in Holly's eyes, too, but he also saw how the promise helped, so he added his own to it.

"We won't come back until we do," he told her.

The others were waiting for them on the far side of the portal—three poorly-defined shapes seen through the shimmer. Suzi took his hand as they were about to step through.

"Nervous?" she asked.

Aaran nodded. "Guess this is old hat for you."

"I wish it was. I feel like I'm going to pee my pants."

Then, before she could lose her nerve, she stepped ahead, into the wall, into the shimmer of the portal. Every inch of Aaran's skin shrunk from the contact as they went through. But there was nothing there—only a thickening of the air—and then they were on the other side. Vertigo hit Aaran hard. Nausea rose up and he would have stumbled if Bojo hadn't caught his arm.

"It doesn't last," the tinker said. "Here, sit on this rock for a moment and put your head between your legs."

Aaran gave a dull nod and allowed himself to be led over to a jumble of rocks under a large old tree of some kind. He dropped his head between his legs when all he really wanted to do was lie down in the dirt. But Bojo had told the truth. The feeling went quickly away leaving only a slight queasiness in its wake. When he was able to look up he saw that Raul still looked a little ill, too, but the other three appeared unaffected.

"Apparently it doesn't hit everybody the same way," Suzi said.

She had the decency to look a little guilty as she offered him a hand up.

"And some people not at all," he muttered.

"What can I say? It's all in the constitution."

Aaran gave her a weak smile and looked around. So this was the other-world. It didn't look a whole lot different from the landscape north of the city. Big fields. Mountains in the distance. A forest, mostly evergreens, to his right. When he turned the other way, the view was only a variation on what he'd already seen.

Two paths joined each other in the place where they were standing—dirt trails leading off as far as he could see in four different directions. The tree above was some kind of oak, he decided.

"It's not what I expected," he said.

"It changes," Bojo said. "That's probably the most disconcerting thing about the otherworld. One moment you're in a place like this, the next you're braving a winter storm on a tundra. The transitions can be that abrupt, or as gradual as they are in the consensual world."

Aaran gave a slow nod.

"Now, this is the most important thing you need to know for the moment," the tinker went on. "I can't emphasize this enough. Don't leave the path. It might change underfoot, it may seem to be taking you in the opposite direction than you want to go, but whatever you do, stay on it." He pointed to the open field in front of them. "You might be thinking, how can I get lost over there, well, trust me in this. You can and you will if you stray."

Aaran wasn't so sure it was as serious as Bojo was making it out to be, but he wasn't going to argue. Then he had a sudden thought. He looked around again.

"The portal," he said. "It's gone."

A sudden panic made his chest go tight. How were they going to get back?

"It's not gone," Bojo assured him.

He made a movement with his hands and the portal shimmered back into view. Aaran stepped closer to look back at the basement. Through the shimmer he could see Geordie, Holly and Dick standing by the stairs, talking. Sitting directly in front of them, staring at the wall was Holly's Jack Russell terrier. She barked when she could see them and the others turned around. Bojo waved to them, then let the portal close again.

"Don't worry," he said. "I can easily find my way back here."

Aaran nodded, but he made a point of memorizing the look of the tree and the stones that were jumbled under it in case something happened to Bojo and they had to get back on their own. Of course, then they'd still have to figure out how to open the portal.

"How does the portal work?" he asked.

"It's easiest to find a place like this," Bojo said. "A crossroads—some place where the border between the worlds is thin. And then it's only a matter of concentrating on where you want to be—holding it very clearly in your mind. That's why you need to have been there before. You can't make the same connection with a place you've never been."

"Which way should we go?" Christy asked.

Bojo stood for a moment, looking either way down the path, his brow furrowing as he concentrated on Aaran wasn't sure what. Every direction looked pretty much the same to him.

"This way," the tinker said finally, pointing to the right, where the path led toward the evergreen wood. "Robert's music took us past the worlds that lie back there."

"Any sign of him or the hellhounds?" Christy asked.

Bojo shook his head. "But they'd be many worlds away by now."

"Can't say I'm unhappy to hear that," Raul said.

"I hope he'll be okay," Christy said.

Bojo nodded. "Yeah, me, too." He shifted the strap of his pack to a more comfortable position. "Time we were going."

The trip proved to be as disconcerting as Bojo had described. The first time the landscape shifted, all of them except for Bojo stopped dead in their tracks. The fields and distant mountains were suddenly gone and the path they followed now took them along the top of a dune. A beach, with a vast body of water beyond it, lay on the left of the path. To the right was a heath that went on for miles until it disappeared into a haze on the horizon. High in the sky, a solitary hawk moved in slow lazy circles, riding the wind.

"Jesus," Raul said. "How'd that happen?"

Aaran nodded. The change had come between one step and another.

"The path we're following," Bojo explained, "takes us through an area where the worlds lie smack up against each other, sometimes even overlapping. Some of them are only a few acres in size, others as large or larger than the consensual world. What makes it confusing is that they shift their positions and sometimes their sizes. That's why the otherworld is impossible to map."

"And is there a Rip Van Winkle effect?" Christy asked.

"Time does run differently in some of the worlds—faster in some, slower in others. In some, time spirals, so that when you walk one way, it's into the future, another, and you step into the past."

"What kind of world are we in?" Suzi asked.

"We're not in a world," Bojo told her, "so much as walking along the edges of them. On this path, time runs the same as it does in the consensual world, perhaps a little faster. We won't return to find a hundred years have gone by, though we might be a little older than we're supposed to be, given the amount of time that will have passed. On the plus side, the air of the otherworld offers a measure of longevity as compensation."

"What do you mean by that?" Raul asked.

Bojo shrugged. "It can help you live longer."

"You're kidding."

"No, but it's not as simple as that. Unless you have the right kind of blood—the right kind of genes, I suppose you would say—staying too long in the otherworld can affect the stability of your mind."

"Like in the fairy tales," Christy said. "You come back a poet or a lunatic."

"Something like that."

If you come back at all, Aaran added to himself. In some of those same fairy tales, the characters never come back. Or if they do, as soon as their feet touch mortal ground, they crumple away into dust.

The changes in the landscape, especially the abrupt ones, took some getting used to for most of them. Considering all of his previous experience with the otherworld, it didn't surprise Aaran that Bojo wasn't affected. Suzi seemed to take it all in stride, too. Maybe that was because being newborn the way she was, everything felt new to her and she simply accepted the bizarre along with the mundane. But it was harder for the rest of them, even Christy. And that did surprise Aaran.

"But you've been writing about this stuff for years," Aaran said at one point, when he and Suzi were walking on either side of the writer.

Christy smiled. "You don't really read my books, do you?"

"What do you mean by that?"

"The short story collections are fiction, and yes, there are stories about otherworlds in them, but they don't come from personal experience. They're either based on other people's experiences, which I listened to with the proverbial grain of salt, or they came from my imagination."

"I wasn't talking about them," Aaran said. "And I *have* read your books—or at least the ones I've reviewed. The ones where you collect all those urban myths and make connections between them and old legends and folk tales. In them you allude to personal experiences as well, though you don't go as much into them."

"That's because until now, I could count my truly inexplicable experiences on one hand. I've always been a believer and a disbeliever at the same time."

"It never seems like that in your books."

Christy laughed. "That's because people tend to find what they're personally looking for in them—it's human nature. The believers believe, the skeptics focus on my own questions, and those with a personal axe to grind against me will find what they think makes me look foolish, even when the examples they inevitably pull out aren't actually in the text."

On the other side of Christy, Suzi laughed as well. "I'm guessing Aaran was one of the latter."

"Maybe I was a bit too enthusiastic," Aaran said, "but—"

"You had an axe to grind," Suzi finished for him, still laughing.

"Yeah, I guess I did."

"That's okay," Christy said. "It's not like you're alone. The very idea of the consensual world, never mind discussing what might lie hidden within or beyond its boundaries, pushes a lot of people's buttons."

Suzi gave him a curious look. "You sound pretty accepting of the negative press."

"Oh, I have my moments of bitterness, but really, what can you do? You can't—sometimes I think you shouldn't even try to—change people's minds. It just gets their backs up. Better to put the information out and let them deal with it in their own way, on their own time."

"And if they don't take the time to assimilate the information?" Suzi asked.

"You conduct your own life as a positive example. Always remain open-minded."

"People aren't going to believe in fairies just because you do," Aaran said. "They aren't even going to think seriously about it."

"I know. That's why in my nonfiction I'd rather focus on the World As It Is—as Professor Dapple likes to call it. The idea of a consensual world— that things are the way they are only because that's what we've agreed to. It's something that seems completely preposterous to so many people, but the funny thing is that chaos theory—which science *does* take seriously—is now catching up to the same ideas: how on a microscopic level, it's the presence of an observer that makes a thing be one thing or another. Until that moment of observation, they're simultaneously both and their possibility remains completely open-ended.

"And those same scientists are now actually considering the concept of parallel worlds as viable."

"Well, considering where we are," Suzi said, "that theory is pretty obviously true."

Christy shook his head. "These are *otherworlds*. The parallel worlds theory posits that every time a decision is made, a new world splits off from the original, making for an infinite number of alternate or parallel worlds. They start off very close to one another, but if you think about the decisions in your own life, even the smallest choice can start a ripple effect resulting in utterly changing your life."

"Like how the movement of butterfly wings in China," Suzi said, "can affect the weather here. Well, not *here,* maybe, but back in Newford."

Christy nodded.

Or like stopping to talk to Suzi had been for him, Aaran thought. It had begun with him thinking of himself as usual, wondering what he could get out of her, and ended up with him being here, in this place, risking his life for other people, most of whom he didn't even know.

Was there some other parallel world where he hadn't? Where he'd gone on the way he always did?

Was there a world where he hadn't forced Jackson Hart to write that virus in the first place?

Before he could follow that line of thinking too far he realized that up ahead, Bojo and Raul had come to a stop. He looked past them to see that the path they were following dipped under a freeway overpass. To their right, the highway was lost in a wide sweep of fields and far-off mountains. To their left, the ocean had long since vanished and he could now see a large city in the distance. Traffic sped by on the freeway in both directions, no one seeming to pay any attention to them.

"Okay, this is weird," Aaran said.

"Why's that?" Bojo asked.

"Well, look at this. What's a freeway doing here? I thought fairyland was supposed to be all pastoral, with maybe a castle or some little village."

Bojo smiled. "This isn't fairyland—it's the otherworld. Somewhere in its reaches you'll find every landscape you could possibly imagine, and some you can't."

"Yeah, but that city . . ."

"Is Mabon."

Aaran saw Christy perk up.

"Mabon?" Christy repeated. "Really? That's Sophie's city. Or at least it was when she was a little girl." He turned to look at the others. "She started imagining it when she was a latchkey kid and . . . well, I guess all of that grew up around the few streets she created."

"You know Mabon's creator?" Bojo asked.

Christy nodded. "Sure. She's a friend of mine."

"Wait a minute," Aaran said. "Are you talking about Sophie Etoile, the artist?"

When Christy gave another nod, Aaran was about to argue how that was impossible. *He'd* met Sophie and . . .

But he caught himself and just shrugged instead. Maybe nothing was impossible anymore—at least not in this place.

"I need you all to wait here for a few moments," Bojo said, "while I scout the lay of the land under that overpass."

"Is there something wrong?" Raul asked.

"Don't know yet," Bojo said. "But it looks like a place of power—what with that freeway and all those people travelling over what amounts to another crossroads. You've already had a brief introduction to what you can meet at a crossroads."

He was referring to the hellhounds, Aaran realized, which the others had confronted in Holly's basement. He and Suzi had missed them and he, for one, was happy to leave it that way.

"It won't take me long," Bojo said.

Aaran watched him go ahead, then looked at the city again.

"So Sophie made that," he said.

Christy nodded.

"Does your friend Jilly have a place here as well? When I think about how *she* goes on about fairies and magic . . ."

"No," Christy said. "But she's been to Mabon."

"Bojo's waving the 'all clear,' " Raul said.

Aaran took another look at the city before trailing along after the others. On the other side of the overpass, the landscape did another abrupt change and for a block or two they were walking in a derelict cityscape that reminded Aaran of the Tombs back home in Newford, but this area seemed far older than the abandoned buildings and empty lots of the Tombs. This city appeared to have been deserted for decades—or at least deserted by normal people. By the time they were halfway down the second block, Aaran got the sense that they were being watched, but by whom or what, he couldn't tell. He just had this prickle in the back of his neck, some vestige of alarm handed down from his own primitive ancestors warning of imminent danger.

But then they reached the end of the block and they were walking across a frozen field, snow crunching underfoot. Aaran shivered and wrapped his thin jacket more tightly around him. He was about to ask Suzi if she wanted to see if they could find something warmer for her to wear in the pack that Holly had given them, when the landscape changed once more and they were walking through desert scrub, where every plant seemed to have a thorn, even the trees. But at least it was warm, and the nervousness Aaran had felt in the deserted city had faded.

They'd fallen into a new order as they walked. Bojo continued to take the lead, but Raul was now walking on his own behind him. Christy and Suzi were next, the two of them still talking about consensual worlds and parallel universes. Tired of that conversation, Aaran stayed in the rear.

Trudging along, he continued to fall farther behind the others, distracted over and over again by the changing landscape. By the time they came to another of what seemed like a perennial English countryside, the others were well ahead of him and didn't hear him when he stopped and called out after them. He was surprised that none of them had noticed the little man he'd spotted just off the road. But perhaps he hadn't even been here when they walked by, the landscape changed so frequently.

Aaran studied him curiously, half-disbelieving what he saw.

He was more the way Aaran imagined a fairy-tale character to be than Dick, the hob he'd met back at Holly's store, had been. Barely a foot tall, this little man's features were all sharp angles, his limbs gangly and stick-like. He was wearing a red cloth cap and leather pants, but his jacket seemed to be made of burrs and leaves, held together with vines and braided grasses.

He appeared to have his foot snagged in among the protruding roots of the tree that towered above him. Aaran couldn't identify it. All he knew was that it was a solitary tree with a wide expanse of open fields spreading out from beyond it and some of its boughs overhanging the path. When Aaran stopped, the little man tried to make himself invisible, but without any real luck. He wasn't having much luck freeing his foot, either.

Aaran glanced at where his companions were still foraging ahead. He remembered Bojo's warning when they'd first crossed over.

I can't emphasize this enough. Don't leave the path.

But this wouldn't really be leaving the path. It was only a couple of quick steps to where the little man was trapped.

He gave a last quick look at the backs of his companions, two hundred yards or so ahead on the path, then stepped off, into the field. The little man's almond-shaped eyes went round with fear and he frantically started tugging at his foot again, his whole little body shaking and trembling.

"Take it easy," Aaran said, gentling his voice the way you did with a frightened child. "I'm not going to hurt you."

When he reached forward, the little man stopped moving. He lay there, terrified eyes staring at Aaran, nervous tremors making his limbs jump.

"Really," Aaran told him. "I'm here to help."

He dug with his fingers around the little man's foot, found where the roots had wedged around the tiny ankle. It only took him a moment to stretch the knotty roots far enough apart to pull the foot out. Even with his foot free, the little man continued to lie there on the ground, shaking with fear.

"It's okay," Aaran said. "You can go now."

He moved back, holding his hands open to show that he meant no harm.

"Or did you break something?" Aaran asked.

But as soon as he was an arm's length away, the little man jumped to his feet and went tearing off into the field. In a moment, all Aaran could see was the small wake the little man left behind in the tall grass and weeds. Then that, too, was gone.

"So I guess you're fine," he said, straightening up. "No need to say thank you."

He had a last look into the field, trying to see if he could spot the little man, before he turned around to get back onto the path.

Which was no longer there.

Don't leave the path.

Oh, come on, he thought. I only took a couple of steps.

But retracing those steps didn't bring him back to the packed dirt of the path they'd been following. Instead, he was still in the middle of this enormous field, knee high grass and weeds swaying in a light breeze, the expanse dotted here and there with large trees like the one under which he'd rescued the little fairy man.

And not at all a bright little man, either, Aaran thought. If the fairy hadn't panicked, he'd have discovered that all he had to do was push his foot the other way and he could have worked himself free.

Maybe fairies weren't all that smart.

Right. And look who's talking.

He turned back to look at the tree, trying to judge how many steps he'd taken from the path to get to the roots where the little fairy man had been trapped. He was about to go back and try to retrace his steps when a hand fell on his shoulder and he suddenly understood the cliché of almost jumping out of your skin.

Adrenaline slammed in his chest and he whirled, flailing his arms, only to have them both caught in firm grips. Then he saw who it was that held him. Bojo let go as soon as he stopped struggling.

"Jesus," Aaran said, heart still pounding in his chest. "You just about gave me a heart attack."

"I told you not to leave the path."

"I only stepped off for a minute."

"Maybe for you," Bojo said. "But you were gone two hours for us."

That didn't seem possible.

"Two hours?" Aaran repeated.

The tinker nodded.

"But . . ."

"Trust me," Bojo said. "You were gone for a while."

"But . . ."

Bojo smiled. "I thought a newspaperman would have a larger vocabulary than that."

"He should. I mean, I do. It's just . . ."

"Hard to get your head around. I know. It's always like that at first. But if it makes you feel any better, the four of you are doing much better for a first trip into the otherworld than most people do. Now come on. Let's get back to the others."

He did something with his hand again, a sideways motion, a twitch of his fingers, but Aaran couldn't concentrate on it. And then he didn't care about it anymore because they were back on the path and Suzi grabbed him in a hug.

"I thought we'd lost you forever," she said into his chest.

He put his arms around her and looked over the top of her head at the others.

"Look, I'm sorry," he said. "There was this little fairy man who looked like he was pretty much made of twigs and leaves. He had his foot caught in a tree root and I just stepped off the path to help him out. I really didn't mean to cause a problem."

"Did he have a red cap?" Bojo asked.

Aaran nodded. "Yeah, he did. Does that mean something?"

"Just that you were lucky. It must have been a brownie under the cap instead of a goblin. Goblins get their caps that colour by dipping them in blood, and they get their blood from people like you that they coax off a safe path."

"Jesus."

"But a goblin also wouldn't get itself into that kind of predicament in the first place."

Goblins and brownies, Aaran thought. Next thing you know, they'd see a dragon.

"But it worked out okay, I guess," he said.

Beside Bojo, Raul smiled. "Sure. You got to be like the hero in some fairy tale."

"What do you mean?"

"You know, stopping to help a spoon or an old woman, and later on in the story it turns out they're the only one that can help you?"

Aaran shook his head. "It wasn't like that at all. And I think that the point of those stories isn't that you should help someone now for a payoff later down the road. It's that everyone's important, no matter how insignificant they might seem." He let go of Suzi so that he could look her in the face. "It's like our guardian angel thing," he said. "You do it because you can. Not because you have to, or because you think you should, but because you want to."

Suzi beamed at him, but no one said anything for a long moment. Then Christy stepped up and gave him a light punch in the shoulder.

"Maybe there's hope for you yet," he said.

Bojo nodded. "Only next time, don't do it on your own. We were lucky we found you as quickly as we did."

"I tried calling after you guys, but you were already too far ahead."

"We were probably too distracted to hear you." Before Aaran could ask for an explanation, the tinker added, "We found the Wordwood, but . . . well, you'll have to see it for yourself."

He started off down the road again and the others fell in behind him. Suzi held Aaran's hand.

"You're really doing well," she said.

"High praise," he told her, "coming as it does from my guardian angel."

"Don't wear that into the ground," she told him, but she was grinning.

"So what's Bojo not saying about the Wordwood?" Aaran asked.

"There doesn't seem to be a way in," she said and pointed ahead.

For a moment, Aaran wasn't sure what he was supposed to be looking at. All he saw was the others ahead of them on the path, the path itself leading off into the greying distance. But as they drew closer, he realized that the greyness he saw wasn't in the distance. It was a thin wall of mist with pale, blue-gold lights playing deep inside it. Stepping right up to it, Aaran could plainly see a deep forest on the other side, the path continuing into it.

"You're sure that's the Wordwood?" he asked.

Bojo nodded. "It's giving me the same feeling that I got from the residue the spirit left behind in Holly's store."

"So what are we waiting for?" Aaran asked.

Bojo bent down and worked a small stone free from the border of the path. When he tossed it into the mist, they never saw it land on the other side.

"Where does it go?" Aaran asked.

"Damned if I know," the tinker said. "I guess into some between."

Aaran gave him a puzzled look. "Some between?"

"A space in between where we are and that forest we can see. It could be a few yards wide, it could be the width of a continent. It could drop us into the middle of an ocean or a volcano. Or it could just be an extension of this path we're following—a little detour of some kind."

"But we're sure that's the Wordwood?" Aaran asked.

"As sure as I can be without having a native of the place confirm it for us."

Aaran looked from him back into the mist.

"So I guess one of us should step through and find out for sure," he said.

"That's what we've been arguing about while we were looking for you," Christy said. "It's either step through into the unknown, or leave the path and try to find a way around."

"Which is also a big-time unknown," Raul put in.

Aaran turned to Bojo. "I guess you're the expert. What's your take on it?"

"I can't decide which way is the least dangerous."

"And while we're all standing here wondering about it," Aaran said, "who knows what's happening to the disappeared people, lost somewhere in there."

"Don't think that's not on our minds," Christy said.

"I wasn't saying it for that reason," Aaran told him. "I was just reminding myself." He glanced at Suzi, then shrugged. "I think one of us should follow the path, see where it goes, and I think it should be me."

Robert Lonnie

The hellhounds were travelling too fast to hide their trail, but it wouldn't have mattered if they'd had the time. Robert had developed such an awareness of them from all his years of avoiding their attention that he could have tracked them with his eyes closed and his fingers in his ears.

Their speed didn't help them either.

For every twist and turn they took, Robert knew a shortcut. When he finally caught up with them at another crossroads, he was there ahead of them, sitting on a low wall under the skeletal branches of a bare-limbed hanging oak, guitar on his lap, bones of those unfortunate enough to have been hung from the boughs above scattered among the clumps of dried grass by his feet. He waited until they burst through the rags of mist that surrounded the crossroads, let them get a look at him sitting there, calm and waiting, then he played some music for them.

The first chord dropped them to their knees.

The second chord snaked right into their heads and went rummaging around in their souls.

The third chord left them lying in the dirt as though they were dead.

Robert let that last chord echo and ring. When even the memory of it had faded, he finally laid his hand across the strings. He was about to stand up when a solitary clapping started up behind him.

Robert turned. There was a man leaning against the hanging oak, black-skinned and white-grinned, a gold cap sparkling on one of his front teeth. Like the hellhounds, he was dressed in a white shirt and black broadcloth suit, except he held a cane with an ivory head and had a tall top hat on his head. There was so little warning of his appearance, it was as though he'd stepped right out of the hanging tree. Knowing who this was, Robert wouldn't have been surprised if that had been the case.

"I didn't think you had it in you," the *loa* said.

"Didn't have what?"

"The balls to kill them."

"I haven't gone back on our bargain," Robert said. "They made the mistake of going after some friends of mine."

"I know that."

"And they aren't dead."

"I know that, too."

"I just took all the meanness out of them," Robert said.

"Which is pretty much the same difference as killing them," the *loa* said.

He pushed himself away from the tree and walked over to where Robert was sitting. His movements were stiff, as though there were only bones under that broadcloth suit—no muscle or flesh. He took his time lowering himself down to the wall beside Robert, using his cane to take the weight until he was settled.

"Not that I care," he added. "They were only under my protection if you killed them for yourself."

"Except I didn't kill them," Robert said. "All I did was take away the waste of their lives and give them a fresh start on things. Did them a favor, really."

The *loa* lifted a questioning eyebrow.

"Taking away their meanness," Robert said, "leaves them with less to work through in their next lives."

"Always thinking of others," the *loa* said.

"Well, I try."

The *loa* gave Robert another flash of that toothy grin of his. "And you're doing a fine job of keeping your soul out of my hands, too."

Robert shrugged. "Keeps me busy."

"But I'll have it in the end."

"I've never had an argument with that."

"You just haven't been in a hurry, either."

"Can you blame me?" Robert asked.

"I don't know," the *loa* said, answering what Robert had only meant as a rhetorical question. "I've never lived the way you do, so I've got no way of knowing if it's the kind of thing I'd want to hang onto or not."

Robert gave another shrug. "You hear people talk about immortality like it's a curse, but the way I see it, that only holds if you stop learning. I don't know that there's an end to what there is to find out in that world I'm living in."

"You're not immortal," the *loa* said.

"I'm working on it."

"I can make it happen."

Robert shook his head. "I've only got the one soul, and it's already sitting in that ledger book of yours, so there's nothing left to bargain with."

"Maybe I want you to do something for me."

"Isn't likely I'd be interested."

"You'd be surprised," the *loa* said. "You might find it of benefit to yourself, and I don't just mean me forgetting this engagement we've got concerning your soul."

Robert wasn't about to start working for him and they both knew it, just like they both knew he'd hear the *loa* out. He stifled the impulse to touch the strings of his guitar except to hold them still.

"So what is that you're proposing?" he asked.

"Interesting place, this Internet," the *loa* said.

"I wouldn't know."

"Then take my word for it. Interesting and busy."

"People have time," Robert said, "they do any damn thing with it except look out for each other."

"I suppose you're right. I don't know them as well as you do and it's not something I need to learn. But I'm learning about the Internet. I see a lot of spirits making a home for themselves in that place. It's getting to the point where if you need to contact one of *les invisibles,* all you've got to do is go on-line."

"You're right," Robert said, when the *loa* paused, and he felt he needed to at least indicate he was listening. "That is interesting."

"By which you mean, get to the point."

Robert shook his head. "I don't get a lot of time to sit around and yarn with someone like you. I'm enjoying this."

The *loa* gave him a considering look, them smiled. "Damn, if you're not telling the truth."

"So what's the Internet got to do with you?"

"Think about it," the *loa* said. "When people have a direct line to the spirits through a thing like that, there's not much need for an intermediary like me anymore."

"You really think it'll come to that?"

The *loa* shrugged. "Yes, no, maybe. It's hard to predict something that changes and grows as fast as technology. Ten years ago, mention the Internet and most people wouldn't know what you were talking about. Now everybody's getting on-line."

"Not me."

"Maybe you don't think so."

"What's that supposed to mean?"

The *loa* smiled. "See, the funny thing is, with all these spirits in the wires, the spiritworld's starting to bleed into the Internet. I can see a time— and I'm talking months, not even years here—when it's all going to be one big place."

Robert shook his head. "That's not going to happen."

"Turn a blind eye if you want, but it's already started."

Robert looked away, past the bodies of the hellhounds still lying in the dirt, to where he could catch glimpses of the world beyond the mists that pressed up against the edges of the crossroads. He'd see a shantytown, then the mists would shift, open to show him a hillside grey with rain, shift again and there was a graveyard.

He turned back to the *loa*. "What is it you're planning to ask me to do?"

"I just want to send a message," the *loa* said. "Take down one or two of the bigger spirits setting up house. Let everybody know that contacts between the worlds should be going through me."

"You've never had a monopoly on that sort of thing."

"Maybe not. Maybe that's what's wrong with the world. Maybe we need a little bit of order put back into it."

But Robert was shaking his head. "I'm not killing anybody—not for you, and especially not for my own gain."

"You don't even know the target."

"I'm not interested."

"Even when it was someone you were fixing to deal with anyway?"

Robert gave the *loa* a hard look. "What are you talking about?"

"The Wordwood spirit."

"What makes you think I'm interested in him?"

The *loa* laughed. "What makes you think I don't keep tabs on where you are and who you see? Oh, don't get that look. I play fair. I've never set anybody on your trail. And I'm patient—I can wait till you die. But surely you didn't think I wouldn't pay any attention to the doings of my investment?"

"I'm still not killing anybody for you."

The *loa* shrugged. "Did I use the word 'kill'? Maybe I just want you to play the meanness out of him, like you did with the hellhounds. Send that spirit back to wherever he came from. All I need is to send a message. The Wordwood spirit doesn't need to die for it to be understood."

"Why's he so important?"

"It's not so much that he's important," the *loa* said. "He's just so damn big."

Robert shook his head.

"I don't even need an answer," the *loa* told him before he could speak. "You just think on what we've been talking about when you're standing face to face with that spirit. Could be your need and mine will be the same. All I'm asking you to do is to consider it when the time comes."

"I don't know . . ."

The *loa* stood up, leaning on his cane.

"I'm not the bad guy," he said. "People come to me and I've got no say in what they do with the help I give them."

"I never said you were."

The *loa* nodded. "Just so we're clear on that. Remember, I didn't come looking for you, back when."

"I remember."

The *loa* gave another nod. He tipped a bony finger to the brim of his hat and turned away. Faster than should have been possible with his slow gait, he disappeared into the mists.

Robert sat there for a long time before he finally got up himself. It was time he looked into what kind of trouble the others had gotten themselves into while he was gone, see if he could help out.

He paused by the hellhounds. The one who'd been calling himself Maman was starting to stir. Robert knelt beside him as the big man's eyes fluttered open. He helped the hellhound sit up.

"Take it easy," he said.

"Where . . . where am I?" Maman asked.

"At the crossroads," Robert told him.

"But . . . how did I get here?"

Robert shrugged. "Don't really know. I just came upon you and your friends, lying here in the dirt. Are you going to be okay?"

The big man lifted a hand to his head. "I can't remember anything . . ."

Robert nodded. "How's that feel?"

"It's funny . . . it feels kind of good."

One of the other men made a groaning sound.

"Maybe you should see to your friend," Robert said.

When Maman turned to the other man, Robert stood up. He had stepped into the mists and disappeared by the time the big man looked back.

Christiana

That big eyelid lifts, the hidden gaze finds me, and it's an impossible moment. It's like a tree pulling up its roots to go walkabout. Like a mouth opening in a cliff face and speaking. Like a tidal wave rushing down the central concourse of a shopping mall on the commercial strip of some desert city. It already seems impossible enough that there could be the semblance of a man so immense—a giant statue, a land form in the shape of a sleeping man—but to know that he's alive, that his attention can focus on you . . .

Saskia gasps inside my head. My own pulse jumps into overtime, but it's not for the same reason that Saskia's so shocked. I'm as amazed as she is that the giant man is alive and aware of us, but when that eye opens and his gaze meets mine, I also recognize him. Not who he is, but what he is.

The realization is almost overwhelming. My legs feel weak, knees like jelly. His gaze pulls me in, and I'm about to go falling into the strange and immense mind that lies behind the eye, when the lid slowly droops, closes once more.

I take a steadying breath. I still feel like I need to lean against something.
<What is it, Christiana?> Saskia asks.
This is all wrong, I tell her.
<No kidding. The size of this guy. And when that eye opened, it was . . . I can't explain it, but it felt like we were going to be pulled right

out of your body and into forever. I've never sensed anything so . . . immense and old.>

That isn't the Wordwood spirit.

<What are you talking about?>

I turn to the librarian. "That's a pretty old spirit," I say.

He nods. "And very powerful."

No kidding.

"Is this how he always manifests?" I ask.

"Oh, no," Librarius says. "As I told you before, until the virus struck, he was an invisible presence. He was *everywhere.*"

"And when the virus *did* strike?"

"First that body of water appeared, swallowing a few acres of the library. And then he came stumbling out of the water, dropping to the ground before he could get all the way up onto the shore. The impact when he struck was like a small earthquake. I was certain that the nearest bookcases were going to come tumbling down."

I turn to look at the collapsed giant once more.

<What's going on here?> Saskia asks. <What did you mean by saying this isn't the Wordwood spirit?>

It's a leviathan, I tell her.

I wish I had someone from the borderlands here to help me work this out. Mumbo or Maxie Rose. Or better yet, one of those scholars who would come to the parties at Hinterdale, clustered in gossiping coveys along the walls of the great ballroom in their black robes, arguing over obscure references that no one else would think of, and if they did, they wouldn't care. But that's exactly the kind of attention to detail I need right about now because I am so way out of my depth here.

<Okay,> Saskia says. <I know what "leviathan" means, but you're obviously using it in a context I don't understand. Unless you literally mean it's the spirit of a whale or some sea monster.>

No, no. The original leviathan are so much older, so much more incomprehensible than the word's come to mean.

<I'm not following you.>

Think of how the world came into being.

<Which version?>

The true version. How it was when Raven made the world.

<Can anybody even know the true version? I mean, every culture and religion's got its own take on it.>

I stifle a sigh and wonder what Librarius is thinking as I have this conversation inside my head. Because I know now that he's not the innocent administrator he's made himself out to be. But I don't want to turn to look at him. I want him to think I'm still mesmerized by the leviathan while I talk to Saskia.

<And besides,> Saskia is saying. <What does any of that have to do with what's going on here?>

The leviathan gave Raven the means to make the world—pieces of . . . I'm not sure exactly what. Themselves, I guess. Or the places where they come from. Some kind of energy that can be shaped into anything.

<Sounds like a lot of the world's concepts of God.>

I suppose. But the leviathan don't come from Heaven or Nirvana. They exist in some other place again. They're pure spirit and they shouldn't be here.

<Except this site *is* in the spiritworld.>

Yes, we call it that. And it is the place where people go when they dream, where spirits exist, but it's still a corporeal place. The home of the leviathan is somewhere deeper still, beyond physical matter.

<A spiritworld inside the spiritworld.>

Something like that. More like something that lies sideways or above or below any world in which the physical can manifest.

As I'm talking, some of the conversations I've had with the Hinterdale scholars are coming back to me. It's funny what you don't realize you remember until the information comes slipping up on you in a situation such as this.

The point, I tell her, *is that one of them shouldn't be here.*

<How do you even know this is a leviathan?>

I think of what Delian St. Cloud once told me when he and his brother Elwin were trying to explain the leviathan to me.

"If you should ever meet one," Delian said, in that distinct voice of his, half the scholar, half the amused gadabout, "and believe me, that's a thousand times less likely than Elwin acquiring a sudden penchant for women— you'll know. You'll just know."

I remember thinking it was a cop-out at the time—that neither of them really knew—but I understand now. There aren't words to describe what I met in this giant's eyes. But before I can relate any of this to Saskia, I hear the whisper of movement behind me.

Turning, I see Librarius stepping up to us. Behind him Saskia's body now lies on the floor beside one of those towering bookcases. Across the aisle from her is Jackson's chair, also settled on the ground. Poor Jackson looks a mental mess, staring at the leviathan more goggle-eyed than ever. I feel bad that he's got to go through all of this, tied up, on his own the way he is, but I can't spare the time to babysit him at the moment. Not with the suspicion I see taking shape in Librarius's eyes.

He tries to hide it, but I'm good at seeing through that sort of thing. Almost as good as I am at schooling my own features. I have such a good poker face that I can hardly ever get anyone together for a decent card game anymore.

"I learned something when the virus struck," he says. "A trick if you will."

I shake my head. "I'm not really interested. I'd rather know how you brought this spirit here."

"I told you, he has always been here. It was only when the virus struck that he manifested into what he is now."

"I don't buy it."

He shrugs. "It doesn't really matter what you believe. The truth is I've decided that you're not nearly as useful as I thought you might be. At least, not in your present condition."

I guess the sudden appearance of a blue-gold aura should have been the tip-off, but it takes me a moment to realize that he's starting up some spell. He begins to do something with his hands—the fingers twisting as he moves them through the air like some bad stage magician trying to distract you from what's really going on. I start for him, ready to do some damage. I've gone all the way from being totally in awe of him to wanting to give him a good smack in the head. But I should have moved more quickly. He speaks a word in no language that I know and it's like a lightning bolt strikes the top of my head.

I stand there vibrating, unable to move, every hair on my body standing on end, my eyes rolling back in my head. I feel like there's a hand inside my chest, rummaging around, trying to grab my spirit and pull it out of my body.

And then I get it—what he meant about this trick he learned from the virus. He's figured out how to remove the spirit without killing the body. I guess he watched how the virus short-circuited Saskia and drew only her body into this place.

But I can't imagine what use he has for *my* body . . . unless . . .

Unless he needs one to get out of here. If he's bound to this place, if he wants out . . .

And he does. I'm sure of it.

Saskia's body wouldn't work for him—originating as she did in the
Wordwood—though I don't doubt he tried to use hers first. Maybe that's
what that whole business with the glass coffin was all about. He must have
been the prince that would give her the wake-up kiss, except she'd wake up
with him inside her. The only reason he hadn't gotten to her before was
because of the virus. He had to deal with the virus first. And then, I guess,
he found out that he couldn't use her body.

But I'm different. I was born outside of the Wordwood and I didn't
change like everybody else did when I got pulled into the site. He's probably thinking that I could be his ticket out.

There's only one problem, but he doesn't know it yet. There are two of
us inside this body of mine.

<Let the spell take me,> Saskia says, and I realize that she's figured all
of this out at the same time as I have.

But . . .

<There's no time to pull straws or argue,> she says. <Besides, this is
your body—so you stay.>

So while I continue to struggle with the spell that's trying to rip me
apart, she embraces it. There's this moment of confusion inside my head,
then the pressure eases on me. The spell grabs hold of her, retreating from
my body, pulling her out with it.

Everything snaps back into focus, but I pretend the spell worked and
slump gracelessly to the ground, trying to land so that I don't get too hard a
whack on my head. I shouldn't have worried. Librarius actually has the
decency to catch me before my head hits the ground. Guess he doesn't want
the goods damaged—not if he has to wear them.

He lowers me to the floor where I lie trying to figure out the best way to
catch him off guard. I need a diversion and try to will Jackson to do something—anything—to attract his attention. But when the diversion comes,
it's from a completely unexpected source, though maybe I should have figured this would happen when Saskia was pulled free. My eyes are slits.
Through my lashes I see Librarius turn when he hears Saskia stir. I'm thinking it'll freak him, but it turns out he was expecting it.

"You see," he says to her. "I'm not entirely cruel. If I was, I wouldn't
have provided your spirit with another place it can call home."

I don't know what Saskia's doing. Is she sitting up, everything back to
normal? Or is she disoriented, trying to get her bearings?

It doesn't matter. All that matters is that she's providing the diversion I
need.

I open my eyes wide, then rise soundlessly to my feet once I see that the librarian's back is to me. I guess this is where my boldness comes in handy. I don't even stop to think, I move in close to him and kick him from behind, the toe of my boot going between his legs right into where it hurts.

And what do you know? He's not a eunuch.

He doubles over and actually screams from the pain—not that I blame him. I kicked him hard, and I mean *hard*. But I'll give him this. He's not out for the count yet. Even hurting the way he is, that blue-gold aura of his starts to intensify. His fingers are still twitching. He's trying to spit out a word.

Can't let that happen.

I take down a nice heavy volume from the nearest shelf—an all-in-one volume of *The Golden Bough,* I note—and bash it against his head. It takes me three hits before he finally drops and lies still. My gaze lifts from him to where Saskia's sitting up, leaning for support against a bookshelf.

"Are you okay?" I ask.

There's no response except for a twitch of her lips. Her gaze tracks my voice, finds my face.

"You're in there, right?" I ask. "And everything's in working order?"

"G-give . . . me . . . a . . . minute . . ."

Her voice is raspy from disuse. I can tell that her vision's still swimming.

"Take all the time you need," I say.

I cross over to Jackson's chair and start to work on the buckles of the straps holding him in place.

"How about you?" I ask as I work the straps free. "Think you can stand?"

"Don't . . . know . . ."

He looks in bad shape, too, but I think he's coming back around, the shock starting to wear off. I get the last of the straps undone and he sits there, massaging where they'd rubbed against his skin.

"Is he . . . is he dead?" he asks.

I don't have to ask who.

"I don't know," I say.

I discover that the straps can be worked loose from the chair and I fuss with them until I've got all four free. I take them over to where Librarius is lying and set to work. I bind his wrists behind his back, then use another strap to bind his arms tight against his chest. The third goes around his legs. Tearing a piece of cloth from his shirt sleeve, I ball it up and stick it in his mouth, using the last strap to hold it in place.

"You think that can actually hold him?" Jackson asks.

I shrug. "Have you got a better idea? He seemed to need to move his hands and actually speak to get any magic done."

"But you said he was a god."

"No, I said he was a powerful spirit—*like* a god, but I was only using the word to give you some term of reference."

"But even a powerful spirit . . ."

"I know, I know," I tell him. "He'd still be way out of our league. But unless you can come up with something better, this is going to have to do."

"Throw him in the lake," Saskia says.

I turn to look at her. She seems all here now and back to normal—except for this sudden bloodthirsty turn of her mind. Maybe she's been hanging around inside my head for too long.

"We might still need him," I say.

"What for? He's the real cause of all our problems."

I shake my head. "I don't think he planned any of this. He just took advantage of how the virus screwed everything up."

"You still haven't said what possible use we could have for him."

Before I can frame a reply, never mind actually voice it, we hear a distant rumble. Not like thunder—it's more like the sound ice makes on a lake when it's cracking. Jackson's head whips around, his anxiety immediately flaring.

"What was that?" he asks.

I don't know why everyone thinks I've got the answers to anything.

"Beats me," I tell him.

I go over to where Saskia is and help her stand. I put her arm over my shoulder, my own around her waist, doing what I can to support her. She starts out kind of like dead weight, but as I walk her back to where Jackson's sitting, she quickly starts to improve.

"God, I'm thirsty," she says.

"There's a whole lake over there," Jackson says. I detect more than a touch of hysteria in his voice.

"I'm not drinking from that."

That rumbling crack comes again. It sounds closer, though it's hard to tell for sure. There are too many echoes. I leave Saskia half-sitting, half-leaning on the arm of the chair and turn my attention to the giant.

"We have to do something about the leviathan," I say.

They both look at me, puzzled.

"Its being here is all wrong," I tell them.

I can hear the voice of one of the St. Cloud brothers in my memory, answering my innocent question about what would happen if a leviathan were to appear in the physical world. They went on about cosmic balances and ruptures in space/time continuums which I didn't understand then any more than I'm able to make sense of now. I just remember that it would be a very, very bad thing.

"Our being here is all wrong, too," Jackson says.

He has a point. But I don't see that we can leave—even if we figure out how. We have to deal with the leviathan's presence. We have to make sure that Librarius doesn't get into some new kind of deviltry. We have to round up all the other people that were pulled into this site and try to find a way to get everybody home.

The rumble comes again, closer still. The echoes bounce off the ceiling, invisible in the dark somewhere above us. But this time it's followed by a weird gurgling sound. As one, we turn towards the lake and see the fissure that's appeared in the stone floor right at the shore. Water's pouring into it.

I guess the first thing we have to do, I realize, reassigning priorities, is figure out a way to stop this place from falling apart around us.

Christy

Aaran just keeps surprising me. He's acting so out-of-character, so *not* the cynical, self-serving Aaran Goldstein I've always known, that I can't help but wonder where Suzi's managed to trade him in for this new, improved version. It's either that or she's got to be a seriously effective role model herself.

Take the business with the little fairy man he stepped off the path to rescue. Or how right now he's offering to test whatever lies on the other side of the wall of mist before the rest of us go through. The old Aaran wouldn't have considered either of those courses of action as an option. He wouldn't have even stopped *to* consider them, never mind actually following through on one of them, unless there was some kind of profit in it for him.

"I don't think that's such a good idea," Bojo says in response to Aaran's offer. He turns away from where he's been studying the way the path continues on out of the mist to face us. "The last thing we want to do at this point is to split up."

"So everybody should take the risk?" Aaran says.

The tinker sighs. "Think about it. We don't know what's on the other side of the mist. More importantly, we don't know if, once we go across, we can even come back. Or if we *can* come back, if it'll be to this same place. So, let's say it is safe on the other side of the mist. What help is that to us if you can't come back to tell us?"

"But we don't know that."

"We don't know that it's unsafe, either," Bojo says. "That's why I've been saying that the decision we need to make is: Do we look for a way around, or do we continue on the path through the mist? Whichever way we choose, we should all go. And my vote is to stay on the path."

No one says anything for a long moment. The forest on the other side of the wall of mist draws our gazes. My memory holds the image of the pebbles Bojo threw earlier, the ones that never landed where the path continued on the other side of the mist. I'm not eager to find out where the pebbles went, but if that's the way to the Wordwood, then that's the way I have to go. I don't have a choice. Saskia's in there. And I suppose if I have to go, I'd just as soon have company. Especially Bojo's since he's the only one of us with any real experience in the otherworld.

"I'm with you," I tell him. "My vote also goes to staying together and following the path."

"Count me in, too," Aaran says.

"And me," Suzi says, then she frowns at Aaran and punches him on the arm. "I can't believe you thought you could leave me behind."

"It wasn't like that."

"What about you Raul?" Bojo asks.

"I've come this far," Raul says. "I'm not backing out now."

His gaze finds mine for a moment and I know just what he's thinking. His own lover's lost somewhere in there, just as mine is.

We turn back to the mist. It's so strange seeing that deep forest on the other side, knowing that when we step through, our feet will land in some *elsewhere*.

"Everybody hold hands," Bojo says. "Just for while we're going through. To make sure we all end up in the same place."

I have this sudden incongruous thought. I remember the galleys I was correcting when all of this started, how I never called Alan to tell him I'm going to be late turning them in.

"Christy?" Suzi says.

Her voice makes me blink and I'm back. I put out my hands. Suzi takes my left, Raul my right. We're strung out like beads on a necklace.

"Hold on tight," Bojo says.

Suzi's fingers press harder against my own as one-by-one we follow the tinker through the mist. I find myself doing the same to her and Raul.

Stepping through that wall of smoky grey air is one of the weirdest things I've ever felt. And following the others as they disappear before my eyes might be one of the bravest. I can't begin to describe the panic that tightens in my chest as I watch them go. Bojo, Aaran, Suzi. Then there's just an arm, free-floating in the air, gripping me hard, and it's my turn.

I don't want to go and it's all I can do to not dig in my heels, to pull free of Suzi's grip. But I force myself, wincing as Suzi's fingers are gone and now it's my own hand that's disappearing.

The mist doesn't so much touch my skin as go through my skin. It's like for one moment I'm myself, but I'm also the mist, all our molecules mingling. I hear a sound in my head like faint radio static. The temperature seems to drop ten degrees. I expected another bout of nausea, like when we first crossed into the spiritworld, but it's not like that at all. Instead I feel this intense, penetrating loneliness. An awareness that no matter how many people I surround myself with, in the end I'm alone in the universe.

Then I'm through, Raul right behind me.

For a long moment we all stand there on the other side, still holding hands, trying to see through the gloom. I feel like I have to learn how to breathe again, but at least that awful sense of isolation has eased. The air tastes stale, like in an old basement. There's just a hint of damp.

"Now that's something I don't want to make a habit of doing," Bojo says.

His voice breaks the spell that holds us. We let go of each other's hands and look around.

The light's poor, but once our eyes adjust, it's not as dark as it seemed when we first stepped through.

"Do you know where we are?" Raul asks Bojo.

The tinker shakes his head. "Somewhere underground."

As soon as he says it, I begin to really register our surroundings. We appear to be in a broad corridor or tunnel. The walls are brick, heavily patched with cement. The ground is a mess of rubble and junk: stones, pieces of brick, newspapers, and refuse of all kinds. I pick up the closest paper and squint at the words. Either the light's worse than it seems, or it's written in some language I've never seen before.

I look up, trying to see where the light's coming from. High up on the walls is a phosphorus glow. I can't see the roof. If the air wasn't so still and stale, I'd think there was only sky.

"Look at this," Suzi says.

She's moved a little further ahead and is pointing to what looks like a shelter of some kind: a crude lean-to, the supports made of obviously salvaged wood and covered with tarpaper and cardboard. Beyond it there's a whole village of lean-tos and cardboard shacks, running the length of either wall for as far as I can see.

"People live here?" Raul says.

"More like lived," Bojo says. "It doesn't look like anyone's been here for a while."

"But it's like a sewer."

"More like an old subway line," I say. I toe at the refuse underfoot. "We could probably find rails if we dug under this stuff. Or maybe it's like Old Town, back in Newford."

"Except nobody actually lives in Old Town," Aaran says. "Not since the quake dropped all those buildings underground."

"Are you so sure?" I ask.

Aaran gives me a weary look and shakes his head. "Come on," he says. "I suppose you're going to tell us about those goblins—what did you call them?"

"Skookins."

"Right. Are you trying to tell me they really live down there in Old Town?"

"That's what I've been told."

"And you've actually seen them?"

"No," I say. "But I've seen homeless people. It's safer than the Tombs because you don't get as many of the rougher elements down there—you know, the junkies and the bikers."

"What are you even doing down there?"

I give him a smile. "Looking for goblins."

Aaran shakes his head again.

"So what do we do now?" Raul asks. "Follow the tunnel?"

Bojo nods. "The path's still here. I can't see it, but I can feel it under all this crap."

I know we all have questions, starting with how can this tunnel even be here when all we could see through the mist was an old growth forest, but when Bojo sets off, we fall in behind him, just like we did when we first crossed over into the otherworld. This time Suzi and Aaran walk together behind the tinker, leaving Raul and me to take up the rear.

"You think we're actually going to find them?" Raul says after awhile. "All those people that disappeared."

He means, are we going to find his Benny.

I give him a quick glance. "We have to," I tell him. "Otherwise I'd go crazy."

"I feel like I already am crazy," he says, waving a hand to take in our surroundings. "All of this . . . all these different worlds . . ."

"Yeah, it's not like I thought it would be either."

"I don't know how Bojo makes sense of it all."

"It's what you get used to, I suppose," I say.

"Are you scared?"

I nod. "Though not as much for myself as I am for Saskia. That we won't find her. Or that we will, but . . ."

I can't finish the thought.

"I've been scared my whole life," Raul tells me. "Scared of pretty much everything, from the world at large to the kids beating on me back when I was growing up. I was a skinny little runt, always more interested in drawing than I was in sports or girls or hanging with the guys." He gives me a humourless smile. "They were calling me fag and fairy long before I actually realized my sexual orientation."

I think of Tommy Brown, this kid in junior high, and the chant of "Fairy, fairy, fucking fairy" that would follow him down the gauntlet of halls at the school. I didn't join in, but I didn't try to stop it. Nobody did. Of course I was having my own problems in those days, and not just with bullies, unless you can include your parents in that designation. They didn't treat Geordie or me any better than the kids in school did.

"I know what you mean," I say. "I didn't get to enjoy the golden days of boyhood either, except when I was by myself."

"Yeah, it's always easiest to be by yourself," Raul says. "But it's so damn lonely growing up like that, being on the outside looking in. Back then I'd have given anything to be able to get an erection from looking at a girl."

I have to smile. "I didn't have any trouble with that—not unless you count actually getting a girl to talk to you as part of the equation."

"You think that was tough?" Raul says, smiling with me. "How about having daydreams about the football team? Talk about your unrequited loves. One wrong word or look and they'd really have gone to town on me."

"I got beat up by a quarterback," I say, "but it was only because I was trying to make time with his cheerleader girlfriend."

"Which is acceptable. The law gets laid down, but you're okay because why *wouldn't* you want to score with his girlfriend?"

"Sure. Those guys loved having the girls everybody else wanted."

Raul nods. "Imagine what the quarterback would have done if it had been him you were trying to chat up."

"Your not doing it wasn't fear," I say. "It was just common sense. In those times . . ."

"I doubt it's all that different now."

"Probably not, more's the pity.

Raul shrugs. "But the funny thing is I'm not so scared now. I think it's because for the first time in our relationship, Benny needs me. For once our roles are reversed and he's the one that's counting on me to make everything right. I just hope I don't screw it up."

"We're doing everything we can."

"I know. But it still doesn't seem even close to enough."

I understand exactly how he's feeling.

The tunnel saps at our spirits. It's hard to see all these lean-tos and makeshift shelters, knowing that people have actually had to live like this. In some places they still do, under even worse conditions. Bojo can't explain where the tunnel exists—somewhere in between the worlds in a kind of borderland—but he says it echoes a real place in the World As It Is.

It's probably another half-hour of trudging through the litter and rubble before we see a different light, far ahead of us in the gloom. As we get closer, we hear a sound that it takes me a moment to recognize. Then I realize what it is. Rain.

Another few minutes brings us to the end of the tunnel and for a long moment we stand there under our shelter, looking out at a rain-drenched forest. I don't know if it's the same one we saw through the mist, or another one. It might just be a different view of that first one we saw. The rain falls heavy and steadily, the kind that would soak you to the skin in minutes if you were caught out in it. The leaves of the trees are all slick and dripping. The air smells so good—earthy and wet. The path that we haven't been able to see emerges from the rubble and junk underfoot and heads off under the trees.

"Is that the Wordwood?" Suzi asks.

Bojo nods. "Or at least it has the feel of that spirit. Let's rest up here for a few minutes. Maybe if we're lucky the rain will ease off."

I'm not happy about the idea—I can hear that clock ticking in my head—but everyone else seems in favor of a break, so I don't say anything. But once we do stop, I find my own body betraying me—all those days of sitting at my computer haven't prepared me for the long hours of hiking that we've already put in today. My calves and thigh muscles are aching. The small of my back and my shoulders breathe their own sigh of relief when I remove my backpack and set it on the ground.

We find places to sit in the mouth of the tunnel and break out granola bars and trail mix, washing them down with bottled water. There's not much conversation. Mostly, we watch the rain come down, listening to the steady drum as it hits the ground. I look into those dark, wet woods and think of how Jilly's always talking about the journeys the characters make in fairy tales, how their passage through the dark woods is an analogy for the struggle one has to go through to reach one's goal.

Right about now, I think I'd rather have an analogical wood than the real one waiting for us in the rain.

After a moment I pull out my cigarettes and shake one out. Light it. I see there are only a couple left in the pack and who knows where the nearest corner store is? Looks like I'll be giving up the habit again.

"How do you think Robert's doing?" Raul asked after a time.

Bojo shrugged. "Robert seemed to me to be the kind of man who can take care of himself."

"But those guys . . . the hellhounds . . ."

Bojo gives a slow nod. "Yes, I know. I've seen their kind many times before. Town sheriffs and tavern bullies. And those three were not only large and strong. They had real power to back up their threat." He hesitates for a moment, then looks around at us. "I have something to confess," he says after a moment.

I get a sinking feeling hearing those five words and my imagination goes into overtime, thinking of all the terrible things the tinker might be about to tell us.

"I remember the old stories from when I was young," Bojo says, and then he smiles as though we've caught him out at something. "Oh, I don't mean from books. I'm not much for reading now and was even less so then. But when I was a boy, there were always stories being told around the campfires and in the wagons, and like any boy, I was eager to hear them.

"They weren't about the heroes and kings like you might expect. They were about ordinary folk, usually tinkers like ourselves. What I liked the most were the stories about my namesake, Borrible Jones. Among the tribes, there are whole story cycles about him."

"Are we about to get another origin for your name?" Raul asks.

Bojo chuckles. "No, but it's interesting in that among other things, my name—Borrible—is old tinker slang for an alchemist. It comes from *borrib-lal,* which means pot or crucible."

"So you're an alchemist?"

"No. But supposedly the Borrible Jones of story was. He was also a soldier of fortune, an itinerant musician, a wizard, and any number of other occupations, depending on the need of the particular story. But mostly he was a kind of Trickster, though I suppose saying he was a tinker is saying enough since there's a bit of the Trickster in every tinker."

"Does any of this have to do with your confession?" Aaran asks.

"Yes, no." Bojo sighs again. "It's just that I feel I've been leading you all on. You see, I'm no expert in any of this." He waves a hand out toward the forest. "It's not that I'm unfamiliar with spirits or the otherworld—I've spent the better part of my life travelling these roads among them. But I know about as much about dealing with one of these old spirits as any of you do."

My heart sinks. I thought between him and Robert, we had a chance. Then we went and lost Robert. . . .

"Then why *did* you offer your help?" Raul asks.

"Because of Holly." He ducks his head a moment, then looks at us. "I'm . . . interested in her and I suppose I wanted to impress her, so when she first mentioned her troubles, I promised her I'd help. The one thing a man shouldn't do is go back on his word."

"Well," Suzi says, "if you had to confess something, I'm glad that's all it is."

Bojo gives her a surprised look. "All? Don't you understand? *None* of us are prepared to go up against a being as powerful as the Wordwood spirit appears to be. But I let you believe that I had a solution."

Suzi smiles. "Well, you could have said you were in league with the spirit, and we were all your captives or something. Or that you've been deliberately leading us in the wrong direction."

"I would never do that."

"And," she goes on, "I think it's kind of sweet that you'd be doing all of this just because you have a crush on Holly, who seems very cute, by the way."

"I don't know what it is," Bojo says, "but it came on me like it never has before—just hit me from the first moment I saw her through the door of her shop. It was all I could do not to simply take her in my arms, right there and then."

"Just as well you didn't," Suzi says. "We like a little courtship."

"Of course," Bojo says. "But the way it came over me so suddenly was a curious thing, nevertheless. It's not as if I haven't met other attractive women before." He gives her a grin. "Like you, for instance."

Suzi laughs, but I see Aaran bristle at her side and realize that Bojo, Raul, and I aren't the only ones doing this for love. And it also explains Aaran's complete change of personality over the past day or so. Love begs changes from us—it can be as small a thing as our taste in music, to everything we are.

"Easy, cowboy," Suzi tells Bojo. "Don't waste that tinker charm on me."

With the riddle of Aaran's involvement solved—I never quite took to his claim that he just wanted to make amends—that leaves only Suzi's presence unexplained and gives me a new puzzle to worry at.

"The rain's letting up," Raul says.

He's right. The downpour's eased to a misting rain. Bojo stuffs his water bottle and the wrappers from his food back into his pack. He stands up and shoulders his pack.

"Good," he says. "It's time we were back to doing rather than talking."

I get to my feet as well, feeling nowhere near as spry as the tinker seems to be. I start to bend down to get my own backpack when we hear a loud rumbling in the sky overhead.

Thunder, I think. Not so odd, considering the rain we had earlier. Looks like we're in for another downpour.

But then the ground trembles in an echo to the thunder—enough that I have to hold out my arms to keep my balance. I hear the sound of shifting rocks and we all look back down the tunnel.

"Out, out!" Bojo cries.

He grabs Raul's arm and steers him to the mouth of the tunnel. Thunder booms once more and again we feel the ground shake. This time it knocks me down to one knee. I hear the grinding of stone from deeper in the tunnel and an ominous crack. I picture a fissure opening in the ground, racing toward us.

"Move!" Bojo calls to us.

I don't need to be told. I'm back on my feet, helping Aaran to his. Suzi grabs the backpack that Holly gave them and then the rest of us scramble out of the tunnel and into the rain to where Raul and the tinker are waiting for us. We only just get outside before there's another rumble of thunder, except this time it comes from the tunnel. We run for the trees. When we get under the canopy, I turn to look back. I'm just in time to see the mouth of the tunnel collapse in a deafening crash, spitting rubble and debris out onto the grass where we were standing a moment ago.

The misting rain puts a sheen on our faces and starts to work its way into our clothes. My hair's already wet and lying flat against my head. But all I can do is look at where the mouth of the tunnel had been. If we'd hesitated a moment longer, we'd be buried under that mountain of debris.

It's a long moment before anybody speaks.

"Jesus," Raul finally says. "That was too close."

Aaran nods. "But at least we all got out in time."

That's when we hear another rumble like thunder, and the fissure I imagined when we were in the tunnel comes snaking out of the rubble, darting to the left just before it reaches us. We all grab tree boughs and each other to keep our balance. We stare at where the ground has opened up, stare down into some unimaginable depth that wasn't there a moment ago.

"What . . . what's going on?" Suzi says.

"It's this world," Bojo says. "The Wordwood. It's collapsing."

There's another rumble and another fissure opens from the side of the one in front of us.

Nobody waits. As one, we turn and bolt into the forest, following the path.

Holly

Holly came back from walking the dog to find the bookstore empty. She wasn't surprised, although she had left Geordie and Dick on the main floor not fifteen minutes ago, sorting through and filing the new arrivals that had come in yesterday, before all of this began. She didn't bother to see if they'd gone upstairs to the apartment. Letting Snippet off her lead, she followed the little dog down the stairs to the basement where, as she expected, she found them sitting side by side on the bottom riser. The hob's toes just touched the basement floor, while Geordie's knees were raised high enough that he could comfortably rest his chin on them. They studied the blank wall that hours ago had been a portal into the otherworld. Now it was simply concrete once more.

Snippet squeezed in between the pair and went to sniff at the wall before returning to the stairs where she waited for Geordie to pay some attention to her.

"Watching that wall's not going to bring them back any quicker," Holly said.

Geordie nodded. He reached out and tousled the stiff hair between Snippet's ears.

"I know," he said. "But they've been gone so long."

It was well past midnight by now, closing in on two. The streets outside had been quiet while Holly took Snippet out to do her business. Holly liked to refer to it as Snippet "checking her pee-mail."

"It just seems like a long time," she told Geordie. "It's actually only been a few hours. We have to be patient—they could be gone for days."

"I know. Maybe we should have gone with them."

Holly sat down on the stairs a few risers above them. She thought about her friends, trapped somewhere in a world on the other side of that wall. Of the handsome tinker that she'd hardly gotten to know, gone looking for them with Christy, one of her best friends.

"Maybe we should have," she said.

"Oh no, Mistress Holly," Dick said. He turned to look at her, his broad face earnest. "It's too dangerous a place for the likes of us."

Geordie gave a short humourless laugh. "Well, doesn't that make me feel better about how the others are doing."

Dick got a horrified look. "Oh, I didn't mean—"

"That's okay," Geordie told him. "I know what you meant. We knew it was dangerous going in, but it wasn't like we had a choice. Somebody had to go."

"But the waiting's hard," Holly said.

"The waiting's really hard," Geordie agreed. "And I guess what has me worried the most is that it's not just the otherworld that they've gone into. There's also this whole business with Web sites. I mean, I can barely get my head around the idea that they can have a physical presence in the otherworld."

Holly nodded. She understood exactly what he was feeling.

"But if we accept that it's possible," Geordie went on, "then that means that part of Christy's and the others' safety is dependant upon computers, and I don't know about you, but I'm not exactly overjoyed with that idea. I mean, think about it. The damn things seem to crash if you just blink at them wrong. Would you trust your life to one? And that's without even adding magic into the equation."

"The Wordwood was always stable," Holly began.

"Until a virus took it down," Geordie said.

"You're not making me feel any better."

"I'm sorry, but this is just eating at me. When it comes to computers, you don't even need outside glitches like a virus to screw things up. Just think about what it's like when you're trying to install some new piece of software. You can do it ten times in a row and it's only on the tenth that it actually works, though nothing's changed and you've been following the exact same procedure each time. Magic doesn't even have to be there to screw things up, but we *do* have magic."

"Yes," Dick agreed. "Computers are very dangerous and home to pixies and goblins and every manner of unseelie creature."

Geordie sighed. "You see what I mean?"

"But there's nothing we can do," Holly said. "Is there?"

When Geordie shook his head, she turned her attention to Dick.

"I don't know anything about computers, Mistress Holly," Dick said.

Having had the hob as a roommate for more than a year now, Holly knew when he was being evasive. She could tell that he knew something, but just didn't want to say it.

"And?" Holly prompted him.

Dick wouldn't look at her. "Oh, don't ask me, Mistress Holly."

"Dick!"

"It's . . . it's just . . ."

"Just what?"

The hob looked miserable.

"Another kind of dangerous," he finally said.

Geordie was about to say something, but Holly held up a hand to stop him. By now, she'd become used to coaxing Dick to tell what he didn't want to share.

"And what kind of dangerous is it?" she asked.

Dick sighed. "Talking to Mother Crone kind of dangerous."

"That's her name?"

"No. You should know by now, Mistress Holly, that names hold power. Never give a fairy your real name. You'll notice that they only ever give you their *use* names."

Holly gave him a nervous laugh. "I haven't actually met enough fairies to be able to judge that. And I think I'm just as happy to leave it that way. Fairies and me seem to spell trouble—present company excluded, of course."

Dick nodded.

"So, *use* names," Holly went on. "I guess they're kind of like user names on a computer."

As Dick gave her another nod, she thought of Bojo with all the different origins of his name, depending on who he was talking to.

No, she told herself. She shouldn't think about him, because that just led to the confusing welter of the immediate attraction she'd felt for him when he came to her door; the fact that he and the others were gone, most likely into some terrible danger; and the worry that she might never see him again . . .

"So, why should we talk to this Mother Crone?" she asked Dick.

"She's a seer. She might be able to help us—for a price."

"Why does there always have to be a price?"

"I don't know, Mistress Holly. There just does."

"I wonder if it's a good/bad fairy thing," Holly said. "When Meran helped us, she didn't want anything in return."

"What kind of price would Mother Crone want?" Geordie asked.

"I don't know that, either," the hob said. "I just know that the bigger the favour, the more dear the price will be."

"Maybe this Mother Crone can tell us why there's always got to be this trade-off," Holly said.

"Oh no," Dick said. "You mustn't ask her questions the way you do me. Most of your Good Neighbours have no patience for them and consider prying to be an insult."

Holly nodded. "I won't pry," she assured the hob. "So tell me, where can we find her?"

"At the mall."

"At the mall?" Geordie said.

Holly had to laugh. "Well, it stands to reason, doesn't it? If there are going to be pixies on the Internet, why not a seer at the mall?"

"Which mall?" Geordie asked. "The Williamson Street Mall?"

Holly knew why he'd picked that one. It was the oldest one in the city and it stood to reason that if some old fairy seer lived in one of their malls, it would be in the oldest one they had.

But Dick shook his head. "No. She lives in the new one up on the highway." He turned an anxious face to Holly. "But you have to understand, Mistress Holly. Someone like Mother Crone uses a widdershins magic. No good can come of it in the long run."

"But you think she could help."

"If she doesn't turn us all into toads."

Holly shivered. "She can do that?"

"Someone like Mother Crone can do that and more," the hob said. "It's why going to her is a last resort."

"Well, I think we've pretty much entered last resort territory, don't you?" Holly looked from Dick to Geordie. "I mean, look at where we stand. We have a Web site that's gone feral and has swallowed a big chunk of the people using it, including a whole bunch of our friends. Christy and the others could be lost forever by now, for all we know. And then the real magic worker we had on our side has gone chasing big scary men and still isn't back."

"Meaning, Robert," Geordie said.

Holly nodded. "The bottom line is, we're now down to three and not one of us really has a clue as to what's going on or what we should do next. So I'm ready to talk to some seer."

Geordie nodded.

"What should we bring to give her?" Holly asked. "I've probably got a couple of hundred dollars in petty cash. Or maybe she'd like a book . . . ?"

"It will probably be something more personal that that," Dick told her. "A favour, to be called in later."

"What kind of favour?"

"I don't *know.*"

"It's okay," Holly said. "I know this is upsetting you and I'm sorry. But you see where we're going crazy doing nothing?"

The hob nodded. "Just remember," he said. "Being around widdershins magic puts your shadow behind you, out of your sight where anyone can steal it. So if you do nothing else, keep a good hold of it."

Holly blinked in confusion. "My shadow? You mean like Christy was talking about earlier?"

Dick shook his head and pointed to where the basement light was casting her shadow on the stairs behind her.

"That shadow," he said. "The one that guards the door to your soul."

"Now I'm really confused," Holly said. "How am I supposed to hold onto it? There's nothing to grab."

"It's more that you have to stay aware of it," Dick explained. "Even if you can't see it, remember that you have one and imagine what it's like, how it stretches from you, dark against the light."

"Because if we don't . . . ?" Geordie asked.

"Some errant spirit could use it to step into your body."

Holly sighed. "Lovely."

"So you've changed your mind?" Dick asked, hope rising in his voice. "We can stay here and wait for the others to get back?"

Holly shook her head. "You can. Just tell me how to find Mother Crone once I get to the mall."

Geordie stood up and smoothed his jeans down where they were bunching at his knees.

"I'm coming, too," he said.

"Oh, why is it always the one thing or the other?" Dick said, standing up as well.

"You don't have to come," Holly said.

"But I do. You'd never find her on your own, Mistress Holly."

"Okay. We can go now, right? Even though the mall's closed for business?"

"Nothing is ever closed to fairies," Dick told her.

As Holly started up the stairs, Snippet went scrabbling by her, claws clicking on the wooden risers.

"What about Snippet?" she asked Dick. "How's she going to know that she's supposed to keep thinking about her shadow?"

"She should stay here in the store," the hob told her. "Not all fairies like dogs the way I do."

That managed to pull a small smile from Holly. It wasn't so much that Dick and Snippet didn't get along. But they didn't exactly seek out each other's company either. It also told her that Dick was reasonably certain that they wouldn't be gone for long.

Woodforest Plaza, situated in the southeast corner of where Richards Road intersects Highway 14, had once been the shopping centre pride of the city's northern suburbs. But early last year, developers had bought up the farmlands north of Richards Road, leveled the fields, including a sixty-year-old crow roost, and before you could say "shop till you drop," they had constructed a two-storied glass and concrete shopping centre so big that it could easily be its own small town. There were certainly people who spent their whole days there, from when the doors opened first thing in the morning until they finally closed at night.

Geordie drove Christy's old Dodge wagon around the Cineplex at the south end of the mall to the shipping bays in the back. He pulled into a parking spot by the eight-foot retaining wall that had been constructed to keep the still-untouched farmlands at bay. When he turned off the engine, they all got out. The banging of the car doors when they were closed seemed loud and to echo forever.

"This is creepy," Holly said. "I've never liked shopping centres at night. There's just something about these huge empty parking lots that doesn't seem right."

Geordie nodded. "I used to have a friend that lived on one of the farms that's now somewhere under all this concrete. I think it was over there, by the grocery store."

"And that's another thing," Holly said. "All those old farms gone—plus the roost."

"Yeah, the crow girls were really ticked off about that. Someone told me that, after it happened, they stole one of those huge cement mixer trucks, drove it to the home of one of the developers, and dumped the whole load of wet cement in his living room. But I don't know. There was never anything in the news about it."

He turned to Dick, who was standing close to the car. The hob's already large eyes seemed bigger than ever as he stared at the folding metal doors of the closest shipping bay. New as the mall was, the door was already covered with graffiti.

"Where do we go?" Geordie asked him.

The hob pointed to the doors. "In there."

"Okay. So what do we do? Just go up and knock on them or something?"

"Or something," Dick said.

Squaring his little shoulders, he set off across the parking lot, the leather soles of his shoes clicking softly on the pavement. Holly and Geordie exchanged glances, then followed the hob.

Holly wasn't sure what she expected when they reached the metal doors. She had little enough experience with magic or fairies, for all that she had a hob for a partner in the bookstore. It wasn't as though Dick's friends came by for a visit—at least they never came around when she was there—and Dick never did anything more magical than his bit where he sat so still he became invisible. So when the hob laid his hand on a part of spray-painted spiral, opening a portal like the one that had opened in her basement, she let out a gasp.

"Is . . . is that the otherworld?" she asked.

Dick shook his head. "It's just a bodach door to take us inside the mall."

"Right. And a bodach is?"

"Like me, a hob. Or like a brownie."

Geordie was still looking at the big metal door.

"Doesn't the iron in the metal bother you?" he asked.

"No, Master Geordie. I've lived among men too long for it to trouble me the way it would my country cousins." He started to step through, then paused, looking at them. "Are you coming?"

"Right, um, behind you," Holly said.

She closed her eyes as she stepped into what her mind still told her was a great big solid metal door, but her hands met no obstruction and then she was inside, Geordie behind her. When she opened her eyes, she saw that they were in a receiving facility of some sort. It must be for one of the department stores, she decided, because all around them were stacks and stacks of cardboard boxes holding everything from kettles to lawnmowers.

Dick took her hand.

"Come on, Mistress Holly," he said. "Mother Crone is supposed to hold court in the main courtyard. Where the swans fly."

It took Holly a moment to understand what he was talking about. Then she remembered the sculptures of the great white birds hanging from the big domed ceiling by the mall's central doors, their long necks stretched out, metal wings outspread, as they appeared to soar across the vault of the dome. She couldn't recall how many there were—a fairy-tale seven?

Dick led them to the far side of the warehouse and out into a hallway that eventually took them into the mall itself. Holly had always thought that it might be fun to have the run of one of these places at night, but right now it felt as creepy as the empty parking lot outside. Plus all the individual stores were locked up, so it wasn't like you could go rummaging around in them or anything.

"Do you hear something?" she asked as they walked down the cavernous hallway toward the central court.

They walked by shuttered carts, wooden benches, waste dispensers and small temporary kiosks, locked up for the night. Their reflections, caught in the windows of the dark stores, kept pace on the other side. Holly glanced behind her, looking for her shadow. Because the light came from above, it was pooled around her feet. But still there.

"It's music," Geordie said. "Something with a hip-hop beat."

Holly nodded. At first she'd thought it might be coming from the mall's sound system. She supposed there was no reason for them to turn the Muzak off at night. But then she realized it came from further up the hallway, growing steadily louder as they approached the courtyard.

"It's revel music," Dick said.

Holly was about to ask what he meant, but then she could see them ahead of her, figures of all shapes and sizes dancing to the music, and from their enthusiasm, the word "revel" became pretty much self-explanatory. It was only when they got right to where the hallway spilled into the courtyard that she saw that the source of the music was a prosaic boombox. Considering the dancers, she would have expected it to be far more exotic: some sort of outlandish elfin creatures creating the music live, rather than having it come from a simple recording.

But the dancers made up for the mundane source of the music.

There were little people half Dick's size that seemed to be made of twigs and moss and grass, although here and there she spied a few similar creatures that looked to be made of wiring, with sparkplug noses and circuitry board torsos.

There were tall men and women with pointed ears, dressed in stately gowns and Victorian waistcoats and suits. Others the same size in rough fabrics with vests and cloaks that were as much leaves and moss and feathers as they were cloth. Others still, in skateboarders' baggy cargo pants and T-shirts.

There were beings that seemed as much animal as human. Gangly monkey creatures with bird-like features. Tubby pumpkin bodies topped with the faces of raccoons and badgers. Straw-thin beings with lizard and snake faces.

There were creatures that Holly recognized from the illustrations of fairy-tale picture books. Goblins and brownies and pixies, and even what seemed like a small trow dressed in rustic browns and greens, with a nose too big and legs too squat and short.

There was, in short, every sort of fairy that Holly had ever imagined, and many she couldn't have begun to. But one thing they had in common: they were all light-footed and graceful—even the stiffest looking of them, which was a creature that appeared to be nothing so much as an ambulatory log with spindly arms and legs and a face that pushed out of the bark at the top. And they were quiet on their feet.

Holly spied soft-soled slippers and running shoes and bare feet, which might have explained the quiet to some degree, but surely there should have been some sound. Whispers and scuffles, the slap of a bare foot on tile or even the faint pad of paws. But the soft-stepping fairy revelers made no sound at all when they moved. There was only the music, the infectious groove of a hip-hop beat that seemed to allow for any kind of dancing, from ballroom to break, all of which were evident.

The revelers completely ignored them until Dick cleared his throat. Then the music continued, but all the dancers stopped and turned to look in their direction. Finally a little twig and leaf girl standing close to the boombox, her vine-like hair pulled back into a thick Rasta ponytail, reached over and turned off the music. Utter silence fell over the courtyard and they were looking into the dozens of fairy gazes turned in their direction.

At that moment Holly felt very exposed and not a little afraid. There was something about the eyes of the fairies that woke a shiver at the base of her spine, that had the hairs standing up on her arms and at the nape of her neck. There was nothing threatening about them—not yet, at least—but nothing human either. They were cat eyes and hare eyes and bird eyes. They were the eyes of wild things, but a sharp, knowing intelligence burned in them as they did in no ordinary animal.

"Well," someone said, breaking the tableau. "I've been expecting you."

She came walking through the crowd, a tall woman with her dark hair hanging halfway to her waist in a dozen or so thick braids. Holly couldn't figure out why she hadn't noticed her among the dancers earlier, she was such a striking woman, with her piercing gaze and fine-boned, narrow features. She wore black cargo pants, platform sneakers, and a tank top that was sized so small it lay like paint against her skin and bared her midriff.

"You . . . have?" Holly managed to get out. "But how could you know we'd be coming?"

"She's Mother Crone, Mistress Holly," Dick said.

"*You're* Mother Crone? But you don't look at all . . ."

Holly let her voice trail off.

"Cronish?" the woman said.

Standing in front of her, the woman towered over Holly.

"I guess," Holly said. "I was going to say 'old.' "

Mother Crone smiled. "It's only a name. You're not made of holly, are you?"

"Well, no . . ."

Though right at this moment, Holly wouldn't have been surprised to find that she was, in fact.

"Why were you expecting us?" she asked.

"I'm a seer."

"Oh, right," Holly said. "Of course."

Mother Crone laughed. "But that said, I'll admit that I only knew someone was coming. Not who, or what you might want from me."

She lowered herself so that she was sitting cross-legged on the floor—a quick, graceful movement that made it appear as though she'd simply floated down. Holly hesitated a moment, then took a seat on the floor herself, although she didn't feel nearly so graceful doing it. Geordie and Dick sat down on either side of her.

"So tell me how I can help," Mother Crone said.

The fairy woman seemed so friendly that Holly had to wonder why

Dick had been nervous about coming here. Then she remembered how he'd been around Meran, who he thought was a princess of some fairy wood.

"Don't be shy now," Mother Crone added.

Holly started, realizing that she let her thoughts drift. She gave Dick a quick glance, but he seemed to be content to leave everything in her hands. Great. And then she remembered something else he'd said about Mother Crone. Better get that out of the way first.

Holly cleared her throat. "Um, could you tell me what the price will be?"

"I need to know the problem first."

"Oh, right. Well, it's a little complicated."

"By the time a problem comes to me, it usually is," Mother Crone said. "It's best to start at the beginning."

So Holly did—but not right at the beginning, all the way back to when pixies had first come stepping out of her computer monitor. Instead, she started with Aaran Goldstein getting his friend Jackson to send a virus to the Wordwood, backtracking a little to explain her own connection to the Web site, then outlining the high points of all that had befallen since.

Mother Crone listened well, asking few questions, and then only to clarify something that Holly hadn't properly explained. But when Holly was done, she cocked her head and gave Holly a puzzled look.

"I understand the problem now," she said, "and it certainly is a messy one. What I don't understand is why you've come to me for help."

"Well, it's just that Dick . . ."

Holly gave the hob a glance and saw a look she knew well; it was the one where the last thing in the world he wanted was to have what he considered some higher class of fairy pay any sort of attention to him.

"I thought you might give us some advice," Holly finished. "You know, as to what we can do to help."

"Hmm."

Mother Crone glanced over her shoulder and singled out one of the little circuit and wire men.

"Edgan," she said "Do you know this place that our guest is talking about?"

The little man nodded. He scurried off, opening a bodach door in a nearby computer store. He returned with a laptop under his arm and set it down on the floor. While he got it up and running, the fairy with the Rasta ponytail who had been operating the boombox approached Mother Crone, handing her a wooden bowl and a plastic bottle of water.

"Thank you, Hazel," Mother Crone said.

Holly watched in fascination as Edgan pulled a credit card-sized circuit from out of the tangle of wiring and circuitry that was his chest. He stuck it in the PCMCIA slot of the laptop and pulled a little aerial out of the card. His narrow wire fingers danced on the laptop's keyboard, then he looked up.

"Here it is," he said.

Holly leaned forward so that she could see what was on the screen. All that was visible was the "This page cannot be displayed," message that they'd been getting ever since the virus had taken the site down, but Mother Crone gave a thoughtful nod.

"Better disconnect it," she said.

The little man hit a key, then removed the PCMCIA card from the slot and inserted it back into his chest. Holly blinked—that was just *so* weird—and turned her attention back to Mother Crone. The seer set the wooden bowl on the floor between Holly and herself. Untwisting the top from the water bottle, she poured the contents of the bottle into her bowl.

"Did . . . did you see something?" Holly asked. "On the computer screen?"

"Not exactly. Just enough to know that there's something very wrong there. I'm not much good at scrying with technology. But now that I have a touchstone to that place, I can use this—" She indicated the bowl of water. "—to look in on it through more traditional means."

Holly was beyond surprise by this point. "Will you be able to see our friends?" she asked. "Can you tell us how they are?"

"I can try," Mother Crone replied, which promised nothing.

She moved a hand over the water and a ripple in the water followed the motion, back and forth across the surface. Lifting her hand, she studied the water as it stilled.

"Hmm," she said.

Holly leaned forward as well but saw nothing, only water in a bowl.

"What do you see?" Holly asked.

The seer made no response. She pursed her lips, all of her attention on whatever invisible drama was being enacted on the surface of the water in her bowl. When she finally looked up, her gaze was troubled.

"I'm sorry," she said.

Holly's chest went tight. "Why? What is it?"

"There is . . ." She looked away, her gaze going inward. "I'm not sure how to explain," she went on when she focused on Holly once more. "Do you know much about the otherworld, how it isn't one place so much as many places—a patchwork of worlds, some large some small, but all connected like some enormous quilt?"

"Vaguely . . ."

"And that this Internet site has become one of those worlds?"

Holly nodded. "That's what—I can't remember who. I think it was Christy who figured that out."

Mother Crone gave a slow nod. "This Wordwood is closed from the rest of the otherworld at the moment and it's a good thing. There is something in it—I can't say exactly what. I just know that it's old, and it's dying. And as it's dying, it's taking the Wordwood with it. Or perhaps it's the Wordwood itself that is dying, taking everything inside it along with it. All I know for sure is that it's too late to do anything about it now."

"But our friends . . . ?"

"What's this thing inside?" Geordie asked.

Mother Crone turned to him. "I don't know. Something ancient. Something I've never met or seen before, though there are stories about its kind."

"And it's evil?"

She shook her head. "It's neither good nor evil on its own. But it's very powerful."

"I guess it doesn't matter," Geordie said, "whether it's the Wordwood or this spirit that's dying. We just have to get hold of the others and get them out of there. . . ."

His voice trailed off as Mother Crone shook her head.

"You won't help us?" he said. "Just tell me the price."

"It's not a matter of price."

"That's my brother in there. Our friends."

Mother Crone sighed. "I know. I understand. But to open any gate into that world at this time means allowing whatever's happening inside loose into the rest of the otherworld. I won't be responsible for that."

"But—"

"Would your friends . . . would your brother want to live at the cost of the death of the millions that would die in the otherworld if whatever this thing is gets loose? And that's saying you could even do anything at this point." She pointed at her scrying bowl. "All I sense in that world is the ancient one. We don't even know if there's anybody else even alive in there at the moment."

"But we can't just abandon them all."

Holly saw the pain in Mother Crone's eyes. "Yes, I know. Hundreds have been lost. But unless we leave the struggle contained as it is, it could truly be millions. It might even spread into this world."

Holly thought she was going to be sick. Geordie stood up beside her. For a moment she thought he was going to hit someone, but instead he stalked off to the glass windows that overlooked the mall's parking lot. He stood there, looking out into the night, his fists clenched at his side.

"I'm so sorry," Mother Crone said.

Holly gave a slow nod. "I . . . I understand. Not what's going on. But why you can't—why we can't do anything. But it's hard to just stand by . . ."

"There is nothing harder than a moment like this," the seer said. "When you would give anything to help those you love, but there is absolutely nothing that can be done."

Holly gave another nod. She wished they'd never come. Better to have stayed at the store, living with ignorance and the hope that ignorance allowed, than to have to deal with this awful feeling.

"There's got to be something we can do," she said, knowing there was nothing. "Someone we can talk to."

Mother Crone hesitated. "I don't know if it would make things better or worse," she finally said, "but we could go the edge of the Wordwood. Perhaps something'll come to us when we're standing there, seeing it firsthand."

Holly scrambled to her feet. "I'm ready to go. Geordie!"

Mother Crone arose as well.

"This could be harder on you than waiting here," she said.

"Harder than dying in the Wordwood like our friends are?"

Mother Crone shook her head.

When Geordie came back to where they were standing, Holly quickly explained what they were going to do.

"I'm in," he said as she knew he would.

"You should go back to the store," she told Dick.

The hob shook his head. "I won't, Mistress Holly. I won't let you go alone."

"I won't be alone," she said. "And someone needs to look after Snippet in case, you know . . ." We don't come back, she was about to say. "We're gone for a while."

Dick began to shiver, but before Holly could comfort him, Mother Crone stepped forward and put a hand on his shoulder.

"Don't worry, Master Hob," she told him. "I'll bring them back."

He gave a glum nod.

"I knew coming here was a bad, bad idea," he said. "I just knew it."

In the end, Mother Crone sent Edgan back to the store with Dick. Under the protests of some of the other fairies that had been following the various conversations and were determined to come as well, she would only allow Hazel to accompany Geordie, Holly, and herself into the otherworld.

"But if it's so dangerous . . . ." one of the human-sized fairies began.

"It's not," Mother Crone said. "We're going to scout, not to fight a war."

"But if it's not dangerous," the fairy went on, "then there's no harm in us coming."

"I would prefer not to have a crowd," Mother Crone said.

She spoke in a tone of voice that was mild, but would brook no argument, and there were none. She turned to Holly and Geordie.

"Have either of you crossed over before?" she asked.

They both shook their heads.

"Then be forewarned," she told them. "The crossing can make you a little nauseous."

No more than she was already feeling, Holly thought. She couldn't stop thinking of the others, trapped in this stupid dying Web site/magic world that she'd had a hand in creating. It made her sick to her stomach. Her chest so tight it was hard to breathe.

"What do we do?" Geordie asked.

"Do?" Mother Crone said. "You don't have to do anything."

"Are you going to use this . . . this widdershins magic?" Holly asked.

"Widdershins to what?" Mother Crone replied.

"I don't know. I just heard . . ."

Holly's voice trailed off.

"You will be safe with me," Mother Crone said. "Just so long as you stay by me and don't go straying off on your own."

She lifted her hands above her head and brought them down with a sweeping arm-wide motion on either side of her body. When her hands touched just in front of her knees, there was a shimmer in the air, like the wall had shimmered in the store's basement, and then they were looking in at a place that shouldn't be there. Here in the middle of a mall, with the night still dark outside, they were looking through a portal at a sunny field, mountains in the distance beyond them.

Another world.

Mother Crone and Hazel stepped through, followed by Geordie. Holly bent down and kissed Dick on the forehead, then took a steadying breath and followed after.

Robert

It was a longer trek than Robert had thought it would be, walking to the Wordwood from the crossroads where he'd left the three transformed hellhounds. But he knew how to pace himself, and he knew how to make good time, taking shortcuts where he could, so it was a quicker trip for him than it might have been for another. Quick, but rough going in places. When he finally drew near enough to see the grey mists in the distance, his fancy shoes were scuffed and dusty, his suit wrinkled, with sweat stains growing under the arms and on his back where his guitar hung, slung from the thin braid of leather that he used as a strap on the odd occasions when he needed one.

He could sense the passage of the others where they'd made this same journey, hours ago. Saw where Aaran had left the road, where Bojo had gone after him, where they'd both come back on the road again. He paused for a moment, studying the fields, wondering what had drawn Aaran away. When he looked back in the direction of the Wordwood, he saw a figure on the road approaching him. He swung his guitar around in front to give him quick access to it and patted the holster under his coat where his Peacemaker hung. But as the figure drew nearer—and when he could finally reach out with his thoughts and read her—he knew neither would be necessary.

She was a big woman—easily as tall as Bojo and twice the tinker's weight. Her hair was thick and brown, a waterfall of curls and ringlets that splayed out over her shoulders and halfway down her back and chest. She walked with a rolling gait, her feet bare, the mass of her body covered with a brightly-coloured muumuu. Instead of the usual large flowers one might expect on such a garment, hers was decorated with large cabalistic symbols and astrological signs.

Everything about her was large, but especially her spirit. That spirit was so big that even a body her size was unable to contain it. When Robert looked at her, she seemed to shine as bright as a sun.

As they drew near enough to each other to exchange words, the woman lifted a meaty hand and favored him with a smile so infectious that he couldn't help but grin back at her.

"Hey there, stranger," she said. "I sure hope you're not on a pilgrimage today."

"Why's that?" Robert asked when they came abreast of each other. He gave a tug on the braid of leather that held his guitar so that it swung around onto his back once more.

"It's all blocked up a-ways from here," the woman told her. "Damnedest thing I've ever seen in this place. I don't think there'll be anything going in or going out for a while, which might be a good thing, considering."

"Oh?"

"I don't know what all's going on behind the wall of mist, but I know it can't be good. It just *feels* wrong, you know what I'm saying? Name's Lindy, by the way. Lindy Brown."

Robert lifted his eyebrows and she grinned back at him.

"Oh, that's just what people call me," she said. "I know enough not to be handing out to my name to just anybody, even a handsome stranger such as your own self. But it sounds so unfriendly saying, 'You can call me Lindy,' like we've got to drive home the fact we don't trust each other."

Robert smiled and held out his hand. "I'm Robert."

"Pleased," she said, giving his hand a shake. "It's been quiet on these roads, the past few weeks. Seems I've been meeting next to nobody, and I guess I've got what feels like a year's worth of words stored up in my head, just waiting to get out. Oh, don't you worry," she added, holding up a hand. "I'm not expecting you to hear 'em all out. I just mean it's nice to say how-do to somebody for a change."

"Did you see anybody up that way?"

Lindy shook her head. " 'Fraid not. You lose someone?"

"Just had some people travelling ahead. I was hoping to catch up to them soon."

"Well, if you didn't meet 'em coming back already, then they must have gone around that wall of mist, which isn't something I'd ever do. It's all quicktime land on either side and they could be anywhere by now."

"I'm pretty good at finding my way around in here."

"I'll just bet you are. Me, I stick to the realtime routes I know. That's why I'm heading back to find me a cross-path that will take me around."

"Mabon's not that far back."

She nodded. "I know. I passed it coming in. But there's a footpath this side of the city that I mean to take. It'll save me a few hours that I'd lose going through the city. Not that I'm in a particular hurry. I'm just not partial to crowds, most of the time."

"I know the feeling."

"You're welcome to tag along with me, if you have a mind."

"Thanks," Robert said, "but I think I'll pass. I've got an itch to see this wall of mist up ahead."

"Just be careful you don't get too close. I surely mislike the feel of that place, damned if I can tell you why. It's just *wrong*."

"I'm always careful," Robert assured her.

But he understood her concern once he'd left her behind and reached the mist. It was definitely the Wordwood in there behind that grey wall. He had no trouble recognizing the feel of the place from the little of it he'd tasted back in Holly's store. And he could also see that Christy and the others had gone into it. He studied it for a long moment, then just as Bojo had done earlier in the day, he bent down, picked up a stone and tossed it into the mist.

And never saw it land.

He nodded to himself. He'd seen this before, some piece of the between cozied up along the borders of the world. He reached in with his thoughts to see if he could find any of the others, but this piece of the between was either too deep, or the others had already travelled out of range. He couldn't get a clear connection inside the Wordwood, either. The whole area behind the mist was swollen with an annoying buzz of static that made it hard to focus on any one thing in particular. But distracting as it was, he could still sense the presence of some enormous old spirit in there, and one other thing, another presence that reminded him of Papa Legba.

It took him a moment to figure out why. Then he had it.

It was because this second presence was also a gateway spirit.

Neither it nor the other, older spirit seemed healthy. There was a rot in the air of the place, a feeling that it was sliding into some deep and lasting darkness. Like Lindy had told him, there was something *wrong* in there.

Robert could fix it. He knew the notes he had to coax from his old Gibson, the music that would reach in and clean that place out. But he hesitated. He wasn't sure that it made much difference which gateway spirit nested in that place, the one that was already there, or Papa Legba. The trouble was, if the *loa* wanted him to do this thing, then there was probably something he was missing. A being like Papa Legba usually had more than one reason behind his side of a bargain. There was the one he'd tell you up front, all open about it. But more often than not there was another, or others, hidden and secret. Twisty reasons that would give the *loa* some extra advantage over you.

He went back over his conversation with Papa Legba. The bargain the *loa* had offered appeared straightforward. If he got rid of the gateway spirit inhabiting the Wordwood—allowing the *loa* to take the place over, Robert assumed—Papa Legba would renounce all claim on Robert's soul. Nothing complicated about that. If there was a trick, Robert couldn't see it. And he supposed that the advantage of being rid of this competitive spirit and the subsequent control Papa Legba would have over the Wordwood far outweighed his loss of one old bluesman's soul.

Robert studied the mist some more, peering through its grey haze at the forest of old growth trees that lay behind it. If he squinted, the trees lost some of their definition and he could see towering bookcases superimposed over them, with aisles in between that seemed to go on forever. He blinked and the library was gone.

There was still no sign of the others, but he wasn't sure if that was because they were elsewhere—taken by the vagaries of the between to some distant world—or if the static was stopping him from being able to sense their presence.

He swung his guitar around in front of him and closed his fingers around the neck. Muting the strings. Still thinking.

Did it really matter which gateway spirit used this place? One was pretty much the same as the other, at least so far as he could see. And if he did use a bit of gris-gris to clean this place out, did it matter if he was doing it for himself, or because he'd promised Bojo and the others to help fix what was wrong with the Wordwood?

That, he could answer. Of course it mattered. He wasn't so naïve as to forget that with magic, intent was everything. Using it for self-gain was never nearly so potent as a selfless act. Though that went with pretty much anything in life, and there was no rule against combining the two, was there?

Still, he hesitated.

"Having second thoughts?"

He turned to see that the crossroads *loa* had joined him. Papa Legba with his black hat, leaning on his cane, still playing up the fiction of his infirmity. Robert wasn't surprised that he'd missed the sound of the *loa*'s approach. Gateway spirits had the whole business of popping in and out of thin air down to a fine art. Robert could do it, too, here in the otherworld, but it wasn't something that came naturally to him.

"I'm just wondering what it is that you aren't telling me," Robert said.

"Well, now," the *loa* said. "Considering the few times we've had the chance to talk, there's a whole world of histories and stories we haven't even started to touch on yet."

Robert indicated the mist. "How about, specifically, what do you have planned for what lies behind this wall of mist?"

"What do you want to know?"

Robert regarded him for a moment. The complete lack of guile in the *loa*'s dark gaze. The half smile playing against that same apparent honesty.

"What do you hold sacred?" Robert said.

The question actually appeared to puzzle the *loa*.

"Sacred?" he repeated.

"You know what I mean."

"I suppose I do. I guess I'd have to say Kalfou."

Robert didn't know if the *loa* literally meant "crossroads," which was one meaning for the word, or if he was referring to the name that the Petro people gave to the more dangerous aspect of his spirit. Legba was the *loa*'s designation as a member of the Rada nation, the revered gatekeeper who provided the only means for voudoun practitioners to contact other spirits. Kalfou was his other aspect, a trickster who delighted in upsetting the natural order of things and caused unexpected accidents.

He supposed it didn't matter, so long as the *loa* held it sacred. He studied Papa Legba for a long moment, still considering. The *loa* returned his gaze with that deceptive mildness in his own eyes, his earlier half smile still tugging at his lips.

Robert gave a short nod. "That'll do. Swear to me on Kalfou that replacing the gateway spirit inside this place with you isn't going to hurt anyone."

"Besides that other spirit?"

"I can get rid of it without hurting it."

"I suppose you can," the *loa* said.

"So swear it."

"I can swear that it's not my intent to harm anyone, but you know how it goes. Supplicants come asking for favours, I can't guarantee what they do with them."

"Then swear that, to your knowledge—"

The *loa* interrupted. "Now I'm supposed to know everything?"

"You're being evasive," Robert said.

"And you're being excessively particular."

"I like to think of it as careful."

The *loa* nodded, but instead of responding, he changed the subject.

"Can you feel it?" he asked. "Something's gone bad in that place. It smells like a stagnant pond and it's getting worse all the time."

"What about it?"

"I can take it away," Papa Legba said. "Whatever's gone wrong in there, I can make it better."

"Out of the goodness of your heart?"

The *loa* smiled. "Yes. Oh, I stand to gain—I won't hide that. But surely you know this much about me: I can't abide disorder."

"Except when you're Kalfou—and then you're first in line to . . ." Robert hesitated a moment, looking for the least confrontational way to put it. "To make things interesting."

"Do I look like Kalfou?"

Robert shrugged. "I wouldn't know. I've never met you in that aspect."

"Well, I'm not. And time's wasting. Every moment we stand here and argue, the rot behind that wall of mist grows stronger."

That was certainly true. Even through the static that kept him from making clear contact with anyone behind the mist, he could tell it was worsening. The old spirit he sensed . . . its power was turning dark and restless. And he was inclined to believe that the *loa*'s intentions, at least in this particular instance, were honest.

"Just tell me," Robert said. "*Swear* that you don't intend to cause any harm."

"That I can do. On Kalfou, my shadow's name."

"Then I'll clean that place out," Robert said.

When he loosened his grip on the neck of his guitar, the strings gave a small hum of anticipation—low, almost inaudible, but there came an answering echo from deep underground. He shaped a chord, fingers stretching in for what most players would be an extremely awkward shape, but for him was as simple as a basic C chord.

"I learned this from an old woman," he said softly. "Back in the delta. She could sing a piece of this chord all on her own, harmonizing with herself."

"What did she use it for?"

"Cleaning out bad spirits from a place," Robert said.

Then he drew the thumb of his right hand across the strings. The chord he played rang out with far more volume and power than should have been possible from the small-bodied Gibson he played. It rumbled, deep and throaty, and that faint echo that had come a moment ago, from deep underground, returned and grew into a sound like distant thunder.

"You be careful," Papa Legba said. "That kind of music could do some real structural damage."

Robert nodded. The chord he'd played was a piece of the music that had sounded when old, black-winged Raven pulled the world out of nothing, back in the long ago. It was the sound of continents rising out of the sea, of mountains shifting and valleys shaping. It was the whisper of rain on the seedling first forest. It was the voice of water flowing, wind blowing. Of the first bird cries and a canid's howl. It was a lonely sound that called community into being.

In the long ago, language was still a part of the great mystery and every word held power. Speaking was a ceremony. What was said then had weight because its effects could carry on for generations. The world wasn't spoken about; the world was spoken into being, word by word.

But older than that ceremonial tribe of words, was music. The first music.

Robert had never played it before, hoarding the little he knew of it against a time just like this. But he hadn't been worried about using a chord of the first music. He'd put the right intent behind it, kept it focused and on the problem. It didn't even need to be repeated. It just kept on sounding, cutting into the mist and going deep into the world that lay behind it.

But what he hadn't taken into account was the static. The same static that made it impossible to get a clear picture of who all was in that world, was messing with the harmonics of the chord. Changing it.

Too late, he saw that it was doing something other than what he'd intended. He damped his guitar strings, but the chord continued to resound. It was out of his hands now and he couldn't take it back.

"This is a little more extreme than I was looking for," the *loa* said.

"I know," Robert said. "Something's changing it—something inside the world."

"Can you fix it—play something else?"

Robert shook his head. "If I couldn't control what happened with one chord going through that mist, playing anything else is only going to make things worse."

"So we wait."

"And we pray."

Papa Legba laughed, but there was no humour in it.

"Yeah," he said. "Like it's something I've ever done before."

Robert closed his eyes. "Then I'll do it for both of us."

Saskia

It's weird being back in my own body like this. But I'm not really allowed the luxury of getting used to it. Because on top of all the rest of our problems, it looks like the Wordwood's about to come apart right under our feet.

We all stare at that huge fissure that's opened at the edge of the lake, the way the water is pouring into it. I hear more thunder, coming from deeper in the library. I'm not sure if it's another of these fissures opening up or the sound of these enormous bookcases collapsing. Maybe a combination of both.

"We need to get out of here," I say.

Jackson gives a quick nod of agreement, but Christiana only shakes her head.

"There's nothing we can do," I tell her. "We're so far out of our depth, I wouldn't know where to begin to look for a way to fix any of this."

"Maybe . . . in the books . . . ?" Jackson says.

"We don't have that kind of time," I tell him.

As though to underscore that, there's another huge clap of thunder, and this time the ground shifts right underfoot, making us all struggle to keep our balance.

"Maybe we don't know how to fix it," Christiana says, "but I'm betting I know someone who does."

She gets this look on her face that I recognize. It's the same look that Christy gets when something that should have been obvious finally slips into place—but this is only after hours of worrying at the problem. With Christy, it's usually a matter of research and he just takes a blue pencil to his manuscript. With Christiana . . . well, with Christiana I'm beginning to realize anything can happen.

I've spent time inside her skin, but I was a passenger in her body. I was able to tap into her physical sensations—what she heard and saw and tangibly felt. But I never touched her emotional landscape. All I know is that she can be impetuous and volatile. And unlike Christy, who'll talk a thing out, she makes snap decisions and then follows through on them immediately.

I want to say something now. I don't know what's come into her mind, but I want her to try to be a bit more like Christy for a moment. I want her to stay calm, to talk to me.

But she's not Christy. She looks from the leviathan to Librarius, whose eyes are open, watching us. Christiana stalks over to where we've left him lying, tied up and helpless. Undoing his gag, she picks him up and slams him against a bookshelf. I've forgotten how strong she is.

"Start talking," she says, her voice low and dangerous.

"I don't know anyth—"

Before he can finish, she steps back, then slams him against the bookshelf again. A couple of books on one of the higher shelves come tumbling down, not two feet from where they're standing. Christiana doesn't even look in their direction.

"Maybe you don't get it," she says. Her voice is still quiet, almost conversational. "I don't want to hear any more of your bullshit. What I *want* to hear is exactly what you did to this place."

"You can't—"

She slams him again.

"You get one more chance," she tells him, "and then I'm going to start taking you apart, piece by piece. Look into my eyes. Read what you see there and tell me I'm making idle threats."

She's starting to scare me now. If this is a part of Christy's personality that he gave up when his shadow stepped out of him, I'm just as happy that he did. But I think she's bluffing. I *hope* she's bluffing, but that Librarius will believe her. But he thinks she's bluffing, too.

"I am looking into your eyes," he says. "Torture isn't something you've ever done before."

I find myself letting out a breath of relief that I hadn't been aware of holding. I didn't want to think that she could be that harsh. But my relief doesn't last long.

"So you think I'm not capable of it?" she asks. Her voice is dangerous now, as though she wants him to push her too far.

There's a long moment of silence, then he slowly shakes his head.

"N-no," he finally says. "You could do it."

She lets him go and he falls to the ground, unable to keep his balance because of how he's bound. He curls into a fetal position as though he thinks she's going to hit him. Instead she puts a foot on one of the hands tied behind his back. I see him wince when she applies some pressure.

"I don't want to see those fingers moving," she says. "And all I want to hear coming out of your mouth is the truth."

"I . . . I . . ."

She crouches down, her foot still on his hand. "Now, tell me what you've done."

I don't like what's happening, but I understand why she stepped on his hand. He needs to move his fingers when he speaks a spell. And then I think about how a few moments ago I was ready to just throw him into the lake, bound and all. I guess I'm not so immune to violence as I'd like to think I am.

"I did tell you the truth . . ." He flinches as she applies some more pressure on his hand. "Just . . . just not all of it."

"So do it now. Tell me about the leviathan."

He swallows thickly and looks in my direction. I school my features to remain expressionless.

"The leviathan *was* here already," he says, looking back at Christiana. "I didn't lie about that. He was the spirit called into this place when the Wordwood took shape."

"That's not possible," Christiana says. "I may not know a lot about leviathans, but I do know they don't physically manifest."

"He didn't," Librarius tells her. "He *was* the Wordwood. At least until the virus struck."

"So what happened?"

"You have to understand," Librarius says. "A place like this, so easily accessible to anyone . . ."

"Through the Internet."

He nods. "It's very desirable real estate. It's hard for spirits to develop—let's call it a constituency—these days. Few people have the desire or time for rituals and devotions. The Wordwood is like a gold mine. Every visitor lends credence and potency to the one who controls it."

"You're saying the leviathan wanted to be worshipped?"

"Not the leviathan. Me. Any being such as me."

"And you are?"

"A gateway spirit."

"Ah."

"What does that mean?" I ask.

Christiana turns to me. "People are always reaching for the Great Mysteries," she explains, "but few of them can make contact with them on their own. So they go through intermediaries. It can be religion. It can be private rituals that they create on their own or with a small group of like-minded friends. It can be sacrifices and devotions made to a gateway spirit who will connect them to the spirits they wish to contact. Usually it's some combination of all of that—whatever will take their invocation and deliver it to the appropriate spirit."

"Sort of like using a search engine," Jackson says.

Christiana gives a slow nod. "I suppose. Though it's more personal than that, because—"

She breaks off as another crack of thunder shakes the ground. I grab the nearest bookcase to keep my balance. When the shivering ground settles down once more, Christiana turns her attention back to our captive.

"So you wanted the Wordwood," she says, "and when the virus incapacitated the leviathan, you stepped in and took over."

"Something like that. Except the leviathan wasn't incapacitated by the virus. He was just disoriented. I'd been eyeing this place for ages. When the virus struck and I saw what was happening, I took the opportunity to . . . contain him."

I don't get it, but Christiana nods before I can ask.

"You gave him a physical body," she says.

"I thought it would work. It's not like I—or anyone—has the power to cast something like a leviathan out of a place like this."

"And it's killing him," Christiana says. There's that dark tone in her voice again.

"I didn't *know*," Librarius tells her. "I swear I didn't know."

"And that's why the Wordwood's falling apart around us."

Librarius shakes his head. "The leviathan's dying is turning this place into a shadow world. Anyone looking in on it from the outside would see a place of darkness and despair. Already, steps would have been taken to close off access to it from the rest of the spiritworld—not by any entity, but by the spiritworld itself."

"Because?" Christiana asks.

"If the Wordwood is accessed—if any gates are opened by those departing or entering—the miasma that rules this place now would spread into other worlds."

"So what's causing the Wordwood to fall apart?"

"I don't know. Perhaps someone is attempting to exorcise the spirits from it. I can feel a pushing inside me, a demand, in no uncertain terms, that I leave. It resounds inside me like a piece of the old music, the first music that helped the old ones create the world in the long ago."

Christiana gives a slow nod. "Where will it send you? Back into whatever void spat you out in the first place?"

"Not exactly. I had a life in the spiritworld before I took on this guise. But if this is an exorcism and it takes hold, it could dissipate my essence. It would take me a very long time to pull the parts of me back together once more."

"Well, that wouldn't be any great loss," Christiana says. She studies him for a long moment. "But you don't seem particularly worried about it."

"Why should I be? Whatever is working the spell against me and the leviathan is breaking up against the fact that the leviathan's immense spirit is contained in a physical form. We're all going to die before the exorcism can work on me."

"And dying's a better thing?"

Now Librarius smiles. "It is for me. If the exorcism was to work on me, I might never be able to collect enough of the errant pieces of my spirit to regain this particular life I wear. But I've died before. It takes me no great effort to return from the dead—I am a gateway spirit, after all." His smile widens slightly. "Pity you can't say the same thing."

"Yeah, it's a real shame," Christiana says.

She starts to stand up, but another tremor rocks the ground. We all have to grab onto the bookcases. When the thundering echoes finally start to fade, Christiana gets to her feet.

"One of you put his gag back in," she says. "And watch his hands. If he starts wiggling his fingers, don't screw around. Just break them all, including his thumbs." She looks from Jackson to me. "Do you think you can do that?"

I know why it has to be done, but I don't think I can do it. But Jackson nods.

"Yeah, I can do it," he says.

I guess he finally found some backbone, though maybe I'm not being fair. In some ways, he's had it the roughest of all of us, starting with having to carry the guilt of being responsible for all of this in the first place, however inadvertently it came about.

"What are you going to do?" I ask Christiana.

"Find something I can use to kill the leviathan," she says, then walks away before I can ask her more. A half-dozen paces down the corridor between the bookcases, she breaks into a run.

Christy

It's impossible to find steady footing as we follow the path into the wet forest, but we go slipping and sliding anyway, splashing through mud, banging up against the trunks of these big trees that sometimes, out of the corner of your eyes, seem to shift into enormous bookcases. But when you look at them straight on, they're trees again.

I don't know how long the panic has a hold of us, but Bojo finally grabs my arm, stopping me. Raul collides into us. He starts to fall except Bojo and I each catch an arm and haul him to his feet. Suzi and Aaran come to a skidding stop and only just miss sending us sprawling in the mud.

We're all breathing hard. I don't know about the others, but I've got a stitch in my side that makes me bend over and lean against the nearest tree. I stare at the bark. I don't know what kind of trees these are, but they're huge. Some have trunks so big that all five of us couldn't touch hands around it. And they go up forever. Redwoods are the closest I've seen like them in the World As It Is.

After we stand there for long moments, catching our breath, Aaran starts to say something, but Bojo holds up a hand. He walks a few paces back the way we've come, cocking his head to listen. We hear more thunder, but it sounds like it's a long way from us.

"I think we've outrun the worst of it," Bojo says when he comes back to us, "but let's keep moving."

He sets off and I fall into pace beside him.

"Does anybody else keep seeing bookcases instead of trees?" Raul asks from behind us.

"They really are bookcases," Suzi says.

That brings us all to a stop.

"What?" I say.

"And they're trees at the same time," she adds. "They both exist at the same time. Don't forget, I was born in this place."

Like Saskia, I think, and I feel the sharp pang of loss that comes every time I think of her.

"Do you know which way we're headed?" Bojo asks. "What we can expect?"

She shakes her head. "I just know we're in the Wordwood. It feels very familiar." Then she shrugs. "And very different at the same time. Something's really wrong with the Wordwood spirit."

"Yeah," Raul says. "It's trying to kill us."

"I don't think so."

"Let's keep moving," Bojo says. "We can talk while we're walking."

"How can they be trees and bookcases at the same time?" Aaran asks as we set off again.

"I don't know," Suzi says. "They just are."

"I think I know," I say. "It's a perceptual thing. We see what we're expecting to see."

Aaran chuckles. "So, what are you saying? That this is more of your 'the world is the way it is because that's what we expect it to be' business?"

"Pretty much."

"Except none of us knew what to expect," he goes on, "so why would we all see it as a forest?"

"Maybe because of the name?" Raul offers.

Conversation falls off after that and we keep walking. Slowly our environment begins to change. The ground firms up underfoot. The mud's gone, turned into dry, packed dirt—the way the path was before we entered the mist. The trees are just as big as they've always been, but the constant drip of water from the leaves has stopped. It's like it never rained here.

I don't know about the others, but I keep getting more and more flashes of the ghostly, here-then-gone-again bookcases, of flooring underfoot instead of dirt, like we're walking through the stacks of some huge, deserted library. I'm about to ask if anyone else is feeling the same way, when Bojo brings us to an abrupt halt again.

"What is it?" I ask, pitching my voice low.

"I hear something," he says. "Footsteps. Something's approaching, and moving fast."

We all hear it then. It sounds like one person, running full out. To us, I wonder, or from some new peril? Then she bursts into view, a half-dozen yards ahead of us on the trail, coming out from between the trees . . . no, from a side corridor as the trees suddenly disappear and the bookcases firm up all around us. It's a completely disorienting moment—for all of us, but especially for me. Not just because of the abrupt shift in our surroundings, but because I recognize the woman. When she turns in our direction, I see the same shock of recognition in her features.

"What are *you* doing here?" we both say at the same time.

"Whoa," Raul says. "Is this Saskia?"

I hear the hope in his voice. Because if it is, then mightn't his Benny be somewhere near, as well? I hate to bring him down.

"It's my shadow," I say as she walks toward us.

I've never seen her this disheveled before. She's often scruffy, but I get the sense that's from choice, on a particular day, just as I know that right now she's been too busy to care about her appearance. She looks like she's been sleeping in her clothes, though I'm sure none of us look any better. Especially not after our trek through that old subway tunnel.

Her gaze goes from me to the others. "Do any of you have a weapon?" she asks.

As usual, there's no preamble with her. She just cuts right to the chase.

"What do you mean, she's your shadow?" Aaran asks.

But it turns out I'm not the only one to recognize her.

"I know you," Bojo says. "You're one of Maxie's friends."

My shadow nods. "Yeah, I've seen you around, but I can't remember where. Maybe in Hinterland?"

Who's Maxie? I wonder. Where's Hinterland? What I don't know about my shadow could fill this library.

"Say," she goes on. "Do you have one of those tinker blades you guys are known for?"

Bojo shakes his head. "But I've got something that might be better. A hellhound knife."

"You're kidding."

Bojo sets his pack on the ground and pulls out a shirt that's been rolled into a bundle. Unrolling the fabric, he takes out the knife that the hellhound threw at Robert's guitar, that Robert dropped on the floor back in the basement of Holly's store. I'd forgotten that Bojo had picked it up and stowed it away in his pack.

"Perfect," my shadow says when he hands it to her.

"Who are we fighting?" the tinker asks as he stuffs his shirt back into his pack and reshoulders the pack.

"*We're* not fighting anybody," she says. "But I'm going to try to kill a leviathan."

Then she takes off again, back down the corridor she burst out of. We all stand around like dummies for a long moment, then hurry after her, but she's already way down the corridor, far ahead of us. Too far for us to catch up to her. I wonder why she doesn't do the fade away bit that she normally does with me back at home, then realize it's not even necessary, considering how easily she's left us all behind.

"Okay," Aaran says. "What the hell was all that about?"

Bojo sets a brisk pace and we follow as we can, straggling behind him. We're already so beat it's hard to muster the energy we need. I explain what I know of my shadow's origins as we go along.

"This is insane," Aaran says.

"You can still say that after the past couple of days?"

"I know," he says. "But, come on. Your shadow can go walkabout on its own?"

"Were you sleeping during Philosophy 101? Jung says—"

"I *remember* what he said. But he was talking metaphorically, not literally."

"Give it up," Raul says. "Just because something's whacked, doesn't mean it's not true. Not anymore. And besides, what about Suzi here? What makes her origin any easier to understand?"

Aaran sighs. "I know. It's just . . ."

"It's all still new for a lot of us," Suzi says. She tucks her arm into the crook of Aaran's. "Don't think I'm not feeling a little nuts myself."

"So, what's your shadow doing here?" Raul asks.

"I have no idea," I say. "The truth is there's more I don't know about her than I probably ever will. I don't even know her name."

"It's Christiana," Bojo says over his shoulder.

"How do you—" I begin, but then I remember that he's met her before.

"You tend to make a point of getting her name," the tinker says in response to the question I didn't finish, "when a woman's as attractive and lively as Christiana."

I turn the name over in my mind. Christiana. It's so weird to finally have a name for her. Like, yet unlike my own.

I want to ask Bojo what else he knows about her and her friend Maxie and anything else he'd care to share with me about her life, but Aaran brings up a new concern.

"So she expects to kill a whale with that knife you took from the hell-hounds?" he asks.

Bojo shakes his head. "No, a leviathan."

"That's what I said."

"It means something different here," the tinker says. "Though to tell you the truth, I didn't even think they were real."

"Or that they can have a physical presence," Suzi adds.

"Can we back up here a moment?" I say. "What's a leviathan?"

"They're big, old-time magic," Bojo says. "Precreation spirits. Legend has it that they're the ones who gave Raven the music that let him create the world. And like Suzi said, they're not supposed to be able to manifest in the physical world."

"So they're the gods that made god," Aaran says. "See, I'm getting with the program now. I'm not freaking out or shaking my head."

"Raven's not a god," I tell him. "The way he tells it, it was like you or me starting a car. He just happened to be there and had the key in hand."

"So now you've talked to God?" Aaran says.

I shake my head. "No. He's just this guy that everyone else keeps referring to as Raven. As *the* Raven."

"Man, have I been leading a sheltered life," Aaran says.

I'm about to say something like, that's what I've been trying to tell you all these years, but there's this huge cracking sound that I remember all too well from the subway tunnel. This time it comes directly from the other side of the bookcases to our right. No one stops to argue or even think about it. We just run, and none too soon. Behind us, in the part of the corridor where we just were, a fissure appears, splitting the floor. The bookcases on either side come crashing down, raining books. Except for Bojo, who's further ahead, we all lose our balance and fall against each other, sprawling to the floor.

Bojo returns and pulls Raul up. The rest of us scramble to our feet and then we're all off and running again.

It's funny. Moments ago I could barely keep up with Bojo as we chased after my shadow. But right now I'm running full tilt, fueled by adrenaline and fear.

Holly

The otherworld wasn't anything like Holly had expected. She'd expected . . . well, magic. For everything to be strange and different, like walking into a Dali painting or one of those confusing Escher pieces, where down was up but it was also down, when it wasn't going sideways. The place Mother Crone had taken them to didn't even have some Bavarian-styled castle off in the distance, or the deep ancient woods that Sophie and Jilly were always talking about.

Instead, they stepped from the mall concourse out onto a wide dirt path. Ordinary grass fields stretched away to either side of where they stood, with mountains in the far distance. Some hawthorns and brambles grew along the verge.

The shopping mall with its dancing fairies had been far more magical. The only really strange thing here was the wall of mist that rose up a couple of hundred yards ahead of them, blocking a clear view of what looked like some enormous forest. Holly smiled when she saw the trees. Now *that* was more like Jilly's Cathedral Wood. Her gaze tracked down from the heights of the trees to where the path they were on disappeared into the mist.

Standing on this side of the mist were two men.

"Stay behind me," Mother Crone said, stepping forward to place herself between the strangers and her companions.

"It's okay," Holly told her, realizing that the seer was trying to protect them from the men. "That's our friend Robert."

"And the man with him?"

Like Robert, the stranger was also dressed in a dark suit. He had a hat, too, but instead of a guitar, he had a cane.

"We don't know him," Geordie said.

Mother Crone nodded. "But I do."

Holly didn't like the sound of that. There was something in Mother Crone's voice that said they might have just stepped into a whole world of trouble. Maybe we should go back, she wanted to say, but then the men turned and an unnoticed retreat, at least, was impossible.

Geordie came up from behind to stand beside Mother Crone. He lifted his hand.

"Hey, Robert!" he called.

When he started forward, Holly trailed along behind him. Mother Crone waited a beat, then followed with little Hazel staying close by her side.

Robert gave them a welcoming nod. "You're about the last bunch I expected to meet here."

"We got so worried," Holly said.

"Well, you've got good cause."

Holly sighed. She hadn't actually wanted to hear that. For all Mother Crone's certainty, Holly had still been holding on to the hope that the seer had made a mistake in her reading of the situation.

"What *is* going on in there?" Geordie asked.

"That world in there is going to pieces," Robert said, "and it's pretty much all my fault. I was trying to exorcise the bad spirits that had taken it over, but once my first chord got into that place, the music left my control and it's not coming back."

"Christy's in there," Geordie said. "And the others. Bojo and Raul. And all those other people that disappeared."

"I know," Robert told him. "Don't think I don't know that."

"But if the world's going to pieces—"

"It won't necessarily be completely destroyed," Robert's companion said. "I think the chaos will last just until the spirits are banished. And they will be banished. This is only a little messier than we'd expected."

Robert gave him a sharp look.

"Fine," the stranger said. "Than *I* expected. But once they're gone, I'll slip in and lay down some order. Any of your friends that found themselves a hidey-hole, they'll be right as rain once I'm done."

"Except we don't *know* that it'll work out that way," Robert put in.

Mother Crone had slipped by them and stood inches from the mist—peering in, Holly thought, until she went over to stand by Hazel and the seer, and saw that Mother Crone's gaze was turned inward.

"It's extremely unlikely that anything is going to survive in there," she said finally, turning around to face Robert. "That's a leviathan you've got going to pieces in there."

Robert's eyes went wide. "What?"

"Oh, yes," Mother Crone said. "I've never actually seen or met one—I don't know anyone who has. But that spirit is so ancient and strong . . . what else could it be?" Her gaze moved to Robert's companion. "What do you think, Kalfou?"

"You've got me mistaken with someone else," the man she'd addressed said. "My name's Legba."

Mother Crone nodded. "Today perhaps."

"Look," Legba said. "I don't know what stories you've been listening to, but I'm just a spirit, same as you, trying to get by. I don't look to cause trouble. All I like to do is see that there's some order in the world."

Mother Crone continued to nod. "Not to mention broadening your influence a thousandfold once you're ensconced as the gateway spirit of that world."

"It wouldn't hurt anybody."

"Probably not. But you can't just work your mojo on a leviathan. That's like trying to keep a tornado locked up in a teacup. It can't be done."

"I know that," Legba said. "Don't think I don't. But I didn't know there was a leviathan in there."

Robert was nodding in agreement. "They don't take on physical shape."

"Then *you* tell me what's in there."

"A gateway spirit," Robert said. "Nobody I know or ever heard of before."

"And?"

"Something old and potent," Robert added with some reluctance. "I could sense that much when I got here. But . . . come on. How could anybody have known it was a leviathan?"

"You couldn't have, I suppose," Mother Crone said. "But to have used a piece of the first music on it . . ."

Her voice trailed off and her gaze went inward once more, but Holly couldn't see what had distracted her. Her and the other two men. They were all three staring into nothing now, and so intently.

Holly sighed. The whole conversation between them had gone way over her head and when she turned to Geordie, she saw only the same confused expression on his face that she knew was on her own. Her gaze tracked past him and found Mother Crone's companion, the little twig girl Hazel.

"How about you?" she asked. "Do you have a clue as to what's going on?"

Hazel shook her head. "Something bad."

"Yeah, we got that part," Geordie said. He turned to look at the wall of mist. "It's so damn frustrating, knowing they're somewhere in there and there's nothing we can do."

Holly nodded. "I was really hoping that somehow we'd turn out to be the cavalry."

"Some things can't be changed," Hazel said. "You shouldn't even try."

Holly hated this stoic acceptance that they all seemed to subscribe to.

"Like this whale everybody's freaking about," she said.

"It's not a fish," Hazel said.

"Mammal, actually," Geordie put in.

"It's one of the ancient spirits that the world grew out of," the twig girl went on, as though she hadn't been interrupted. "Like the Grace."

"I've heard of her before," Geordie said, turning to Holly. "She's this spirit that embodies all that's good in . . . well, pretty much anything."

"So, what . . . what does this spirit embody?" Holly asked. "The leviathan that Mother Crone says is in the Wordwood."

Hazel shook her head. "I don't know. I don't think they actually embody anything. They're more like doors into the medicine lands—the place we all came from when the world was being formed."

Holly was still trying to get her head around that when Mother Crone stirred.

"That's odd," the seer murmured.

Then her eyes flashed open. She and Legba looked at each other in shock.

"Oh, shit," Robert said. "We need to get out of here!"

Mother Crone grabbed Hazel by one hand and Geordie by the other and pulled them away from the wall of mist. Before Holly could ask what was going on, Legba had her by the hand, and they were racing down the dirt path after Mother Crone and the others, Robert taking up the rear.

If she'd been looking back, Holly knew she'd have been blinded. As it was, the flare of white light that came from behind them was still a shock to her eyes, leaving her blinking, tear ducts welling. There was no sound, just that awful, searing light. Then a blast of wind picked them up like they were so many leaves and twigs and scattered them along the length of the path.

Christiana

It's getting worse, I realize, as I go tearing back to where I left the others watching over Librarius and the leviathan by the lakeshore. All around me I can hear the thundering crashes of bookcases toppling as fissures open underneath them. A huge one comes from just behind me. I hope Christy and his friends are okay, but I don't have time to go back and look. Then one of the crevices opens right in front of me.

I jump over it, clearing it easily, but the ground's still moving when I land and it's enough to throw me off balance. I crash into a bookshelf, hitting it with my shoulder. Books come flying off, tumbling around me as I fall to the floor. I don't know how, but I manage to hold on to that hellhound knife I got from the tinker.

I start to get to my feet, then see the fissure widen and the bookcases on either side of me begin to slide into it. I put an arm over my head to shield myself from the falling books and scrabble out of the way. The books that hit me are falling from the nearest shelves, but I know that any minute the ones higher up are going to be coming down. If one of them hits me, I'm going to have worse than bruises to worry about.

It's hard to make progress. The floor's at an odd angle, sloping back. Like it's trying to funnel me back into the fissure. I only just make it back to a level section when the bookcase on my right goes sliding into the crevice. I allow myself one look back, hear an ominous, stony crack from almost directly underground, and take off again.

I don't realize how far I'd come in my search for a weapon until now, when I'm making my way back. I don't know how big this place is, but I've been running for miles. I've always had a lot of stamina, but I have a stitch in my side by the time I finally reach the lakeshore where I've left the others. Saskia turns around, eyes widening at the big knife I'm carrying. Jackson's still standing watch over Librarius.

"Don't let him so much as twitch," I tell Jackson as I angle my course to where the huge body of the leviathan lies sprawled, half in, half out of the lake.

"You've got it," he tells me.

I guess I misjudged him because he's proving to be a lot more capable than I would have guessed from when I first met him.

"Christiana!" Saskia calls.

"Don't worry," I tell her. It's easier to pretend everything's under control. "I saw Christy and some other folks back there. It's going to take them awhile to work their way here, what with all those bookcases coming down, but they shouldn't be too long."

She's trailing after me. Now she turns to look back the way I've come.

"Christy's here? Is he okay?"

"He looked fine."

"Who's with him?"

"I didn't recognize anybody, but I guess they're all here on a rescue mission."

"But—"

"There's really no time," I tell her.

I speed up a little to put some distance between us, but I needn't have bothered. She's still looking back to where I came out of the bookcases and not following me anymore. She's obviously thinking about Christy.

And then I'm by the leviathan, his immense bulk rearing up above me.

I can believe how big he is. I mean, I *know* how big he is—you can't miss it, up this close—but he's so enormous that unless he's right in front of me like this, I lose the size reference. It's as though my memory can't hold his immensity, so it brings him down to something manageable—you know like twenty feet tall instead of the two hundred or so he really is.

But he's not twenty feet tall. He's a mountain, lying there. A behemoth.

I look at the knife in my hand.

Yeah, like it's going to do the trick.

But there's nothing else. Until I ran into Christy and his friends, the only thing I could find were books. Lots of books. So what was I supposed to do? Tear out some pages and paper cut him to death?

Though I'm not planning to actually kill him. I just want to set him free of the weight and burden of the flesh that *is* killing him. Semantics, I suppose, but it makes sense in my head.

I take another look at the knife, then put it between my teeth—which feels really weird—and start up the side of one enormous arm.

I've experienced worse things in my time, but not many. Quickly heading the list is this: grabbing fleshy handfuls of the putrid skin of this monstrous man to haul myself up onto his chest, handhold by handhold. It's making my stomach do little flips.

I keep expecting him to rouse. Not get up and lumber around—I think he's too far gone for that. But to lift a giant hand to brush away some bothersome insect crawling up his arm? I can see that happening. I can really see that happening. My imagination's way too good.

But I get up onto the slope of his chest and he doesn't even twitch. There's just the slow rise and fall of the spongy flesh underfoot to tell me that he's still alive. Barely.

I take the knife from between my teeth and slowly make my way up to his throat, arms held out to keep my balance against the movement of his breathing. I get right up to the collarbone, then slide carefully down into the hollow of his throat. I don't have any trouble identifying the twinned carotid arteries I need to sever. I touch the edge of the hellhound knife with my thumb—just enough to feel the edge of the blade. It's sharper than a razor.

I bring it down toward where the arteries pulse just under his skin.

And then I can't do it.

It doesn't matter that I have only his best intentions in mind. I feel too much like I haven't weighed enough other options. Sure, he's dying. And the Wordwood is falling apart around us as he goes. But who's to say that my killing him will free his spirit to go back into the Wordwood the way it was before Librarius bound him? For all I know, I'll just bring about the Wordwood's destruction all that much more quickly.

The Wordwood, and us in it.

I wish I knew what to do.

I wish someone else would step up and take charge.

It's funny. I'm the most independently-minded person I know, but right now I really would give almost anything to have somebody else here to make the decision for me. Or at least for them to give me some informed advice. How come Mumbo didn't prepare me for a situation like this? Some days it felt like she was readying me for everything and anything, up to and including fixing a kitchen sink. But while I know all about passing as human and getting around in the borderlands and the otherworld, when it comes to leviathans, I've got nothing to fall back on.

I look away, over at the rest of the library. It's really getting bad now. The cracks of fissures splitting the stone floor, the crashing of the bookcases coming down, are a steady cacophony that doesn't let up. From my vantage point on the leviathan, I can see great gaping holes where bookcases used to stand.

I think of what Librarius told me. Of how he wasn't afraid to die, because dying he'd just be born again as himself. What he was afraid of was if whatever's destroying the Wordwood also tore *his* spirit apart, because then there was no telling when, or even if, he'd be himself again.

I guess that's what answers my dilemma. If the leviathan dies—if I can summon the courage to use this knife—he'll get to go on as himself. But if I don't kill him, then he'll be torn apart like Librarius when the Wordwood completely falls to pieces around us.

I know that I can't let that happen. The leviathan doesn't deserve it. For all I know, he's the very one who gave Raven the tools to make the world of which this little corner of the otherworld is only a tiny part. Wouldn't that be horribly ironic?

Before I can chicken out, I take a deep breath, then plunge the knife down into the artery and tear it across. The knife goes into his skin like I'm cutting a pudding. There's no resistance at all. And then the hole I made explodes. Blood fountains out, a grotesque, red geyser. The immense body underneath me shifts and I fall down, sliding across the blood-slick skin.

It's weird. My perceptions go slow-mo, like in a car accident. I feel a huge change . . . in the air, inside my chest. Something shifts inside me. Deep. Bone marrow deep.

The blood rains down on me. I'm covered in it. Sliding in it.

I'm going over the edge of the leviathan's shoulder. I try to grab a hold of something, anything, but his skin's covered with blood and too slick.

Then I'm airborne.

Falling.

And everything goes white.

Christy

We almost lose Bojo in the next fissure. It starts to open under our feet, separating Suzi and Aaran from the rest of us. Aaran makes the leap across, then turns back to help Suzi, Bojo at his side. The gap keeps widening, stones grinding deep underfoot. The bookcases are tottering, sliding into the fissure. Suzi makes the jump and Bojo and Aaran each catch her by a hand, pulling her to safety. But before they can get to level ground, the floor does a dip under their feet.

Bojo gives Aaran and Suzi a shove to where Raul and I can grab them, but he goes sliding down into the fissure. All that saves him is that he manages to grab on to a bookcase that's wedged into the crevice at an angle. Books are falling, hitting the floor and sliding past him into the growing gap. Bojo starts to climb back along the bookcase, but it suddenly drops another foot and he almost loses his grip.

"Hang on to me," Raul says.

He stretches out on the floor and flings his knapsack toward Bojo. Aaran, Suzi, and I hold on to his legs. One of the straps on the knapsack reaches Bojo. Raul's holding on to the other with both hands. Another shower of books comes down—luckily slim folios. It's pretty much a miracle that no one's gotten a concussion yet from one of the larger books.

Bojo grabs the strap and then we all start hauling Raul back, which also pulls Bojo toward higher ground. We manage a couple of yards before

Bojo finds some purchase for his feet. He pushes himself forward and crawls to safety. And we all scramble to our feet on the level ground. I don't know about the others, but my heartbeat's doing double-time in my chest.

But there's no chance for us to take a breather.

There's another crack of splitting stone.

"Look out!" Suzi cries.

Another fissure is opening right in front of us. We dart down a side corridor to avoid it. The gap widens faster than before and the bookcases are crashing down, swallowed into it in moments.

"This way," Bojo says.

He leads us down the side corridor. We cross, one, then another passage. At the third, he has us heading back in the same direction that we'd been going earlier, the direction that my shadow took. All around us we can hear the grind of stone, the thundering crashes of the bookcases coming down.

"This is the way I've always figured things would end," Raul says as we trot behind Bojo. "If a person was to get caught up in something as big as this, I mean. You can be brave, and you can do your best, but in the end all your efforts prove to be ineffectual."

"I don't believe that for a moment," Suzi says from behind us. "When we expend the effort, we make a difference. We might not solve the big problem, but at least we'll have done something to improve the small aspects of it that lie closer to home."

"Which is really comforting when you're dead," Aaran puts in. Then he adds, "Ow," and I assume Suzi's given him a whack.

I want to add something to the argument, but then Bojo calls out from ahead of us.

"I think it's opening up!" he says.

We all look forward. In between the bookcases, far ahead, I get a glimpse of what seems to be an impossible sight. A lake, in the middle of the library. A giant man with blood fountaining from his throat.

Then there's a flare of white light. Blinded, we stumble into each other and fall in a tangle of limbs.

As I try to stand up, I realize that my eyes are still open, but I can't see anything.

And then the world goes completely away.

Holly

Holly picked herself up from the dirt, moving gingerly. It took her a long moment to remember where she was and what had happened. Her body still held an echoing tremor of the blast. Her mouth was full of dust and stars flashed in her eyes, blinding her. There was a ringing in her ears and her whole body felt bruised, although the bruising seemed to be on the inside of her skin. But after a brief spell of dizziness, the stars finally faded and she was able to find her glasses. She put them on and looked around.

Not far from her, Legba was already standing up, brushing dust from his suit with a gloved hand. When he bent lower to get at a patch on the pant legs below his knees, the sleeve of his jacket rode up. Holly's eyes widened. Instead of an arm, there were only bones there, held together by she didn't know what.

I didn't see that, Holly thought and she turned away. But she couldn't forget that he'd taken her hand earlier. It had certainly *felt* real.

On the other side of her, Geordie was helping Mother Crone stand. Little Hazel sat in the middle of the path, her legs splayed in front of her, her eyes unfocused and a confused expression on her pixie features. Past them, Robert was using the sleeve of his jacket to clean the dust from his guitar. He looked up and caught her gaze.

"She's taken quite the beating this trip," he said. "Between a hellhound's knife and a handful of new cracks from this fall, we're talking some serious repairs."

Holly nodded, not knowing what to say. She felt guilty about what had happened to his guitar, but the guitar was the least of their worries. She felt guilty about everything. Except for Legba, everybody was here because of her. Not to mention Christy and the others, trapped in the Wordwood.

She finally let her gaze go to where the wall of mist had been veiling their view of the Wordwood's forest.

It was different now. Completely opaque. She had no idea what that meant, but it couldn't be good.

"What . . . what happened?" she asked as she got to her feet.

Mother Crone shook her head. "It's changed," she said. "But how, or from what, I have no idea."

She turned her attention to Hazel, stroking the little twig girl's locks of Rasta vines until Hazel finally blinked and came back from wherever the blast had sent her.

"I can tell you how it's changed," Legba said. "The leviathan's left his physical shape and swelled to fill the world behind the mist. He's that world and it's him. There's no place for a gateway spirit in there now because there'll be no going in or out anymore."

"Making it useless for you," Robert said.

Legba shot him a quick humourless smile. He gave his sleeve a last brush—

Don't think of what's under the cloth, Holly told herself. Or better yet, what's *not* under it.

—and picked up his cane.

"I doubt I will see any of you again," he said. His gaze went to Robert. "Except for you, of course. We'll meet at least once more."

He touched the brim of his hat with gloved fingers, tapped his cane in the dirt, then stepped away, disappearing. Holly blinked in surprise.

"What did he mean by that?" Geordie asked.

Robert shrugged. "Oh, you know these old spirits. They like to be cryptic."

Holly didn't bother trying to work that out. There was only one thing that concerned her at the moment.

"Can you tell what happened to our friends that were inside?" she asked Mother Crone.

The seer had trouble meeting her gaze.

"I'm sorry," she said. "I can sense the leviathan, but nothing more."

"So they're all . . . gone . . ."

An enormous ache filled Holly as the realization hit home. All those people who had disappeared. Christy and the others . . .

Their deaths opened a deep pit in her chest and she didn't know if she'd be able to stop herself from falling in. She didn't know that she could bear the weight of this much sorrow.

"I don't know," Mother Crone replied, her voice gentle with sympathy. "It's like Legba said. It's impossible to reach inside and see anymore. I can't ignore the leviathan—he has such an enormous presence—but nothing else is clear."

"But . . ." Geordie had to clear his throat before he could continue. The anguish in his features was too much a mirror of what Holly was feeling and she had to look away. "The danger you were talking about earlier . . . ?"

"That, at least, has passed."

The seer took Hazel's hand. She looked as though she was about to add something more, but Robert caught her attention. Holly turned to see him cocking his head. What now? she was about to ask, not sure she could bear anything else. Not sure she even cared. But then she heard it, too. It was like in the basement of the store—the sound of a distant howling. She was surprised to discover that she could still feel afraid for herself with all that had been lost.

"I really thought he'd give me a little bit of grace," Robert said.

"Legba's rarely generous," Mother Crone said.

"Tell me about it."

"Those are the hellhounds, aren't they?" Geordie asked.

Robert nodded.

"But I thought you dealt with them."

"I dealt with one batch of them, but the otherworld's thick with crossroads spirits, looking to cut their own deal with the *loa*. There will always be more."

He slipped the strap of his guitar over his shoulder and let the instrument hang at his back.

"They'll follow me," he said. "But that doesn't mean you should still be here when they arrive."

Holly looked down the path. She had a long view, but while she could still hear the howling, there was nothing in sight yet.

"What will you do?" she asked.

"Don't worry about me," Robert told her. "I'll be fine. I'm an old hand at this game."

Then, just as Legba had done, he stepped away and disappeared. Here one moment, gone the next.

"He's right," Mother Crone said. "We should go."

"But our friends . . ." Holly began.

"There was nothing we could do for them before," the seer told her, "and even less now. They've either escaped or . . . or not."

Holly turned to look at the wall of mist. Nothing had changed. It was still impossible to see through.

"Come," Mother Crone said.

She held Hazel by one hand and took Holly's hand with the other.

"Stay close to us," she told Geordie.

"Can . . . can you just take us back to my store?" Holly asked.

Mother Crone nodded. "Keep an image of it clear in your mind."

"I'll try."

Holly looked back at the wall once more, trying not to think of their friends trapped or dead behind it, unable to think of anything but.

The sound of howling rose up, closer now.

"I'd rather not have to confront those hellhounds," Mother Crone said.

Holly wanted to say, "Right," or "Of course," but she couldn't seem to shape the words properly, so she simply nodded.

Mother Crone repeated what she'd done back in the mall, lifting her hands above her head and bringing them down with a sweeping arm-wide motion on either side of her body. The air went iridescent when her hands came together and then they were looking through a shimmering portal. They could see the bookstore, lit only by the streetlight coming through the front window.

"Is this the place?" Mother Crone asked, taking Hazel and Holly's hands once more.

"That's it," Geordie said when Holly still couldn't speak.

Her grief was unbearable.

She let Mother Crone lead her and Hazel through, Geordie following close behind. The portal closed behind them as silently as it had opened, and with it, all their hopes of ever seeing their friends alive again.

Christiana

I was pretty sure I was dead when I went sliding off the shoulder of the leviathan and that flare of white light blinded me. I remember thinking it was a version of the light you sometimes hear people talk about, the one they see at the end of some tunnel when they're dying. It starts out like a dot, burning far in the distance. They're rising up to and falling into it at the same time. Then they finally disappear right into it and everything goes white.

I don't know. I didn't see a tunnel. But I was falling, spilling right off the leviathan's giant shoulder, and everything did go white.

And then I came back.

I'm completely disoriented at first and become aware of things all jumbled out of their order of importance:

I realize the blood's all gone. I was drenched in it, but there's not a drop on me now.

I have a really sore shoulder, like I landed on it when I fell from the leviathan.

The lake is gone.

The *leviathan* is gone.

The library . . . the library is different. I sit up and look around. The rows of bookcases still go on forever, but I can see a tall, vaulted ceiling now, with chandelier lights hanging at regular intervals. Carpets with an

Oriental pattern run on forever, up one corridor, down another. The rows of bookcases are broken by various little reading islands made up of two or three leather club chairs with ottomans, reading lamps, and side tables.

I look back to where the lake had been. I get up slowly and walk to the bookcase that's right where the shore should be. When I touch the bookcase, it's solid. I pull a book off the shelf, flip through a few pages, then replace it. Same deal. The books are real.

So then the leviathan . . .

Intellectually, I remember his sheer enormity, but my memory calls up a figure in the twenty-foot range. Still improbable. But not the sheer impossibility that I clambered up and stuck with a knife . . .

I see the hellhound blade, lying on the carpet.

And then I remember my companions.

I turn around, but I'm alone. Saskia and Jackson are both gone, like they were never here. Librarius is gone, too, but I see a heap of cloth where I remembered him lying before the world went white on me and everything changed yet again.

I walk over and toe the fabric with my foot. It's his clothing. Mixed up in the folds of cloth are the straps I used to tie him up.

I guess he got taken apart after all.

I can't say I'm sorry, but what does that mean for Saskia and Jackson? And if they got taken apart, too, then where are their clothes? And why am I still here?

It's so quiet in this place that every sound I make echoes loudly—the shuffle of my feet on the carpet, the sound of my breathing. I don't know why I should worry about it. It's not like anybody's going to come along and *shush* me. Then I hear voices. Somebody—a bunch of somebodies—are approaching. It takes me a moment to figure out what direction they're coming from.

I wonder if I should hide, but then it's too late and I realize it doesn't matter anyway, because I recognize them. It's Christy and the tinker and three other people I don't know—the ones that were also there when I got the hellhound knife from the tinker. They all look pretty much as bewildered as I'm feeling and stop dead when they see me.

I figure I must look a sight, but then I remember that the blood's all gone.

Did any of that even happen? Was there a lake and a leviathan? Did I actually kill him?

I remember the blood fountaining from the wound and my stomach does a little flip.

Then I remember something else, how this strange sensation swelled inside me as the leviathan died. Something shifted in me. Changed me. But I'm not sure exactly what. I just feel different. I'm aware of every cell in my body, from my skin to the blood in the marrow of my bones.

Christy and the others have started walking toward me again. They stop a half-dozen feet away.

"Christiana," Christy says. He pauses. "Is it okay if I call you that?"

I have to smile. Trust him to keep a sense of propriety, even in the midst of all of this. He's wanted a name for me forever, but I never wanted to give him that box to put me in. I guess the tinker must have told him. It doesn't seem to matter anymore.

I might have been born as his shadow, but for all I don't know or understand, I do know that I'm my own person and have been since I stepped out of him, this seven-year-old tomboy shadow that got taken under the wing of a ball with arms and legs all those years ago. He can't put me in a box, except for one that he carries in his own head. It's not going to change who I am inside of *me*. He can't know me any more than I know him, except for the things we tell each other, and the trust we have to hold on to to believe that what we're saying is true.

The only box I can be in now is the one I make for myself.

"Sure," I tell him. "You can call me that."

"Are you okay?"

I nod. "How about you guys?"

Now it's his turn to nod.

"Have you seen anybody else?" I ask.

They shake their heads. We're doing real good in the nonverbal communication department here. But I don't blame them. Something like this is so big that it's hard to get your mind around it. I don't know if you ever can.

"Who else was here?" the tinker asks.

At the sound of his voice, I find myself remembering his name. Bojo, short for Borrible Jones. He had this really funny story about why his father gave him that name.

"Saskia was with me," I say. "And this guy named Jackson."

Christy and one of the guys with him both speak at the same time.

"Saskia was here?" Christy says.

"Jackson?" the other one says. "Jackson Hart?"

I nod a yes to both of them and then we do a quick catch up on how Saskia and Jackson and I got here, on who they all are and what brought them.

I give Aaran a hard look, trying to see the monster in him that Saskia told me about, but he's wearing a congenial mask and it's not slipping.

Christy smokes a cigarette, his hands shaking a little while he lights it. It must be hard for him to have been so close to her and then lose her again. He seems pretty messed up, but I don't know what to tell him. There's nothing I can tell him.

Raul asks after some friend of his, but all I can say is that I never saw him. At least, not that I know. He could have been one of the ghosts I saw when I first got here, the ones with voices like radio static.

I find Suzi fascinating. She's got the same energy as Saskia, except she's . . . I don't know. Edgier. I think of the story Saskia told me, about how hard it was for her to fit into the world at first. To assimilate herself with all of its complexities. That's what's different with Suzi. She's not as integrated with the world as Saskia is now.

Bojo's been along for the ride, like me, but he hasn't come close to seeing what I've seen. Doing what I had to do.

"So this librarian," he asks, then pauses. "He actually called himself Librarius?"

I nod.

"He was the one that caused all the trouble?"

"Not the virus, but otherwise, yes. Though to be fair, I don't think he meant it to get so out of hand."

"Do you believe it happened the way he said it did?"

I nod. I don't explain how I was ready to beat the information out of him. It's not something I'm particularly proud of. I don't mean my threatening him. I mean that I was completely ready to go through with actually hurting him if I had to.

"And the Wordwood spirit," Bojo goes on. "He was really a . . . leviathan?"

"I think he still is," I say.

The words come out of my mouth without me even thinking about what I'm saying. But as soon as I do, I realize I'm right. I don't know how I know. I just do.

"When those friends of yours," I say, looking at Christy—I'm working it through as I speak. "When they were making the Wordwood site, either something they did drew him into it, or there was something about it that just appealed to him. So he came . . . across, I guess. From wherever the leviathan exist."

"Like Isabelle's numena," he says. When I nod, he looks at the others, explaining. "A friend of ours has this . . . gift that lets her paintings literally come to life."

"Are you talking about Isabelle Copley?" Aaran asks.

Christy nods.

"So all those weird abstracts she does . . . ?"

"No, this was before them," Christy says. "When she was doing stuff like Jilly used to do. Fantastical creatures and portraits."

"So they just stepped off the canvas?" Aaran says. He holds up his hand as Christy starts to answer. "I'm not arguing," he adds. "After everything I've seen recently, nothing much can surprise me anymore."

"They didn't step off the canvas," Christy says. "What happened was that as she painted, spirits were drawn to inhabit the same shapes as what had been depicted in the final versions of Isabelle's paintings. They were separate from the paintings, but still connected to them."

"Connected how?" Aaran asks.

"You remember the big fire on the island when her studio burned down? When she lost all her studio and all that art?"

Aaran nods.

"The numena died when their paintings went up in flames," Christy says. "They all died, except for the few whose paintings weren't at the studio."

The look Aaran gets really makes me wonder about the things Saskia had to say about him. There's so much honest empathy and distress coming from him—it's nothing like you'd expect a freak to be feeling.

"Jesus," he says. "So when she switched to abstracts . . ."

"It was so that she wouldn't be responsible for any more numena deaths," Christy says.

"I get it," I say then. "So, if Holly and her friends brought a leviathan across in the same way, then whatever happened to the Web site, also affected him."

"Except," Raul says, "I thought you said that a leviathan couldn't take on a physical presence."

"I didn't think so either," I tell him. "And maybe he still can't. Look what happened to him when Librarius forced him into a shape."

"But if he's the Wordwood—"

"Except," I break in, "it's not really physical either, is it? I mean, we're standing inside it, but it's really just digital information."

"I guess," Raul says, but he doesn't look convinced. Or maybe he's just confused. I know I am.

"Who knows, really?" I say after a moment. "I don't want to say any-thing's possible, but I've seen enough things in the spiritworld to know that whether or not something actually exists isn't a question that comes to mind. If it's in front of you, you believe. And think about it. There's so much that we don't know about the consensual world—you know, the one we all came from. You have to multiply that a thousandfold when it comes to spirits and this world."

We all stop to digest that for a moment. I'm thinking of Mumbo and how quickly it didn't seem weird to have a ball with arms and legs to be my friend. How I still don't think it's weird. She's not this freak. She's just Mumbo.

"So it—he's still here?" Bojo asks, bringing us back to the question of the leviathan.

"I can feel him," I say. "Can't you?"

Except for Suzi, they all shake their heads.

"I feel something," she says. "But it's not the same as it was before."

"Maybe that's because Librarius was the one who gave you a shape and then put you out into the world."

"I guess," she says.

But she doesn't sound sure. Or maybe it's that she doesn't want that to be the case. I can't say I blame her. Given a choice, I'd much rather be think-ing of the leviathan as my daddy than to know I'd been put into the world by some freak like the gateway spirit that called himself Librarius.

"Can we talk to him?" Christy asks. "I mean, the spirit of the Word-wood. Can we ask him what happened to the people that disappeared?"

What he really means is, how can we find Saskia?, and I'm with him on that. The trouble is . . .

"I don't know," I have to tell him.

"Maybe we need to be connected through a modem," Raul says. "Well, that's how it worked before," he adds, when we all look at him.

"So," Suzi says. "Anyone bring a laptop?

I can tell she's joking. How would you dial up to a server here? What would you plug the phone jack into? Unless you had a cordless connection, you wouldn't be getting on-line, and I doubt there are any communication satellites floating around in the skies beyond the vaulted ceilings of this library.

"Maybe there's some ritual that will work just as well," Bojo says.

He looks at me, like I'd know, but I can only shrug.

"Maybe," I tell him. "Or maybe we just need to open our thoughts to him."

I see Aaran shaking his head.

"What?" I ask him.

"Nothing," he says. "I'm just not going to be any help if you start getting into the woo-woo stuff, that's all. No offense."

I have to smile. "I know what you mean," I tell him.

"But you're . . ."

"A shadow. Yeah. I know. But Christy's the one who puts all that stuff
up on a pedestal. I just take it on a day-by-day basis."

I'm about to expand on that when I get distracted. I lift my head. I
thought I heard something, but I'm not sure what. Then I realize that I'm
still hearing it except it's not so much a sound—or *just* a sound—as a feeling. A pressure inside me. The more I concentrate on it, the less I can tell if
it's something in me, trying to get out, or something outside of me, trying to
get in.

I look at the others, but it's as though time has stopped. They're frozen
in place—Christy lifting a hand to brush his hair back from his brow.
Aaran turning to say something to Suzi. Her eyes are half-closed, in the
middle of a blink. I can't see Bojo or Raul and that's when I realize that I
can't move either. All I can see is what's directly in front of me. All I can
hear is that whisper feeling of pressure, a sound that's not a sound.

This is too weird.

For some reason I don't panic. I'm pretty sure that the Wordwood spirit
is doing this. The leviathan. Librarius told me that before its spirit was contained in the body I killed, the leviathan was everywhere, permeating this
place. Maybe he's trying to contact me.

Hello, I say, shaping the word in my head the way I talked to Saskia
when she was in me. *Is anybody there?*

There's no response.

But the pressure continues to build.

They say our largest organ is our skin, which I always thought was a
bizarre concept, because you don't really think of your skin as an individual
thing, an organ like your heart or your liver. But I believe it now. I can feel
every cell and pore of my skin, all at once, trembling like a drum's membrane in sympathetic vibration to some bigger sound that I can't actually
hear.

It's an eerie feeling. Like turning a familiar corner, but everything's
changed—not the way it is in the borderlands, where you expect that sort of
thing, but how it works in the consensual world, where everything's locked
into what it is by the agreement of a hundred thousand wills.

It's like I'm tuning in to something, dialing through the static.

Or like something's tuning in to me.

I remember the shift I felt inside me just before the leviathan died and the white light blinded me. Something changed for me then, but I still don't know what. I can only recognize that a change occurred and that maybe what's happening to me right now is a result of that subtle transformation—a transformation so subtle that I can only sense the results. I can't connect to what it is.

But I don't want to change. I don't want to be someone else. Truth is, the idea of it kind of scares me. I remember, growing up, how I'd hear other people wishing they were someone else—and I still overhear that in conversations—but I've only ever wanted to be me. Me, with all my faults and scraped knees and bruised heart and all. I know I've done some dumb things, and gotten into more trouble than I should have, but those mistakes and escapades helped shape who I am.

And I like who I am. Or was. I don't feel like I know who I am right now.

Because there's something else inside me. It's not like it was with Saskia, a recognizable foreign presence. It's something that's not me, but it's me at the same time, if that makes any sense. It doesn't to me, but that doesn't stop it from happening all the same.

At some point—

Moments? Minutes? Hours?

—I find my—

Attention? Gaze?

—turning inward.

I can't see anything anymore. I feel like I'm floating in water, but under the surface. Encompassed in . . . I don't know.

Thick air? Some kind of gel?

I just know it's peaceful. So serene. I could float here forever and not worry anymore about who I am or if I've been changed.

But then the sound that's not a sound, the *pressure,* builds inside/outside me again, a choral rhythm that thrums on both sides of my skin, and this time I can sense a sort of communication. It's not like how you or I talk to each other . . . with words, in sentences. Instead, I suddenly acquire all this information that I didn't have before, all at once—like a data dump, Jackson would say—and I understand that—

The leviathan is changed, too.

He's been damaged by either the virus, or what Librarius did to him—it doesn't matter how it happened. What matters is that the leviathan is . . .

I'm not sure how to explain it. He's expanding. That's what the pressure I feel is. It's the leviathan, his spirit swelling, pressing against the borders of the Wordwood. He needs us—or at least one of us—to stay here and provide an ongoing conduit to the world outside the Wordwood, allowing the pressure building up inside him to dissipate at a regular, steady pace instead of all at once.

Without that conduit, he'll implode like a black hole, sucking the spiritworld with him into the wormhole the implosion will create. Eventually, the whole of spiritworld will be gone and when that happens, the consensual world, *our* world, will start to be sucked in along behind it.

Cause and effect, domino-style.

So the leviathan needs to ease the pressure in small amounts through contacts outside of the Wordwood, and he can't do it himself because he has no connection to either the spiritworld or ours. But those of us trapped in here with him at the moment . . . we do.

I think of Librarius. It figures. While this wasn't the case before I freed the leviathan from his fleshy prison, a being like Librarius is now necessary: a gateway spirit, opening lines of communication between the worlds. Librarius was just planning to go about it the opposite way from how it needs to be done. He wanted the attention, the input of the people in the worlds outside the Wordwood to feed him. The leviathan needs to send his own attention *out* of the Wordwood.

Through one of us.

But I'm not a gateway spirit, I find myself saying. *None of us are.*

The reply comes, not in words, but I understand it all the same:

Gateway spirits don't have to be born; they can be made.

He means one of us.

One of us needs to stay.

I run through the options in my mind.

It can't be Christy—he needs to be with Saskia. He's been willing to sacrifice everything to see her safe and be with her again. We couldn't possibly ask this of him.

The same goes for Raul who's here for his lover Benny.

Suzi can't do it because she hasn't got a strong enough connection to the consensual world yet, and no connection at all to the spiritworld.

As for Aaran, not knowing his history, you'd think he was a good man. But I can't forget what Saskia's told me about him. How could he possibly be trusted for something this important?

That leaves only Bojo and me.

And it's obvious who it has to be. Bojo's far more of an innocent by-
stander than I am. He only got pulled into this because he likes Holly and
wanted to help her. I started out the same, wanting to help Saskia figure out
who she was, but then I started messing around like I always do. Breaking
Saskia's glass coffin. Busting Librarius. Freeing the leviathan from his
prison of flesh.

But the most important difference between Bojo and me is that he's not
a shadow.

He's real.

And I'm not, no matter what I try to tell myself.

I mean, think about it. The truth has been sitting there right from when
I was that little seven-year-old girl cast off from Christy, and Mumbo came
along to show me the ropes. She was teaching me to how to *pass* for
human.

I hate to give up my independence, but really, who's got the least to
lose? Except for Suzi, at least the others stuck in here with me are all real.
And Suzi's too newborn to be of any use to the Wordwood spirit, for all
that she looks like she's in her twenties. I'm the only one of the two of us
with the right kind of connection to the outside world.

After coming to my—admittedly reluctant—decision, my head fills
with directions on how the others can leave the Wordwood and what I need
to do here once they're gone. It's like the leviathan's monitoring my
thoughts and isn't *that* creepy.

You know, I say. *If we're going to have any kind of a decent working
relationship, the first thing we need to do is work out some boundaries. It's
bad enough I'm going to be stuck here like this. The least you can do is
allow me a little privacy. Because really, nobody likes—*

I don't get to finish. As suddenly as I found myself unable to move and
ended up wherever it is I am, it all goes away, and just like that, I'm back in
my body.

My eyes feel dry and I blink. I see Bojo making the sign of horns,
thumb holding down his two middle fingers, the remaining two standing
straight out. It's a tinker's ward against bad luck. The others just look the
same way I feel: stunned.

"Wow," Christy says after a moment, Mr. Words reduced to the vocabulary of a doper.

Aaran gives a slow nod. He looks around at each of us, gaze finally settling on me.

"Was that . . . was that *him?*" he asks. "The Wordwood spirit?"

Suzi answers before I can. "I think so. It must have been. But it didn't feel like the spirit I knew . . ."

"He was right inside my head," Raul says. "No, he was totally a part of me, but separate at the same time."

That's when I realize that everybody's had the same experience as me. Good. It makes what I have to do easier.

"That was the leviathan," I say. "And I take it you all know what has to be done?"

Raul nods. "Someone has to stay behind, or he . . . what? Implodes? Did I get that right?"

"Pretty much," I tell him. I look at the others. "And you all learned how to leave?"

Christy finally finds his voice. "We open a door back to our world—" He starts to shape the spell with his fingers, but stops before the sequence of finger movement is complete. "—staying focused on where we want to go while we're doing it."

"But who stays?" Raul asks.

"That's easy," I say. "It's going to be me."

I see the looks that cross their features: relief that someone else has stepped forward, which then shifts into guilt. Christy's the first to argue the point.

"Why does it have to be you?" he asks.

"Because I've got the least to lose," I tell him. "I might as well be here as in my little hidey-hole in the borderlands. Being here's not going to make that big a change in my lifestyle."

"Bullshit," Christy says. "You're the original free spirit. This'd kill you."

He's right. It might. But I'm not about to admit that. Not till they're gone and the deal's done.

"No, I should do it," Suzi says. "I don't have a life to lose—not a real one, at least. All the memories in my head were put there, except for what's happened in the past day or so."

"And that's the problem," I tell her. "You don't have a strong enough anchor to the consensual world. A day or so in here, on your own with the leviathan, and you could completely lose what little connection you have."

"Not if I stayed with her," Aaran says.

She gives him a warm look. I can't tell from Christy's expression if he trusts Aaran or not, but I still don't.

"Or I can stay on my own," Aaran adds. "After all, what's happening here is my fault."

"I'll give you that," I tell him. "But do you have the background or stamina for this kind of thing?"

He shrugs. "I could ask the same of you. I know books."

"This isn't going to be about books."

"No, but it will be about spending a lot of time in this place and it looks like the only distraction will be the books. My whole life's been about books." He glances at Christy. "Even if I could never write one worth a damn." He turns back to me. "And as for stamina, none of us know how well we'll do until we give it a try. Unless you've done this kind of thing before?"

"Yeah, right."

He nods. "So there you go. I should be the one that stays."

"No," I say. "I'm doing it and I'm not arguing about it anymore. Like I said, I've got the least to lose."

"What about me?" Bojo says.

I shake my head. "You've got something to go back to—or at least the potential for something, which is more than I'll ever have."

"Playing the martyr doesn't become you," Christy says.

"I'm not playing at anything. Now go. You know how to leave. The leviathan showed you, the same as it did me."

There's a long moment of silence. I look at them, one by one, trying to stare them down into agreeing with me. When I get to Christy, I can tell he's about to start in again, but Aaran interrupts him before he can get the first word out.

"No," Aaran says. "She's made her decision. Who are we to argue the sacrifice she's willing to make? It's a hard enough thing she's got to do as it is, without our making it harder by not giving her our support."

I really don't see the creep in him that Saskia does. Who knows, maybe he's changed for real. Whatever. I'm just happy to have someone backing me up. And one by one the others come around.

It's hardest for Christy, I can tell. He's torn between wanting to be with Saskia and stopping me from doing this. We've always had a weird relationship—I mean, just consider how I came into the world. He probably thinks he's alone in this endless fascination he has for his shadow twin, but that's only because I've never shared my own curiosity for him. I just go sneaking through his journals and observing him from a distance instead of asking questions the way he does of me.

"You can always e-mail me, care of the Wordwood," I tell him. Then I smile. "Just think, you'll finally have a way to contact me whenever you want. Won't that make a change."

"But I'll never see you again."

"Oh, this gig won't last forever," I say.

Everybody knows I'm lying—including him. After all, we all got the same telepathic message from the leviathan. Whoever stays becomes a gateway spirit and there'll be no coming back from that. For all I know, the change already started for me, back when I fell off the leviathan and into the light. Something happened to me then.

So we won't be seeing each other again.

But he doesn't call me on it—he knows how stubborn I can be once I make up my mind about something—and neither does anyone else.

"Say hello to Saskia for me," I say.

He nods. "Thanks for keeping her safe."

"It was my pleasure," I tell him and I mean it.

Then we all say our goodbyes and they open a door in the air to take them back into the consensual world—a one-way trip back. I want to look away, but I find I need this one last glimpse of what I'm leaving behind. All I see is some basement. A worktable. Stairs leading up.

I lean closer as they start to step through, one after the other. Then, just as the door's starting to close, I feel a shove from behind me and I'm falling through, arms flailing for balance.

And the door in the air whispers shut behind me.

This, Too, Shall Pass

Were we always
strangers,
or did we only
learn to become
this way?
—SASKIA MADDING,
"Strangers" (*Mirrors,* 1995)

Christiana

We land in a tangle of limbs on a cement floor. I suppose I should be grateful that I'm not on the bottom, but all I'm really concerned with is figuring out who gave me the shove and took my place back in the Wordwood. I have my suspicions.

Because I'm on top, it's easier for me to extract myself from the pile. I do a quick head count. Christy. Raul and Bojo. Suzi.

I was right and I get a little nervous twitch in the pit of my stomach.

It was Aaran.

No wonder he was so helpful and ready to take my side when we were arguing about who should stay. He must have had this planned from the moment the leviathan came into our heads and told us what we needed to do. What *one* of us needed to do.

And it wasn't me after all.

I can't tell what's stronger: relief that I'm not stuck back there in the Wordwood with the leviathan, or the worry about what Aaran will get up to in there.

Christy and Raul regard me with some confusion, but Bojo and Suzi get it right away.

"Oh, you fool," Suzi says softly, and I know she's not talking about me.

"He made his choice," I say.

I'm feeling a little weird. Do they all feel that way? That I was supposed to be the one to stay behind?

Suzi seems to understand what I'm thinking because she looks right over at me and gives me a half-hearted smile.

"He means well," she says. "But from everything I've come to know about him, he hasn't had that much experience at playing the good guy. And I don't know that he's strong enough to take on something like this. He's not like you in that way."

I've never been good at compliments so I don't acknowledge it. But it sure makes me feel better.

"This is going to be hard on you," I say. "You two had a thing going, didn't you?"

She shakes her head. "We had the start of something, but I'm not sure what. I like him—I like him a lot, actually—but we met under circumstances that could have gotten in the way of a long-term relationship. You know, once we got past the rush of getting to know each other."

"Like your being born in the Wordwood."

"Not to mention his picking me up while I was panhandling."

"That wouldn't make a difference," Christy says. "Not if you care about each other."

Suzi looks away from me, but not before I see the wet shine in her eyes.

Way to go, Christy, I think. Here we are trying to downplay Suzi's feelings for Aaran, and you have to come out with something like that. But I know he didn't mean to make her feel bad. He's thinking about himself and Saskia, trying to show how this kind of thing can work out. Trouble is, we're way past the chance of that happening.

"So does anybody know where we are?" I ask.

Adding anything to what we've just been talking about is only going to make Suzi feel worse, so I opt to change the subject.

"The basement of Holly's store," Bojo says.

I've been in the store before, but never down here. There's something in the air I can't quite place. A hint of the otherworld that goes beyond the fact that the basement has been used as a place to cross over. Now that I think of it, I got that same feeling upstairs the few times I've come into the store. I just put that down to all the books. They've always seemed like magic to me. I mean, talk about your doorways into other worlds.

"I need to use the phone," Raul says. "To call . . . home . . ."

That makes Christy perk up. Raul wants to check on his lover Benny. Christy needs to see if Saskia made it back. Because none of us know what happened to all the other people who disappeared into the Wordwood. Did they get away before the white light burned everything away?

We troop up the stairs just in time to see yet another otherworld door open in the middle of the bookstore. Holly and Geordie come through it, along with a tall woman dressed like a skateboarder with a little twig girl by her side. I recognize the woman from revels in Hinterland. Her name's Galfreya, but I think she calls herself Mother Crone when she's here in the consensual world.

There's all sorts of confusion as our two parties meet—which is only heightened when a door opens at the back of the store and a hob and a little yapping Jack Russell terrier are added to the mix. As soon as I see the hob, I realize what that hint of the magic I feel here is. Holly's got a bookstore hob living in her store.

While Holly picks up her dog and tries to calm it down, I catch Galfreya's eye. She nods hello and has the same "funny to see you here" look in her eyes that's probably in my own. Then I do a quick fade into the borderlands and leave them all to sort it out.

I just want to go home, but first I have to check in at Christy's apartment to make sure that Saskia's okay.

I don't know why I assumed that Saskia was back, safe in the apartment she shared with Christy. I just did. So I have a moment's panic when I slip in—stepping sideways from the borderlands as I always do—and she isn't there.

I call her name. Soft. Then louder.

My heartbeat becomes a quick thunder in my chest as I go from room to room in the apartment.

The sudden ringing of the phone makes me jump. Christy, looking for Saskia. I don't pick it up. What could I say to him?

I remember the white flash when I was falling from the leviathan's shoulder. Had it burned her away?

Then I see clothing scattered on their bed. The jeans and T-shirt she was wearing in the Wordwood the last time I saw her.

She just got cleaned up and went out looking for Christy.

The sense of relief that floods me is almost physical. I find myself sitting on the edge of the bed and reach over to touch the jeans as though to assure myself that they're real.

I wonder if she knows he went to Holly's store? Probably not. So, where would she go? Geordie's place, I decide. Or the professor's house,

where Jilly's still recuperating from the car crash that took her out of com-
mission last year. I decide to try Geordie's first because it's on the way to
the professor's house.

I take another shortcut through the borderlands and step back into the
consensual world in the alley behind the apartment, startling an old orange
tom with a torn ear. He goes skittering off through a hole in the fence of
one of the yards backing onto the other side of the alley, while I walk
around to the front. My heart lifts when I see Saskia going up the steps of
the building. She jumps when I call her name. A huge grin lights her features when she sees me and she hurries over to give me a hug.

"You made it," she says as she steps back. "I was so worried about
you."

I nod. "I was worried about you, too."

"I was just looking for Christy . . ."

"I figured as much. He's at Holly's store."

She turns to look for the bus stop, but I take her arm and walk her back
into the alley with me.

"I really have to see him," she says.

"I know you do. That's why I'm taking you the quick way."

I step her into the borderlands, get my bearings, then pop back out with
her into the consensual world at the same place I left Holly's store a few
minutes ago. Christy's on the phone—calling home again, I guess. Everybody else is still talking a mile a minute, except for Bojo, who's leaning
against the front door, a half smile on his lips as he takes it all in.

Saskia turns to me. "You'll have to teach me that trick."

"Any time," I tell her.

Then I leave her to run over to where Christy's trying to reach her by
phone, and I finally get to go home.

Okay, here's what happened, or at least what I remember and was able to
find out later. Some of it's been confirmed by news reports, back in the consensual world. A lot of it, for obvious reasons, can't be. The funny thing is
what people actually remember, which isn't a lot. You can still find the original reports of the disappearances in newspaper morgues and on-line, but
there isn't any of the follow-up you'd expect from a story this big. If you
were paranoid, you might think it was a government cover-up, or if you
know what I know, you might think the leviathan had something to do with

it through his on-line resources now that he's got Aaran on board to make contact with the outside world again.

But *people* don't remember. It's like there was some little blip in reality and now that it's over, no one's willing to even think about it anymore. No, that implies choice. What we have here is like it never even happened in the first place.

All those people who disappeared reappeared from wherever they'd originally vanished. At least, I think they all made it back. I know Holly's friends did, but they don't remember any more of what happened than anybody else does. Even Jackson's clueless. I went by to see him and he just stood there in the doorway of his apartment looking at me—the way you do when you've opened the door on a stranger and you're not quite ready to let them in, but you're still willing to see what they want.

I'd have turned around and walked away, except for the faint puzzle of recognition I see in the back of his eyes.

"You don't really remember me, do you?" I say.

He shakes his head. "You seem a little familiar. . . ."

"Guess I really made an impression."

"I'm sorry, I just—"

"It was a joke," I tell him.

He still doesn't seem too big in the sense of humour department.

"It was a long time ago," I say. "We met in a library."

He shakes his head again. "I can't remember the last time I was in a library." He pauses for a moment, then steps aside. "Do you want to come in?"

"No," I say. "I just wanted to see if you were okay."

He gets a nervous look. "Why wouldn't I be?"

I wonder at his nervousness, then I remember him telling us about the prank he played on some bank, the one that let Aaran blackmail him. So he remembers that much.

"No reason," I tell him. I start to turn away, then look back at him. "A word of advice: Next time someone tries to blackmail you into sending a virus anywhere, maybe you'd be better off owning up to what you did and taking your medicine."

"What do you know?"

I smile. Not "What do you mean?" but "What do you know?"

"Nothing that's going anywhere. Just remember what I said."

"But he—"

Jackson stops himself.

"Don't worry about Aaran," I say. "He's out of your life now. Just don't get into any more trouble."

"Who *are* you?"

I shrug. "Maybe I'm your conscience," I tell him.

"Do you have something to do with the bunch of people I found in my apartment when I . . ."

"When you what?"

I can see the confusion deepening in him as he tries to work it out.

"I was going to say when I got back," he says, "but that's not right. I haven't been anywhere . . ."

"Don't give yourself a headache," I tell him. "And maybe try to find yourself a better hobby than hacking bank computers and sending out viruses."

"Wait a second . . ."

But then I do walk away, down the stairs and out of his life.

Christy has a theory about all of this forgetfulness. Of course, Christy has a theory about everything, bless his heart, but this one makes a certain amount of sense. I can't remember how we got to talking about it. I wasn't even planning on having a conversation with him that morning. The shades and curtains are all drawn, and it's comfortably gloomy inside when I slip into their apartment. I thought they'd both still be asleep—I just came by to stand at the end of their bed like the shadow I am, reassuring myself that, yes, they're still safe. I don't realize that Christy's awake and lying on the sofa in the living room until his voice comes to me from out of the darkness.

"I wanted to thank you again for rescuing my girl," he says. "I was so worried."

He's not being disrespectful, calling Saskia his girl. No more than she is when she refers to him as her boy. I think they'll still be doing it in their eighties. At least I hope they will.

"You don't have to," I tell him. I sit down in the wing-backed chair so that we can see each other without Christy having to get up from where he's lying. "I like her and I wouldn't want to see anything happen to her either."

"You do? Like her, I mean."

"Why wouldn't I?"

"Well, you're my shadow. I just assumed you wouldn't't."

"Because I'm supposed to be all the things that you're not?"

He nods his head.

"Jeez, will you get with the program," I tell him. "That happened when we were seven years old. You've had plenty of time to reacquire all sorts of bad traits since then. Just like I've had the time to acquire some good ones."

"So, do you think we're more the same than not these days?"

What I want to say is: No. You're real and I'm not. But I don't feel like getting into a discussion about that at the moment. And I don't want to make it sound like I'm feeling sorry for myself.

"I think we're like twins," I say instead. "We're individual, but we still have this birth thread linking us to each other. We know how the other thinks and feels. We can feel each other's presence in the world, no matter the distance between us."

And that's true, too.

He smiles. "I never have the slightest idea as to what you're thinking about."

I laugh. "Yes, but that's only because I'm so mysterious."

"Christiana Tree," he says, and laughs with me. "Which makes you Ms. Tree." At my raised eyebrows, he adds, "Saskia told me."

"Has she left me any secrets at all?"

"You'll be happy to know that she was most circumspect. She said your secrets weren't hers to tell."

"I'd just as soon people didn't think about me at all," I say.

"Why's that?"

I shrug. "Life's just easier when you're anonymous—when people have no expectations about you."

"You're not exactly forgettable," he says. "Look at Bojo. He only met you the one time, but he remembered you right away."

"Maybe I was doing something outrageous."

He smiles. "Were you?"

"I don't know. Probably not. I find that people remember me more when I act just like them. Half the time I can step away into the borderlands right in front of someone and the next time I see them, it's like it never happened." That makes me stop and think for a moment. "Which," I go on, "is pretty much like what's happening with this whole business of the people who disappeared."

"It's a mental self-defense mechanism," Christy says, "that seems to have been bred into the species. Sometimes it works just on the level of individuals, other times, society itself convinces itself to forget."

"Is this more of your 'consensual world' theory?"

He nods. "The World As It Is exists the way it does for most people because they've agreed not to accept exceptions to what's been decided is impossible."

"So who decides?'

"No one person," he says. "It's something that becomes ingrained in the fabric of society as a whole. And there will be variations. It's why religious sects exist. They've all agreed to a different take on some aspect of the accepted canon of how the world's supposed to be. That agreement— that view into a different version of the World As It Is—becomes a rallying point for their beliefs and draws them together."

"So nobody remembers that all these people disappeared because it contradicts the way the world's supposed to be."

It's not a question, but Christy answers it as though it were with one of his own.

"Can you think of a better explanation?"

"Besides some vast hidden conspiracy?" I say.

He nods.

"Not really," I say. "But why do *you* remember?"

I don't have to ask about myself because I already know the answer: I'm not part of the consensual world in the first place. Considering my origin, my life, and where and how I live, I'd be in therapy forever if I didn't accept that little bit of information as true.

"There are different reasons why people remember," he tells me. "Someone like Jilly just expects the world to be more than it is, so she's never surprised when reality strays from the acceptable norm. Holly won't be forgetting because there's too much magic in her life now, starting with having a hob for a business partner and friend.

"As for me, writing it down has helped a lot in the past, but it's not foolproof. Looking at the words on paper is often too great a distance from what they're describing and rationality kicks in, convincing me it probably didn't happen."

"But in your books . . ."

"For some reason, the anecdotal evidence I collect for the books is easier for me to accept than what I experience myself. I mean, how long did it take for me to accept that you're real?"

"I didn't help."

He smiles. "No. But then we also *expect* the supernatural to be mysterious and speak in riddles."

"And now?" I ask.

He shrugs. "I'm starting to have more and more hands-on experience with the supernatural. It's coming to the point where I can't *not* believe, the whispering voice of reason inside me be damned."

I start to snicker and a puzzled frown crosses his features.

"What?"

" 'Hands-on experience,' " I repeat and then start to giggle. When he gives me a blank look, I manage to add, "You. Saskia," before I dissolve into laughter.

"Oh, for God's sake."

But he has to wait until I can get myself under control again.

I don't know why I'm feeling so giddy. It must be relief that even though we were all so far out of our depth, we not only managed to survive, but we also set things right again. How often does that happen, in this or any world?

Finally I'm able to stop, though laughter's still bubbling up in the corners of my bones, just waiting for any silly little thing to set it off again. I wish that for just once Christy would loosen up and let himself go. But though he's smiling with me, he doesn't lose it the way I do. Maybe he just doesn't think it's very funny, but I'm guessing it's more because he's always so in control of himself. It's funny, we're the same age, but sometimes our relationship seems more like parent/child. Right now he's looking at me the way a father might his errant daughter.

I clear my throat and try to feel serious.

"So Saskia's okay?" I say.

He nods. "She must be. She's able to sleep while I'm still sitting up. I thought I'd work on those galleys for Alan, but I can't seem to concentrate on anything."

"I can't help but feel that all of this is my fault," I tell him. "If I hadn't convinced her to try to make contact with the Wordwood spirit, none of this would have happened."

Christy shakes his head. "It was in motion long before that."

"I guess. But would *we* have been involved?"

"Maybe not. But think where that would have left the people who disappeared."

I give him a slow nod. "Not to mention the leviathan."

Christy closes his eyes for a moment. When he opens them again, I see they're filled with wonder.

"I only caught a glimpse of him," he says. "Before the flare. But he seemed immense."

"Like a mountain. I can't imagine him standing up."

Christy nods. "I don't think I've ever experienced anything so *other*."

"Me, neither," I say.

"Even with living in the borderlands and all you've done?"

"Even with that."

"That was a pretty brave thing you did," he says.

"Or pretty stupid. It could have all gone wrong. But I was running on instinct and there just didn't seem to be anything else I could do."

We fall silent awhile then, Christy lying on the couch, me slouched in the chair. He lights up a cigarette and offers me one. I shake my head. I feel like I should go and let him get back to bed, but I don't want to be alone yet. And he doesn't seem to be in any hurry to get up.

"So how is everybody else?" I ask.

He shrugs. "Oddly enough, Geordie's taking it the best of all. Considering his past history as our resident skeptic, I would have thought he'd be the quickest to put it all behind him, but the experience seems to have . . . I don't know. Loosened him up, certainly. He was talking about how much he was going to relish telling Jilly about all of this." Christy pauses for a moment, then adds, "And I think there's a little mutual attraction thing happening between him and Mother Crone."

I lift my eyebrows. Everybody knows that—his last long-term girlfriend notwithstanding—Geordie's always carried an unrequited torch for Jilly. Well, everybody except for Geordie and Jilly. But one of them always seems to be in a serious relationship when the other's not. At the moment it's Jilly. So Geordie being interested in Galfreya could be a good thing. Especially if she's interested in him.

"How mutual?" I ask.

"Well, when Holly asked her what payment she required for helping them cross over, she said his coming to play at one of their revels." Christy smiles. "Then added that she'd also consider it a favour and an honour."

I nod in understanding. Knowing Galfreya, she'd only offer such an invitation to a potential lover.

"I guess everybody's pairing up," I say.

"Traumatic experiences can do that. When you make it through, you find you just want to hold on to someone—you know, to feel grounded again."

That probably explains why I'm here.

"And how about Holly?" I ask.

Christy shakes his head. "You'll have to ask her yourself. But Bojo was still there when we all left."

After awhile I sit up from where I've been slouching. I uncurl my legs from under me and set them on the floor. Christy sits up as well.

"I should go home," I say.

"Home."

"I do have one."

"I never doubted it. It's just . . ."

I smile. "You're curious about where and what it is."

"Saskia said it was like a room in a meadow."

"It is," I say. "But she wasn't actually there. That was when she was riding around inside my head." I hesitate for a moment, then say, "If you're not doing anything, I can show it to you."

"You mean right now?"

"Why not?"

"I . . ." He looks to the closed bedroom door. "I'd love to," he says, "but it's too soon since all of this happened. I know Saskia's sleeping, but I want to stay close in case she wakes up. It's all I can do not to pull up a chair by the bed and just sit there, watching her sleep."

I wonder what it's like to have someone feel like that about you.

"It's okay," I tell him. "Some other time."

I reach over to the coffee table and pick up the notepad and pencil that are lying there. I write my phone number on it and put it back down.

"Call me when you're ready," I say.

"You've got a phone?"

"A cell phone."

"And it works over there?"

I nod. "I had to trade to get an ever-charge spell for the battery and rewire it. Don't ask me to explain what satellite the signals are bounced off of now, but yes, it works just fine."

"An ever-charge spell."

"Don't start banging up against the idea of magic again," I tell him. "Not with all of what we've been through."

"I'm not. It's just . . . you don't expect magic to be used for something so mundane."

"Here's a news flash," I say. "Most magic is used to enhance the mundane."

When I stand up, he does, too. He starts to put out his hand, but I give him a hug instead. I've never been very demonstrative with him for a whole bunch of reasons. I want to maintain my air of mystery with him and I know all too well that he's not one of your touchy-feely people. And then there's also that warning of Mumbo's not to get into physical contact with the person whose shadow you once were.

But nothing happens except he hugs me back.

"Don't be a stranger," he says into my hair.

"I never was," I tell him.

Then I let myself fade away into the borderlands and he's left holding only air.

Holly

It seemed to take forever before the last of them left the bookstore. Not that Holly was unhappy to have them here—these were her friends, after all. Or at least most of them were. And those that weren't—Mother Crone and Hazel, Benny's boyfriend Raul—were the sort of interesting people she could easily become friends with. But right now Holly was tired and the crowd of people—talking over each other, using the phone, vying for her attention as they retold some part of the story she already knew too well . . . it was all too much for her.

She needed to come down from the adventure, not relive it.

But finally it was simply Dick and Bojo still in the store with her. She stood holding Snippet, the little dog drowsing in her arms. Bojo leaned against her desk, looking handsome as ever, while Dick appeared asleep on his feet. When Christy closed the door behind him and the crowd that was going back to the mall to get his car, the hob blinked suddenly. He gave Holly and Bojo each a considering look.

"It's time for this old hob to get himself to bed," he said.

Which seemed odd to Holly, because she had the impression that Dick never slept. When he retired to his room, it was only to read until the morning when he could get up and go about his business in the store—when he wasn't dusting and organizing in the middle of the night. But then she realized what the considering look had been about and found herself blushing.

"I'm glad you're back, Mistress Holly," Dick told her.

There was a knowing smile in his eyes, reminding Holly once again that while Dick might be no larger than a child, he was actually much older than her. And probably far more experienced, too. She remembered seeing little men not so unlike him, dancing close to pretty little fairy maids at the revel in the mall concourse. There had been nothing innocent in the way they rubbed up against each other.

Dick turned from her.

"And goodnight to you, Master Borrible," he said.

He gave Bojo a nod, tipped a finger against his brow, then turned and went upstairs to the apartment. When the apartment door closed behind him, Bojo and Holly looked at each other.

There were a hundred things Holly wanted to say, but all she could think about was how handsome the tinker was.

"Well," Bojo after a moment. "Here we are."

Holly nodded.

Speak, she told herself.

But she was too shy.

"I should probably go see what the bodachs and piskies have been up to at Meran's house," the tinker added. "I was supposed to be looking after the place, after all."

But he made no move to leave.

Or you could stay here a little longer and kiss me, Holly thought.

But she seemed to have lost her voice again.

"So I was wondering," he said, "when I was off with the others on our adventure. Do you have a motorcycle?"

Holly shook her head, but the question was curious enough to surprise words from her. "Whatever for?"

"A red-headed girl in black leather on a motorcycle . . . could there be anything more a tinker could ask for?"

Heat rushed up Holly's neck, but she still managed to smile and keep her voice.

"The hair I've got," she said after a moment. "And the leather's doable—at least the look is. I think I'd prefer pleather." At his blank look, she added, "It looks and feels like leather, but you don't have to kill an animal to wear it."

"Not killing is good."

She nodded.

"What about the motorcycle?" he asked.

"You're going to have to settle for a bicycle."

He studied her for a long moment, then smiled.

"If I just had the red-haired girl," he said, "I wouldn't feel like I was settling for anything. I'd already have it all."

Something seemed to melt, deep inside Holly. Her pulse quickened.

Whoa, slow down, she told herself. Think this through.

Granted, there seemed to have been an immediate attraction between them from that first moment when he came through the front door in response to the call she'd left on Meran's answering machine. And she couldn't remember the last time a man this handsome had seemed so interested in her—it surely hadn't been in this lifetime.

But she also knew that surviving danger made people feel the need to be close to each other—and what was closer than sex?

And then there was the fact that he was a tinker. A travelling man. He could leave for parts unknown—*very* unknown—at any time. It could be tomorrow morning. And if not tomorrow, then next week. Next month.

And that, her heart asked her, was relevant to the moment at hand . . . how?

She took his hands and tilted her head.

"Don't make any promises," she said as he leaned down to kiss her.

He stopped, those gorgeous eyes of his with their long lashes so close to hers.

"I always keep my promises," he said.

"I know. You've told me that. But I don't want you to be bound to anything beyond right now. We don't even know each other."

"We know what's important."

Holly smiled. "No, we just know that, right now, we want to be close. We don't know anything beyond that."

"So, what is it that you look for in a man?" he asked.

"Someone who can stick around," she said. "Who can be here for me."

"Ah. Now I—"

Holly reached up and put her finger against his lips.

"No," she said. "No promises, no figuring anything out."

She took her finger away.

"But—" he began.

This time she stopped him from talking by pressing her own lips against his.

Suzi

They were kind and they meant well. There had been offers to give her a place to stay—from the couch in the apartment upstairs to the spare room at Christy and Saskia's place. And that feeling of being disliked for no reason except that she didn't seem to belong in this world, appeared to have faded—at least among these people. But Suzi still needed to get away and be on her own.

There was too much to think about.

She had a head full of memories—not simply from the past few days, the ones that she knew were real, but a lifetime of others that had been implanted in her upon her creation. When she considered them—the abusive husband, her family turning on her—she felt they must have come from a novel, filed somewhere in the Wordwood. Something teary and a little over-the-top, but nevertheless absorbing for all that it was fiction.

But knowing that didn't stop the memories from feeling real. It also created a whole other world of confusion, because now she had to live with the idea that underneath the implanted memories there was only a blank slate of a life. There was *no* life. She'd been "born" full-grown, just the way she was now.

She didn't know how to begin to deal with it. And since she didn't know where to start in understanding and getting along with herself, how could she possibly interact with others right now, no matter how well-meaning they might be?

It would have been different with Aaran. She might have told him that there wasn't much hope for a relationship between them, but that didn't mean there couldn't have been once she'd had the time to figure out who she was, which would, in turn, let her figure out who they could be.

But the chance for that was gone.

She had only herself.

And that became increasingly clear as she listened to Raul's side of his conversation with his returned lover Benny.

". . . know what I'm doing here," Raul said. Then he laughed. "I know. It is pathetic, isn't it? But I'm on my way home. I'll be on the first flight to Boston in the morning."

He didn't remember—not anything of what had happened. Neither did Holly's other friends who'd found themselves inexplicably in Jackson Hart's apartment. Listening to Holly's side of the conversation when Estie called the store, Suzi made up her mind. She slipped upstairs and retrieved Aaran's laptop, then said her goodbyes and left the store. They had protested—especially Saskia, who'd mysteriously arrived out of thin air when everyone had their backs turned.

"I know how hard this can be," Saskia said.

Suzi knew she meant well. And there was a kinship between them, considering their origins. But she was only interested in one piece of information from Christy's girlfriend.

"Can you show me how to step between the worlds the way you just did?" she asked.

Saskia shook her head. "I have no idea how it's done. Christiana brought me here."

And Christiana had already stepped away again, back into the otherworld.

"I tried to adjust on my own, too," Saskia went on. "Trust me. It just makes it harder."

Suzi nodded. "I'm sure you're right. But I still feel like it's something I have to do on my own."

"If you need help—you'll call us, right?"

She found a piece of scrap paper on the desk and scribbled her name and a phone number on it.

"I will," Suzi told her.

Suzi was impressed. It was an awfully generous offer for Saskia to make, considering how she felt about Aaran herself, and what she must know of Suzi's own friendly relationship with him.

"Really," Suzi added when Saskia gave her a dubious look. "I will."

And then she was finally able to escape all of their good intentions, stepping out of the store and onto the quiet street. It was early morning— she wasn't sure exactly what time it was, but the skies were still dark and there was very little traffic. She walked briskly down to Williamson Street, not stopping until she got to the bus stop. She wasn't sure if the subway ran this far north, but she wouldn't have taken it anyway. She only knew her way back to Aaran's now-empty apartment from how they'd gotten here. By bus.

That was her big plan. She had to go back to collect her duffel bag anyway, but she might as well stay in the apartment for a little while. Why not? Nobody else would be using it. Not Aaran—that much was certain. It was near the end of the month, but surely no landlord would come looking for his rent cheque for at least a few days. She might even have a week. All she really needed was a quiet refuge while she tried to figure out what she was supposed to do with her life.

Sitting on a bench while she waited for the bus, she closed her eyes and tried to make a connection back to the Wordwood. But it was still gone. Severed as though it had never been.

She thought about Raul back in the bookstore, confused as to what he was doing here in Newford. Not to mention Holly's other friends, who'd not only found themselves far from their homes, but in some stranger's apartment with no clue as to how they'd gotten there.

The past was real for them, except for the last couple of days. *Those* they didn't remember at all. She, on the other hand, remembered the recent past as true, and all the rest of her life as a lie.

How were you supposed to be absolutely sure what was real and what wasn't? What if the past few days were the false memories? What if she really had walked out on Darryl after one physical attack too many? What if she really had a sister who now hated her because of that? A family that had pushed her out of their lives?

How were you supposed to know for sure?

She opened her eyes and stared across the street.

Maybe you weren't. Maybe people who grew in their mothers' wombs could get just as confused.

A southbound bus arrived then and she got on, finding a seat among the sprinkle of sleepy-eyed early morning commuters already on board. She sank back in her seat and tried to remember if there'd been a fire escape outside of any of the windows at Aaran's apartment. At least there hadn't been an alarm system.

Christy

All things considered, there's an unspoken decision made to take a bus over to the mall to pick up my car. I don't know what it would do to Raul if we suddenly took him on a shortcut through the otherworld. He's already forgotten everything that's happened in the past couple of days. He doesn't even register Dick—the hob disappearing from his awareness in that way that Faerie can do so well. Mother Crone's little friend Hazel doesn't register for him either, while Mother Crone just looks like a skateboarder, albeit one in her twenties. He never questioned Saskia's sudden appearance in the store.

Saskia.

I can't believe how my heart swelled to see her standing in front of me. Real. Unhurt. I took her in my arms and didn't want to ever let her go again. We might have still been there if she hadn't patted my back.

"Time for me to breathe now," she said in my ear.

I let her go, but after that it was hard for me to concentrate on much else of what was talked about until Geordie said something about getting the car from the mall's parking lot.

I know we tried to convince Suzi to stay here with Holly, or in the guest room at Saskia's and my apartment. I was aware of Estie and the others calling from Jackson's apartment, totally messed up about what they were doing there. Suzi left. Raul booked a flight that needed him to get to the airport in a couple of hours. Holly told Estie what hotel she and the others were staying at. She told them they could come over, but they, too, were intent on returning to their own homes.

"They're going back to their hotel to check out," she said when she got off the phone. "Then they're also going to book the first flights they can get out on."

Which is when Geordie mentions that we should pick up the car and I realize that we really should go. I'm dead on my feet.

I let go of Saskia's hand long enough to give Holly a hug and to shake Bojo's hand.

"Do you need a ride?" I ask the tinker.

He shakes his head. "I don't have far to go. I'm looking after the Kelledy's place."

"But that's—"

All the way downtown, I was going to say. Miles from here. But Saskia nudges me in the ribs and I get it. Holly and Bojo. They've been making moony eyes at each other ever since we got back.

"A good gig," I say. "They've got a beautiful house."

I glance at Saskia and she smiles approval at my recovery. She hooks her hand in the crook of my arm and gives me a little tug toward the door where Geordie and the others are already waiting. She's probably worried that I could still put my foot in my mouth.

I nod to Dick and then we all troop out into the early morning air, leaving the three of them behind in the store.

We trail along the sidewalk as we make our way down to the bus stop on Williamson Street.

"Oh, I never thought," Geordie says to Mother Crone. "Will you be okay on the bus?"

He worried about Faerie and iron—never a good combination in the old stories. But I figure any Faerie living in the city must have acclimatized themselves to the metal by now.

"We'll be fine," Mother Crone says.

"You don't like buses?" Raul asks.

"I'm just not used to them," she says and manages to sound sincere. "They don't have them where I come from."

"Jeez, where's that?"

"The place that they don't have buses," she says, but she smiles in a way that lets him know that she just doesn't want to talk about it. She's not mad or anything.

Raul shrugged. "I think I'd like it there," he says. "I've always hated public transportation."

The bus comes then, sparing us any further conversation. Hazel goes scrambling up the steps as soon as the doors open, invisible to Raul and the bus driver alike. I dig in my pocket for change, but Geordie produces a handful of tokens and pays for all of us.

I hand the car keys to Saskia when we finally reach our old beast. I know I'm too tired to drive and for all she's been through, she seems a lot more alert. Raul gets in the back on the driver's side, while Saskia slides in behind the wheel. I walk around to the other side.

Mother Crone takes Geordie's left hand and runs a finger over the calluses his fiddle strings have left on his fingertips.

"I meant what I told Holly," she says, her smile, her eyes, promising more. "Come play music with us—any time. Tap on the shipping bay doors that Dick took you through. The revels usually start after midnight."

"I will," he says. "Should I bring any other musicians?"

"So long as you bring yourself," she says.

She leans forward and says something that I can't hear, then she gives him a kiss on the brow and a little push towards the car. Hazel's sitting on the hood, staring in through the window at us and making faces. She jumps down when Saskia turns the ignition and then we're heading for the airport.

A couple of hours later we've dropped Raul off, then fought the growing commuter traffic back into town. Saskia pulls the car up in front of Jilly's building where Geordie's staying. I lean over the seat to look at him before he gets out.

"You okay with all of this?" I ask him.

He gives me a slow nod.

"I went to an actual Faerie revel," he says with a grin. "And I've been invited back."

"So you're not freaking anymore about things that aren't supposed to exist?"

"No. Should I be?"

"Not in my book," I tell him.

"What do you think of Mother Crone?" he asks.

"I think she needs a new name," I say.

"She has another one," Geordie says.

"What is it?"

He shakes his head. "I don't think I'm supposed to tell. You'll have to ask her yourself the next time you see her."

I shake my head. "She's no better than the rest—all riddles and mystery."

Saskia gives me a look but I can tell she's only mildly exasperated. "I think she's nice," she tells Geordie. "A little spooky, but nice."

"She's a seer."

"That would explain the spooky." She looks as if she wants to add something to that, but then she reaches back to ruffle his hair and only says, "Be careful."

"Because of Faerie glamours?" he asks.

He's still grinning. Saskia smiles in return.

"Because of whatever," she says. "Thanks for coming to look for me."

"Hey, you're like my sister. I couldn't *not* come."

He leans forward to kiss her cheek. Then, giving me a light punch on the shoulder, he gets out of the car. Saskia pulls away from the curb and we're finally alone.

We don't say much on the drive home, but I guess we don't need to.

Later, our positions are reversed. Usually I'm the one who drifts off after we've made love, but this morning I'm wide awake and she's the one who's fast asleep. I lie there beside her for a long time, marveling that I could be so lucky as to have her in love with me, but finally I get up.

I'm feeling restless and I don't want to disturb her. I wander around the apartment a bit and half-decide to do some work on those galley corrections that I owe Alan, but eventually I just lie down on the couch and think about all the strangeness that's filled my life these past few days.

I'm still awake when my shadow arrives. I smile as I see her slip into the apartment. I have a name for her now. Christiana. Christiana Tree.

"That makes her Ms. Tree," Saskia said before she fell asleep. "Get it?"

Suzi

Everything fell together for Suzi as though arranged by some higher power. Not God, of course, but when it came to manipulating data and finances electronically, the Webmaster at the Wordwood was certainly more than humanly efficient. She wanted to call him Aaran, but that was only who he'd been.

Now he was an anonymous Webmaster.

She hadn't needed to break into Aaran's apartment. There was a fire escape outside the bathroom window and the window had been open, covered only by a fine-mesh bug-screen. The window was too small for a regular-sized burglar to crawl through, but she'd been able to push in the screen and squeeze through without too much trouble. There were benefits to being small.

She searched through the drawers in the kitchen, then through the two in the maple washstand in the hall by the front door. One of the drawers in the latter rewarded her with a set of Aaran's spare keys. This was good. The next time she entered the apartment, she could come in through the front door.

Once she had the apartment key, she went back out to the alley and climbed up the fire escape to retrieve the laptop. She set it up on the mahogany writing desk in the corner where Aaran had kept it. Finding the right place to plug in the phone jack had her puzzled until she realized that the back of the machine opened up to reveal a hidden panel of sockets, one of which fit the phone jack. It took her longer to figure out how to get on the Internet. She couldn't remember the protocol Aaran had used and she wasn't computer-savvy enough to figure it out on her own. In the end, she tried simply opening Explorer, then clicking on "Yes" when the prompt came up asking her if she wanted to work on-line.

As soon as she was connected, she typed the Wordwood URL into the address bar near the top of the screen. After a moment's pause, a new window opened with a still picture of a forest rather than the streaming video that used to normally be there. There were no options to click on and no matter where she moved the cursor, it never changed from an arrow to the hand with a pointing finger indicating a link that could take her elsewhere.

She stared at the screen for a while, then returned the cursor to the address bar where she typed in the URL that would take her to her Hotmail account.

Besides the usual spam, there was only one new message.

Her pulse quickened when she saw whom it was from: Webmaster@ TheWordwood.com. But her happiness dampened as she read through the businesslike list of what had been provided for her:

The apartment was now in her name. Rent and all utilities were covered and would continue to be covered if she decided to move elsewhere.

A bank account had been opened in her name. A debit card was on its way to her by mail. If she needed money now, she could go to the bank to withdraw it from a teller. There was also some cash in the nightstand drawer on the left side of the bed.

She blinked when she looked at the amount that was in the account. Where had all that money come from? As though Aaran had expected the uneasy feeling rising up in her, the source of the funds was described in the next paragraph, something about skimming fractions of interest accrued on hundreds of thousands of accounts—each on its own amounting to nothing, but collected together it became a very tidy sum indeed.

The e-mail ended with the hope that she'd be happy in her new life and was simply signed "the Webmaster."

It was like getting a letter from a lawyer. Just the facts, ma'am.

Her first impulse was to walk away from it all. But reason prevailed. Yes, it made her feel like she was a kept woman, but there were no strings attached here. And really, did she want to go back to the streets and its dangers?

You never really lived on the streets, a part of her argued. That was only an implanted memory.

True. But that didn't make living on them any safer or easier.

She reread the e-mail and sighed, remembering an early conversation with Aaran when they'd decided that maybe they were each other's guardian angels.

He was certainly hers now.

Her distant, unapproachable guardian angel.

Because there hadn't been any warmth in the message. She supposed she should take comfort in the knowledge that seeing to her welfare had been one of the first things he had done once he'd established contact with the world outside the Wordwood, but why couldn't there have been something personal?

Something. Anything.

Because Aaran needed to cut himself off from human concerns, she realized. It would be the only way he could survive in the alien symbiotic relationship of which he was now a part.

She supposed she understood.

But it was small comfort, alone as she was in the world.

In the days that followed, she avoided everyone who'd been involved with the events that had led up to Aaran's disappearance into the Wordwood. Mostly, she stayed in the apartment. Reading, watching TV. As often as not, she simply pulled a chair up to a window and sat staring at the view. No one knew she was here—no one besides the Wordwood's Webmaster, she supposed—so no one tried to contact her.

But eventually she had to get out more often than simply slipping off to the corner store for staples.

She knew her past wasn't real—she was an active person, not a reactive one, no matter how the memories she was carrying around in her head said otherwise. The Wordwood spirit might have created a background for her in which she had docilely accepted Darryl's abuse until finally standing up for herself, but that wasn't who she was. Or if it was—if that was how she was *supposed* to be—then the conditioning had failed.

Or she had overcome it.

There was no point in looking for a job. Aaran had provided enough money for her to make the simple earning of money not an issue, and she had no burning desire to follow any particular career. At least not yet. That might come, but for now she thought it best to concentrate on experiencing more of the consensual world firsthand. Build up a store of her own *real* memories.

So she visited museums and galleries. She went into cafés and ate out, watching people as they interacted with each other. She tried shopping, but she didn't need much, not with everything Aaran had in his apartment. She did shop for clothes, but found that after picking up some new cargo pants and T-shirts, a nice jean jacket, underwear and even a couple of dresses, she wasn't mentally equipped to do any more. She carried around a pocket full of change and parceled it out to panhandlers and buskers that she passed on the street.

She discovered libraries and found them fascinating, both for the people-watching they provided as well as for the books. Aaran had a whole spare room devoted to his own personal library, but it held mostly fiction and she was more interested in nonfiction. How things worked. How history unfolded. How people, famous or not, lived their lives.

It was on one such expedition to the Crowsea Public Library, walking by the computer room, that she spotted a familiar face. She stood in the doorway watching Christiana, her face bathed in the light of the monitor, her fingers tapping away on the keyboard. She almost turned and walked away, but at that moment Christiana sat back from the computer and looked up. Their gazes met.

Suzi hesitated. Christiana smiled a greeting, but she seemed to sense how close Suzi was to bolting and she made no move to get up and come over. Finally, Suzi closed the distance between them. She pulled an unused chair from another table and sat down beside Christy's mysterious shadow, not sure why she was doing it. Not sure she even liked the woman. Christiana was the only one of them, other than Aaran, who had argued to stay behind. She was the one who should have stayed behind.

"So, how are you finding the consensual world?" Christiana asked.

Suzi shrugged. "It's interesting."

She glanced at the screen. It showed an in-box from a Yahoo account with as many messages as her own. None.

"Funny how that word's changed," Christiana said.

"What do you mean?"

"Well, people used to say something was interesting when it really did grab their attention. It'd be something remarkable. Or appealing. Or at least out of the ordinary. Now it's just a polite way of being noncommittal and usually means you don't find it interesting at all."

Suzi blinked.

"So which is it for you?" Christiana asked.

"A bit of both," Suzi admitted. "There are a lot of things that can keep my attention, but at the same time I feel distanced from it all."

"What have you been doing?"

"Mostly just watching people."

Christiana gave her a knowing look.

"Well, what's wrong with that?" Suzi asked.

"Absolutely nothing. But when I was learning how to be real, the first thing I was told was that I needed to interact with people."

"I don't have to learn how to be real."

"I didn't say you did."

Suzi smiled. "No, but you inferred it."

"I suppose I did. I guess I just assumed you'd be experiencing some of the same problems with self-identity that Saskia and I have."

"You don't think you're real?"

"I don't know. I was born as the cast-off shadow of a seven-year-old boy. How real is that?" Christiana smiled suddenly, but the humour didn't reach her eyes. "But it's funny. Until I first ran into Saskia and we had the long talk that got us involved with this whole Wordwood fiasco, I never really questioned where I came from. That's just who I was."

"And now you do."

Christiana nodded. "I feel kind of adrift. Rootless."

"Well, I may not be so good at interacting with the world at large," Suzi said, "but I'm sure about this much: It doesn't matter where any of us come from, or even what we look like. The only thing that matters is who we are now."

Christiana didn't say anything for a long moment. Her gaze traveled away from Suzi's face, and Suzi wasn't sure if she was looking inward or across the library.

"That's pretty good," she said finally, looking back at Suzi. "It puts the onus on yourself, instead of on where you came from. It suits what I like to think of as my independent temperament with the added bonus of making good sense. How can your genetic history or your past even begin to compete with who you are today?"

Suzi took that as a rhetorical question, so she didn't worry about an answer.

"But you're also right about my needing to interact more with people," she said instead. "There's something weird about living your life in a cocoon. There's only so much you can get out of books and art galleries."

Christiana nodded. "How are you doing for living expenses? Have you got a place to stay yet?"

"I'm in Aaran's apartment. He set it up so that everything of his is in my name, plus he's opened up a bank account for me with a ton of money in it."

"Probably ill-gotten gains," she said, but there was a smile in her voice that let Suzi know she wasn't not supposed to take it seriously.

"Only semi-ill-gotten," Suzi told her.

"Do you ever hear from him?"

Suzi sensed more than simple interest in the question.

"Just one e-mail that first day," she said. "It was very businesslike and just signed 'the Webmaster.' "

"That's harsh."

Suzi nodded.

"Have you ever run into any of the other . . . scouts the Wordwood sent out with you?" Christiana asked.

Suzi smiled at Christiana's momentary hesitation. She'd probably been about to say "spies."

"No," she said. "I can't sense their presence any more than I can the Wordwood's, but then I haven't been looking for them."

And she realized she wasn't particularly interested, either. That was all part of an old life. She wanted to concentrate on the new one. What she had now.

Christiana was looking at the monitor. "Funny to think how we were all right in there only a few weeks ago."

"In where?"

"The Wordwood. The Internet. Where it was a place instead of pixels on a screen."

"But it's nothing we have to worry about now," Suzi said.

Christiana nodded.

Suzi decided that she liked sitting here, interacting with someone other than the voice in her head. She also liked Christiana, even if it should have been her that stayed behind in the Wordwood.

"Do you want to go and grab some lunch?" she asked, surprising herself.

Christiana pretended she had to think about it. "But only if you're paying with those ill-gotten gains. It'll make me feel more piratical."

"And that's good because . . . ?"

"It means I can finally get a parrot and who knows? There might even be a treasure map tied to its leg."

"Except you'll have to change your name to something like Long John Silver."

"I suppose," Christiana said. "Say, did you ever wonder if he got that name because he always ran around in his underwear?"

That made them both giggle. The woman sitting at another computer station nearby shushing them only made it worse. So they got up and left before a librarian came over and threw them out, the two of them leaning against each other, bending over from having to stifle their laughter.

Christiana

So, remnants of our journey into the Wordwood continue to impact on my life.

I've got a new friend in Suzi—I love her observations about other people when we're out at a café or a concert, or just walking down the street. She can be serious and funny and she never hesitates at the thought of trying some new adventure. In that way, she's more like my friends in the borderlands than most of the people I meet here in the consensual world.

During that first lunch we had together, she asked me to teach her how to travel between the worlds. I knew why she wanted to learn, but I couldn't argue her out of it. She needed to talk to Aaran. So did I, but going back into the Wordwood didn't strike me as the answer.

Why did I teach her?

Partly because if I didn't, someone else eventually would. But mostly because I didn't see her getting into the Wordwood anyway. Even if Aaran—or what was left of Aaran in the Webmaster he'd become—wanted to let someone in, I doubt the leviathan would allow it to happen.

So I taught her how to find the borderlands by tricking them into existence in her peripheral vision. It's easy, really. What we actually observe is such a small part of what's going on around us.

Try this some time. Hold your hands out at arm's length and make a circle with your index fingers and thumbs that's about the size of a dinner plate. *That's* all you really see at any given point. Everything around it your brain makes up from its memories of what your eyes have taken in as you generally scan your surroundings. And that's why it's so easy to find the borderlands in your peripheral vision. All you have to do is to trick your mind into believing that they're actually there and then step sideways into them.

Though I guess that doesn't explain how you can catch something in your peripheral vision, like someone approaching, or a car as you're about to step off a sidewalk. But mostly it holds true. And I know for sure that the borderlands are always there, waiting for you.

The otherworld's tougher—at least crossing over to it from this world is. But it's simple to reach once you're already in the borderlands. The membrane, veil, whatever that lies on the edges of both our world and the spirit realm is so much thinner when you're looking through it from a vantage point inside the borderlands.

It took Suzi awhile to get the hang of it, but before too long she was moving through the worlds like a seasoned pro.

"I love this," she said the first morning she appeared in my meadow apartment.

She was polite enough to stand outside in the cedars and clear her throat, waiting for me to notice her and invite her in.

I smiled at her and beckoned her in.

"Yeah," I told her as she sat on the end of my bed. "It never gets old."

Christy and I treat each other more like brother and sister now. He's stopped putting me on a pedestal, and I try to be more straightforward with him and not feel like his weird little shadow. But there are still things I won't tell him. Like Galfreya's name. I side with Geordie on that one because when it comes to Faerie, names are a big deal. It's like that in most of the borderlands and the otherworld, too. Giving someone your name is a gift; it says "I trust you."

How come I know her name? That's a whole other complicated story involving whiskey and Maxie—never a peaceful combination—and this is neither the time nor the place for it. One thing at a time, Mumbo always tells me.

So as I was saying, mostly I try to be more forthcoming with Christy. We've even had these family dinners—Christy and Saskia, Geordie and me. I enjoy them more than I thought I would. There's none of the awkward tension of needing to make conversation that I was expecting. We just sit around and yak, stuffing our faces with some new wonderful meal that either Saskia or Geordie has put together. Neither Christy nor I can do much more than boil water and burn toast, though we make a fine clean-up team when the meal is done.

When Bojo's in town, I'll often hang out with Holly and him, though most of the time when I go by the bookstore I spend talking to Dick. We'll sit up into the middle of the night and talk about obscure books long after the others have fallen asleep. He loves the fact that I actually know a lot of the characters that started out their lives in the pages of those mostly forgotten stories. I think I've actually got him convinced to tag along with me to the next party at Hinterland, which is a big deal for a stay-at-home fairy man like a hob.

As for the others . . .

I never went back to see Jackson. He came through in the end, back there in the Wordwood, but I think knowing me would just cause him more problems than not. Every time he'd see me, he'd have that weird feeling of unwanted memories pushing up against the calm complacency of his life.

For some people that would be a good thing, but Jackson struck me as someone who expects to find order in the world, and knowing me tends to put a little chaos in your life instead. Look what happened to Saskia within a day of introducing herself to me in that café.

I didn't even meet the other Wordwood founders, but Holly tells me that they and Raul are fine. I did get her to ask if any of them had heard from Aaran, but they didn't know who he was and none of them will have anything to do with the Wordwood site anymore. When Holly asks why, they don't really have an answer and she doesn't press them.

I remember liking Raul—maybe because he was gay. He looked at me like I was an individual instead of evaluating my attractiveness the way so many men do with women. It's weird how refreshing a lack of sexual energy can be in this overly-charged world where even kids' cartoons seem to be selling sex, though it's not something I'd ever want to give up in the long term.

And it's not like I think Raul's some kind of prude. He's just got a different orientation. If I was a guy, he'd probably have been checking me out.

The only one I never met before the Wordwood business began was Robert Lonnie, but both Christy and Geordie talk so much about him that I've been keeping an ear out for that guitar playing of his wherever I go, whether it's wandering through the city or in the borderlands.

"You'll know it when you hear it," Geordie tells me when I ask him to describe it. "Trust me."

And he's right.

I'm on Palm Street late one night, walking past this run-down bar, when I hear a bluesy guitar playing a familiar twelve-bar like I've never heard it played before. I know exactly who this must be and stop dead in my tracks. The place has been closed for hours. It's dark inside and the door is locked—like that has ever stopped me. Drawn by the music, I step into the borderlands, then back into this world, but take a few steps so that when I reappear, it's inside the bar.

The guitar playing stops immediately.

I see this handsome black man sitting in a booth at the back of the bar, a guitar in his lap, a big revolver in his hand, the muzzle pointed straight at me. We stare at each other for a long moment before he finally lowers his hand and lays the weapon on the table.

"Either they're making hellhounds too pretty to resist," he says as he starts to play again, "or you've got some other good reason to come creeping around at this time of night."

"Can I sit?" I ask.

He smiles. "I don't know. Can you?"

I don't rephrase my questions into a "may I." I just take his smile as a yes and pull a chair from a nearby table and sit near his booth.

"I'm a friend of Christy and Geordie's," I tell him. "Kind of like a sister, really."

He cocks an eyebrow and his index finger does a hammer-on up around the seventh fret, bass string, that sounds like a question.

"Kind of how?" he asks.

"I'm Christy's shadow."

"You look pretty substantial to me."

I shrug. "He cast me off a long time ago—when he was only seven."

"How's that make you feel?"

"I don't know. Most of the time I never really thought about it, but lately . . ." I give him another shrug. "I just don't know."

Robert gives a slow nod.

"I've known a shadow or two," he says. "The one who usually comes to mind was cast off by this brother who ended up on death row for killing I don't know how many people. Back in my time they'd have just lynched him."

"What was he like?"

"Meanest mother I've ever had the misfortune to run across."

"I meant the shadow," I say.

"That's who I was talking about."

"But . . ."

"You don't really believe you're locked into whatever personality you were born into when you were cast off, now do you? That you've got to stay the opposite of the one that cast you off?"

It's the same argument I gave Christy. Somehow it seems to have more weight coming from someone else.

"Not really."

He nods. "In my limited experience, shadows have as much control in how they turn out as do the people who cast them off—and that's more than anyone thinks. Especially the people who like to use genetics as an excuse when they mess up."

"I'd like to think it's not all been laid out for me."

"Everybody makes their own way in this world," he says.

He falls silent then. Or at least he stops talking. His fingers make magic happen from that beat-up old guitar of his, and I just sit there and listen to him until the morning comes banging up against the windows of the bar.

Here's the one thing I can't seem to let go: Aaran in the Wordwood.

What's he *doing* in there?

I know it's partly morbid curiosity centering around the fact that it could have been me. That maybe it should have been me. But there's also a huge helping of worry in the mix because the Aaran I met doesn't jibe with the one Saskia and everybody else knew.

Christy said that Aaran appeared to undergo a genuine change of heart. He thought it had to do with Suzi, that somehow she got inside where no one else could. That just the example of her was enough—for whatever reason—for him to want to make amends for the way he'd been living, the way he treated people. That her coming into his life was an epiphany, though we shouldn't belittle his own efforts to change and make a difference either.

Suzi's in Christy's camp, though she thinks the changes in Aaran were all his own. That all he'd ever needed was for someone to accept him at face value. To look past the bullshit face he offered the world and just believe in him.

Saskia doesn't agree. She wants to be more generous, but I guess the wound he dealt her way back when cut too deep.

Me, I can't make up my mind. I need to talk to him some more first. So I keep e-mailing him in care of the Wordwood. I go on-line on Christy's computer when he and Saskia are out, or asleep. I become a regular at the Cyberbean Café, stopping in every other day for a cappuccino and to use their Internet resources. I slip into the Crowsea Public Library and use their machines, usually at night when everybody's gone home, but sometimes during the day, too.

Maxie says I should just get a machine of my own. Apparently there are ways to get them to work in the borderlands, the same way my cell phone does. But I don't really want one. Except for this one little cyber quest of mine, I've about as much interest in owning a computer as I do staring at the way little bugs scurry away when you lift a rock. No, that's not true. I actually like looking at little bugs.

So I keep borrowing other people's machines, and one day when I'm in the Cyberbean, there's finally a response waiting for me in my in-box:

To: MsTree@yahoo.com
Date: Tue, 26 Sept 2000 15:04:21 –0400
From: Webmaster@TheWordwood.com
Subject: Re: Are you there?

Hello Christiana,

I've been wanting to write for ages. And I would have gotten back to you much sooner, but . . . well, it's complicated. I've spent the last month or so completely caught up with the need to assimilate myself with this strange new reality I find myself in.

I guess the thing I really need to tell you . . . no, it's more that I need to share it with someone and, except for Suzi, you're the only one who keeps making an effort to contact me. I'd tell Suzi, but I don't know how to put it in the right words. And I know what she'd say, anyway: You make your own destiny, or some other positive thing like that. But I'm not sure she would actually understand. I'm not sure you will either, but it won't hurt as much if you don't. And maybe you will. You were inside the leviathan. Not just like the others, but like me. We were deeper inside him, I think. The others couldn't have been or they'd have put up a bigger argument to stay and do what I'm doing.

I'm not making much sense, I guess. It's funny, I can multitask like you wouldn't believe now. But it's all Wordwood business. Dealing with e-mail and downloads and running _serious_ scans for viruses on uploads. But when it comes to something personal . . . well, there's not a whole lot of personal left.

But what I need to tell you is this: Librarius lied to you. He didn't come from outside the Wordwood when the virus struck to take advantage of the situation. Oh, he was trying to take advantage, all right, but not like he let on.

He was trying to separate himself from the all-pervading spirit of the leviathan. He was in here all along, just like I am now. He was the Webmaster.

I guess what I'm trying to say is that I'm afraid that I'll give in just like he did.

I know it's different. I have foreknowledge. And I'll try to do this right like I've never tried to do right before. But I've only been here a month or so and I already know _exactly_ what Librarius was feeling. You don't get a moment's break. Not a moment to be yourself.

I don't feel real anymore. Hell, I'm _not_ real, am I? I'm no more than interactive software creating a conduit between the leviathan and the world outside.

So I guess what I'm really trying to say is, it could happen to me. Some new crisis like the virus Jackson sent could show up and, even though I know better, already I can see myself taking advantage of it and trying to figure out how to separate myself from the leviathan.

Not today. Or tomorrow. Or even in a year. Don't forget, Librarius was here for years before he broke.

I'm just scared that I'll break, too.

I don't know if I'm strong enough not to. I don't know if anybody is.

Aaran

http://www.thewordwood.com/

I realize as I'm reading his e-mail that he's not the only one having a crisis. I'm having one, too. An identity crisis, which is kind of funny when you think of how all of this started. Or at least how all of it started for Saskia and me: she was having the crisis and I convinced her to contact the Wordwood because it seemed the best way she could answer the question once and for all: Is she real or not?

But I'm the one who's been circling around that question ever since we got back.

No, that's not true. I've never stopped wondering about it from the moment I got pushed out of Christy. It's just that meeting Saskia—carrying her around inside me and with what I've been through with the leviathan and all—has brought it to a head and I don't know how to deal with it.

I'm still looking at the screen when someone sits down beside me. I look up and there she is. Saskia with her golden hair and sea-blue eyes, so effortlessly beautiful.

I get her to read Aaran's e-mail.

"You have to let this go," she says when she reaches the end and turns to me. "There's nothing we can do about it now."

"I know. It's just . . . worrisome."

She cocks her head and gives me a considering look.

"And what's bothering you more?" she asks. "That it's a worrisome situation, or that you're actually worrying about it?"

How can she know me so well? Like Christy said, I'm the original free spirit. No cares, no worries. Something bad's happening? Tra-la-la. I'll go somewhere else where it's not.

"How much did you get out of me when you were inside my head?" I ask.

"Only what your physical senses told you," she says. "I couldn't read your mind or know what you were feeling about something unless you shared it with me."

"Well, that's a relief."

"And you're avoiding the question. Which of the two worries you more?"

"Both," I have to admit.

"Well, it's good that you can worry about it," she says, "but you still have to let this go."

"But . . ."

"What are you going to do? Figure out a way to get back into the Wordwood and take his place?"

"Maybe that's not such a bad idea."

She shakes her head. "And you wouldn't be affected by the same thing that's happening to Aaran because . . . ?"

"I'm a shadow?"

"Oh, please. What happened to that independent streak of yours?"

She reaches past me and pushes the delete button. Another e-mail pops up in place of Aaran's, some spam telling us that we really do want men's penises to be bigger. It's exactly what I need to put everything into perspective. There's *always* going to be someone or something that thinks it knows you better that you can know yourself.

We grin at each other. I exit my account and we leave the computer free for another customer. Saskia gets us each another cappuccino and we sit at a table by the window.

"With all our adventuring," I say. "We didn't really find anything out, did we?"

Saskia smiles. "You noticed?"

"So, are you okay with it? Not knowing for sure what coming from where you did means?"

"In terms of who I am now?"

I nod.

"I think so," she says. "I've decided that it doesn't really matter. That it shouldn't matter for anyone. Maybe this is sour grapes—you know, because *I* don't know what I really am any more than you do. Or maybe it's like a poor person saying money can't buy happiness because they don't have any themselves, but if we take it down to basics, it doesn't matter where we come from, or even what we look like. The only thing that matters is who we are now."

I smile. "That's almost word-for-word what Suzi told me."

"You've seen her?"

"Mmhmm. And I still do. I see all kinds of people in the consensual world now."

"You're becoming a regular little social butterfly."

"I always was."

"Only not here. Not in this world."

"Christy's world," I say.

"Why does it have to be his world?" she asks. "Why can't there be room for both of you in it?"

"No reason, I guess."

I feel a little lighter as I say it. Like actually using the words can make them true. Maybe that's the change I felt coming over me when the leviathan left his physical body. Maybe I'm finally accepting that I can have a place in this world, that I can make lasting relationships here, instead of always being the traveller, passing through.

I smile at her and repeat the words again, enjoying the taste of them as they leave my tongue.

"No reason at all."